LITTLE
GIRL
GONE

Stephen Edger has been writing crime thrillers since 2010. An avid reader, Stephen writes what he likes to read: fast-paced crime thrillers with more than a nod to the darker side of the human psyche. In all, he has published over a dozen novels – four trilogies, and the rest standalone psychological thrillers.

The one common location to each of the novels is the city of Southampton, where Stephen has lived since attending the university there. This local knowledge gives each of the stories a unique and edgy realism that few can match.

Stephen was born in the north-east of England, but grew up in London, meaning he is both a northerner and a southerner. By day he works in the financial industry using his insider knowledge to help shape the plots of his books. He also has a law degree, which gives him a good understanding of the inner workings of the UK justice system.

Stephen is married, and has two children and two Westie dogs. He is passionate about reading and writing, and cites Simon Kernick and Tony Parsons as major influences on his writing style.

www.stephenedger.com
 /AuthorStephenEdger
 @StephenEdger

Also by Stephen Edger

The DI Kate Matthews Series
Dead to Me
Dying Day
Cold Heart

The PI Johnson Carmichael Series
Trespass
Fragments
Downfall

Standalones
Snatched
Blackout
Then He Was Gone

STEPHEN EDGER

LITTLE
GIRL
GONE

KILLER
READS

A division of HarperCollins*Publishers*
www.harpercollins.co.uk

KillerReads
an imprint of HarperCollins*Publishers* Ltd
1 London Bridge Street
London SE1 9GF

www.harpercollins.co.uk

This paperback edition 2019

First published in Great Britain in ebook
format by HarperCollins*Publishers* 2018

A catalogue record for this book
is available from the British Library

ISBN: 978-0-00-832061-4

Set in Minion by
Palimpsest Book Production Limited, Falkirk, Stirlingshire

Printed and bound in the UK by CPI Group (UK) Ltd, Croydon CR0 4YY

For Hannah, Emily, and Ethan, my world

1

The wipers squawked as they battled to keep the windscreen clear.

'I'm going to be late,' Alex Granger muttered to herself, as she strained to see through the gap in the condensation rapidly rising in front of her. Glancing down momentarily she switched the blower to full, the sound of the rushing warm air drowning out the radio.

A giggle from the back seat caused Alex to look up at the rear-view mirror. 'At least you're happy enough,' she said, adding a smile as her eyes met the blonde girl grinning back at her.

A car horn sounded from behind, the driver gesticulating that the traffic lights had finally turned green. Raising her hand in acknowledgement, Alex lowered the handbrake and moved forward, looking left and right for the name of the road where the car park was located. And as if her prayers had been answered, she spotted a large blue 'P' on the next street sign, and indicated to the right. The driver behind gave a second blast of his horn as he swerved around her.

'What's the hurry, arsehole?' Alex shouted at the window, suddenly realizing that Carol-Anne could hear. Looking back at the reflection of her two-year-old daughter, Alex quickly apologized. 'Just ignore Mummy's crazy words.'

Carol-Anne giggled again.

The windscreen still wasn't clearing, and as Alex spotted the entrance to the car park up ahead, she realized the car's fans weren't even aimed at the windscreen. Adjusting the dial, she silently cursed Ray for not putting them back. Her husband had borrowed her car the night before to go to the gym, and she was certain he must have interfered with the way she liked the car to be set up; she'd had to move the seat forward when she first got in that afternoon. She'd remind him when she saw him later, she thought. Right now there were more important things to worry about, like finding a parking space, dropping Carol-Anne at the crèche, and running to her interview. She should have phoned ahead and postponed the interview when traffic had been far heavier than she'd anticipated. It had been the only interview she'd been offered out of the dozen or so jobs she'd applied for in the previous three months, and she hadn't wanted to make the wrong first impression. Arriving late wouldn't be a good start though either, she knew.

'Think positively,' Alex reminded herself, as she pulled the car through the entrance and began to hunt for a free space.

Carol-Anne giggled and sang away to herself in the back.

'Tell Mummy if you see an empty space,' Alex hummed along, as she glanced left and right, completing a full tour of the single-level car park, reaching the exit without luck. She was about to give up when she spotted a yellow umbrella, moving towards one of the cars behind them. Reversing towards the bright glow, Alex lowered the passenger window and called out, 'Are you going?'

The woman beneath the umbrella looked over and smiled. 'Yes, in a minute. Do you want my space?'

'Please, you're a lifesaver.' Reversing further to allow enough space for the SUV to pull out, Alex waited for the woman to lower the umbrella, duck into the car and finally drive away.

'Someone up there must be smiling down on us today,' Alex mused at Carol-Anne's reflection; although whoever it was, they could have done something about the weather; arriving looking like a drowned rat wouldn't help her nail that first impression.

With the SUV finally clear of the space, Alex manoeuvred into it, and killed the engine. 'Right, that's the first task complete, now to get a ticket ...' Her words trailed off, as she scanned the car park for the ticket machine, eventually spotting the bright orange machine back over by the entrance. It seemed so far to have to carry Carol-Anne in such horrible weather. There seemed no let-up in the rain sweeping wildly across the car park.

Deciding there was only really one option that would save time and keep Carol-Anne dry, she swivelled round in her seat. 'Do you think you could be super good for Mummy? I need to go and buy a ticket from that machine over there,' she said, pointing to where she meant. 'If I lock the doors, do you think you could sit here really quietly while I go and get it? You'll have to sit perfectly still so you don't trigger the alarm. Can you do that for Mummy?'

Carol-Anne blinked back, oblivious to what Alex had asked.

'No, I can't do that,' Alex answered for herself biting her nail. 'I'll just have to get you out and bring you with me. It was a stupid idea.'

Turning back, she checked the handbrake was on and ran through the checklist in her mind, before snatching up her handbag from the front seat and reaching for the door handle. But as she prised the door open, a strong gust forced it closed again.

'Oh, this is just crazy! Does the weather not realize I have a really important interview in twenty – no, correction, *eighteen* – minutes?'

Her phone bleeped, and the display showed that Ray had sent her a good luck message. He knew how much this opportunity meant to her, and he was doing his best to be supportive, even if he didn't agree that her returning to work was the best thing for them at this point.

Staring at Carol-Anne's reflection in the mirror again, she reconsidered her options, before biting the bullet. Removing her purse, she dropped the handbag on the passenger seat, forced her door open and darted into the rain, remote locking the car as she sprinted through the puddles, cursing as the water splashed against her suit trousers.

Was it too late to phone and let them know she was running late? Would they judge her as a poor time-keeper? She'd always been so punctual when she'd worked before giving birth. Ever since Carol-Anne had arrived, she'd found getting anything done on time a struggle. It wasn't that she'd suddenly become disorganized overnight, there just always seemed to be some kind of hurdle she'd failed to envisage. Like Carol-Anne soiling her nappy the moment they'd got in the car this afternoon, and the mad dash back into the house to change her.

Blinking against the rain, she shielded her eyes as she stared back at her small grey hatchback, tempted to run back and check that none of the hideous outcomes her paranoid mind was picturing had befallen her daughter. And as if to heighten her paranoia, the car's alarm sounded in a flurry of orange light. Carol-Anne would be terrified by the sudden cacophony. Splashing back a few steps, she killed the alarm with the remote.

Scanning the full car park, she saw there wasn't a soul in sight, and with time against her, she hurried back to the machine, opening her purse and fishing for change. The rain continued to blind her as she struggled to read the sign and calculate how much she needed, finally dropping three £1 coins into the slot and pressing the green button, forcing herself to look back at the car every few seconds. The orange machine finally whirred and spat out her parking ticket. Snatching it up, she charged back towards the car, relieved to get back in, and take a moment to catch her breath.

'It is such a minging day,' she said, finally opening her eyes and wiping rain from her face.

Looking up at the rear-view mirror, the breath caught in her throat.

Spinning around, she stared at the empty child seat, unwilling to believe her own eyes. It had to be some kind of joke. Where the hell was Carol-Anne?

Alex rubbed her eyes, and then dug her freshly polished nails into her skin to wake herself from the sudden nightmare.

The seat remained empty. Turning back to face the front, the ticket machine was barely visible through the rain-soaked windscreen.

This couldn't be happening. Not again.

Her heart raced, as her mind desperately tried to connect the dots and determine why her daughter was no longer strapped into the chair.

Pushing her door open, Alex stepped back out, no longer noticing the rain as it splashed against her suit and pressed blouse. Still there was no sign of a single person in the car park. She scanned the area for any sudden flash of colour. Was it possible the alarm had frightened Carol-Anne so much that she'd managed to unfasten her belt, get out of her seat and leave the car in search of her Mummy?

It seemed so ridiculous, but what other explanation was there?

Darting to the back of the car, Alex stooped to look beneath it, scouring the floor, only finding puddles where the rainwater had settled. Then stalking along the row, looking in the gaps between the cars, the feeling of dread continued to grow in the pit of her stomach.

'Carol-Anne? Carol-Anne?' she called out, hoping that the sound of her terrified voice would find its way to her daughter's ears.

There was still no sign of Carol-Anne, as she reached the end of the row, and so she turned and sprinted back towards her car, thick raindrops scraping against her cheeks, mixing with the tears that were already flowing uncontrollably.

'Carol-Anne!' she screamed at the top of her voice, until her lungs burned.

And as she spun around, desperately hunting for some tiny glimmer – some explanation – her thoughts returned to the car. What if she hadn't got out? What if she'd been playing a game of hide-and-seek?

Yanking open the rear passenger door, she dived into the back of the car, pushing at the bags on the mats in the footwell, already knowing that she was wasting time, and that her little girl wasn't there. What was the alternative? Nobody had been near the car.

Had they?

Alex choked down the urge to vomit, her pulse now dangerously high, and the world began to spin around her head.

'Carol-Anne!' she screeched at the top of her voice, calling out for the wind to carry her voice to the far edges of the earth.

There wasn't a soul inside the car park, the only sound that of the rain falling.

Carol-Anne was gone.

2

'You playing squash tomorrow night, Ray?'

Detective Sergeant Ray Granger looked up at the desk to his right. 'Not this week, Owen. Shoulder's still not recovered from the last time.'

'You pull something?'

Ray ground his teeth to stop himself revealing the real reason he wasn't going to make squash this week, the same reason his appearances at the fortnightly meet-ups had been so inconsistent for the last few months: the guilt was eating him alive, but he was like a puppy whenever she called him.

Pressing a hand against his right shoulder, Ray made a windmill gesture with his right arm. 'No idea, mate, it hasn't been right for a few weeks.'

A glimmer of concern flickered in Owen's eyes. 'You seen a doctor about it?'

Ray pulled a face. 'You kidding? Hard as nails, me.'

Owen smiled and nodded. 'Of course, I forgot you old-timers *think* you're invincible.'

Ray cocked a sceptical eyebrow, knowing his younger colleague was teasing. 'For one thing, less of the old; I'm only forty. And secondly, just because I don't panic over every sniffle and self-diagnose a tumour like you wet-nosed graduates, doesn't mean I think I'm invincible. I guess I just have a better pain threshold than you.'

Owen offered a slight bow out of courtesy, standing and lifting his mug. 'You want a brew?'

Ray handed over his mug with a nod. 'Cheers.'

'No worries. Wouldn't want you to develop a hernia by moving too quickly.' Owen grinned, leaping out of the way as Ray pretended to take a swing in his direction.

DC Owen Hargrove was proving to be a decent copper, and his ability to deliver banter and stir shit was second to none in the unit. Leaning back in his chair, Ray observed his own reflection in the tall window next to his desk. Although he still felt like a man in his twenties, his appearance put him at double that age. Hair thinning from the age of nineteen, he'd shaved his head clean at twenty-five, choosing not to waste countless hours of his life worrying about the developing bald patch and ways to cover it. His father had also lost his hair at an early age, so what was the point in fighting against genetics?

Of course the bulging midriff wasn't something he could blame on his father. Too many processed meals, grabbed on the hop when time allowed, and too many nights spent sinking beer after beer to reduce stress, had taken their toll. It was lucky he wasn't applying to join the force today, as he'd struggle to meet the fitness requirements.

'You thinking about making your comeback as a model, Ray?'

Looking up, he spotted the detective inspector hovering over the soundboard. 'They couldn't afford me, ma'am.'

'Underwear, wasn't it?' DI Serena Trent laughed slyly.

Ray grinned back at her. 'That's right.' He paused, as he considered her statement. 'You know I could have you done for sexual harassment for a comment like that, ma'am. I mean, picturing me in my underwear isn't exactly professional, is it?' He laughed to show he was kidding.

Trent pulled a disgusted face. 'I wasn't picturing you in under-wear, but I am now. Eurgh, the image is ingrained on my eyelids. Thanks for that, Ray.'

He chuckled. 'Always aim to please, ma'am. Did you want me for something?'

Trent regained her composure. 'Team brief in a few minutes to check where everyone is with their caseloads. Got something big on the horizon and I'll need all hands on deck. How was your training course last week?'

A week away from home, staying in a hotel with meals on expenses: it had been just what he had needed. The training itself had been less exciting. When he would ever need to use the hostage negotiation techniques was beyond him, but the DI had recommended he go to aid his development. Not that he could see himself climbing the career ladder anytime soon.

'It was interesting, ma'am. I appreciate you sending me.'

'I'll get you to give the rest of the team an overview in the next few weeks. And if any nutcase decides to rob a bank around here and take hostages, you'll be the first one I call.'

He mock saluted as she moved away from the desk, calling together the rest of the team. Glancing at the framed photograph on the corner of his desk, he suddenly remembered that Alex's interview was approaching. Pulling the phone from his pocket, he typed a quick message of support and pressed send.

He grabbed the frame and held it tight. He loved this picture: Alex with her shoulderlength brown hair was positively glowing, while Carol-Anne nestled in her arms, as they both relaxed on holiday. He could still remember taking the picture, and how proud he'd been of his little family. It was the day Alex had told him she was expecting their second child. He lowered the frame back to the desk face down; so much had happened in the six months that had passed since then, yet the pain felt just as raw as the day the sonographer had told them she couldn't trace a heartbeat. Alex had later admitted to fearing something wasn't right.

Pocketing the phone, Ray locked his workstation and made his way to the group of ten forming a semicircle around the main board. Perching on one of the desks, Owen handed him his mug of tea, as Trent quietened them down.

'First of all,' Trent began, standing in front of the board allowing her to make eye contact with each of them, 'can we welcome back DS Ray Granger from his trip to Hendon? Ray has been learning the Met's latest negotiation techniques from an instructor who has been working in Asia and the Middle East for the past decade.'

Ray nodded as his colleagues acknowledged his return. It seemed a bit staged, particularly as he'd only been away for a week, but it was Trent's way of micromanaging her team.

'So, when it comes round to the annual pay review, I'll be delegating to Ray to negotiate on my behalf, and I'll be expecting a bumper pay rise, Ray.'

'They won't know what's hit them, ma'am,' Ray smiled.

The group laughed.

'Onto other matters,' Trent continued, 'we've had a tip-off that a new crew are smuggling counterfeit goods through the docks. The chief super has signed off a two-week surveillance op with overtime available for those who want to be involved. It'll mean working all hours, with a view to crashing the ring by the end of the month.

'I'll be leading the surveillance, and we'll be working closely with our colleagues in Organised Crime to identify the main players and set up further surveillance on their activities. The potential return on this one could be in the millions, which is why it's been sanctioned. I want names on the board by the time I finish today so I can coordinate who's doing what over the next fortnight.'

Ray pressed a hand to his pocket as his phone vibrated.

'Everything okay, Ray?' Trent asked.

All eyes fell on Ray as the phone continued to vibrate in

his pocket. Trent was a stickler for keeping work and personal lives separate. She acknowledged that her team all had lives outside of the office, though she didn't like it encroaching on her time.

'Sorry, ma'am,' Ray replied, lowering his eyes.

'Right, where are we with the armed robbery at the post office in Portswood last Friday?'

An arm shot up. 'CCTV has four masked men making their escape in a Transit from Portswood,' DS Jodie Crichton explained. 'Plates are false. We tracked the vehicle as far as the M3 before we lost sight of it. Having spoken to colleagues in Dorset and Berkshire, this could just be the latest in a string of robberies. It has the hallmarks of raids in Swindon, Bournemouth and Reading. The group are heavily armed – four men and a getaway driver – and only hit post offices, focusing primarily on their foreign exchange booths. One stands watch at the main door, keeping a check on the time via a stopwatch around his neck. He seems to be the one in charge. Each time, when it gets to exactly three minutes, he signals and the rest of the group haul tail out of there. They are very efficient from what I can see, using a different van each time, always with false plates, and always abandoned and torched with no DNA or fingerprints discovered at any of the wrecks or crime scenes.'

'Do the other teams have any idea who the group are?' Trent asked.

Crichton shook her head. 'None, ma'am. The group are masked in all of the footage from the post offices.'

The phone was vibrating again, and this time Ray pulled it out and dropped it into the drawer of the desk he was sitting on.

Trent fired a look at him, before turning back to Jodie. 'What about MOs of other crews?'

'Still checking for similarities. I'll keep you posted.'

'Ray, you've got some free time on your hands. I want you to work with Jodie on this. Okay?'

Ray nodded as the sound of the vibrating phone echoed quietly in the drawer.

'Good. Owen, what have you got for us in terms of news on the streets?'

Owen Hargrove stepped forward. 'Uniform have reported a string of muggings in the precinct area of Shirley. Victims have described a tall girl, aged maybe fifteen or sixteen, with long brown hair. There's also been three burglaries at properties in Hedge End. Can't say for sure if they're connected at this stage.'

'Anything else?'

'The only other thing they mentioned was the release of Jack Whitchurch, ma'am: convicted sex offender. He's been released on bail and has been relocated outside of the county; they're wary of reprisals, and have been asked to keep a watch on his property. We also need to make contact with his previous victims and advise them of his release. I'll see if uniform can do house visits.'

'Okay, thank you for the update. Don't forget, names on the board by tonight. Back to work.'

Ray waited for the team to disperse, and in particular DI Trent, before opening the drawer and pulling out his phone. Five missed calls from Alex, and voicemail. It was unlike her to be so persistent when she knew he was working. Pocketing the phone, he headed for the exit.

3

Six calls and messages to Ray had yielded no results.

Where the hell was he, and why wasn't he answering?

He should know that she wouldn't keep calling unless it was an emergency.

The rain was still heavy. She no longer cared that her hair looked like she'd just stepped out of the shower and that her eyeliner had left streaks down her cheeks. None of that mattered anymore.

Returning to the back of the car, she opened and checked the boot for a second time. She knew it was impossible that Carol-Anne could have figured out how to lower the rear seats and crawl through to the boot, but she was fast running out of ideas about where her daughter could have gone.

She'd never felt so scared in all her life. What if Carol-Anne had somehow managed to get out of the car, and rather than walking towards Alex had taken a wrong turn? What if a car had hit her? Or what if she was out there now, lost and alone and wondering why her Mummy had abandoned her?

Why hadn't she just taken Carol-Anne to the ticket machine with her? That would be the first question Ray would fire at her, and he'd be right to blame her for the moment of madness. She'd thought she was doing the right thing. She'd locked the car so Carol-Anne would be safe. And then the alarm had sounded. She hadn't looked away for any real length of time, she was sure of that.

She replayed the two-minute period over and over in her mind, hunting for any detail or clue that would help her see through the fog of uncertainty clouding her every thought. She was certain she had strapped the harness around Carol-Anne before they'd set off from home. She would have noticed otherwise, wouldn't she? Even so, there was no way Carol-Anne could have figured out how to unclip the harness herself. God knew, it was struggle enough to put the damned thing on each time, how could a two-year-old manage to undo it? Why else wouldn't she be there now? As ridiculous as it sounded, if Carol-Anne hadn't unfastened the harness that could only mean someone else had, and Alex was doing everything in her power to keep those thoughts from her mind.

Realistically it was the most likely explanation, but to cave in to that conclusion was to invite a whole new world of pain. The urge to vomit was returning, and this time she stooped over and dry-retched.

Wiping her mouth with the back of her hand, she looked at her phone. Ray still hadn't replied. He'd know what to do. He was always so much more pragmatic than she was. And given his experience in the force, he'd know what steps to follow. She desperately hoped – even though deep down she knew she was kidding herself – that Ray had stopped by, seen Carol-Anne alone, and he'd been the one to take her, and that was why she couldn't now get hold of him. He was playing some kind of twisted game; that had to be it! He hadn't been that keen on her coming for the interview, and so rather than supporting her decision, he was retaliating in the cruellest way.

Slamming the boot, she moved back to Carol-Anne's window and stared in. When she had last turned to look at her daughter, there had been no sign to suggest the harness had been loose or not clipped together. She never would have considered leaving her alone in the car if she had thought there was some way Carol-Anne could have fallen from the seat.

How could anyone else have taken her?

She retraced her steps back to the ticket machine, playing the memory in real time. She had locked the car with the remote as she had darted through the rain. It had beeped as the alarm had cut in. And then when she'd got to the machine the alarm had sounded, meaning Carol-Anne had to have been in the car then.

She froze halfway to the machine, and the hairs on the back of her neck stood on end; what if Carol-Anne hadn't been the cause of the alarm being triggered?

Alex had looked over at the car as the alarm had sounded. She would have noticed somebody lurking at the side of the car, wouldn't she? And there had been no sign of anyone anywhere in the car park. She would have seen a stranger snatching her daughter, wouldn't she?

Having switched the alarm off, she couldn't have been by the ticket machine for more than twenty seconds – thirty at most – and then she'd hurried back. If somebody had opened Carol-Anne's door, unfastened the harness, closed the door and snuck away, Alex would have spotted them. There had been no colour among the drab view of cars as the rain had thundered down; she was sure of that. There had to be something else she was missing.

Alex jumped as her phone burst into sound. 'Oh, Ray, thank God, where have you been?'

'Sorry, babe, I was in a team meeting. How'd your interview go? Do you think you got it?'

'I need you, Ray. Right now! It's Carol-Anne … she's-she's-she's …' but Alex couldn't bring herself to say the words as her eyes filled with tears, threatening to burst at any second.

'Carol-Anne. What's wrong? Is she okay? Has something happened?'

Alex tilted her head back, desperate not to burst the damn holding the tears in place.

'Alex? What's going on? Where are you?'

'She's gone,' she managed, her voice barely a whisper, as the tears ran down her cheeks.

'She's what? I didn't hear what you said. It sounded like—'

'She's gone, Ray. I think someone's taken her. Oh God,' she sobbed.

'What do you mean someone's taken her? Where are you, Alex?'

'I came to town for my interview, and I was in the car park w-w-when …'

'What car park, Alex? Tell me exactly where you are and I'll come across straight away.'

'The Woodside Road car park. Please hurry, Ray.'

The line disconnected, and Alex buried her head in her hands, willing Ray to arrive and save her fragile mind.

The sudden sound of a child's laughter caused the sobbing to stop almost immediately, as she strained to hear where it was coming from. Scanning the car park once more, Alex saw a woman in a long, hooded jacket, loading something into her back seat. Setting off without a second's thought, Alex splashed through the puddles in the uneven surface.

The hooded woman was now fewer than twenty yards away. She was closing the rear door of her estate car, and already had a hand on the driver's side door handle. Alex had never been much of a runner, but from somewhere deep she found the drive to move her legs quicker, almost colliding with the car's bumper, as she tried to steady herself. The woman jumped as Alex rested both hands on the bonnet; this woman wasn't going anywhere with *her* daughter.

The woman pulled her hood down to reveal a mop of tight strawberry-blonde curls. Winding her window down, she leaned out and called to Alex. 'Can I help you with something? Do you want my space?'

Alex sucked in lungfuls of air, as she tried to steady her breathing. Rather than replying, she stalked around to the rear passenger door, and tried to stare through the rain-covered and misted glass. A bob of fair hair could be seen in a child seat.

Alex pulled on the door handle, but it was locked.

'Hey, what the hell do you think you're doing?' the woman demanded, now standing with one leg in the car and one outside. 'Get away from my car.'

'Give me my daughter back,' Alex demanded, standing firm. 'Open this door.'

The woman stared back at her, puzzled. 'I'm warning you: get away from my daughter's door. I'll call the police,' she threatened holding her mobile aloft.

'Good,' Alex fired back wide-eyed with anger. 'Call them. Then you can explain to them why you took my daughter from my car and tried to drive off with her.'

The woman looked around the car park, as if she was expecting a film crew to appear at any moment and reveal Alex's behaviour was all part of an elaborate practical joke. 'I won't tell you again: back away from my car so I can leave.'

'Give me back my daughter!'

'I don't have your daughter!' the woman screamed back. 'That is my daughter in the car.'

Alex stepped back uncertainly. 'Of course you'd say that.'

The woman's anger boiled over. Straightening, she slammed the door behind her and stomped past Alex, opening the rear passenger door. 'Take a look yourself!'

Alex hurried forward, stopping only when her eyes fell on the blue eyes of the toddler staring back at her, clearly worried by the raised voices.

Alex stared from the toddler to the angry mother.

'Well? Satisfied now?'

Alex wobbled, before falling to her knees despite the wet ground, and allowing her terror to escape in a sorrowful scream.

The other woman closed and locked her daughter's door, before crouching down beside Alex. 'Are you okay, love?'

'My-my-my daughter,' Alex wailed. 'She's missing.'

The woman gasped, understanding the sheer terror that had driven Alex to behave so irrationally. Suddenly all the anger was gone from her voice. 'Missing? You poor thing. When did you last see her?'

Alex couldn't respond, as the sobs returned with a vengeance. The woman opened the front passenger door and manoeuvred Alex into it, before racing around and diving into her own seat.

Offering a packet of tissues, she said, 'Is there anything I can do? Can I call someone for you?'

'My husband is on his way,' Alex replied, through stilted breaths, accepting one of the tissues and blowing her nose, embarrassed by her outburst and accusation.

'When did this happen?'

Alex did her best to steady her breathing, but she might as well have not bothered. 'Just now ... I left her in the car while I went to get a ticket ... one minute she was there, and the next ...' Her eyes stung as further tears threatened to fall.

'Oh my, you poor thing. Have you called the police?'

Alex nodded. 'My husband's in ... I mean, my husband is a detective.'

'You're welcome to wait here until he arrives,' the woman offered. 'What does your daughter look like? Was she wearing a coat?'

'She has blonde hair and the cutest face ... she was wearing a bright red anorak.'

The woman's eyes darted left and right as she too began to search helplessly for any sign of Carol-Anne. 'She can't have gone far. Have you tried heading out to the main road in case she wandered off?'

Alex shook her head.

'That's probably what's happened,' the woman concluded, trying to sound positive for both of their sakes. 'I know what kids can be like. My little one wandered off in a supermarket once. Scared me to death, she did. I was searching everywhere for her, and when I returned to the trolley there she was, totally oblivious to the years she'd shaved off my life expectancy. I'm sure your daughter will turn up too. The important thing is to remain focused.'

Alex looked up at the woman through clouded eyes. 'I'm sorry about what I said—'

'Don't be silly. I imagine I'd have been far ruder in your situation. I'm sorry I was so abrupt with you initially.'

'How old is your little one?' Alex asked.

'Eighteen months,' the woman replied, turning and smiling at her daughter to reassure her. 'And yours?'

'Two years.' Alex paused. 'What kind of mother would allow her daughter to be snatched like this?'

Neither answered the question. Alex stared back out into the rain-washed car park, her paranoia going into overdrive.

4

Ray was still squeezing the phone as Owen returned to his desk.

'Everything okay, Ray?'

Ray took a deep breath, trying to suppress the blizzard of questions racing through his mind. 'Um, no … I don't know …'

Owen frowned at his colleague. 'You look like you've seen a ghost. What's going on?'

Ray blinked several times, his mind in limbo somewhere between reality and disbelief. 'That was Alex … she said that someone has taken our daughter … I need to go.'

Owen's eyes widened at the admission. 'Someone's taken her? Like, as in, *taken* her?'

The computer on the desk blurred as Ray tried to focus on where he was and what he needed to do next. Nausea swept through him as the room began to spin. Reaching out for his chair, he steadied himself.

Sensing the seriousness of the situation, Owen lowered his mug to the desk and grabbed a set of keys from the tray on one of the cabinets. 'Come on, I'll drive you.'

Ray allowed Owen to lead him from the office, down the double set of stairs and into the yard where the team's unmarked squad cars rested.

Holding the key aloft, Owen pressed the remote and looked to see which unlocked, nodding towards the Focus. 'That one,' he said, as he grabbed Ray's arm and put him in the passenger seat.

It was like he was watching a film of his life, with some not-so-attractive actor playing him. He knew what was happening, but had no control over where the script would take them.

Among the questions to be considered was whether he should report the phone call to DI Trent immediately, but he needed to assess the situation first. It wouldn't be the first time Alex had overreacted to a simple situation.

Things hadn't been right with her since the miscarriage, and he'd urged her to see a counsellor after the loss. She'd assured him she didn't need it, and had focused her attention on Carol-Anne and then hunting for a new job. But she'd been on edge, flying off the handle at the littlest of irritations, constantly lethargic. And then two weeks after it happened, he'd found her in what would have been the nursery holding a knife. She insisted she'd been washing up and had become distracted by the sound of crying, which is why she'd climbed the stairs. Thankfully, Carol-Anne had been with him at the shop, and was oblivious to her mother's delicate state of mind.

Then there was what had happened in Manchester with the girl at the park. He'd insisted on counselling after that, and she'd had no choice but to go, though he couldn't remember the last time she'd talked about her progress, or even the last time he'd seen her take the medication the GP had prescribed.

Calling to tell him someone had taken Carol-Anne: could her mind have finally snapped? Alex was many things, but could she really have done something to put their daughter's life in danger? Ray desperately hoped he was misjudging his wife, although only time would tell.

'Where are we headed?' Owen asked as he started the engine.

'The car park off Woodside Road, down from the Civic Centre.'

'I know the place. Belt up.' Owen nodded, engaging the lights built in to the grill. 'What else did Alex tell you?'

Ray tried to recall the conversation. Usually his memory was good; however a flurry of questions interrupted every time he tried to hear Alex's words again. 'She was going to town for an interview. She was supposed to be dropping our daughter at a crèche, heading to the Civic Centre for the interview, picking up Carol-Anne and then coming home.'

'What time was the interview?'

'At three, I think.'

Owen noted the time on the dashboard display. 'Well she either didn't make it, or it was the shortest interview in history. Do you think someone took your daughter from the crèche? I mean, do you think it could be a simple mix-up? Like the supervisors gave the wrong child to the wrong mother?'

Ray could only hope it was that simple, but the anxiety in Alex's voice had suggested something far worse had happened.

'Either way,' Owen concluded, 'we should probably call it in. You know how vital the first hours are in abduction cases. At the very least, we should see if there are any units in the area. If someone *has* snatched your daughter, we should get a description out there as soon as possible.'

Owen put the radio to his mouth and called it in, requesting backup at the car park.

'I really appreciate your support,' Ray said when the radio quietened.

'Listen, mate, you don't need to say thank you. You know we take care of our own. And if some nutcase has snatched your daughter, we'll do everything to get her back.'

Ray appreciated the sentiment, even if it was scant consolation. He couldn't stop picturing a future where a tiny coffin was lowered into the ground, and it was all he could do not to break down.

The patrol car was first on the scene, swiftly followed by Owen and Ray, with a third joining moments later.

'Do you see Alex?' Owen asked, scanning the immediate vicinity.

Ray couldn't, at first, surprised at how busy the car park was. 'There's her car,' he said, recognizing the registration number and pointing at the hatchback.

Owen brought the car to a halt immediately in front of Alex's, and the two of them jumped out. Noticing that Alex wasn't behind the wheel, he pulled out his phone and called her, and she was soon running over to them, throwing her arms around his neck.

'Oh, Ray, thank God, I only looked away for a moment, and ...'

Ray wrapped his arms around her waist, holding her still for a moment, knowing that he needed to be pragmatic. Now wasn't the time for emotion. 'Tell me what happened.'

Alex steadied herself before recounting the story, retracing her steps, explaining her actions throughout. 'I couldn't have been looking away for anything more than twenty to thirty seconds, I swear to you.'

Owen was examining the door handle, shining his phone's torch on it, looking for any obvious fingerprints or smudges. 'And you said the car was locked?'

'Yes. The alarm sounded while I was at the machine, but I couldn't see anyone, and assumed it was Carol-Anne moving about that had caused it.'

Ray remained standing in front of the car, scouring the horizon for potential security cameras that might have captured what had happened, only spotting one some distance behind the car park.

For the first time his blood ran cold. His little girl – his bundle and joy – was out there alone and needed him more than ever.

Ray called Owen over as his training kicked in. 'Do me a favour:

get Alex out of this rain; put her in the back of our car and take her to get a cup of tea or something, will you? There will be a mountain of questions to scale, and she needs to be calm and rational.'

Owen nodded and moved over to Alex. She looked at Ray as Owen spoke to her, and he gave her a nod to confirm she should go with Owen. Waiting until the car had pulled away, he instructed the uniforms to set up a perimeter, preventing access to the car park, and to take the names and identification of anyone returning to collect their vehicle. And then with trembling fingers, he searched for Trent's number, placing the phone to his ear.

5

In the back of the police car, Alex was helpless as she watched the scene around her unfolding.

'You'd be better off waiting at home,' Ray had said after Owen had brought her back from the drive-thru. 'I promise I'll phone as soon as we know more.'

How could she return home and pretend that everything was normal? What did he expect her to do: make the dinner like usual? She had no idea of the time, but as the darkness was drawing closer, it had to be gone six. Where had the time gone?

As she watched technicians in protective paper suits carefully examining the ground in and around her car, none of it felt real. Her nails were chewed to the quick and her wrists red raw from scratching; no matter what she tried, she couldn't wake from the nightmare.

Who would have taken Carol-Anne, and why? She could understand an opportunistic thief stealing a handbag left on a seat, or a mobile device left unattended; it wasn't right, but she could understand the mentality. Maybe they could sell their loot to fund drugs or drink. What could someone possibly gain from taking Carol-Anne?

And how had they known where to get her from? There was

no way anyone could have foreseen that Alex would be running late for the interview, that she would choose that particular parking space, or that she would be stupid enough to leave Carol-Anne unattended, while she dashed through the rain to purchase a ticket.

So, what did that leave? Some predator who just happened to be in the vicinity? It didn't ring true. Someone sick enough to abduct a child had happened to be in the car park, near her car at the right moment? That didn't tally in her mind.

What else did that leave?

She could see from Ray's reaction what he was thinking. He'd hardly said more than two words to her since he'd arrived. Why wasn't this affecting him in the same way? Why wasn't he pulling out his hair with worry? Instead, he was busying himself talking to the technicians, doing anything that kept him away from the car she'd been shepherded to. Couldn't he see how much she needed him right now? Couldn't they just temporarily forget all the arguments and focus on supporting each other? Isn't that what relationships were all about? Wasn't that what they'd promised on their wedding day?

Maybe it was just more evidence of his infidelity. She had no doubt he'd loved her once, but in reality they'd been going through the motions for months. The miscarriage had stolen more than just their unborn child.

If she was right about the real reason he was avoiding her, what did that mean for their future together? She'd seen it when she'd explained what had happened. That look, so subtle, yet so apparent to someone who had shared so many tender moments with him.

He thought she was lying.

As the minutes continued to disappear into the mire of history, even she was beginning to question her version of events. Had Carol-Anne definitely been in the car? Or had Alex's fragile psyche snapped and her mind created the memory to cover up the truth?

After what had happened at that park in Manchester, she knew it was a possibility, yet the memory was so real. She couldn't have fabricated Carol-Anne giggling, could she? And if she had, where the hell was Carol-Anne now? Already Ray had been home and confirmed she wasn't there.

'You're not crazy,' Alex muttered under her breath, failing to convince even herself. 'You're not crazy,' she said, firmer this time.

She felt numb to the anxiety now. Troubled thoughts continued to flood her mind, each one like a paper cut, inflicting pain; eventually they would kill her. Her pulse and heartbeat had slowed drastically, as her body subconsciously came to terms with the prospect that there was nothing she could do to fix this terrible occurrence. The pill she'd found in the bottom of her handbag had probably helped, the last of her prescription from Dr Kirkman. Maybe that was why the scene outside the car was occurring in slow motion despite the minutes on the clock passing so quickly.

At least Ray hadn't blamed her yet. He had to be thinking it behind those dark brooding eyes of his; however he hadn't uttered the words, and she appreciated that. Carrying the guilt was hard enough, and having him to share the burden was a blessing. She wished he was sitting in the car with her now, but Ray wasn't someone who could just sit on the sidelines and watch the game unfold. Especially not where Carol-Anne was concerned. He needed to be involved, even though he would probably be assigned to other duties as the full investigation launched. For now, at least, his DI was allowing him to observe.

The driver's door opening snapped her back to reality. The woman who took the seat was older than Alex, and with a slender frame and taut shoulders, she carried a confidence suited to her role.

'Alex? I'm Detective Inspector Serena Trent,' the woman said, extending her hand. 'I've read the statement you gave earlier, and I'm hoping you can clarify a few points for me.'

Alex nodded, her pulse already quickening.

'In the statement you said you had to wait for that particular space?'

Alex nodded again, terrified that the detective could read her mind.

'Did you speak to the woman whose space you took?'

Alex coughed, and when she spoke sounded croaky. 'Briefly, just to check she was leaving.'

'And can you describe what this woman looked like?'

Alex frowned. 'I don't remember.'

'Hair colour? Eye colour?'

The only thing she could remember was that bright yellow umbrella. She wasn't even sure they'd spoken anymore.

'Did she have any other distinguishing features? Glasses, distinctive nose, anything like that?'

Alex stared blankly back at her, too exhausted to cry again.

'Can you remember the make and model of her car? Or any part of the registration plate?'

Alex watched DI Trent. Was she being serious? Did she really think the woman with the yellow umbrella had taken Carol-Anne? Was that even possible? Alex had seen the SUV pull away, but had it actually exited the car park? What did Trent know that she didn't?

'Alex? I said, can you remember the make or model of the car?' Trent repeated.

Alex shook her head, staring down at her hands as they scratched at the scars on her wrists.

'Given the proximity of her departure and your dash to the ticket machine, she could be a potential witness. It would be good if we can identify her in case she saw anyone strange hanging about the place.'

Alex raised her head, considering the woman before her, in whom she was expected to put all her trust. Ray had mentioned Trent's name in passing, although he'd never said how attractive she was. The skin around her eyes wasn't as smooth as her neck, and she didn't look as old as Alex was certain she was. Her face bore little by way of make-up, and her bleached hair seemed to hang effortlessly, without need of grips or spray.

'I'm sorry,' Alex eventually said.

Trent narrowed her eyes. 'And there was a second woman you interacted with too?'

Alex blushed at the memory.

'In your statement you said you thought *she* might have taken your daughter,' Trent encouraged.

'I thought I heard Carol-Anne's voice.'

Trent watched her in silence for a moment. 'I'm going to apologize in advance for my next question, but I need to know, Alex, have you taken any pills or consumed any alcohol today?'

Alex ground her teeth, her nails scratching feverishly. 'No.'

'Are you taking any medication, prescribed or otherwise?'

How could she know about that? Surely Ray hadn't told his boss what they had been through this past year? If he had, it would explain why Trent was looking at her so strangely.

Trent ran a hand over her face, as if wiping away the guilt of having to ask the question. 'It's a strange case for me to be involved with – knowing Ray so well – and vicariously knowing you through his eyes.'

The hairs on the back of Alex's neck tingled. 'What's he said?'

Trent raised her hands in a calming gesture. 'Nothing bad. As his superior I'm obviously aware of what you both went through a few months ago, and—'

'My miscarriage has nothing to do with this.'

'I'm not saying it has, Alex, I just meant I know the pressure the two of you have been under, and stress can do strange things; the mind can play tricks.'

'I didn't imagine this! Someone took my daughter.' For the first time Alex wanted to believe the words, even if Trent would take more convincing.

'Our Scene of Crime specialists have been searching for forensics in and around your car, and so far they've not found anything to suggest anybody else had access to the car. The only prints on the rear door handle are a match to your own, presumably created fresh today when you put Carol-Anne in the back of the car. What's also odd is they've found no loose hairs anywhere in the back of the car; has it been cleaned recently?'

It had been at the garage for a service yesterday, but what did that have to do with this?

'Do you keep a spare key for the vehicle at home?' Trent continued.

Alex nodded.

'Does anyone else have access to your home who might have used the key to get to Carol-Anne in the back?'

'I unlocked the car when the alarm went off.'

Trent smiled thinly. 'We have to consider the possibility that whoever took your daughter came here with that intention. We have to investigate every possibility. Where do you keep the spare key?'

'It's in a drawer in our bedroom.'

'Have you had any friends or family around socially recently? Or do you have a cleaner or regular babysitter who's been in your home?'

Alex couldn't think of a single friend or relative who would deliberately take Carol-Anne. 'No.'

'And when did you last check the key was there?'

Alex opened her mouth to speak. She had no idea when she'd last seen the spare key. It wasn't something that had ever crossed her mind. It was just *there*. In the unlikely event she ever lost her keys or somehow locked them in the car, she would know where to find the spare.

'I'm sure it was there when I last checked.'

'Which was when?'

Alex shrugged. 'I don't remember. Only Ray and I have access to our home.'

'I'm just doing my job, Alex. I need to establish the facts if I'm to investigate what really happened here. I don't mean to be blunt, but the sooner we cut through the bullshit, the better it'll be for Carol-Anne.'

Alex looked away as she felt the sting of tears at the corners of her eyes.

'I want you to give me a list of guests – friends, colleagues, *and* strangers – who may have visited your home in the last month.'

Alex felt embarrassed that the list of names could be counted on one hand with fingers to spare.

Trent sighed. 'I'm going to assign one of my best Family Liaison Officers to stay with you and Ray for the next few days. She's experienced in dealing with family traumas and will be able to keep you informed of progress on the investigation. Do you have space at home where she can stay?'

The thought of a stranger in her house filled Alex with dread, but she nodded regardless. As the darkness continued to envelope the horizon, she was certain Carol-Anne was still alive, and very much in danger. If having someone in her home would keep her up to date with what was going on, that's what she would do.

6

Ray watched as Trent exited the patrol car and headed over to the Crime Scene Manager. Alex was staring at him from the back of the car, and although he could see the pain in her eyes, he turned away.

She needed comfort and support, but he didn't trust himself to provide it. Maybe once upon a time it would have been easier, but not anymore. He wanted to reassure her: to tell her that he wouldn't rest until Carol-Anne was back safe and sound. He knew if he went over there now and tried to empathize, he would allow his own anxiety and terror to seep through the cracks in his armour, and then he would be no good to anyone.

He had to remain strong for Carol-Anne, and if that was at the expense of Alex's delicate emotions then so be it. He didn't want to turn his back, but he didn't have enough strength for both of them. Carol-Anne was his priority, and getting her home safe his only objective.

'Can I have a cigarette?' he asked, as DC Owen Hargrove approached.

Owen reached for the packet and opened the lid. 'Thought you quit.'

Ray drew a cigarette from the packet and placed it between his lips. 'I did.' He leaned in as Owen held the lighter forward.

Taking a deep drag, Ray had forgotten how toxic that first inhale tasted. Like a mixture of antiseptic and faeces. He quickly exhaled and took a second pull, the endorphins beginning to bubble somewhere in his head. 'Thanks.'

Owen squashed the lighter into the carton, and handed it to Ray. 'Keep them. I get the impression that won't be your last.'

Owen was giving him that look, a mixture of pity and relief that he wasn't the one suffering the pain. Ray knew the look as he'd offered it to victims of crime on so many occasions, yet he'd never realized how tough it was to face. He could feel the lump growing in his throat, and took another drag on the cigarette. There would be a time for him to deal with the toll of the emotion and stress of the situation. Not yet.

Ray nodded his thanks. 'Where are we with locating local security camera footage?'

'No street cameras in the local area, and considering where the car park is – off a residential street – there are no local businesses with cameras pointed in this direction.'

'What about that one?' Ray asked, pointing at the tall pole directly behind the car park that he'd spotted on arrival.

Owen's face contorted. 'It points directly at the ticket machine, and the cars in the immediate vicinity, though that's only about five or so of them. It was set up to capture anyone trying to steal from the machine. And the footage isn't great. It isn't a live stream, rather still images captured every ten seconds.'

'Have you watched it?'

Owen nodded. 'Alex can be seen approaching the machine, then leaving the shot, which is presumably when she turned the alarm off, and then returning to purchase her ticket.'

'At least that proves she isn't lying about what happened.' He inhaled deeply, welcoming the burn in his throat. 'And there are no cars or people seen entering or leaving the car park in that time?'

Owen shook his head. 'It's as good as useless, mate. It isn't even in colour. I think the owners must have put it up more as a deterrent than to actually serve a purpose.'

'Can I see it?'

'Trent has instructed us not to share any information with you, unless she clears it first. You know how it is.'

Ray fixed him with a look, forcing eye contact. 'Come on, Owen, what harm can viewing the footage do? Please?'

Owen returned the look, before finally relenting. 'Okay, but it stays between the two of us. Trent can be a Rottweiler and I don't want her on my arse.'

Ray remained where he was while Owen moved across to one of the SOCO team vans, returning a moment later with an iPad, holding it to his chest, and standing directly in front of Ray so nobody would see what they were doing.

Tapping the screen, Ray watched as Alex came into view, the shot captured at 14:47:20. She could be seen studying the sign above the machine, calculating how much she would need to pay. In the next image, Alex could be seen staring back at the vehicle, before disappearing in the next shot, as Owen had described, and then returning at 14:47:50. At 14:48:40, Alex was facing the car, and at 14:48:50, she was out of shot.

'I want to watch it again,' Ray said, discarding the cigarette and squashing it under foot.

'Why?' Owen asked. 'I've watched it a dozen times, and there is nothing going on in the background. Just Alex and the machine.'

Ray glared until Owen tapped it again and the first shot appeared on the screen. The grainy image wasn't ideal; and it was only because they knew the figure to be Alex that they could actually be certain it was her. Even if another figure had appeared in the background, there was no way they'd be able to identify who it was.

'A two-minute window,' Ray concluded when the footage once again stopped.

'How do you figure that?'

'At 14:47:20 she is looking at the machine, and she isn't heading back to the car until 14:48:50.'

'Yeah, but she moves away to switch off the alarm at 14:47:40, and is staring at the car a minute later, leaving a fifty-second window at best.'

'Not if the culprit was already ducking down behind the car when Alex left. Let's say for a moment that whoever took Carol-Anne had it all planned. Somehow they knew Alex would be here and would leave Carol-Anne in the car. It's what, a twenty to thirty second walk to the machine from where she's parked? Which would mean she first turned her back on the car at 14:46:50. If the culprit opened the door, and pulled Carol-Anne out, they could have been well away by the time Alex first turns back to look at the car at 14:47:30. Even if they were still crouching down by the car at that point, there's still another minute to get away.'

'And go where? Alex didn't see anyone.'

'Another vehicle more than likely. She didn't look in every car. What if the perpetrator was already in the car park waiting for Alex to arrive? He or she could have returned to their car and waited until Alex wasn't looking again, then driven off.'

'You're basing this on no evidence whatsoever.'

'It's like a magician's trick: smoke and mirrors. With the heavy rain, condensation on the windscreen, a car park packed full of cars, and a mother under extreme stress, it's the only explanation that fits.'

'It doesn't narrow down who took her or why.' Owen quickly apologized for the remark, having briefly forgotten how involved Ray was. 'I'd better get the iPad back to the van before anyone realizes it's missing.' Owen paused and squeezed Ray's arm. 'We'll get her back, mate. You have to let us do what we do best.'

Ray wasn't listening, his imagination already working through a list of suspects who would want to see him suffer such cruelty. He'd locked up his fair share of villains over the years, but none who would devise a revenge as complex as snatching a child from an open car park. Yet what else did that leave?

For now he needed answers from the only witness at the scene. Making his way to the patrol car, he climbed into the back, unable to bring himself to meet Alex's eyes.

'You said you looked away for thirty seconds at most.'

The confusion on Alex's face revealed she hadn't been expecting this to be his opening gambit. 'It's true.'

Ray shook his head, hating himself, yet unable to stop the words leaving his lips. 'Thirty seconds from the car to the machine without looking at the car. Then twenty seconds initially until the alarm sounds, and then another fifty seconds buying your ticket. Almost two minutes where you weren't watching our daughter.'

'No, Ray, it couldn't have been that long—'

'I've seen the security footage! How could you be so reckless, Alex?' He still couldn't meet her gaze as he uttered the words, feeling her pain as much as his own.

'I-I-I,' she began, unable to string together the words needed to explain her actions.

'I'm going to have you driven home,' he continued, not prepared to listen to anything more she had to say; at least not yet. The pain burned deep in his chest, and to remain in her presence would only lead him to say something he would later regret.

'I see you're smoking again,' she said bitterly, as if trying to strike back.

It was like waving a red rag at a bull. Turning, he glared at her, pointing his finger just inches from her face. 'You have no right to judge me for anything right now.'

And with that, he climbed out, wanting to hug his wife and tell her everything would be okay, and equally wanting to berate her for losing their daughter. Lighting a second cigarette, he stalked off into the darkness.

7

'I don't want to go home,' Alex growled as Owen watched her from the front of the car. 'Let me help search for her. I'm her mother, and she needs me.'

It wasn't Owen's fault, he'd been told to drive her home. As far as DI Trent was concerned, they'd taken and questioned Alex's statement, and now she was just getting in the way of their investigation.

'Someone will call as soon as there is any news,' Owen tried to reason, but calming highly strung women clearly wasn't one of his strengths.

'Wherever she is, she'll be frightened because I'm not there. She's never spent a night without me nearby. Even when Ray puts her to bed, I still kiss her goodnight. There hasn't been a single night when I haven't held her close and kissed her.' She didn't like the look of pity shrouding the young detective's face.

'What about a public appeal?' she blurted. 'You could put her picture on the news and tell everyone in the city to look out for her. Or the radio? Maybe I could speak to the local radio and put her description out there. Maybe someone would come forward and say they've seen her.'

She couldn't keep the desperation from her voice, nor could

she sit idly by and wallow anymore. A time for grieving might come eventually, but while she could still feel Carol-Anne's life force, she would keep fighting.

She was fighting a losing battle as far as Owen was concerned, though. His DI had ordered him to drive Alex home and no amount of reasoning or valid arguments would deflect him from that course of action.

'Can I get you anything?' Owen asked, as he pulled into the driveway and killed the engine.

Alex didn't answer, instead staring out the window at the big brick building that had never looked so alien to her. If it wasn't for a slight recognition, she would have said he'd brought her to somebody else's house. With no lights on, and the curtains open, the building looked unloved and abandoned. Hadn't it been a loving home? Carol-Anne had known she was loved by both her parents, right?

'I could pick up a takeaway for you,' Owen continued, watching her from the mirror. 'Or if you need me to go to the shop, then—'

'Thanks, I'll be fine,' Alex replied, avoiding eye contact. She was determined not to cry in front of him. The rest of the journey home had been filled with awkward silence; awkward because she didn't feel like engaging, and he clearly hadn't known what to say to someone experiencing a living grief.

She clamped her eyes shut as her fingers brushed against the door handle, but they refused to coil around it, her body fighting against going in and her worst fears being realized. Even though Ray had already confirmed Carol-Anne wasn't at home, to see it with her own eyes would be to finally admit that her daughter was gone, maybe never to return, and the weight of that would crush her soul.

'Is there anybody I can call to be with you?' Owen asked.

With no brothers or sisters, Alex's circle of friends had dwindled since she'd given up work to be a full-time mum, and although her social media feeds listed dozens of 'friends', there was no one she would want to see now. Sophie was her closest friend these days; even so, she didn't deserve to bear the brunt of Alex's current emotional state.

She shook her head, forcing her fingers around the plastic handle.

'I think DI Trent said she's assigning a Family Liaison Officer to support you. I can wait until she arrives if you'd like?'

There was desperation in his voice, but it suited her best to decline the offer, much to Owen's evident relief. Pushing the door open, she stepped out into the cool and damp air. The rain had stopped and the atmosphere made it clear a reprisal could be imminent at any time. Reaching into her handbag she removed her house key, grimacing at the 'World's Best Mum' key ring that dangled between her fingers. It was all she could do to stop herself tearing it off and throwing it to the gutter.

Owen was still in the car, waiting for her to enter, so as she pushed the door open, she waved without looking, then pushed the door closed with her bottom before crumpling to the floor, her head in her hands.

She couldn't have been there for more than a few minutes when there was a gentle knocking at the door. Had Owen heard her wailing and come to check on her? That was the last thing she needed: the pitying look of her husband's colleague.

Or maybe Ray had finally come to his senses and had come home to offer the support she needed. Wiping her face with the backs of her hands, she forced herself up and took several deep breaths to compose herself, before pulling the door open.

'Oh you are home,' the woman on the doorstep said cheerily, clutching a bottle of white wine. 'I wasn't sure as your car isn't in the drive and all the lights are off. Have you just got home?'

Alex frowned at her friend. 'Sophie? What are you …?'

Sophie's puzzled expression mirrored Alex's. 'It's Tuesday

night? You said Ray was going out to play squash and I should come over for a girly catch-up. Sorry, am I too early? You did say come after seven.'

The memory fired to the front of Alex's mind. 'It's Wednesday.'

Alex studied Sophie's face. Her elfin-like bob curled at the fringe, and despite the bright choice of eye shadow, she wore little other make-up to accentuate her high cheekbones and silky-smooth skin.

'Yes, it's Wednesday, silly! Oh, and before you ask I had a text from Noemi, and – *surprise, surprise* – she can't make it. That woman is such a flake. For someone who works in IT, she is so disorganized.' Sophie continued into the house, oblivious to the pained expression on Alex's face. 'I would understand if she had children or a man in her life, but once again she's bailed at the last minute.' Sophie paused when she saw Alex was still by the door. 'Don't tell me you forgot! Have you made other plans?'

'No, not exactly, it's just …'

Sophie was already through to the living room, turning on the main light and looking around, pausing when her eyes fell on Alex's swollen face still sheltered by the front door. 'Oh gosh, what's happened? Are you all right?'

How could Alex begin to explain the magnitude of what had happened that afternoon? They'd been friends for two years, since Alex and Ray had moved in next door to her. As a single woman with little responsibility other than her lease, how would Sophie understand the torment?

'Is it Ray?' she pressed. 'Has something happened? You can tell me, sweetie. You know I'm discreet.'

Alex allowed Sophie to lead her through to the living room; it didn't feel like home as she sank into the armchair. Carol-Anne's scent still filled the room, and for a moment Alex allowed herself to pretend none of the last few hours had occurred.

Sophie reappeared a moment later with two large glasses and the bottle of wine she'd brought over. Pouring a generous measure into each, she handed one of the glasses to Alex. 'Take your time, sweetie, I'm not going anywhere.'

Alex took a sip from her glass, before taking a much larger gulp, almost draining the contents. It tasted crisp and dry, and for the first time that evening, the weight of events lifted a fraction as the alcohol numbed the pain.

'Someone's taken Carol-Anne,' she said, in one quick breath, hoping that admitting the truth would be less painful if spoken quickly, like removing a plaster.

Sophie's mouth dropped, as deep crevices sank in her forehead. 'I … what do you mean? Ray's taken Carol-Anne?'

Alex took a deep breath. 'I was parked in town; one minute she was strapped into my car, and the next …'

Sophie gasped, her eyes widening, the shock of the words hitting home. 'Oh, sweetie, I don't know what to say.'

Alex lowered her near empty glass to the table. Alcohol wasn't the answer. She needed to keep her wits about her, and if the police needed to speak to her urgently, she didn't want her breath smelling of wine.

Sophie took a nervous sip of her own drink. 'I'm so sorry, Alex. What have the police said? I'm sure they'll find her. Whatever you need in the meantime just say.'

This was precisely why Alex hadn't wanted to inform her. Sophie was a sweet girl, and not the sort of person you'd rely on in a crisis. She was younger, and a free spirit, not someone who worried about a career, a family, the trappings of a regular life. They were polar opposites in terms of aspirations, and that was probably why they got on so well. That, and the fact that Alex had supported Sophie when a previous relationship had turned sour.

Sophie was perching awkwardly on the edge of the sofa, not knowing where to look or what to say. It would have been kinder to allow her to slip away, and although originally Alex had wanted to be left alone, the presence of someone – anyone – in her home would distract her from the silent reminder that Carol-Anne wasn't home.

She didn't expect to see Ray anytime soon. He would stay at the crime scene until he was forced to leave. Either that or he would be seeking solace in someone else's company. Although she had no proof that he had been seeing someone behind her back, the distance between them was too vast to ignore.

'What's with the suit?' Sophie suddenly asked, her attempt at small talk showing again how ill-equipped she was to deal with such an awful situation.

Alex stared down at the damp clothing, which she'd picked out especially for today's interview. She'd woken with such high hopes this morning; it now felt like a lifetime away.

'I should probably get changed,' she admitted.

And that was Sophie's trigger to spring into action. 'You sit still, and I'll grab your pyjamas and dressing gown.'

Alex didn't argue, knowing Sophie would have done anything to escape the tension in the room. And as silence once again returned to the house, Alex found herself staring at the large print of Carol-Anne on the wall above the television. The photo shoot had been a present from Ray's sister and husband. The photographer had done such a good job of capturing Carol-Anne's sweet, glowing innocence. And as Alex studied each line of her daughter's face, she made a silent vow that she would get her back, whatever it took.

8

The area immediately surrounding Alex's grey hatchback had now been covered with a tent to keep it out of sight of curious bystanders, but more importantly to protect the evidence it contained from being washed away by the elements. A large mobile generator whirred away in the background, powering the temporary brilliant white lights that had been erected and pointed at the scene as the technicians continued to examine and collect samples from the surrounding area.

The sky overhead was pitch-black, the moon hidden somewhere behind the thick blanket of clouds. At least the rain was holding off for now.

Ray finished the last of the cigarettes Owen had given him and scrunched up the packet, tempted to throw it into the gutter, but conscious that an eagle-eyed technician would probably take it back to the lab for later examination.

He was standing between the inner and outer cordoned areas. An area of ten cars either side of where the tent was stretched over the hatchback marked the width of the inner cordon – the area where the technicians' focus was – while the depth stretched almost to the edge of the car park. The residential street where the car park's entrance and exit stood had been taped off, with a uniformed officer standing guard at both ends, allowing access only to residents who could provide documentation showing they lived there. Several residents had been watching the scene unfold from the safety of their windows; free entertainment for the curious mind.

Ray hated waiting for news – he felt so useless since DI Trent had made it abundantly clear that she didn't want him anywhere near her investigation. It wasn't personal discrimination – he understood the rules – but who better to have on the team than someone who knew the victim so well?

His phone vibrated, and he allowed himself the briefest smile when he saw who it was from, before the guilt took over. He deleted the message – as he always did – and this time didn't reply. It was important to keep his mind focused on the job at hand.

'What are you still doing here, Ray?' Trent called out, ducking beneath the inner cordon and heading over to him. 'I asked you to go home and wait for our call. I can't have you anywhere near the crime scene. Please don't make me have you escorted from here.'

He pulled the overcoat tighter around his midriff. 'Please, ma'am, I don't want to interfere or slow you down, I just want to stay close by to react when there's a break. I swear you won't even know I'm here.'

'The rules are there for good reason, Ray, as well you know.' She softened her tone. 'I understand that you want to help, and if it wasn't for your close involvement there's nobody I'd rather have by my side, but it isn't possible. I have assigned a Family Liaison Officer who'll help keep you informed. Please just go home and await my call.'

'I could be useful, ma'am. I'll go out of my mind with worry if I go home. Let me chase down some leads. Anything? I don't care how mundane it is, I'll do it. What about searching for any possible dashcams that might have captured something? Please?'

She reached out and rubbed his arm. 'You know I can't. We have all available resources searching the properties near to your home, canvassing for witnesses, and searching for Carol-Anne.' She sighed. 'I can't even begin to imagine what you're going through and how you're feeling, and you know we're good at what we do. And because you're so well-liked in the team, you know everyone will give a hundred per cent to get little Carol-Anne back to you and Alex.'

She steered him towards the outer cordon, and gave the uniformed officer there strict instructions not to allow him back within the area.

'I'll call as soon as we have something,' she called after him, but he was no longer listening, stalking off to a nearby off-licence to buy more cigarettes and a small bottle of vodka.

If he had to go home and try not to think about his daughter's peril, then he couldn't do it sober. As he unscrewed the cap, though, and moved to put it against his lips, he had a fresh idea, and quickly resealed and pocketed the bottle.

Any detective worth his salt knows who the key figures in the city are: the people who exercise control over large-scale criminal enterprises. One such figure in Southampton was Gianni Demetrios, the product of a Greek father and Italian mother, raised in the UK but with strong family connections in his parents' countries of birth. A self-professed crime lord, he made it his business to know everybody else's; no major activities occurred in Southampton without his prior approval.

Like most men in his position, Demetrios liked to create the impression that he was just an honest businessman trying to scrape together a living. And among his less-than-savoury busi-nesses, he did indeed run several above-the-counter companies, paying his taxes and providing pension benefits to his employees. The rumours about Demetrios's wider interests were well known to every detective in Hampshire Constabulary. The trouble with rumours is they're worth nothing in court. Which is why Demetrios continued to run his operation from the comfort of the outside world, rather than behind bars.

Most evenings Demetrios could be found sitting behind three feet of mahogany, watching as the hard-working residents of Southampton gambled their wages in his casino. If anyone could provide alternative insight into what might have happened to Carol-Anne, it was Demetrios; which is why Ray was now sitting behind the wheel of his car staring up at the brightly fronted building that welcomed gamblers of all varieties to bet against the house.

Two large bouncers with shaved heads – one black with thick arms, and the other EasternEuropean-looking – were checking memberships at the main door as Ray approached.

'It's a members-only club, pal,' the larger of the men said, sticking out an arm to block Ray's approach to the door.

Ray eyed him cautiously. With a good six inches height advantage, it didn't look like he'd have too much trouble flattening Ray.

'I'm here to see your boss,' Ray said, as he pulled out his police identification and held it aloft for both to see.

'You got a warrant?' the bouncer fired back, not even bothering to look at the credentials.

'It's not official business,' Ray countered, puffing out his chest as much as he could and pushing himself up on his toes to reduce the height difference. 'I don't want any trouble. Can you just ask Mr Demetrios whether he will see me? It won't take long.'

The black guard nodded for his colleague to make the call, and peeling away, the call was placed, leaving Ray and the larger man where they were.

He eventually returned and led Ray in through the doors, past the cloakroom and past the well-dressed members squealing in equal measures of despair and excitement as they won and lost their bets.

The lift carriage deposited them on the top floor of the

building, where Ray was led through two solid oak doors with gilded door handles.

'Mr Demetrios said you should wait here and he will be along shortly,' the bouncer said, indicating the large leather sofa against the far wall. 'I'll be just outside in case there's any trouble.'

A moment later, two other doors opened and in walked the olive-skinned, dark-haired businessman, resembling a young Al Pacino in *The Godfather*.

'It's Detective Sergeant Granger, isn't it?' Demetrios asked, extending a wary hand as he joined Ray by the sofa.

Ray looked at the hand, before reluctantly shaking it. Ray wasn't the sort to go cap in hand to anyone, let alone an individual with Demetrios's shady background, but formalities had to be observed in such quarters. 'Thank you for seeing me.'

'I'm always happy to make time for the upstanding law enforcers of our fair city,' Demetrios purred, his coal-coloured curls slicked back. 'What is it I can do for you?'

Ray was taking a huge risk being anywhere near Demetrios's casino; desperate times called for desperate measures. He would worry about the fallout once Carol-Anne was back home and safe.

'I need information,' Ray began carefully, conscious that Demetrios was the sort of snake who would probably be recording every word of their exchange. 'You know people, and I need to know the name of the person or persons who have abducted my daughter.' The words cut his heart to ribbons; it was all he could do to keep himself upright as his knees buckled under the weight of expectation.

It was hard to tell if the look of confusion on Demetrios's face was as a result of Ray's appearance or the words he'd spoken. 'I'm sorry about your loss, but I'm afraid I really have no idea—'

'Cut the crap!' Ray barked before he could stop himself. 'Nobody would sanction something like this around here without your say-so. Was it someone I locked up? Someone looking for revenge? Going after me is one thing, but to snatch my daughter, it's … *give me a name!*'

Demetrios took off quickly, moving back through the doors he'd emerged from, ushering Ray to follow him. Lifting a framed photograph from the corner of the desk, he showed it to Ray. 'This is my daughter Gabriella. She's ten now, and lives with her mother and grandparents in Sicily. I miss her every day. I swear on her life, I have *no* idea who would make a move against you. I would never be involved in something so cruel.'

Ray examined his face, looking for any twitch or hint of deceit. Finding none, his heart sank. 'Then can you find out who would do it? She's only two and I'm terrified that …' He couldn't finish the sentence, as he struggled to keep his composure. 'I will do anything to get her back. Any amount of money, I'll pay it. I just want my daughter back.'

And in that moment, their conflicting backgrounds were forgotten about as they shared the pain and joy of paternity.

'Leave it with me, detective. I will see what I can find out. And then maybe one day in the future, you can return the favour.' There was a momentary glint in his eyes as he spoke, but it was gone seconds later. He pressed a buzzer somewhere beneath his desk, and the bouncer returned and led Ray away by the arm.

9

The sound of urgent banging woke Alex from the few disrupted hours of slumber she'd managed on the sofa when her hours of impatient pacing had yielded no news. Ray's keys weren't in their usual spot suggesting he'd never made it home, and as she reached for her phone to check for any news on Carol-Anne, her heart sank to find no messages or missed calls. He may not have verbally blamed her, yet his actions were speaking far louder.

Further banging quickly lifted the fog of drowsiness, and she raced to the front door, yesterday's suit creased and hanging from her aching body. As she opened the door to see a tall woman in a long skirt and grey cardigan holding her identification aloft, the hope of seeing Carol-Anne bounding towards her faded.

'I'm PC Isla Murphy,' the woman in the cardigan said, her silhouette framed by the early morning light. 'I'm your assigned Family Liaison Officer. You were expecting me, weren't you? DI Trent said she would phone ahead and tell you I was coming.'

Alex strained her neck to look beyond the woman for any sign of her daughter, but finding an empty and lifeless street, she stepped to one side. 'You'd better come in,' she said, allowing Isla to enter before closing the door. 'Is there any news?'

Isla headed into the kitchen, making a beeline for the kettle and promptly filling it. 'Tea? Coffee?'

'Tea,' Alex said, subconsciously biting at her nails, oblivious that she was chipping yesterday's coat of polish.

'Where would I find that? And mugs?'

Alex pointed to the cupboard hanging above the kettle's stand on the counter.

Isla removed two fresh mugs, depositing teabags in each. 'Do you take milk and sugar?'

'Just milk,' Alex replied, not one who enjoyed being fussed over, yet desperate to keep her only contact with the investigation onside.

'Have you had breakfast yet?' Isla asked, while waiting for the kettle to boil.

'I'm not hungry,' Alex replied, shaking her head. 'Please, just tell me what's happening. Does DI Trent have any new leads? Have they worked out who took my daughter yet? Please, I need something.'

Isla cocked her head sympathetically. 'I have nothing new I can tell you yet,' she said. 'I am due to have a check-in call with Detective Inspector Trent in the next hour, and then hopefully I will be able to provide you with an update. In the meantime, we should get some breakfast. It's important to take care of yourself during situations like this. I've seen firsthand how the stress takes a grip, and you need to stay strong for your daughter's sake. There's no knowing when she is going to need you again, and you'll be no use to her if you're exhausted. In my experience the best thing you can do to help us is to eat three square meals per day, get eight hours' sleep and keep yourself well-hydrated.'

There was something so familiar about Isla. Standing at over six feet tall, her grey hair was scraped back over her head and held in a bun with a grip. The cardigan was the same shade of grey as her hair, and the skin around her face and neck was so pale she looked washed out; like someone had plucked a character from a black-and-white movie and deposited her in a Technicolor universe. Facially she couldn't have been much older than her late-fifties, but her plain clothes and dour attitude reminded Alex of an old headmistress.

'I'll fix you some toast,' Isla continued, lifting the lid of the bread bin. 'Butter and jam?'

'In the fridge,' Alex said, nodding at the unit in the corner behind the door.

'I hear your husband is in the force, is that right?'

'He's a detective sergeant in Trent's team. You don't know him then?'

'Not personally. Southampton isn't my regular patch. I'm usually based on the Isle of Wight, but DI Trent requested me specifically to come and be with you.'

'Why?'

'I like to think it's because I'm good at my job,' Isla said as she dropped two slices of bread into the toaster. 'I'm here for whatever you need for as long as this takes, Alex. I'm not a spy, as some families choose to believe. I'm here to keep you informed of the investigation's progress, to answer any of your questions, and to shield you from as much of the stress and drama as I can.'

Isla turned away to make the tea, placing the mug on the breakfast bar in front of Alex when it was ready. When the toast popped up, she spread the butter and jam ferociously, handing the plate over.

Alex dutifully took a bite of the toast, struggling to generate enough saliva to swallow.

'How did you sleep last night?' Isla asked, brushing a stray hair from her face.

'Hardly at all,' Alex admitted. She wasn't one who easily shared with strangers, yet Isla struck her as someone who wouldn't take no for an answer.

'That's to be expected. It might be an idea to get your head down for a nap later on this morning or early afternoon. There's no knowing how long or short the investigation will be, and I should warn you there will be a lot of hanging around waiting for updates. I will do everything in my power to keep you as well informed as I can, and if there is anything specific you want me to ask the investigation team, please tell me and I will make a note of it.'

Alex wasn't sure she wanted to know the answer to her next question, but asked anyway. 'Have you worked on any child abduction cases before?'

Isla studied her face, as she looked for the right words. 'I have, and before you ask me how many of those cases resulted in the safe return of the child, you should know that no two cases are ever the same. My track record as a Family Liaison Officer has absolutely no bearing on how your situation will turn out.'

'How many ended well?'

'I told you, it doesn't matter; it has no bearing on—'

'How many?' Alex interrupted, fixing her with a firm stare.

Isla sighed. 'Okay, in the interest of establishing a circle of honesty with you, I will answer your question, but I cannot stress enough that you should not read anything – either positive or negative – into it.' She paused. 'I have been liaison in five separate child abduction cases, and in four of those, the child was safely returned.'

Alex couldn't prevent the trace of a smile breaking out across her face.

'You need to understand that none of the five cases bore any of the hallmarks of yours,' Isla cautioned. 'In those successful cases, we identified the perpetrator as a relative or family friend, and the circumstances surrounding the holding of those children were not as complex as what occurred yesterday.'

'You got them back?'

'I didn't personally, but the investigating team did manage to reunite the child with the parent.'

'And the fifth?' Alex interrupted. 'What happened with the one who didn't make it home?'

Isla's forehead tightened. 'Why do you want to know?'

'I just want to know what to expect.'

'There's no way to know what to expect. Every missing child case is different.'

'What happened to the child?'

Isla sighed again, raising her eyes to the ceiling. 'I'm not at liberty to—'

'Please just tell me!'

'He died,' Isla sighed, and the heavyset frown revealed she instantly regretted it.

Alex wasn't prepared for the answer, and had to steady herself on the stool. 'What happened to him?'

'I've already said too much. I will repeat that what happened then was totally different to what you are going through. You need to remain positive. The police will do everything they can to find your daughter.'

Alex fought against the nausea building in her stomach, pushing the remains of the toast to one side. 'I'm going to take a shower and get dressed. I want you to interrupt me the second you hear something.'

Isla promised she would, and then watched as Alex headed for the staircase, a mutual understanding already growing between them.

10

Tired eyes stared back at him from the large mirror above the basins. Ray wasn't accustomed to sleeping slouched over a desk, and as he straightened and rotated his shoulders, his lower back ached from the uncomfortable position. Running the hot tap, he allowed the sink to fill with water before lowering his hands into it and splashing handfuls of warm water against his stubbly cheeks.

It didn't bother him that he was still in yesterday's clothes. He doubted his colleagues would comment even if they did notice. None of them would judge him, not after what had happened. Although Trent had made it clear she wouldn't involve him in the investigation, he hoped she'd have softened her resolve overnight and might at least allow him to hang around in the office. He didn't want to interfere, but he wanted to be the first to know the moment a break was made. Somebody would have to collect Carol-Anne from wherever she was and he couldn't think of anyone better.

Emptying the sink, he reached into his trouser pocket and removed the spare tie he always kept in his desk drawer, slipping the pre-tied loop around his neck before straightening the knot. At least the tie would make it appear as if he had been home and changed.

Exiting the bathroom, he proceeded along the corridor to the large office the team worked out of. There was no sign of Trent, and he guessed she was probably further along the corridor setting up the Major Incident Room, where the team would operate from primarily as the investigation developed.

'Ray?' DC Owen Hargrove said as he approached, a quizzical look on his face. 'What are you doing here? I thought—'

'What's the latest?' Ray quickly fired back, ignoring the question.

Owen glanced nervously around like he could sense Trent nearby. 'I can't … I mean, we're not supposed to discuss the investigation with you; DI's orders. Has she seen you here yet?'

Ray shook his head, unsurprised by Owen's reaction. Leaning closer, Ray whispered, 'Whatever happens, you'll keep me in the loop, right? I'm not asking you to break any rules, just keep me updated with what's going on. That's all I'm asking.'

'I can't,' Owen replied through gritted teeth.

'You owe me, Owen. Okay? I won't stitch you up; just let me know when something new breaks.'

Owen's eyes widened as he spotted Trent approaching the two of them over Ray's shoulder.

'Ray, can we have a word in my office, please?' she said calmly.

He nodded and followed her through the banks of desks to the small enclosure at the far end of the room, closing the door quietly behind him. 'I'm ready to do whatever you need, ma'am.'

She looked at the creased shirt, crumpled suit jacket and stained tie. 'What I need is for you to go home and wait for us to call.'

'Please, ma'am, I'll go stir crazy at home. You know me: I need to keep busy. I promise I won't get in anybody's way.'

'I know that, Ray,' she said empathetically. 'My stance hasn't changed from last night. You can't be anywhere near what is going on for your sake as well as the sake of the rest of the team. We need to consider *every* angle in cases like this, and I don't think any of the team will feel able to speak freely knowing you are nearby.'

He knew what she was implying, even if she hadn't used the term. He'd been a detective long enough to know that Trent would have already instructed the team to pull together a list of registered sex offenders from the area so they could start checking alibis. The thought of some slime ball being anywhere near Carol-Anne made him want to pick up the chair in front of him and hurl it out of the window. And that was precisely why Trent didn't want him anywhere near the investigation.

'Please, ma'am, give me anything else to do. I'm not asking to work the case, but just let me be nearby. I could work from my desk here. We've got dozens of unsolved cases that I could slowly work through.'

She considered him silently, but he couldn't tell if she was pondering his request or trying to find the words to let him down gently.

'How's Alex coping?' she eventually asked.

He thought back to the reprimand he'd delivered in the back of the patrol car before Owen had driven her home. The guilt must have been written over his face, as Trent said, 'Ah, I see.'

'I'll check on her when I go home,' he said, lowering his eyes.

'And how were things between the two of you before yesterday? When you were both at the car park I couldn't help noticing frostiness.'

'Everything's fine,' he lied.

She laid her palms flat on the table. 'Take it from someone who's been through two divorces, what I saw was far from fine. This job … it puts a strain on even the strongest of relationships. The hours can be shit, but it's more than that. It's the knowledge that the world is a terrifying place, and being unable to share those experiences with the ones you love for fear of dragging them into the mire.' Her cheeks flushed as she realized she'd overstepped the mark. 'You need each other more than ever now.'

He forced eye contact. 'Please don't keep me out of the picture, ma'am. I can be useful. Nobody knows my daughter better than I do. I promise not to go off half-cocked, and to work as part of the team, but please don't leave me out in the cold.'

'Ray, you know I don't have a choice in the matter. It's a massive conflict of interest to have you anywhere near the Incident Room.'

'I can provide valuable intelligence, ma'am. Like-like-like mine and Alex's schedules and the places we've been where the suspect may have first seen her.'

'And as her father, I would expect you to provide those details to one of the investigative team, but you're too close to this, Ray. Come on, don't make this any harder than it already is. You're a valuable member of my team, and I'd love your determination and experience on the case, but my hands are tied. If you push me on this, I'll have no choice but to put you on leave until the case is closed.' She paused and stared empathetically. 'Of course, I don't want to do that.'

He knew there was no point in arguing with her, and he wasn't surprised by her stance, but Trent had always been a reasonable governor, and he had hoped to convince her of his usefulness.

'Before you go, there's something else I need to ask: what were you doing at Gianni Demetrios's casino last night?'

His head snapped up and eyes widened. 'How did you—?'

She cut him off by dropping an A4-sized colour photograph on the desk. Ray immediately recognized Demetrios's office from the night before. He could see why Trent had concerns.

'Where did you get this from?'

'It was emailed to me in the early hours of this morning. It was a taunt, with the subject line, "Who polices the police?". Do you realize how badly this reflects on me and the unit? I've spent two years trying to nail that son of a bitch, and now it looks like members of my team are cozying up to him.'

'It's just a photograph. It doesn't mean anything.'

'No, but it's what it implies. What were you talking to him about?'

'He knows the worst of the worst,' Ray tried to explain. 'And I thought if anybody had been planning to get back at me for something, then he might know about it, or be able to point me in the right direction.'

She narrowed her eyes. 'Is that what you think happened yesterday? That someone you once banged up snatched your daughter to … what … get revenge?'

He looked at her sheepishly.

She ripped up the photograph and dropped the pieces in her waste bin. 'I've seconded PC Isla Murphy to act as Family Liaison. I sent her to your place this morning and she's messaged to say she's made contact with Alex.' She paused, standing and offering him a sincere look. 'Take my advice, Ray: go home, and get yourself cleaned up. Maybe it would be better if you took a couple of days off. Spend it with Alex. Console and reassure her. She needs you now more than ever; you need each other.' She pointed at the door – her cue that the meeting was over.

Pulling the tie back over his head, he walked to the exit. Stumbling out into the fresh air, he made his way along the road to a newsagents where he purchased a sandwich, a bottle of juice, a packet of gum and a fresh carton of cigarettes. He needed to focus. Despite Trent's reservations, there was no way he was prepared to sit back while his daughter was still out there needing him.

11

Stepping out of the shower, Alex couldn't ignore the overwhelming feeling of guilt sweeping through her core. How could she be acting so normally when Carol-Anne was out there, alone and in huge danger? As much as the sheer terror remained, no further tears would flow; as if she had no more tears to give. What did that mean? Had some part of her subconscious mind already given up hope that Carol-Anne would return safely home?

Taking a deep breath, she shook the thought from her mind and, wiping condensation from the mirror with the edge of her towel, she stared at the tired-looking reflection in the mirror.

How could you be so stupid? How could you turn your back on her? How could you allow someone to take her?

It still didn't feel real. Tying a smaller towel around her wet hair, she almost expected to hear the sweet giggle coming from the bedroom next door. As she opened the bathroom door, she was only greeted by silence.

Isla had decided to dial into the team brief from her car, and Alex could see her head bobbing inside the small red car in the driveway. She could only hope that there was positive news. For a city supposedly covered in security and traffic cameras, one of them had to have captured the moment it had happened. Or the vehicle the culprit had used to make their escape.

Alex had replayed the events over and over in her mind as the hot water had thundered against her neck and shoulders. Could she have done something differently? As soon as she'd realized Carol-Anne was missing, could she have done more? She had checked the immediate vicinity, but why hadn't she gone from car to car, looking for anyone who might have been restraining a frightened child?

Reliving the nightmare was doing nothing to ease the pain and guilt of her reckless choice. Even if her face was masking that burden, every muscle could feel it weighing her down.

Ray had yet to return any of her calls or messages. She knew his words in the back of the car had been delivered in anger, and that he had probably regretted them the moment they had spewed, yet that didn't make them any less hurtful. Why hadn't he come home yet? Was he chasing down a lead? Maybe it was a positive sign that he had yet to message her: maybe Trent and her team had already identified the culprit and were fast on their way to make an arrest. And maybe that was why Isla was nodding in the car.

Throwing on tracksuit bottoms and a vest top, Alex didn't have a clue about how to spend the day. Her car was still with the police technicians, so she couldn't go anywhere, and even if she had the car, she wasn't sure there was anywhere she would want to go. It was at times like this that she missed her mum and dad the most. And having been an only child, she had no close family she could speak to. She probably should call Ray's sister and tell her what had happened, but how could she even begin to explain?

As she prepared to head back downstairs, she couldn't resist the urge to go into Carol-Anne's room, inhaling her daughter's smell. The tiny bed was neatly made, as it had been yesterday, and each of Carol-Anne's favourite teddies were resting against the edge of the frame.

Apart from one.

Carol-Anne had insisted on taking Ballet Bunny in the car with them. The bunny, about ten inches long, wearing a bright pink tutu, was the first toy Alex had bought when she'd learned she was expecting a girl. To Alex's amazement, Carol-Anne had never been without it. She had tried to clean the bunny in the washing machine last year, but Carol-Anne had sobbed at the prospect. As a result, she'd chosen to handwash the bunny since then, with Carol-Anne attentively supervising the procedure.

Alex made a mental note to ensure she collected the bunny from the team scrutinizing her car. She would give the bunny an extra-careful wash, so she would be fresh and clean for when Carol-Anne returned. Taking a final look around the room at the array of photographs on the wall, Alex tried to focus on her positivity; assuming the worst would only invite negativity into their lives; she had to believe that Carol-Anne would be found, and for the first time since the incident, Alex felt a glimmer of hope.

The sound of knocking at the door indicated that Isla's call was probably over. Galloping down the stairs, and opening the door, Alex was surprised to see Sophie on the doorstep, holding a cardboard tray of coffee cups, and a bag of fresh doughnuts.

'Oh good, you're up,' Sophie said, smiling awkwardly. 'I wanted to apologize for last night. You needed a friend and I wasn't much help. I'm here whenever you want someone to talk to or vent at. Okay? You can call on me at any time of the day, and I'll be there. It's the least I can do after what you did for me before. Have you eaten yet? I brought breakfast.'

Alex stepped back and allowed her to enter. 'Aren't you working today?'

'I'm not due in until this afternoon. To be honest I didn't sleep well last night after what you told me, so I got up and went for a run to clear my head. And then I spotted the bakery on my way back and thought you might need something to keep your energy levels up.'

Alex pulled her into a grateful hug.

'What was that for?'

'For not telling me I'm a lousy mother who deserves everything she gets.'

Sophie handed her one of the cups. 'What kind of friend would I be if I did that?'

Before Alex could reply, Isla appeared on the doorstep.

'Any news?' Alex asked hopefully.

Isla gave Sophie a cautionary look. 'Nothing so far … the team have a number of avenues they are going to be pursuing today, which is positive. DI Trent plans to hold another briefing later this evening, so we should know more then.'

Alex introduced the two women.

'There's something I need to talk to you about privately, Alex,' Isla began, giving Sophie another cautious look.

Sophie gave Alex a quick hug. 'I'd better get out of your hair anyway. If you need anything – and I mean *anything* – just call me. I'm meeting Noemi at the gym, but I'm only a phone call away.'

Alex had hoped Sophie would stay, but felt awkward asking; the last thing Sophie needed was a neighbour on the verge of a nervous breakdown, particularly if she'd already made plans with Noemi.

'DI Trent thinks it would be a good idea to make an early public appeal for information,' Isla said when they were alone.

'You want me to go on television?'

Isla shook her head. 'No, we would handle it in-house at this stage: a formal statement released to various UK media outlets, a copy of Carol-Anne's picture shared for publication in news-papers and regional news programmes. The thing is: the CCTV footage of the area isn't great, and while the team will continue to search for any images from the surrounding area at the time

Carol-Anne was taken, a public appeal might help identify potential eyewitnesses who either saw the act, or maybe can describe anyone suspicious hanging around the car park.'

'Great. Okay. Do it,' Alex said enthusiastically. 'If it helps bring her back sooner, then go ahead. I'm surprised you've even asked for my permission.'

Isla's nose wrinkled. 'I have to advise you that there can be repercussions from an appeal of this nature.'

Alex frowned. 'What kind of repercussions?'

Isla considered her next words carefully. 'For all the benefits of social media connectivity in situations like this, trolling is still a major issue that's hard to manage. Even if we don't name you in the campaign, and only share Carol-Anne's image and story, nothing stays secret forever, and these things can spread like wildfire.'

'That's a good thing, isn't it? I mean if everyone is talking about Carol-Anne and sharing her picture that can only be good.'

Isla ground her teeth. 'You need to be prepared for an almighty backlash. Given the nature of what happened yesterday, there are plenty of mothers who will empathize with what has happened, and there will also be plenty who will call you names and deride you for leaving your daughter unsupervised in that car. I'm not judging you, Alex, but others will. So, to that end, our advice is for you to delete, or at least suspend any of your social media accounts: Twitter, Facebook, Instagram, or wherever else you have a digital footprint. Such an appeal is going to thrust you firmly into the spotlight, and once it's out there, there will be no going back.'

'I'm prepared to do whatever it takes to get her back,' Alex said firmly. 'Even if it means I get lynched, we've got to try *everything*.'

Isla nodded her understanding. 'Okay, well can I ask you to find me a recent picture of Carol-Anne that we can distribute? It should be a full-body shot if possible, and preferably something which captures her essence in your eyes. Whoever has her may be using larger clothes and hats to disguise her appearance, so we need something that would shine through disguises like that. Okay?'

Alex raced up the stairs, bursting back into Carol-Anne's room and immediately scanning the walls for something suitable. As her eyes danced over the images, she heard a noise that chilled her bones: the unmistakeable sound of a little girl giggling.

12

The bus, packed full of antisocial children on their way to school, finally dropped Ray at the stop at the end of his road. He already had a cigarette between his lips as he stepped off the vehicle, and it was lit before his second foot hit the pavement. Public transport wasn't his preferred method of travel, most usually bumming a lift home from Owen, but at least he'd managed to grab ten minutes' kip before the first of the screaming and chattering groups had got on. He couldn't imagine anything worse than being a school teacher and being subjected to six continuous hours of enthusiastic disobedience. He'd far rather spend a day sitting outside a suspect's premises waiting for something to happen; surveillance was boring, yet peaceful.

The air felt fresh this morning, and the only clouds that remained in the bright blue sky were thin and white, offering little threat of the downpour they'd experienced yesterday. The surrounding countryside was now firmly in autumn's grip and winter was only just around the corner. Piles of wet leaves lined the edge of every kerb, and the puddles on the road had yet to evaporate under the bright sun. A cool breeze offset any warmth of the sun's rays.

His phone beeped to inform him of a new message.

Are we still on for tonight? I miss you x

Why had he brought this additional complication into his life? Didn't he have enough on his plate already balancing an intensive job, a wife, and child? His guilt exploded once again as he pictured Carol-Anne; maybe if he hadn't started the affair she would still be here. Had his behaviour indirectly led to Alex's momentary lapse of concentration yesterday? Was this karma's way of getting back at him?

He deleted the message without responding, telling himself that cooling things would be the right thing to do, at least until Carol-Anne was safely returned. After that, he would need to sit down with Alex and resolve their future once and for all.

He didn't recognize the small red car parked on the driveway, but as he remained on the doorstep finishing his cigarette, he couldn't help wondering who would choose such a vibrant colour. Stamping out the cigarette, he popped two pieces of gum into his mouth, dropping the now empty juice bottle in the recycle bin.

Opening the door, he wasn't prepared for the sound of chattering coming from the kitchen. Poking his head around the door, he caught sight of Alex with a grey-haired woman in a matching cardigan, who had police written all over her face.

Alex rushed over to him, throwing her arms around his neck. 'Thank God you're home.' She peeled away and fixed him with a stare. 'I heard Carol-Anne giggling upstairs.'

He frowned sceptically. Of all the things he'd thought she might say, this hadn't been one of them. He'd expected admonishment for staying out all night and for stinking of cigarettes, though neither of these things seemed to be bothering her.

'DS Granger,' the grey woman said, extending her hand. 'I'm Isla Murphy. DI Trent assigned me as your Family Liaison.'

Ray shook the hand, still not able to comprehend the mixed

look of excitement and horror on Alex's face. 'Please, call me Ray. What's going on here?'

'I heard her, Ray,' Alex blurted. 'I heard Carol-Anne's voice in her room. I swear it!'

He raised an eyebrow at Isla.

'Your wife *believes* she heard the sound of a child laughing upstairs,' Isla confirmed.

'Giggling,' Alex corrected. 'Just like Carol-Anne. I swear it was her, Ray.'

'As I explained to your wife, it was probably a by-product of the stress she's been under.'

'I didn't imagine it,' Alex said, glaring.

'With respect, Alex, we've both searched the room and there is no sign of Carol-Anne up there.'

'I heard her,' Alex repeated, annoyed at the exchanged glances between Isla and Ray.

Gripping her arms, Ray held Alex firmly. 'What exactly did you hear?' he said, his frown still heavy.

Alex took a deep breath to compose her out-of-control emotions. 'Just now. I was upstairs in her room, and I swear to you I heard her voice, as clear as I'm speaking to you. I was standing at the foot of her bed, looking at the photographs of her on the wall when I heard it. It was like she was actually *in* the bed. I'm not making this up, Ray.'

He blinked several times, his detective's mind trying to connect dots that couldn't be there. He had to accept that one of two truths were real: either somebody had abducted Carol-Anne as Alex had claimed, or his wife really had snapped.

He'd been home and searched for Carol-Anne and she hadn't been anywhere in the house. He froze. In the panic of rushing home from the scene yesterday afternoon he'd checked all the *obvious* places – the bedrooms, living room, kitchen and bathroom – but he hadn't torn the place apart.

His heart bursting with hope, he pulled himself away from

Alex and raced up the stairs, turning at the top and diving into Carol-Anne's bedroom, stopping in the middle of the room and straining to hear anything. His heart skipped a beat as he momentarily saw Carol-Anne snuggled under her thin duvet, before his mind snapped back to focus, and he realized the bed was empty.

Alex burst into the room right behind him. 'I was just here,' she began, before he lifted a hand to silence her.

It was almost impossible to hear anything above the sound of his rapidly beating heart. Dropping to his knees, he searched the carpet for any kind of audio device that could have been inadvertently triggered, or a toy with the capability of making a noise like laughter, but all he found was a box of books and clothes his sister had donated to them that had belonged to her own daughter. Certainly nothing obvious that could have been mistaken for a child's giggle. He then lifted each of the stuffed toys from around the edge of Carol-Anne's bed; none of them made a noise as he squeezed their middles and limbs.

Climbing back to his feet he went through each of the drawers in the chest, and finally the soft bag of baby toys Alex had packed up to donate to charity. Although this bag did make a variety of noises as he lifted it, none came close to the sound Alex had described. And that's when his eyes fell on the small open window behind the partly drawn curtains. Moving across to the window, he was about to close it when the noise of two chattering children in school uniforms stopped him.

Reaching for Alex's hand he pulled her towards the window and pointed at the two girls in the street. 'That's probably all it was: kids on their way to the bus stop.'

Alex pulled her hand free of his. 'You think I misheard? *It was Carol-Anne*,' she repeated through gritted teeth.

Ray shook his head sceptically. 'I know you want to believe that, but how could it be? We've all checked and she's not in her room. Some bastard has taken her, and what you heard was your body's way of telling you that you're missing her. I'm sorry, Alex.'

She stormed from the room, and stomped down the stairs. Ray remained where he was, taking a final glance back around the room, disappointed that he'd allowed Alex's imagination to let him believe that Carol-Anne was hiding somewhere in the property. To be safe he moved out to the landing, pulled down the loft ladder and, using the torch on his phone, he scoured the floor space, searching behind dusty boxes of Christmas decorations and old photograph albums. He found nothing more than silence and cobwebs.

Closing the hatch he headed back downstairs, his heart heavy at the prospect of Alex's previous psychological issues returning en masse. Finding Isla alone in the kitchen, he nodded when she offered to put the kettle on.

'Trent says you're one of the best FLOs she's worked with,' he said to finally break the silence.

'That's very kind of her. She's one of the better SIOs I've come across,' Isla smiled back. 'You couldn't have asked for someone better to be in charge of your case.'

'Trent said you were dialling into the morning brief; anything to share with us?'

'It was a standard primary briefing, leads they're going to pursue and that kind of thing. She did also say she wants your permission to appeal to the public.'

'What did Alex say?'

'She gave the go-ahead.'

'Did you tell her to delete her Facebook account?'

'I did. Standard procedure in these circumstances. You should do the same.'

He grunted. 'I don't have time for all that sort of thing. My digital footprint is as clean as they come.'

Isla looked as though she wanted to say something else and was holding back.

'Spit it out, whatever it is,' he finally said.

Closing the door, she leaned in closer, her voice barely more than a whisper. 'You're not going to be trouble for me, are you?'

His cheeks reddened at the implication.

'DI Trent warned me that you aren't likely to sit quietly and wait for my updates, and she has asked me to remind you that you are not authorized to be directly involved with this investigation. Any contact with her or the rest of your team is to be social only, and kept to a minimum. In this morning's brief she warned everyone not to engage with you on matters pertaining to the investigation.' She sighed. 'Listen, I know better than anyone how hard it is to leave others to the job, but that's precisely what you need to do. Is that clear?'

Ray didn't answer, instead heading out of the room and stepping outside before he said something he knew he would regret.

13

Alex was by the back door, staring out at the patio and small muddy lawn beyond it. 'He thinks I'm losing my mind.'

Isla was standing in the doorway, holding a tray with two mugs. 'It may seem like that, but this can't be easy for him either. No matter how many families I support I find each is different, and one partner's reaction is rarely the same as the other's. Both of you are terrified about what might have happened to Carol-Anne and feel helpless to prevent the unfolding drama. How you deal with those elements is bound to be different. In these situations it's always best to be extra patient with each other; it serves nobody well to allow your frustration to boil over.'

Isla raised a tablet from the tray and passed it to Alex. 'This is the statement DI Trent's team have prepared. She needs you to review it and give the green light.'

Alex read the first paragraph three times, before rubbing her eyes. 'I'm sorry,' she mumbled, 'I'm reading the words but they just aren't going in.'

Isla lowered the tray to the table. 'Why don't I leave you to read it alone for a few minutes? Give you some space. If you have any questions, I'll do my best to answer them when I return.'

* * *

Resting the tablet on her lap, Alex sat on the sofa and began to read the first paragraph again. It seemed fairly straightforward, explaining that Carol-Anne was a two-year-old who was snatched from a car park around 3 p.m., and that they were looking for witnesses who may have seen something.

It felt like she was reading about some other family's misfortune, even though each word was like another nail in her own coffin.

The sound of the front door closing was followed by the sound of Ray's footsteps thundering up the stairs. She hated the tension that had been hanging in the air between them these last few months, even before the shock of yesterday.

They hadn't been intimate since they'd learned of the miscarriage, apart from that one drunken fumble in the dark on his birthday. At first she'd thought he was being patient and understanding, allowing her body to recover; however, on the two subsequent occasions she'd tried to instigate foreplay, he'd made up excuses for not wanting to. He was tired, or had an early alarm call and just needed to sleep. There was only so much rejection she was able to handle.

There were other signs, too, like growing the goatee beard. He'd always kept his face clean-shaven, and then all of a sudden he'd bought a new trimmer and just started growing it. And it wasn't until she asked why he suddenly had a moustache that he admitted what he was doing, like it was none of her business. And then he'd started playing squash or going to the gym to swim a couple of times a week. In itself it wouldn't have been a problem, as it was important for them to have sociable interests outside of the marriage, but who splashes on cologne to go and hit a ball against a wall?

Even so, she had no evidence that he was seeing anyone else. He kept his phone on him at all times in case the office needed to call him in urgently, and if she'd asked to see it he would know she was on to him and he would most likely deny it. He didn't have many female friends that she knew about – her gut told her the woman was probably somebody he worked with. Maybe that DI Trent, or someone else in his team. He didn't tend to talk to Alex about his job, claiming she wouldn't want to know about half the things he saw on a daily basis.

She still loved him though, and deep down she knew she always would even if he had betrayed their marriage vows, because without him she never would have had Carol-Anne. The now familiar sting of tears threatened to break free, and she took a couple of breaths and looked away from the screen until they cleared.

'How are you getting on?' Isla asked, coming in to the room.

Alex still couldn't say for certain whether she approved of the statement, and handed the tablet back. 'It's fine,' she said. After all, they were the professionals who were used to preparing such formal statements. 'When will it be on the news?'

'Tonight, I believe. I'll check with DI Trent when I let her know you've given your consent.' She locked the tablet and was about to leave when she remembered something else. 'Have you suspended your social media accounts? As I said earlier, it's best if you put a temporary freeze on them. People can be quite cruel.'

Alex pulled out her phone and nodded. 'I'll do it now.' She'd barely had the app open for a minute when she suddenly gasped, and felt her eyes water instantly. In her hands the photograph of the ultrasound she'd uploaded three years earlier stared back at her as a memory, the app asking if she wished to re-share the post.

The blur of light and dark, blobs that clearly represented her baby's head, body, arms and legs, made it look almost as though Carol-Anne had been waving at them. She'd never felt as excited as she had the day she'd seen the images on the screen of the ultrasound machine. Ray had been speechless, and in that moment everything had felt so perfect and life-affirming. It was the start of their family life together.

The longing and ache in her heart now felt so intense. What she would give to go back to that day of the ultrasound and just warn herself never to take her daughter or husband for granted, to never allow them out of her sight.

Isla appeared behind her, staring down at the phone. Rather than offering words of understanding, she simply put an arm around Alex's shoulders.

Alex couldn't speak, desperate to hold back the growing storm. She didn't want to cave in to her emotions. Not again. She had to stay strong. Taking a deep breath, she held it for a moment, before exhaling, and then repeated the process.

Ray appeared in the doorway, clearing his throat. 'I'm going out. Work. Call me if there's any news.'

He was wearing a fresh – albeit creased – shirt, and the cloud of antiperspirant spray he'd applied seemed to hover around him. Alex could barely look at him. How could he think about working at a time like this?

'When will you be back?'

He shrugged. 'I'll message you.'

And without offering her a hug or a kiss, he turned and headed for the front door, leaving Alex alone with a woman she'd known for only a few hours.

14

It was just after nine, and the street was finally quiet. Taking a last drag on his cigarette, Ray brushed the ash against the brickwork.

A squad car pulled up at the bottom of the driveway, and he spotted DS Jodie Crichton behind the wheel. Incredibly, she was two years younger than Alex, her fresh face reflecting her relative inexperience. She was part of the new breed of detectives. No longer was it a requirement for all new recruits to undertake a minimum of two years on the beat before applying for the Detective-in-Training Course. For graduates like Jodie Crichton, the career path was more streamlined. She would go far, he had no doubt, but for Ray an analytical mind wasn't the same as honing skills with experience. He knew he was fighting a losing battle, though. The force had changed a lot since he'd first joined; it was more progressive than ever and Jodie fitted the mould they were evolving.

He knew little about her background, and wasn't sure they would have many shared interests that didn't revolve around the job. She hadn't been in the department long enough for them to have worked closely together on a case, yet he'd heard the rumours about her brownnosing up to Trent and the chief super. He was all for ambition and admired detectives who were keen to progress swiftly along the career ladder; however, she needed to understand that teamwork was still a vital part of detection.

Jodie offered a non-confrontational smile as he climbed into the passenger seat. 'I really appreciate you offering to support my case. I'd understand if you'd rather not work. With everything you've got going on—'

'Let's just get out of here,' he said as he spotted the net curtains twitching in the front window of the house.

'Sure,' she said, smiling thinly, the concern on her face all too apparent. 'A bookies got done over late last night, and the MO is a match for the Friday raid on the post office.' She squinted against the embers of sunlight peeking around the visor. 'Listen, Ray, I know it's none of my business, but if you feel like talking about what you're going through, I don't mind lending an ear.'

He didn't want to talk about his feelings of fear and despair, nor about how he felt impotent to protect and save Carol-Anne. Pushing thoughts of her from his mind, he said, 'Just drive.'

The pavement outside the bookies was coned off and littered with fragments of glass from where the pane in the front door had shattered when one of the robbers had fired a shotgun at it. SOCOs hadn't yet managed to locate the shell casing, suggesting the robbers had potentially taken it with them. Again, it underlined the professional nature of the crew: a single shot fired to show they meant business; nothing left to tie back to them.

'From post offices to bookies?' Ray mused. 'Seems like a backwards step if you ask me.'

'Didn't realize you were such a snob,' Jodie replied, picking up on his dismissive tone. 'I'd bet they picked up more loose cash in this raid than their last three post office jobs combined.'

Presenting their identification to the uniformed officer standing closest to the cones, they ducked below the cordon tape as he lifted it for them.

'Is the shop manager inside?' Ray asked, and the officer pointed towards a short, rotund man with a rapidly receding hairline. Although he was wearing a shirt and tie, his belly hung over his trousers and he gave the impression of someone who tried hard but would never look professional.

Keeping his identification aloft, Ray approached him with a welcoming smile. 'Mr Papadopoulos? I'm Detective Sergeant Ray Granger, and this is my colleague, DS Jodie Crichton. Would you mind telling us what happened here?'

Papadopoulos gave them both a withering look. 'Some twats robbed me.' The voice lacked any semblance of an accent, despite the foreign name.

'Can you tell us exactly what happened?'

Papadopoulos sighed. 'Can we do this outside so I can smoke?'

Ray nodded and followed as Papadopoulos led them through to the office behind the counter and then out of a back door into a small bricked yard, barely large enough for the three of them to stand without rubbing shoulders.

'Every day we cash up at four p.m. and nine p.m.,' Papadopoulos continued as he sparked up, 'but yesterday one of my girls called in sick, and I didn't have resources to do the early bank drop, so I put it in the safe. At 8.57, the shop was empty, save for me and the student who does the evening shift, so I made a start. Which is when the three men burst into the place.'

'Can you describe the men to me?' Ray asked, pulling out his notebook and pen.

'One of them, the one who shot out the window, he seemed to be in charge. He stayed by the door the whole time, and kept looking at his watch.'

'Can you describe the watch for me?'

'I didn't get a good look. A wristwatch.'

'Was he tall, short, fat, thin?'

'Average. Taller than me; muscly.'

'Taller than me?'

Papadopoulos considered Ray for a moment. 'Yeah, maybe a couple of inches taller than you. It's hard to remember as I was shitting my pants at the time, you know?'

Ray watched him cautiously. 'I understand. What about the other two men?'

Papadopoulos shrugged. 'They were about the same height, but one was much thinner than the other two; kind of weedy. He was the one who pushed the tip of the gun against my nose.'

'Is there anything else you can remember about them? Any distinguishing scars, tattoos, unusual accents? Anything at all?'

'They were dressed in black clothing and wore balaclavas. You could have been one of them for all I know.'

Ray wasn't laughing. 'I noticed you have security cameras inside. Can we have the footage from those for the last week? If they were casing the joint in advance, it's possible your cameras captured them without their disguises.'

Papadopoulos looked like a man under intense pressure as he finished his cigarette and immediately lit a second. 'Sure. Take whatever you need.'

'Have you managed to calculate how much was taken yet?'

Papadopoulos fixed him with an angry look. 'Close to eighty thousand.'

Ray was surprised the figure was so high. 'Is that a regular intake for a weekday?'

'Average. Ordinarily two-thirds of that would have already been deposited at the bank.'

'Who's the girl who called in sick yesterday?'

'Delilah.'

'Surname?'

'I'll write it down for you. She's Polish.' He grabbed the pen and scribbled the name in the pad.

'Have you heard from her today?'

'She's still sick.'

'And you trust her?'

'Of course.' He raised his eyebrows. 'You think she's involved?'

'I wouldn't rule out anything at this stage, Mr Papadopoulos. Could just be coincidence, so don't jump to any conclusions. Can you jot down her address for me too?'

Papadopoulos obliged, and Ray left him where he was chain-smoking his third.

Jodie was already in the office studying the security footage on the monitor. They stood and watched as the three men burst through the door, reminiscent to the footage captured at the post office on Friday, which Jodie had showed him on the way over. The leader remained by the door, the window bursting as he fired into it, glass dispersing into the shop as well as onto the street outside. A vehicle bumper could be seen just outside the window shrouded in orange as the indicator flashed.

The thin guy was carrying a semi-automatic, although it was hard to distinguish make and model from the grainy footage. Papadopoulos was just off camera, but his trembling hands were in shot as the lad pushed the weapon into his face and demanded the takings from the safe. The third guy disappeared from shot, presumably filling his bag with proceeds from the till out of frame. As three minutes approached, the man by the door raised his arm and the other two followed him out of the shop. The bumper outside pulled away and Papadopoulos tentatively appeared on the screen.

Ray paused the screen. 'Well?'

'How much did he say they took?'

'Reckons close to eighty grand.'

'I told you so,' she said. 'People don't realize just how much these places make.'

Ray ejected the disk and scanned the shelf, reading the labels on the DVD cases, before picking out the most recent five. 'I said we'd review last weeks' worth in case they've been casing the joint.' He passed her the cases, and she placed them inside a large evidence bag. 'Are there any traffic cameras outside? We need to get an ID on the getaway vehicle.'

'Already put a call in to the ROMANSE centre for that. They're going to send over everything they've got.'

'Do you really think this is connected to the crew from Friday?'

Puzzlement gripped her face. 'You don't?'

He shook his head. 'The MO is certainly similar, but there are too many discrepancies for me. For one thing, there are only three of them inside. You said it's usually four inside and one getaway driver.'

'Maybe they decided they only needed three because the venue is smaller than the post offices. Or maybe one of them was ill.'

'Okay, how do you explain the timing discrepancy?'

'What discrepancy? They were in for exactly three minutes again. You saw the timer as well as I did.'

'Not the time, but the method of measuring it. You said the leader used a stopwatch hanging around his neck, whereas this guy is looking at his wristwatch.'

She blushed at having missed that detail. 'Again, maybe he left it at home in error. Criminals are prone to making mistakes.'

'Okay, why did they shoot out the window?'

'To show they meant business.'

'Have they fired a shot on any of the other jobs?'

Jodie thought for a moment. 'No.'

'And finally, you said they always use a stolen van with false plates as their chosen getaway vehicle. I know it isn't obvious from the video, but I would put serious money on that bumper belonging to a hatchback, rather than a van. The traffic cameras should confirm it. That's four rather significant details if you ask me. I think we're looking at a copycat gang here.'

'How would they know all the other details about the MO?'

Ray shrugged. 'Newspaper coverage maybe? I'm telling you, my gut says this is not the same crew. And my gut is also screaming that this lot are far worse: they're going to shoot someone eventually. We need to catch up with them sooner rather than later.'

'Okay, where do you propose we start?'

'The ill shop assistant. Let's go and see what Delilah knows about what happened yesterday.'

Jodie nodded and peeled out of the office, and Ray realized that for the briefest of moments, Carol-Anne's face hadn't been the only thing on his mind.

By the time they reached the car, it was all he could do not to crash to his knees as the pain and fear for her tugged at his heart strings once again.

15

'I need to clear my head,' Alex said, suddenly standing.

'I'll come with you,' Isla offered.

'No,' Alex quickly replied. 'Please, I'd rather be on my own.'

Isla gave her a curious look. 'Where will you be going? I need to know how and where to get hold of you in case of any sudden developments.'

'I'm just going to walk to the local shop,' Alex explained. 'I'm sorry, I know it's selfish, but I just need some kind of normality for a moment. I'll only be ten or so minutes.'

Isla didn't look convinced, though eventually nodded. 'Very well, but if you're going to be longer, I want you to call and let me know.'

Alex pulled on her trainers at the front door. Although cloud coverage was heavy, she opted not to reach for a coat.

One of the neighbours across the road was washing his car and waved in Alex's direction as she passed. She nodded in his direction, but didn't stop to chat. The air smelt heavy with damp, a sign that more rain wasn't far away. She ignored the urge to return home.

It felt so strange being outside in the daytime on her own

buying milk and bread from the shop. Usually leaving the house was a carefully devised operation – making sure she had changes of clothes, spare nappies, snacks and drinks for Carol-Anne, all carefully secreted in various compartments in her pushchair. It was hard not to imagine what she would have been doing now if Carol-Anne was with her. Wednesday was when the two of them usually went to a local playgroup for toddlers. Carol-Anne loved playing with the musical instruments provided by the group organizer.

They usually walked to the event, stopping at the nearby bakery for bread on the way home, and if Carol-Anne had been good – or more likely when Alex fancied it – she would buy them a cake as a small treat.

Having eaten one of the doughnuts Sophie had brought round with her for breakfast, it didn't feel right to visit the bakery now. The pressure had just got too much to bear – she'd needed to get out of the quiet and empty house.

How many times had she wished for a few minutes of peace and quiet when Carol-Anne had been having a tantrum? She now felt so guilty about ever wishing for time away from her daughter. Although she'd enjoyed being a full-time mother, and was grateful that Ray's salary had allowed such a move, she had missed the daily routine of work, which was why she'd been so keen to find a part-time job that allowed her to have the best of both worlds. Now it felt like karma or some other force had taken its revenge for her wanting to be more than just a mum.

She stopped still.

What was wrong with her? All morning she'd been telling herself to remain positive, yet every second thought was focused on dealing with a future without Carol-Anne in it. Isla had said in four of the five cases she'd been involved in the child had been returned unharmed. Those were good odds, and it was far too cynical to fear the worst.

With that thought, Alex left the shop, spun on her heel, and upped the pace as her house came into view once more. It was time to stop feeling sorry for herself and focus on reestablishing her routine. There was a ton of washing she needed to do, and once the appeal was broadcast later, there was bound to be at least one witness who would come forward with details of who had taken Carol-Anne.

Right?

When they did, there was a chance Carol-Anne could be back home with them that evening. And when her daughter was back, she would sit Ray down for a proper conversation about their future. Carol-Anne should have both her parents in her life, and Alex felt ready to fight for that stability for her little girl.

She was practically buzzing as she stepped back in through the front door, until she saw the blood drain from Isla's face as she tentatively held a phone to her ear.

'You'd better sit down,' Isla said as she hung up the call. 'There's been an arrest.'

16

Tower blocks dominated the skyline as Ray and Jodie arrived in Millbrook, after an uncomfortable silence on the journey over. It wasn't that he didn't want to talk to her, he just couldn't figure out what to say; small talk had never been one of his strengths, and he couldn't concentrate on anything but his daughter.

'I grew up on an estate like this,' Jodie mused, staring up at the thirty-storey building directly above them. 'It was always worse in a storm. You could literally feel the building shaking as the wind buffeted it.'

'You're from Millbrook then, are you?' It was rhetorical; an acknowledgement rather than an attempt to stimulate conversation.

'No, I grew up near Streatham, in south London. Lived there with my dad until I was eight, before we moved down this way.'

Ray feigned interest. 'Was he from this neck of the woods?'

'No, he was concerned with gang culture in London, and when his employer decided to relocate offices to Southampton, he decided it was the fresh start we needed.' She opened her door to get out before pausing and looking back at him.

'He sounds like a sensible man.'

'He was. He died when I was still young.'

Ray looked at her, feeling the need to apologize, but she spoke again before he had the chance.

'I wanted to tell you how sorry I was to hear about ... you know. You're certainly coping better than I would be.'

It didn't feel like *he* was coping. If he was any decent man he'd be home supporting his wife as she needed, rather than conceding to the emotional strain to show. 'Let's just get on with this, shall we?'

She nodded, accepting that their one and only conversation about his situation was now closed off, not to be revisited.

Grey clouds swirled overhead in stark contrast to the early morning clear skies. The grass verges bordering the pavements were torn up with tyre tracks from the variety of vehicles that parked up on them overnight. The door into the tower block was boarded up where the glass should have been. Finding Delilah's flat number, Jodie pressed the door buzzer, and despite two attempts and two minutes' wait, there was no response.

'Maybe she's out,' Jodie offered.

'Or hiding,' Ray replied, noticing a shiny new black Mercedes parked in a disabled bay not far from the communal bins. 'Looks a bit out of place, doesn't it?' he said, nodding at the car.

Jodie considered it with a shrug. 'Could just be visiting someone.'

A young woman struggling with a pushchair appeared on the other side of the door, pushing it open with her bottom. Jodie held the handle while Ray lifted the pushchair out. The woman thanked them with a wary look.

'Don't worry, we're police,' Ray said, showing his identification, before following Jodie through the door. He cursed when he saw the 'Out of Order' notice hanging from the lift doors. 'What floor is she on?'

'Seventh. Could be worse.'

As they reached the seventh floor Ray was puffing badly, and he suddenly remembered why he'd given up smoking the first time. There wasn't a bead of sweat on Jodie, who'd taken the fire escape stairs two at a time and had been waiting for him to catch up.

'Do you need a minute before we proceed?' she teased, but he didn't have the breath to argue as she set off along the balcony, reading the door numbers until she reached '7H'.

Banging on the door, they were surprised when it opened a moment later and a tall black man dressed in a thick dark overcoat, with a nose that looked bent out of shape, ducked beneath the doorframe.

He didn't stop to consider them, pushing past Jodie. Ray recognized him as one of the bouncers from Demetrios's casino last night; a fact he held back from sharing with his colleague.

He continued to watch as the man left the building, climbed behind the wheel of the shiny black Mercedes and pulled away.

'Problem?' Jodie asked, her foot keeping the door to Delilah's flat open.

'Not sure yet,' he replied heading inside, leaving the door open.

Rolling her eyes, Jodie proceeded into the flat, explaining who they were. With peeling wallpaper, the tiny corridor was dimly lit, with a small living room to the right, and a kitchendiner to the left. Delilah was in the bathroom at the far end, the bruising beneath her left eye fresh.

'The guy who just left do that to you?' Ray asked, ready to put a call in to uniform and have the Mercedes pulled over.

Giving her eye a quick glance in the mirror doors of the medicine cabinet, Delilah washed her hands in the basin before leading them back to the living room. 'Can I ask why you're here?'

'Your boss, Mr Papadopoulos, gave us your address,' Ray explained when she was seated. 'Your place of work was hit by an armed gang last night. Did he tell you?'

She looked from Ray to Jodie, and back again, before shaking her head.

'They stole close to eighty grand,' Ray continued, running his tongue over his front teeth. 'Your boss was still pretty shaken up this morning.'

Delilah's face remained unmoved by the news.

'You were lucky not to be there,' he concluded, narrowing his eyes, hoping for any kind of reaction.

Delilah continued to stare blankly at them.

Squeezing into the sofa next to Delilah, Jodie deliberately allowed their knees to touch. 'In robberies like this, where the perpetrators seem to have inside knowledge of procedures and are able to strike at the most opportune of moments, well …' she allowed the implication to hang in there, before confirming it. 'The first place we look is employees with an axe to grind with their employer.'

'You think *I* had something to do with the robbery?' Delilah asked, her eyes widening with the horror of what was being suggested.

'Did you?' Jodie asked evenly.

'No!' It was barked, rather than offered calmly.

'Do you enjoy your job?'

'Does anybody?'

'I like my job,' Jodie replied honestly. 'Ray? You enjoy yours, right?'

He didn't answer, watching Delilah's reactions.

Delilah looked from one to the other again, before glaring at Jodie. 'Mr Papadopoulos is a good boss; he lets me take time off when I need it without much of a fuss. I wouldn't do anything to see him off bad.'

'How long have you worked for him?' Jodie asked.

'Three years now.'

'That's a long time to stay with one employer these days. You must have a good understanding of the place and his routine?'

She shrugged. 'I guess so. I trust him and he trusts me.'

'So you'd know if anyone had a grudge against him? Maybe

an unhappy punter? Or someone else who doesn't get on with him?'

Delilah glanced at the door, like she was expecting someone to burst in at any moment. It remained closed. 'I don't know. We have lots of regular customers; none that I think would do something like that.'

Ray studied his phone as it buzzed with a message.

It's Isla Murphy. Please call me urgently. An arrest has been made.

17

Alex felt like the rug had just been pulled from beneath her feet. 'They've found her? They've found Carol-Anne?'

'It's best if we go and sit down first,' Isla suggested, taking Alex's arm to support her.

Alex pulled the arm away. 'No! Tell me now!'

'Please, Alex, I really think it would be best—'

Alex could feel her face burning up, desperately fighting the growing dread starting to shadow her every thought. 'No! I know how these things work. You – police, doctors – you're all the same; you all have to deliver bad news while the recipient is seated. What's happened to Carol-Anne? Just tell me!' She hadn't realized she was shouting, and lowered her voice. 'Please?'

Isla looked up at the ceiling, as if appealing to some higher being, before eventually sighing. 'Nothing has happened to Carol-Anne; at least nothing that I'm aware of. I have no news on her specifically. Please, can we just go and sit down and I'll try to explain what DI Trent has told me?'

Alex's watering eyes studied Isla's face, looking for any tick or tell to suggest she was lying just to get Alex into a calmer place. The wrinkles around the older woman's eyes remained fixed.

'Fine,' Alex said reluctantly, 'I don't need you to lead me; I'm not incapable.'

Isla lowered her hands and headed towards the living room, leaving Alex feeling the edges of the walls for support. For all her bravado, her legs were like jelly, and she thought she might topple at any moment, but she had to remain strong. Her daughter deserved that.

When seated, Isla made a show of flattening her palms against her legs, a technique she'd learned to show she was speaking honestly. 'One of the team just called to advise they have made an arrest. Ordinarily, she wouldn't share such information so early in a case; however, given Ray is on the job, and DI Trent can't control rumours, she thought it better if you heard it from her first.'

'Who is it? Someone we know?'

Isla's eyes apologized for her. 'I'm not at liberty to give any names at this stage.'

'I don't understand. What's the point in saying anything then? And why don't you have any information about Carol-Anne? If someone has been arrested, surely they've found her too, haven't they?'

Despite years of training and experience, it was clear Isla was struggling just as much with the limited details she'd been fed. 'DI Trent said the person they arrested is known to them – the police, I mean – which is our way of saying he's someone with a criminal record.'

Alex blinked several times, the walls of the room somehow seeming to close in around them. 'A person with a criminal record? For what? They've done this before?'

Isla's lips remained tight, though her eyes were speaking volumes.

Alex's hand shot up to her mouth. 'You mean a paedophile, don't you? Oh Jesus!'

Isla was quick to shake her head and deny the inference, but the nervous edge to her voice failed to convince Alex.

'They've arrested a sex pest, haven't they?' she said from behind her hand, willing Isla to vehemently deny it. 'Please just tell me.'

Isla looked at the wall, as if trying to get her own thoughts straight.

'So if you've arrested him, where's my daughter?' Alex continued.

'I have nothing more I can tell you right now. An arrest has been made and, as far as I am aware, Carol-Anne has yet to be located. Please try to stay calm, Alex. This arrest doesn't necessarily mean this man is connected to the abduction of Carol-Anne.'

Alex was struggling to contain her rage. If Trent had made an arrest, why wasn't there any news on Carol-Anne? If this person had taken her, where was she now? Had he killed her?' Alex shuddered at this thought. Had he just abandoned her somewhere, fending for herself? Or had he passed her on to someone else as sick as him?

Closing her eyes, protecting herself from the possible answer, she took a deep breath. 'In your experience, why would they arrest someone if Carol-Anne wasn't with him?'

Isla frowned, thick crevices forming in her forehead. 'It really isn't helpful for me to speculate, Alex. I'm sorry.'

'That's what I'm asking you to do. I need to understand what is going on, and my brain just can't process why they would arrest someone but not know anything further about where Carol-Anne is. You have to help me. That's what you're here for, right? To help? So *bloody* help!'

Alex knew it wasn't Isla's fault that she didn't have the answers, and she didn't like taking out her frustration on a virtual stranger, but with Ray absent, who else did she have?

Isla stood suddenly. 'What I'll do is try and phone DI Trent back and see if there's anything else she can tell me. I'm afraid that really is the most I can do.'

It wasn't the answer Alex was craving; she didn't want to

alienate the only person who genuinely seemed to be on her side. 'Thank you.'

Isla remained where she was, studying Alex's reaction.

'Does Ray know?' Alex asked, wondering whether he was privy to information that she wasn't.

'I sent him a message, asking him to call me, but he hasn't replied yet. Can I ask you a personal question?'

Alex nodded reluctantly.

'Well it's more of an observation than anything else … you and Ray, is everything okay between the two of you? I mean before what happened yesterday.'

Alex didn't know how to begin answering that question. 'We're fine.'

Isla didn't look ready to accept such a non-committal response. 'Have the two of you talked about yesterday?'

'We spoke at the car park. Why?'

Now it was Isla's turn to be evasive. 'It's nothing … well, not really … it's just … in my experience of these situations, the shared loss and fear usually brings couples closer together. And yet with you two …' She allowed her words to trail off, maybe hoping Alex would fill in the blanks.

Alex wasn't ready to discuss her marital issues with a perfect stranger, though, especially when they had nothing to do with getting Carol-Anne home.

Isla remained where she was for a moment longer, until it became apparent that Alex wasn't going to share anything further. Then, excusing herself, she headed into the kitchen to call Trent, closing the door behind her, leaving Alex alone with her thoughts.

Alex moved across to the portrait frame hanging on the wall next to the doorframe. It was a picture Ray had taken almost a year ago that he'd had blown up onto a large canvas so it could hang in that very spot. They'd been in Marseille, soaking up a week's sun, while back home the country had been hammered by storms. Closing her eyes she could remember the smell of the hotel and feel the plastic bars of the sun lounger pressing into her shoulders. She hadn't cared about the discomfort: Carol-Anne had just fed and fallen asleep in her arms, the warm glow of sunshine falling across the two of them. Alex's face had been clear of make-up, having only recently woken, and at first she'd been cross that Ray had taken the snap, but it had turned out to be better than she'd anticipated. He told her he loved the picture; now, though, for her, it was a painful reminder of what could have been.

Having just announced she was pregnant with their second child – a son, they would later discover – everything had seemed so perfect. Then the bubble had burst.

The pregnancy with Carol-Anne had gone so smoothly: Alex had had few cravings, limited discomfort, and Carol-Anne had even been born on her due date. Looking back on that nine months, Alex couldn't recall a single moment where she'd felt like she couldn't cope. After this particular photograph had been captured, she couldn't remember a day when she'd felt she *could* cope. The pressure of the miscarriage was self-inflicted, she knew, and yet it didn't seem to matter how many times she was told it wasn't her fault, she still relived every day of that pregnancy, evaluating whether she could have done *anything* differently to alter the course of events. Had she drunk more water, or rested more, or just taken more care of herself, rather than taking the pregnancy for granted. Carol-Anne's delivery had gone so well, so why wouldn't the second one?

Alex forced herself to look away from the portrait, suddenly needing to busy herself. Grabbing the pile of laundry that had been sitting on the dining table for three days, she marched upstairs, not even stopping to eavesdrop on Isla's secretive conversation in the kitchen.

Once in her bedroom, she separated the pile into three, leaving Ray's pants, socks and shirts on his pillow for him to put away on his return. She didn't mind washing and folding his clothes, but he was a grown man and more than capable of putting fresh laundry where it went. She then folded her own tops and squashed them into a drawer, once again reminding herself she really needed to go through her clothes and throw away or donate to charity anything she no longer wore. There had to be plenty of clothes she'd kept from her thinner days that with the best will in the world she would never squeeze into again. To undertake such activity now would probably result in her throwing away virtually everything. After all, what good were clothes without her daughter around?

Her eyes fell on Carol-Anne's bibs and tiny vests. Each one so petite compared to the other piles of clothes. And each one sparking a different memory of an occasion when Carol-Anne had worn it. The T-shirt which had looked so large the first time she'd slipped it over her daughter's head that she hadn't been able to imagine it ever fitting. The last time she'd struggled to squeeze Carol-Anne's head through the opening, realizing how much her little girl had grown.

Pressing the T-shirt to her nose, she could still smell Carol-Anne's fresh scent on it, and her cheeks were suddenly wet as the flood of tears she'd been so desperately trying to keep at bay broke free. And then her knees went, unable to sustain her body beneath the weight of emotion. She collapsed onto the mattress, the pile of Carol-Anne's cloths softening the blow. Each fresh tear felt like a wasp's sting against her face. As much as it hurt to accept her own vulnerability, she was powerless to stop the tears.

Then she heard a noise that made her blood run cold – the unmistakeable sound of Carol-Anne giggling.

Opening her eyes and pushing herself up, she raced from the bedroom into her daughter's room, straining to find the source of the sound. Only silence greeted her.

Moving swiftly to the window she stared out, looking for any sign of a child who could have made the noise; the street was empty and both windows closed and locked.

Spinning around, she checked every inch of the small bed. The still faces of the stuffed toys stared back at her.

She had *definitely* heard Carol-Anne's unmistakeable laugh. *Definitely*.

It was impossible. Carol-Anne wasn't here.

Maybe Ray was right. Maybe she was losing her mind.

18

Ray took the stairs two at a time as he charged up to the third floor, trying the door to Major Incident Room-1. He wasn't surprised to find it locked. Procedure meant Trent would have allocated a new PIN code to the door, but that didn't stop him trying the last one they'd used only a week before. The door remained closed, and with the small window in the door frosted, it was impossible to see inside. The whole point in having a secured area for developing major cases was to keep unwanted eyes from the room.

Jodie was parking the car, and he was supposed to be meeting her on the next floor up where she'd set up the smaller MIR-2. He hadn't told her why he'd been so keen to get inside, though she wouldn't need to be much of a detective to figure out it related to his missing daughter.

'You shouldn't be here, sarge,' Owen said, shaking his head as he approached the locked door. 'Trent will go ballistic if she catches you within a hundred yards of this room. Or within a hundred yards of me for that matter.'

'Who's been arrested?' Ray said, ignoring the warning. 'That's all I want to know. Who and how are they involved?'

The lack of information in Isla's text message was enough for him to safely conclude that Carol-Anne had yet to be found. An arrest meant they were narrowing the net.

'You know I can't tell you that,' Owen replied, looking up and down the corridor as if Trent would somehow be able to sense Ray was too close for comfort.

Ray fixed him with a pained look. 'Please, Owen. What would you do in my situation? Imagine if you had children, and then imagine if one of them was snatched out of thin air. You'd be going out of your mind with worry.'

Owen took another glance down the corridor. 'I could lose my career if anyone sees us talking here.'

'Then meet me elsewhere,' Ray pressed. 'Please? I didn't want to do this, but you owe me, Owen.' He raised his eyebrows. 'Remember?'

Owen's cheeks flushed. 'Jesus! I can't believe you'd even think about bringing *that* up.'

Ray shrugged. 'I'm sorry, I'm desperate. We both know you'd never have made it through the interviews without me feeding you the answers. I only helped you because I knew you had the potential to be a great detective. Help me now.'

Another check of the immediate perimeter was followed by a guttural sigh. 'Give me twenty minutes and then meet me at the Wetherspoon's in Ocean Village. I'll tell you what I can, but if you drop me in it, I swear—'

Ray wasn't listening to the rest, practically skipping down the corridor as he raced away, hoping to get the keys from Jodie before she'd signed the car back in.

Ray was starting to think he'd been stood up when there was no sign of Owen after twenty minutes, when the young DC eventually darted in through the door, picked up the orange juice Ray had bought for him and headed for a dark corner of the small bar. They would be less likely to be disturbed here by the men poring over the racing pages of the newspaper, nursing their fourth or fifth straight pint.

Owen's hand was trembling as he sipped from his glass, clearly wishing he hadn't agreed to come. Every time the door opened, his head shot up, as if expecting an armed response unit to storm the place and drag him away in handcuffs.

'Just relax,' Ray encouraged, as he squeezed himself into the booth and put his own glass of juice to his mouth.

'I shouldn't have come here,' Owen said, clearly debating whether to leave before he breached anymore of the rules he'd sworn to uphold.

'I'm grateful you did,' Ray replied. 'What can you tell me? Have they found any further forensics in the car?'

Owen shook his head. 'Forensics is a virtual dead end. Alex said the car was valeted the day before, right? Well the only prints on the door handle are Alex's and the only fibres inside the car are a stray hair belonging to Alex, and saliva that has been matched back to Carol-Anne. The team will keep searching every nook and cranny. If someone else was in the back of that car, they did a great job of covering their tracks.'

'What do you mean *if*? Of course someone else was in the back of that car. Where else would Carol-Anne be?'

Owen apologized quickly. 'I didn't mean anything by it; I'm just telling you what the evidence is saying. You know what it's like, we have to explore *every* possibility and assume nothing.'

Ray was struggling to contain his rising ire. 'What does *that* mean?'

'Shit,' Owen said, 'I didn't want to be the one to say this.'

'Say what?'

Owen took a long gulp of his drink, his hand still trembling as he lowered the glass. 'The only evidence we have that your daughter was anywhere near that car park is your wife's statement. There is no camera footage that we have as yet identified—'

'You think she's lying?' Ray interrupted.

'No, *I* don't, but we have to consider *everything*. Listen, if it's any consolation, I drove Alex back to your house last night, and if she was making up the events, she's a world-class liar. I'm as certain as I can be that it happened as she described. I'm just telling you what's going on.'

'So what do they think happened to my daughter if she wasn't taken?'

Owen drained the rest of his drink. 'I don't know, mate. Maybe something else happened prior to Alex arriving at the car park. I really didn't want to be the one to say that. Listen, that's just one angle under consideration. Of course, we all *believe* Alex wouldn't lie about what happened.'

Ray was angry Trent would even consider the possibility that Alex had invented the abduction to cover up something else, and now he couldn't think about anything else. 'Who's been arrested?'

'Terry Thornby.'

Ray recognized the name; though he had never come into direct contact with Thornby, he knew him to be one of a number of registered sex offenders. Reaching for his glass, he was desperate for anything to steady his nerves. 'Go on.'

Owen looked at the door again. 'Trent had us knocking on known offenders' doors all morning. Richmond and Farris called at his, and when he answered the door, he was acting *suspiciously*, so they exercised caution and went in. They found a child's cot in the back room, a number of stuffed toys and a digital camera. After reviewing the images on the camera, they discovered Thornby has been taking photographs of children in two local playgrounds, including the one that's only yards from the Woodside Road car park.'

Ray slammed his clenched fist onto the table, and this time Owen's glass wobbled and fell against the varnished top. 'Was Carol-Anne in the photographs?'

Owen raised his hands in sympathy. 'I don't know, mate, I

100

wasn't there and the camera is under review with Scientific Services Technicians.'

'Was Carol-Anne at the house? Was there any sign he took her?'

'Listen, Ray, I've told you everything I know. Okay? Farris and Richmond have just finished the first interview with Trent observing. It was a standard "No Comment" response from Thornby. He's in with the duty solicitor now, and then they'll reconvene.' Swinging his legs out of the booth, Owen stood unsteadily. 'Listen, I've already been too long. I need to head back. Go home, Ray, and wait for Trent to call there. It's the best thing you can do right now. Cheers for the drink.' He paused, fixing Ray with an assured look. 'We're even now. No more favours.'

And before Ray could ask him anything else, Owen headed for the door.

Instead of following his colleague out, Ray remained where he was, opened his wallet, and pulled out the picture of Carol-Anne he kept in there. Dropping it to the table he buried his head in his hands and wept for the first time since Alex had called yesterday.

19

'I don't understand why I feel so nervous,' Alex mumbled, clutching the hot mug of tea like it was life itself.

Isla strained a reassuring smile, something she'd been doing all day, and now it seemed to be finally taking its toll. 'That's understandable given what you're about to watch. Just remember that DI Trent will be dealing in cold, hard facts. I know the last thing you want is to relive the memory of what happened yesterday afternoon, but public appeals can do wonders for providing valuable intelligence in cases like this.'

Alex nodded, watching as Isla turned her attention back to the advertisements, and the clock ticked closer to six. It was hard to believe that twenty-seven hours had already passed since the event that had turned her world upside down. It had felt like time had deliberately slowed as one second dragged into another while they'd waited for further updates from Trent and her team, yet considering it now, it seemed to have flown by. The reality was Alex had little concept of time, trapped in a mournful limbo, somewhere between life and death.

She'd phoned Ray to see if he would be home for the televised appeal, but he hadn't answered and according to her phone he had yet to read either of the messages she'd sent him. She wondered if he was still working, if he had actually gone to the gym to work through the stress, or if he was with *her*.

Isla turned up the volume as the opening credits rolled and the two presenters introduced themselves, summarizing the headlines. The breath caught in Alex's throat as Carol-Anne's face filled the screen, and the newscaster announced a televised appeal for a missing toddler from the area. Alex would have given anything to have Ray at her side, wrapping one of his large arms around her shoulders, telling her everything would be okay.

The anchor, with his shiny head and tufts of hair above his ears confirmed the two remaining headlines, before the shot cut to him and his female colleague staring directly at her, like they could see her sitting there and were silently judging her lapse of concentration.

'*Hampshire police are appealing for witnesses,*' the female began, '*who were in the city centre around three p.m. yesterday, particularly anyone in the vicinity of the Woodside Road pay-and-display car park. That's where two-year-old Carol-Anne was last seen, strapped in a child seat in a grey hatchback. Detective Inspector Serena Trent, who is the Senior Investigating Officer on the case, had this to say to reporters earlier. We should warn viewers that the following footage contains flash photography.*'

The scene cut to a table covered with large microphones, behind which sat DI Trent, looking fresher than she had when she'd briefly questioned Alex at the car park yesterday; her hair and make-up clearly fixed for the cameras. Behind her hung two enormous photographs of Carol-Anne: the one Alex had provided and another that Ray must have supplied. Alex's hand gripped the arm of the sofa as she struggled to breathe.

Trent cleared her throat. '*Please look carefully at the beautiful toddler behind me. Carol-Anne is two years old, has bright blonde and curly hair, chestnut-coloured eyes, and an infectious giggle when she is happy. She answers to her name and can say yes and no to questions, though her conversational speech is otherwise limited.*

Carol-Anne was last seen in the Woodside Road car park at three p.m., by her mother, who was away from the car momentarily, and upon her return Carol-Anne was gone. We are currently reviewing security camera footage from the time period. This is an urgent appeal for anyone who was either in the car park or in the near vicinity at around three yesterday afternoon and may have witnessed someone taking Carol-Anne from the car park.'

A flurry of camera flashes reflected off the hanging images.

'I also want to appeal directly to the individual who took this innocent little girl. Her parents miss her dearly and want nothing more than for Carol-Anne to be returned unharmed. While abducting and incarcerating a child is a serious crime, if you come forward and return Carol-Anne safely to us, you will be given the opportunity to explain what happened without pre-judgement. We just want this little girl home to her parents before any serious harm befalls her.

'Finally, we would like to appeal to anyone who may know who took Carol-Anne. You would know if one of your friends has suddenly welcomed a young child into their life or home in mysterious circumstances. There is an emergency contact number at the bottom of your screens now where you can pass on information in confidence to one of my officers. This isn't about apportioning blame or making headlines with a series of arrests; it's about bringing this little girl home.'

The two newscasters reappeared on the screen with the two images of Carol-Anne superimposed in the background.

'So, to recap,' the bald male said directly into the camera, *'Carol-Anne is two years old, has blonde hair and chestnut brown eyes. Were you in the Woodside Road car park yesterday around three o'clock? Did you see anyone urgently leaving the car park with a little girl who may have been crying? Have you seen Carol-Anne since yesterday afternoon? Carol-Anne is a vulnerable child who needs to be reunited with her parents urgently.'*

'Such a horrific crime,' the woman agreed empathetically. *'I*

can only begin to imagine what those poor parents are going through right now.'

'*The police hotline will remain on the screen for the rest of the programme,*' the man continued. '*If you have any information that may aid the police in their investigation, please call as a matter of urgency.*' He paused. '*And in other news …*'

Isla switched off the television and made eye contact with Alex for the first time since the report had started. 'I know that can't have been easy. Do you have any questions about the appeal, or anything you'd like me to raise with DI Trent?'

Alex stared at her, fighting the urge to yell out in angst. 'It's just so …' she began as her voice cracked under the strain. 'It's so-so-so cruel. Who could …?' The words came out in a high pitch.

Isla waited for Alex's stuttering breaths to ease. 'If my experience has taught me anything, it's that there are some vicious and sick people out there. People who do unimaginable things that any reasonable person wouldn't dream of doing. Do you know what? We catch them in the end. It's not always as efficient as we'd like, but we catch them. Rest assured, nobody will give up on Carol-Anne.'

The words were empty promises, but Alex appreciated the sentiment.

Isla glanced up at the clock. 'We haven't discussed sleeping arrangements. Every one of these cases is different and your feelings on the subject will undoubtedly be unique to you. As I have been designated as your Family Liaison Officer, I am at your disposal for whatever you require until such time as the case is concluded or I am reassigned. To that end, I can stay here with you tonight and going forward so I can be at your beck and call twenty-four-seven. Some victims prefer their own space, and if you'd prefer I check in to a hotel and return at an agreed time in the morning that's also fine. It really is up to you. What would you rather I do?'

Alex dabbed her eyes with a tissue. 'You want to stay here? As in sleep?'

Isla nodded. 'If you'd like me to. If you want space then I can go elsewhere.'

'We don't have a spare room. There's only ours and … and Carol-Anne's.'

'I've slept on plenty of couches in my time. I also have an airbed I can inflate if you don't mind me using the floor in here. I promise I'm very tidy and will live out of a suitcase until we're done. And I'm house-trained,' she added with just a hint of a smile.

'Um, yeah, okay, I guess. If you're happy on the floor then you can stay.'

Isla clapped her hands together and stood purposefully. 'Great! Then if you don't mind, I'll nip home and pick up a few things and will be back here in an hour?'

Alex wasn't really listening, nodding as Isla left the room, the front door closing a moment later.

20

Hours had passed since Ray had last smoked, and although the craving was tearing through his mind, he didn't cave, knowing that Carol-Anne wouldn't want to see him on a path to selfdestruction. She knew far more than she was able to communicate, and she would know that what he was doing was wrong, and that Mummy wouldn't like it. She would fire him angry glares whenever he cracked a rude joke about Alex's cooking, or deliberately went against something she'd asked. How could someone so young be so worldly-wise and see through the façade of bravado that he had cultivated for so many years? How could one so innocent hold the key to his heart and well-being without intending it?

Plenty of people had told him that parenthood would change him, and he hadn't believed them. He'd acknowledged the guidance and had accepted that they were probably right, although he hadn't expected it to have had such a profound effect on him. Carol-Anne's birth had put a lot in perspective, and accepting that she was gone just wasn't something he was able to do. It had only been a day, but deep down he couldn't escape the feeling that he would never see her again. Maybe it was as a result of what he had witnessed over the years as a serving officer; in truth he'd already pictured himself leaving flowers at a plaque in a graveyard.

He was grateful when his phone clattered to life on the table – until he realized who was calling. He was tempted to ignore it, but to do so would only result in a worse outcome.

'Hi, sis,' he sighed, as he put the phone to his ear.

Eight years older than Ray, his sister Verity could be a hard woman to ignore; built like a sumo wrestler and with a voice capable of chilling the bones of any man at fifty paces, she was the epitome of the idiom, 'You can choose your friends, but you can't choose your family'. The significant age gap hadn't helped them build a close relationship growing up, and their father's death last year had only served as a further divide between the siblings. He knew she meant well; however, she was terrible at showing her caring side, coming across as an interfering battle-axe to all who met her.

'*Raymond? Tell me what I just saw on the news is a terrible mistake.*'

Ray glanced at his watch; the public appeal must have aired, and now Verity would want to know why he hadn't phoned her to tell her about Carol-Anne's abduction.

'She's missing. It's true. I'm sorry I didn't—'

'*Oh Raymond, you poor darling. You must be devastated.*'

'The best officers in the force are searching for her. They'll get her back,' he said, unable to convince himself that he was telling the truth.

'*Don't worry, I've packed my bags and I will be over as soon as Henry is back with the car.*'

His eyes widened. The last thing he needed was Verity complicating the already stressful dynamic between him and Alex. 'No, please, that really isn't necessary.'

'*Nonsense! At times like these you need family around you. I won't hear another word about it.*'

'Please, Verity, it isn't that I don't appreciate your offer of support, it's just—'

'*I presume you're still working?*' she said curtly.

'Well, yes, I am, but—'

'*So there's nobody home looking after Alex during this nightmare? Who better than me to provide the love and support she needs?*'

He could picture Alex waving her arms frantically at the prospect of being stuck for hours on end with Verity; the two had never seen eye-to-eye on anything, and Verity's arrival would be like pouring petrol on a bonfire.

Ray squeezed the bridge of his nose, searching for a polite way to put her off. 'What will Henry do without you? He needs your love and support more right now.' Using his brotherinlaw's recent diagnosis didn't feel right, but desperate times called for desperate measures.

'*He'll manage. There's plenty of food in the freezer he can reheat while I'm away.*'

'What if he takes a turn for the worse? You'd hate yourself if something terrible happened and you could have prevented it had you been there. Believe me, nobody knows that better than I do right now.'

A hesitation.

Ray crossed his fingers, hoping it had been enough.

'*No,*' she eventually declared. '*He will just have to manage without me. He's a grown man for goodness' sake, and the nurse said he has Type 2 diabetes, which means as long as he's careful with what he eats, nothing bad will happen.*'

Ray slapped his own forehead in defeat. 'I'm sorry, Verity … I didn't want to say this, but you've left me no choice. The police have told us that we need to act as if nothing has changed. That's why they didn't mention us by name in the appeal tonight. The thing is,' he paused, pushing the mouthpiece closer so he could whisper, 'they think we're under surveillance.'

The shock was apparent in her voice. '*By whom?*'

'I can't say, I'm sorry, in fact I've already said too much; I just hope I haven't now put you in any danger.'

'*I don't understand what's going on, Raymond—*'

'That's probably for the best. Just trust me, sis, please. I'll explain when all *this* is over.'

'*And is Alex okay? She's not had a relapse of her—*'

'She's coping as well as can be expected under the circumstances. Listen, I know I should have called you yesterday and told you what had happened. I was instructed to keep the information on a need-to-know basis.'

'*Will you at least send Alex our love? I remember how awkward it was when all that nasty business occurred last time. What was the name of those drugs the doctor gave her?*'

'She's fine, Verity. She hasn't had any kind of relapse. Listen, I really have to go, my boss is calling on the other line.'

'*If you're sure there's nothing else I can—*'

'I'm sure. Thank you for calling, and I'll keep you posted.' He hung up before she could argue anymore. At least he'd averted one crisis.

He checked his messages as another threatened to blow up in his face.

21

Fifty minutes after the appeal, Alex found herself in the kitchen, stirring some soup as it simmered in the pan. She caught a glimpse of one of her neighbours across the street, wheeling his bin to the bottom of the driveway ahead of the morning's collection. Before turning to head back to his door, he looked across at her. With the kitchen light on, he'd be able to see her and the immediate area behind her. He made no effort to wave or come across; he just stood there, watching.

It had to have been the news. He must have recognized Carol-Anne's picture or name and realized exactly who she was, why she'd looked so familiar. The appeal had gone out on the regional news. Anyone who was tuned in at that time – which could easily amount to thousands, if not hundreds of thousands – would have seen it. The average viewer would have no idea that Carol-Anne was her daughter, although most in this street would, including the neighbour now shaking his head disapprovingly.

Alex's response was to lower the blind, shutting out the rest of the neighbours who were probably sitting in their living rooms debating what a terrible mother she was. Suddenly her memory flooded with every confrontation she'd had with her neighbours, whether it was over parking spaces in the street when friends had visited, or too much noise during the early parties they'd hosted, or waking other children with late-night spontaneous fireworks. She could picture each neighbour she'd argued with now judging her behaviour and saying to their partner, 'I never did like that woman'.

Alex looked down at the soup, her appetite waning. She needed to battle through it and eat something, even if it was just to keep Isla off her back later. Tipping the pan over a bowl, she watched as the warm red soup splashed against the sides, before tearing a slice of bread and dropping it in. Then placing the bowl onto a tray with a spoon, she carried it through to the living room.

Her phone flashed on the coffee table where she'd left it. Placing the tray on the cushion next to her, she unlocked the screen, expecting to see a response from Ray. Instead she saw close to a hundred notifications from her Facebook and Twitter apps. Confused, she opened the Facebook app and saw messages and wall posts from a host of people she'd never met. Isla had warned her of the potential backlash to the appeal, but how had so many strangers worked out so quickly that she was Carol-Anne's mother?

Daring to open the first message, she was relieved to see it was from a Facebook friend – a woman she'd been to school with – offering sympathy, telling her that she too had lost a daughter and understood the pain that Alex had to be feeling. Alex felt her shoulders relax considerably. That wasn't so bad.

As she opened the next one, nothing would have prepared her for what it said:

You ought to be locked up you reckless bitch! Women like you don't deserve children. I hope social services take her off you!!!

Alex was typing a response before she could stop herself.

How dare you be so cruel! You don't understand what happened! Carol-Anne should have been safe. She was strapped into a child seat in a locked and alarmed car. I only looked away for a moment. Nobody can hate me as much as I hate myself right now. What gives you the right to pass judgement on me? I'm a good mother who doesn't deserve to be feeling this pain.

Alex was about to press send when another notification flashed onto the screen. And another. And another.

It was clear that the news was out there, and Isla had been right: it was spreading like fire. Locking the screen, she buried the phone under the seat cushion and reached for the soup. She'd only managed two spoonfuls before she could hear the phone vibrating again. Pulling it out she unlocked the screen, shocked to see the number of notifications had almost doubled. This time she opened the Twitter app to try and delete her account, and that's when she saw her name trending along with the hashtag *#shitmum*.

@alexg200 left her child alone in a car park #shitmum

#mumoftheyear @alexg200 should be locked up #shitmum

Who leaves their child alone in a car? #shitmum

If I ever meet @alexg200 im going to teach her how to be a proper mum #shitmum #southampton #pieceofmymind

#shitmum did @alexg200 have something to with her daughter's disappearance #carol-anne

This kind of abuse wasn't right. Where was Isla? She should have been back by now. Weren't there laws against threats to life? Couldn't these vile people be prosecuted for such horrid rants?

She searched through the settings, looking for anything that would allow her to delete her profile, but nothing jumped out. She'd never been particularly savvy with technology, and unlike Sophie, Alex had little by way of social media presence. She'd only set up the accounts so she could see what old school friends were now doing, so how had so many strangers found her, and so quickly? Trent had promised hers and Ray's names would be kept out of the press, and there had definitely been no mention of their names during the appeal. Who had leaked it?

With no other way of stopping the constant alerts, Alex uninstalled the two apps. She knew it wouldn't stop the onslaught of messages. Until Isla was back and could explain how to delete the profiles, she would just have to bury her head in the sand. If she couldn't see or hear the abuse, she could almost convince herself it wasn't there; at least, she hoped she'd be able to.

Searching through her contacts, she tried Ray's number again. It rang and rang until the messaging service cut in.

'Ray, it's Alex, where are you? Please call me ASAP. Our names are out there. The world now knows Carol-Anne is ours. Please call me. I *need* you.'

She hung up, and was about to switch off her phone altogether, when she saw a message notification on her email app. Opening the app, she saw an urgent message from the office manager of the company she'd been heading to yesterday afternoon. It had been sent at nine this morning, asking Alex to get in touch, questioning why she'd failed to attend the interview, and asking if she wished to withdraw her application for the role.

Alex was amazed they'd even got in touch. No employer would be interested in someone with all this emotional baggage right now, particularly given the campaign of hate slowly building towards her. Yet, it was a job she'd been keen on taking, and the fact that they had messaged her indicated she hadn't blown her chance of still securing the role. As she tried to compose a response in her head, her mind kept wandering back to what she'd read on her Twitter timeline.

She finally gave up trying, deciding she'd give it another bash in the morning, or better still would phone the office manager and try to explain what was going on. They deserved her honesty, and it would be easier to deliver that verbally than in written form.

She was about to close the email app when she saw a second message had come through, from an hour ago. She didn't recognize the sender's name, but opened it, wondering whether another potential employer was interested in interviewing her. As the message opened, and a photograph of Carol-Anne filled the screen, she nearly dropped the phone as she read the message that had come with it:

Simon Says …
   If you ever want to see Carol-Anne, all you need to do is kill a man.
   If you kill Jack, I will give her back.
   Refuse to comply and Carol-Anne will die.
   3 days.

22

The rain splashed against the window as Ray stared out. The sun was low in the sky and barely visible through the thick cloud surrounding it. As weeks went, he couldn't remember any worse, even those difficult days following the miscarriage. At least back then he and Alex had handled it together. They were now in virtual isolation, and while he accepted that that was his fault, he couldn't bring himself to bridge the rapidly growing gap between them.

Despite himself, Verity's words kept dancing around his head: what if Alex had suffered a relapse? He couldn't remember when she'd last had an appointment to see the counsellor. She'd said the meetings with him hadn't helped, though she'd agreed to continue seeing the guy. Now that he thought about it, though, he couldn't recall the last time he'd seen a reference to the appointments on the calendar at home. If she'd stopped going to counselling, what else was she keeping from him? Was she off her medication too? How much didn't he know about?

In truth, he hadn't been at home as much as he'd once been, finding it easier to bury himself in his job than actually deal with the destabilizing effect of the miscarriage on their relationship. If it weren't for Carol-Anne, he suspected they wouldn't now be together.

'Is it okay if I drop you here?' she asked, her accent barely noticeable anymore.

He looked up, only now realizing they'd reached his road. 'Yeah, I guess that's for the best.'

'Safer this way. Sorry, I know you'll get wet before you reach your door.'

The rain didn't bother him as much as the prospect of having to look at Alex with the burden of guilt hanging heavy in his heart.

He reached for the door handle, and she tugged on his arm. 'Aren't you at least going to kiss me goodbye?'

'Someone might see.'

'Not if we're quick,' she said, a twinkle of mischief in her eyes.

He'd agreed to see her to try and cool things off, to explain that he needed to focus on his family, to support Alex and get Carol-Anne back. She'd taken the news far better than he deserved, and had gently massaged his shoulders, helping to relieve the tension. Before he'd been able to stop himself they'd been tearing each other's clothes off as he'd searched for anything to distract him from the pain of not knowing how to find his daughter. Now, though, the guilt of spending any time without Carol-Anne at the centre of his thoughts was eating him up inside.

'Perhaps it's not a good idea anyway,' he said softly. 'I'm sorry, I've been a real downer today.'

She looked away, clearly hurt by his rejection. 'I understand. You need some space.'

He grabbed the handle and pushed the door open, waiting until she'd pulled away from the kerb before jogging along the pavement in the direction of home.

There was no sign of Isla's car on the driveway, and he wondered whether Alex had evicted her for the night.

He was just putting his key into the lock when the door burst open, and Alex grabbed him by the hand, dragging him inside.

'What's going on?' he managed to splutter, as she dragged him through the hallway and into the lounge, not even bothering to close the door.

'Look,' she said, pointing at the laptop screen.

Moving closer he stared at a picture of Carol-Anne. 'What am I supposed to be looking at?'

'The picture: someone emailed it to me.'

He wasn't following why a picture of their daughter had caused Alex's cheeks to flush quite so much. 'Back up a minute. Would you mind filling me in? Somebody sent you a picture of Carol-Anne. Who?'

'I don't know. I didn't recognize the guy's name. I thought at first it was from one of the recruitment agencies I'd joined. When I opened it, I saw the picture and message.'

'What message?'

She scrolled down and read aloud the words he was reading on the screen. '"Simon Says … If you ever want to see Carol-Anne, all you need to do is kill a man. If you kill Jack, I will give her back. Refuse to comply and Carol-Anne will die. 3 days."'

'Who's *Simon*?' Ray asked, unable to keep the frown from forming.

'I have no idea. The person who snatched Carol-Anne presumably.'

'You think it's from the abductor?'

'Don't you? He says he has her.'

Ray raised his eyebrows sceptically. 'It's probably just some crank who saw the appeal on the news.' He stepped away from the screen dismissively. 'Oh, my sister phoned me today, by the way. You'll be relieved to hear that I persuaded her not to drop everything and visit.'

'I couldn't give two shits about Verity right now!' she shouted back, clearly annoyed at his attempt to change the subject. 'You need to find whoever sent me this message.'

'Oh come on, you don't really think this is from the person

who took Carol-Anne?' he said in disbelief. 'It's obviously just from some crank looking to take advantage of your delicate emotional state.'

'No, Ray, you're wrong! I'm telling you it's from *him.*'

Verity's concern about Alex's emotional state flooded to the front of his mind again. Taking Alex's hand in his, he led her back to the sofa, sitting on the cushion next to her.

'You need to calm down, Alex. I'll tell you why I'm pretty sure this isn't from the person who took Carol-Anne, shall I? For starters why would a child abductor reach out to the distraught mother? What's his motive for doing so? What does he gain? Secondly, how does he – or she – even know who you are? As far as the investigative team are concerned, the abduction was totally at random, so how does the abductor know you're the mother or what your email address is?'

Alex buried her head in her hands. 'You're wrong, Ray. The whole world now seems to know that Carol-Anne is our daughter. I know they didn't mention us by name in the appeal, but someone somewhere has leaked the information. My name is trending on Twitter for fuck's sake!'

Ray's shoulders tensed. 'It is?'

Alex opened a new page on the screen and inputted her user-name and log-on. 'Facebook's the same. I've deleted both apps from my phone because it wouldn't stop alerting me to new messages and abuse. It's horrible, Ray. Some of the things people are saying about me are so cruel and untrue. They're saying I'm an unfit mother, that I should be charged with neglect, and that Carol-Anne is lucky not to be with me anymore.'

Ray instinctively put an arm around her shoulder as she began to sob. 'This email is just another one of those things. Vicious; some sicko with nothing better to do with their time than prey on the defenceless. Forward it to DI Trent, and then put it behind you. And you should definitely delete your social media accounts. I'm surprised Isla didn't suggest that to you.'

Alex pulled away, her sobbing suddenly stopping as she reached for the laptop and forced it onto his lap, the fans blowing warm air onto his damp trousers.

'The appeal didn't go out on the news until just after six. Before that time the only people who knew about the abduction were you, me, the investigative team, and the person who abducted her. Look at when the email was received: 17:47; a full fifteen minutes before the appeal went out. I'm telling you, Ray, this isn't a crank. You need to find out who sent us this message!'

He stared at the timestamp on the open email message, and couldn't ignore what she was suggesting. 'Okay, okay,' he said, standing and carrying the laptop to the dining table. 'I'll call Trent now and we'll get this message to the tech wizards. Hopefully they'll be able to trace the IP address of where the message was sent from, and then we should know who sent it. I've never known a child abductor taunt the parents for no obvious reason. Did you hear they made an arrest earlier today?'

Alex nodded, wiping her eyes with the back of her hand. 'Isla wasn't able to tell me much about who it was other than he had a criminal record.'

Watching her, Ray couldn't bring himself to share what Owen had said about Thornby and the photographs from the park. The room blurred in and out of focus as the sound of the ticking clock echoed off the walls. He hadn't shared what was driving his need for distraction: missing children not found within seventy-two hours rarely return home alive.

23

Alex squinted towards the television, determined to put the real world out of mind for just a moment, yet no matter how hard she concentrated, her eyes kept falling back towards the laptop. Ray had switched it off and closed the lid, promising he would forward the message to Trent and have the team confirm it was just the cruel workings of another troll. He'd been on the phone in the kitchen ever since, and from his muffled raised voice, she sensed the conversation wasn't going well.

Presumably, Trent would be keen to know why this updated information was coming from Ray directly and not Isla; as Family Liaison, it was her responsibility to be the bridge between the investigative team and family. She had yet to return from collecting her things. She'd said she'd be back within the hour, and it was now well past that.

Alex glanced at the laptop again, chiding herself, and turned up the television volume instead. It was some sort of crime thriller in the prime-time slot, and although she recognized one of the lead actors, she couldn't quite determine if he was supposed to be the good guy or the bad. Maybe that was the point of the programme and why she couldn't work out what was going on. It seemed to be set in London, judging by the tall buildings and high volume of traffic, yet could just as easily be Manchester or any of the UK's other larger cities.

Ray hated watching shows where the police were portrayed as non-stop crusaders for justice.

'It isn't realistic,' he would say. 'These TV police never seem to sit still, lurching from one crisis to another. There's a lot more sitting around and contemplating than they show.'

Of course, a room full of detectives staring blankly at screens and out of the windows wouldn't make for a tightly plotted and fast-paced show, and Alex was usually happy enough to suspend disbelief. This was just too much for tonight, though. Pulling up the onscreen guide, she flicked through the menu until she spotted a rerun of *Friends* and put it on.

Her eyes returned to the laptop yet again, and this time she caved, leaning forward and dragging it from the coffee table onto her lap. Lifting the lid, she booted it up and inputted the password. The emailed image filled the screen once more. It was definitely Carol-Anne, but those weren't the clothes she'd been taken in. She'd been wearing black leggings, a white frilly Tshirt and a red anorak. The police hadn't shared that information with the public, so maybe that's why she was dressed differently in the image. Staring closer at the screen, Alex couldn't escape the fact that it looked familiar: the way Carol-Anne was staring playfully away from the camera; the way the sunlight seemed to catch on the wall behind her. Alex felt like she had seen this picture before. And that's when it hit her.

Opening a fresh internet page, she logged into her Facebook profile, ignoring the flashing message windows, and clicked on the folder of uploaded photographs. She wasn't someone who posted a lot online. She did share the occasional image of Carol-Anne so that friends and family could see how much she was growing. And there it was, the fifth image down: Carol-Anne in the same outfit and pose as the message that had been sent.

'Ray!' she screamed at the top of her voice.

Ray came bundling into the room a moment later, eyes wide, anxious and searching all about the room in an effort to identify whatever imminent danger had threatened. The phone hung in his hand. 'Wha-what is it?'

Alex turned the laptop screen round, and pointed. 'He must have got the photo from my Facebook page. Look! It's the same image.'

Ray moved closer, snatching the laptop up and dumping his phone onto the cushion next to Alex. 'I told you to stop looking at this.'

He was angry with her, but why couldn't he understand what she was trying to tell him? It didn't matter that she'd gone against his wishes, finding the source of the photograph was an important step.

She took a deep breath. 'There was something about the picture that I recognized. I knew I'd seen it before, and there it is on Facebook.'

He glowered, his eyes narrow. When he spoke again his voice was more even. 'So the picture is one you or I took? I don't recognize it.'

She shook her head. 'Do you remember a few weeks ago I took Carol-Anne to that toddlers' get-fit workshop? It was all about encouraging infants to be more active and educating parents on acceptable levels of television and computer games. You must remember!'

It was clear from his face that he didn't remember as he stared blankly back at her. Alex could have sworn she'd told him about that day, and she was certain she'd showed him the image.

'There was a photographer there – hired by the people organizing the workshop – to take pictures of the children playing and having fun for them to use on their website. All the parents had to sign some consent form to say we didn't mind our child's image being used as part of their advertising campaign. This was the picture they wanted to use of Carol-Anne and I didn't see the harm so I agreed. They put it on their website and Facebook business page, and tagged me in it so I could download a copy.'

Ray was staring at the screen again. There was still no recognition in his eyes. Did he ever listen to any of the things she told him when he returned from work?

'You think the photographer is the man responsible for taking Carol-Anne?'

'What? No! I'm saying that whoever sent the image must have stolen it from my Facebook page.'

Ray grabbed the phone from the seat cushion and unmuted it. 'Ma'am? Can you have someone in the team pull a list of users who have accessed Alex's Facebook profile in the last,' he paused and turned to Alex, 'when did you say this event was?'

Alex racked her brain. 'About five or six weeks ago?' She leapt to her feet. 'It'll be on the calendar. Hold on.' Darting to the kitchen, she unhooked the calendar from the wall and flipped back to last month's page, her finger scanning the boxes until she found it. 'It was on the sixteenth. Last month.'

Ray appeared in the doorway, and looked at where she was pointing before relaying the information back to Trent.

'The image in the email, ma'am, Alex thinks whoever sent it may have downloaded it from her Facebook page.' He paused as he listened to her response.

His face was a conflict of emotions; it was like he wanted to believe Alex's theory, but was holding back, as if there was something he wasn't telling her. He'd always been good at keeping secrets from her, and she knew no amount of pressure or questioning would break it out of him.

Alex leaned back against the counter, allowing herself a brief moment of satisfaction that she'd potentially found a tiny piece of jigsaw puzzle in recognizing where the image had originated. And then she spotted the two open bottles of lager on the counter nearest where Ray had been standing, one empty and the other not far from joining it. This wasn't the first night in recent weeks when she'd caught him drinking on his own. She knew he still judged her for the medication the counsellor had prescribed, but he was just as guilty of using booze as a crutch.

'Yes, ma'am, understood,' he concluded. 'I'll tell her now.'

Hanging up the phone, he stared silently at Alex, his pupils darting slightly like he was trying to read her mind. He finally moved past her, picked up the second bottle of lager and drained it, before resting it back on the counter.

'She said they'll request activity logs for your Facebook and Twitter feeds. I mentioned the abuse you'd received and she said she would forward those on to a team who deal with cyberbullying and verbal assaults. If they deem any of those messages to be in breach of the 1997 Harassment Act, they'll take appropriate action with those involved. I imagine a lot of it will result in nothing more than a slapped wrist and warning over future conduct. How are you feeling now?'

He said it so matter-of-factly, lacking the warmth she knew he was capable of. Did he really care how she was feeling, or was he just going through the motions, doing what he thought she wanted?

'What did she say about the email though?'

'I forwarded it to them and she agrees that it's probably just a crank. They'll trace the IP address that sent it and ascertain that it isn't more serious.' He opened the fridge and stared into it, looking for inspiration. Finding nothing much in the way of food, he pulled out a fresh bottle of lager, prying the lid off with his hand. 'You have to understand that in child abduction cases it's unheard of for the perpetrator to contact the victim. The last thing they want to do is draw unnecessary attention to what they've done. Most will lay low until the heat has blown over, before even venturing out of their house. That's why it can be so hard to pinpoint those responsible for such crimes.' He noticed her staring at the bottle in his hand. 'What?'

Alex opened her mouth to say something, but again chickened out. 'Nothing. How was your squash match?'

He spluttered as the beer caught in his throat. Coughing and looking guilty as hell, he wiped his lips with the back of his hand. 'Um, it was fine. Owen trounced me three times; I guess my mind just wasn't on it tonight.'

She didn't need a polygraph to tell her he was lying. He was now avoiding eye contact, and clearly hoping she didn't ask where his kit bag was. The thing is, if he was going to lie about playing squash, the least he could do was take his kit bag with him. She knew full well that it was upstairs in the bottom of the wardrobe, where it had been for weeks. It was heartbreaking to think of him off with some other woman. It hurt almost as much that he wasn't making more of an effort to try and keep it from her; it was almost as if he wanted her to find out.

She remained silent, waiting to see if he'd take the opportunity to tell her the truth, but as he headed out of the kitchen and into the lounge, she heard the television being switched to the sports channel, and realized the conversation was over.

'I'm going to go up to bed,' Alex called out as she headed for the stairs. 'I've got a pounding headache, so I'm going to take something for it and hopefully crash out. Can you wait up until Isla gets back?'

He nodded, without turning to look at her. As she headed into the bedroom the deathly silence returned, leaving Alex in no doubt that she was on her own.

24

Ray's neck ached as he flicked on the kettle at the wall and dropped teabags into two mugs. His plan to sleep on the couch had been disrupted when Isla had returned shortly after Alex had headed upstairs. She'd stared at the bottle of lager in his hand, the judgement painted all over her face.

He'd peppered her with questions about the investigation, trying to see if she'd tell him anymore than he'd managed to get out of Owen yesterday afternoon. Either she didn't have further information, or she had a great poker face. If Trent was as smart as she seemed, she would restrict the updates to Isla, in order to avoid the FLO having to lie to them. It was standard practice not to offer victim's families false hope, and the best way to do that was to filter which updates were provided through the FLO.

Alex had been fast asleep when he'd made it upstairs, and as he'd tried to go to sleep his mind had been filled with images of his daughter and the unending belief that his affair was the cause of karma's cruel blow. At one point he'd almost shaken Alex awake to come clean, as if somehow that would lead to Carol-Anne's return, then at the last moment he'd stopped himself.

If Alex was in half the pain he was, she wouldn't be able to cope with his betrayal as well. He would tell her everything, but only once he'd got their daughter back. And as painful as it was to leave things up to Trent and the team, he knew deep down it was the right thing to do, even if he wasn't convinced he'd be able to live up to such a demand.

Putting the phone to his ear, he was relieved when it connected and didn't go to answerphone. 'Morning, Jodie.'

'*Ray, good to hear from you. I won't ask how you are,*' she replied, her voice soft and unassuming. '*I take it you're ringing to say you're going to take a few days off? When you didn't come back last night I figured you'd decided to take some personal leave.*'

The truth was he wasn't sure what his next step would be. The thought of sitting around waiting for news filled him with dread. He'd hoped that burying himself in another case would distract him from the constant thoughts of Carol-Anne, spiked by the paranoid imaginings of outcomes that could befall her. He'd seen too many cases of abuse first-hand to ignore the growing sense of anxiety.

'How'd you get on with tracing the vehicle the thieves used on the bookies?' he asked, trying to push thoughts of Carol-Anne from his mind.

'*Uniform managed to get hold of the camera from the shop next door, and you can just about see a saloon pulling past. Unfortunately it's virtually impossible to tell make and model, let alone registration number. The traffic camera on that stretch of road was no use either. However, our gang of four seemed oblivious to the camera on the traffic lights thirty yards further up the road.*'

'Anyone we know?'

'*No,*' she sighed. '*I showed it around the office but nobody recognized the driver. We're running it through facial recognition as we speak and hoping for a hit. In the image, between the two front seats, you can make out two other figures in the back. Their faces are obscured though one looks like he's holding a shotgun. I was going to show the image to Papadopoulos and see if he recognizes him. Maybe he's a regular punter, or has been in casing the joint.*'

'Vehicle licence plate?'

'Not on this particular shot. I managed to trace their movement back to where they collected the car from. The camera at the security barrier of West Quay car park. A 1995 Jaguar XJR in British racing green was stolen from the shopping centre on the morning of the robbery. It seems our crew told car park security they had lost their ticket, then paid the fine and drove away. They hit the bookies minutes later before driving off with the cash and dumping the vehicle in a farm near Ower. Tyre tracks leading from the farm suggest they made their escape in two 4x4s, but we have yet to identify specifics.'

His mind flashed back to the Woodside car park, wondering what sort of vehicle had been used to snatch Carol-Anne, and how Alex could have missed the activity. Unless she wasn't totally with it. Could her medication have clouded her memory? It was worth following up on. Alex used to keep her prescription pills in her handbag, and if he was quiet he might manage to sneak upstairs and check exactly what she was taking and whether there were any side effects.

'The car wasn't torched like the other vans,' Jodie continued. *'Scientific Services have confiscated the vehicle to examine it for forensics. They should have an update by lunchtime.'*

'And you're certain the car's registered owner isn't in on it?'

'Pretty certain. He isn't from the area – he was down visiting his daughter at university – and was out eating a meal in town when the incident occurred. I have uniform checking out his alibi; my gut says he's telling the truth.'

'Sounds like you don't need me then,' he said, keen to end the call and fetch Alex's handbag.

'No, I should be able to handle things from here. Listen, if there's anything you need, or you just want to talk about things, you know where I am. Okay? I don't mind being a sounding board or if you just want to vent and let off steam, I'm happy to be that support.'

He thanked her and hung up, making the tea as the kettle

boiled and tiptoeing back up the stairs, relieved to find Alex still gently snoring in bed.

Creeping around to her side of the bed, he gently rested the mug on her bedside table, listening for any change in the sound of Alex's breathing.

He hated sneaking behind her back, but was equally sure she wouldn't tell him the truth if he confronted her. And so, bending low, he carefully gripped the leather strap of the bag and lifted it, holding it out in front of him like he was carrying an explosive device. The house keys inside the bag jangled slightly as he bumped his knee on the corner of the wooden bedframe, and it was all he could do not to scream as the shooting pain tore up his leg.

Leaving the room, he headed for the bathroom, where he closed the door and unclipped the bag, his fingers trembling as he searched inside the inner zipped pockets.

If she caught him now, he'd have a hard time explaining why he was snooping through her bag, but he had to be certain. There was something about Alex's account of the abduction that had been sitting uneasily with him since she'd first told him. It wasn't just the discrepancy in the timing of her account, nor the fact that she'd been naive enough to leave Carol-Anne unattended for any amount of time. Maybe it was the memory of what had happened in Manchester that was troubling him most.

He froze as he heard movements coming from the bedroom. He listened for any indication that Alex was moving about, and as he heard footsteps approaching he quickly locked the bathroom door.

The handle was lowered a moment later, followed by a banging. 'Babe? You in there?'

'Yeah, sorry,' he quickly replied, breath still held, sweat clinging to the back of his neck. 'If you're desperate, go downstairs.'

'Okay,' she replied sleepily.

He let out the breath with relief as he heard her footsteps padding down the stairs. Pulling out her purse, make-up bag, keys and phone, he searched for any sign of the small bottle of pills he'd seen her with weeks before, but the bag was empty. Cursing, he quickly returned the items and re-clipped the bag, unlocking the bathroom door and stepping onto the landing, leaning over the rail to listen for movements downstairs.

Then, hurrying along the landing, he dived into the bedroom and returned the bag to where he'd found it, before creeping back to the bathroom and flushing the toilet just as Alex reappeared at the top of the stairs.

She still looked half-asleep, her eyes barely open. 'You all right? You're sweating.'

Eyes widened, mind racing, he ran a hand over his stomach. 'Dickey tummy, that's all.'

She nodded, satisfied with the response, before returning to the bedroom.

Ray didn't follow, heading back downstairs and reaching for the calendar as soon as he was in the kitchen. Skimming the pages, he looked for when she'd last had an appointment with her counsellor. Turning over the pages it took three turns to find the last scrawled note.

Three months without an appointment spelled bad news in his mind. If she hadn't been seeing her counsellor in that time, did that also mean she was off the antidepressants? Taking a step back, he considered his options. The right thing would be to inform Trent of this revelation. To do so would mean even greater scrutiny into Alex's troubled past, which he didn't think she'd handle well. And what would it achieve? It wasn't like Alex could have hurt Carol-Anne.

Even as he tried to reassure himself, the niggling voice in the back of his head was starting to grow louder.

25

Poking her foot from under the duvet, Alex was tempted to remain in bed for the rest of the day. After all, what was worth getting up for? Ray would probably make himself scarce for the day again; Isla would probably fuss about the place, offering to make tea, the whole time secretly observing everything Alex said and did, reporting it all back to Trent. Alex wasn't convinced that anyone in Trent's investigative team had formally ruled her name out as a suspect in Carol-Anne's disappearance. And with no daughter to look after, what was the point of getting up? Her mind would freely wander whether she was in bed or in the living room.

She'd be better off staying in bed and trying to catch up on the hours of sleep lost during the night, in part due to Ray's endless snoring. At one point she'd considered taking her pillow and a blanket to the living room for some peace, until she'd remembered Isla was already down there, and the last thing Alex wanted was to give the FLO any further fuel to question the stability of their marriage.

Despite all the arguments for staying where she was and shutting out the real world, Alex eventually pushed the duvet back and quickly dressed, finding a fresh mug of tea waiting on the bedside table, presumably left by Ray.

Isla was folding up the duvet as Alex headed downstairs. Ray was in the kitchen, lost deep in thought.

'Is there any news?' she asked him, but it was like he hadn't heard her.

'Nothing to report yet,' Isla said as she entered the room, looking disappointed to see them both with a drink, and nothing waiting for her. 'DI Trent wants to pop round this morning and ask you both some questions about that email message you received. Ray mentioned it when I got back last night. I should apologize for taking as long as I did to collect my bits and pieces. It was unprofessional of me not to keep you informed of my whereabouts, and I won't let it happen again.'

Ray seemed oblivious to the conversation.

'Have they found out who sent it yet?' Alex asked, sipping the hot tea.

Isla shook her head. 'Not as far as I'm aware. DI Trent will probably update us both when she gets here. Can I fix you some breakfast?'

I'm not an invalid, Alex wanted to scream. It wasn't Isla's fault. She was probably just as lost as Alex, and trying to find anything she could do to justify being there.

A car pulling onto the driveway caught Alex's attention. As the driver's door opened, she immediately recognized DI Trent.

'Your boss is here,' Alex remarked to Ray, and a moment later a knock confirmed Trent's arrival. Alex left it up to Isla to open the door, while she carried her tea through to the living room and slumped into her usual seat.

Isla, Ray and Trent appeared a moment later.

'How are you keeping, Alex?' Trent asked, as if they were friends who hadn't spoken in several months.

How do you think I'm doing? Alex wanted to shout. 'Have you found out who took my daughter yet?'

Trent looked cautiously from Alex to Ray and then back again.

'We're working on a number of leads at the moment. There's nothing concrete yet.'

'What about the guy you arrested yesterday?'

'Unconnected to Carol-Anne's disappearance, I'm afraid,' Trent said regretfully. 'Our technicians have combed every inch of his property and there's no trace of Carol-Anne's DNA anywhere. Also, he has a cast-iron alibi for the time of the abduction.'

'So what you're saying is you were wrong to arrest him and get my hopes up?' Alex hadn't meant the question to sound so bitter, but couldn't help feeling she'd been misled by Isla's optimism yesterday.

Ray was standing by the patio doors, staring out at the lawn, showing no obvious sign of interest. How could he be so indifferent? He should be the one taking charge, demanding more than a hundred per cent from his colleagues.

'What's important in times of extreme stress like this is remaining patient,' Trent continued. 'The suspect we arrested yesterday is in breach of the terms of his release and will likely face a further spell behind bars as a result of what we discovered yesterday. I know it doesn't help you, but the world is a marginally safer place as a result of our actions.'

'I wanted to speak to you directly about the email you received yesterday,' Trent continued without missing a beat. 'I have a specialist trying to trace the IP of where the message originated, and that should hopefully steer us towards whomever sent it. However, it's important for you to realize that the person who sent the message may not be the person who snatched Carol-Anne. Either way, though, I assure you we will take action against whoever sent the message. You have my word.'

'How did the sender know Carol-Anne was missing before the appeal was televised?'

Trent's face remained unmoved. 'There are some twisted people out there who get pleasure from causing distress to others. You have to bear in mind that although the appeal wasn't broadcast until six p.m., it was actually recorded an hour before, so while the information wasn't in the public eye, the story was out there. How so many people learned you were the mum of the missing girl is still being investigated. From what we've managed to deduce so far, someone you used to go to school with was the first to make the link.'

Trent paused and pulled a piece of paper from within her jacket, unfolding it and passing it to Alex. 'At 18:02, this woman tweeted you directly using the hashtag #Carol-Anne, asking if you were okay. Presumably she recognized your daughter, and it spread from there. I'm aware of some of the abuse you received following this message, and I'm sorry that you had to read it. I have forwarded the messages on to the cyberbullying team who will take appropriate action.'

'I know all this,' Alex snapped before she could stop herself. 'I just want to know where my daughter is. It's been almost two days and you don't seem any further along than when it happened.'

It was Trent's turn to look over to Ray. 'I can assure you we are doing everything within our power to find out where she is and bring her home. I wish I had more positive news to share. Believe me when I say we are working flat out. Ray will be able to confirm how hard the team are working.'

Ray looked over at the sound of his name, and for the first time Alex was surprised to see an absent look in his eyes, like a lost child anxiously hunting for a parent.

'Does the name Jack mean anything to you?' Trent pressed. 'Do you know anyone called Jack? Or is there a Jack from your past that the email message could be referring to?'

Alex had asked herself the same question over and over as she had lain awake in bed in the early hours of the morning. The response was always the same.

'No, I don't.'

'You don't have any friends – or enemies – called Jack? What about you, Ray?'

He shook his head. 'Nobody who would do something like this.'

Deep lines formed in Trent's forehead. 'It's just … very specific: "if you kill Jack, I will give her back".'

Alex was beginning to feel nauseous. 'What are you getting at?'

'Well it may be nothing. Let's just say – for argument's sake – that the email was from the person who snatched Carol-Anne. He knows he took her from you, and how to get in touch with you. He's even gone to the efforts of making his message rhyme. What's the point if you don't know who *Jack* is?'

'If I knew I would tell you. I swear!' Alex pleaded, feeling as though nobody was listening. 'There's nothing I want more than to have my little girl back.'

26

After half an hour of questions and challenges, Trent got up to leave, though not before asking Ray to follow her back to the car. A look was exchanged between Isla and Trent. And as they left, Ray could hear Isla trying to comfort his wife.

'My car,' Trent said, a command rather than a question.

She was parked thirty or so yards down the road, away from the house and out of view of the kitchen windows at the front of the property. He couldn't tell whether the chosen space was deliberately parked so far away, or whether it had been the only available option.

He climbed into the passenger side, unable to escape the feeling that he was about to get a bollocking, maybe because Owen had come clean about their private chat yesterday.

Trent climbed in behind the wheel, making no effort to start the engine or fasten her belt. She remained in silence, as if trying to summon the words she wanted to say. Then, allowing her gaze to fall on her window, head turned away from Ray, she said, 'Is there anything you want to tell me?'

It had to be about the chat with Owen. On the off-chance he was wrong, he wasn't prepared to give her anymore rope to hang him. 'Like what?'

'This isn't easy for me, Ray. You're one of my best detectives, and you're also Alex's husband. If there's anything you want to tell me about what happened on Tuesday, *now* is the time to do it.'

He looked over at her in confusion. 'What are you getting at?'

Her head turned so she could look him in the eye, clearly using her own internal polygraph to judge his response. 'Are you aware, or have you become aware, of any information which could directly impact our investigation into the disappearance of your daughter?'

He fixed her with an assured stare. 'Don't you think I'd tell you?'

Her face remained emotionless. 'Okay, let me rephrase, has Alex confessed anything to you since she called to report the abduction?'

She was clearly driving at something. For now he couldn't quite see what.

'You think I'm hiding something? Whatever it is you want to know, just come out and ask me.'

She nodded. 'Okay. There's no easy way to ask this, so I'm just going to spit it out and hope you understand.'

His shoulders tensed involuntarily.

'Why was Alex arrested last year?'

His vision blurred. 'How did you hear about that?'

'Never mind how I found out about it. What happened and why didn't you mention it sooner?'

His throat felt unbearably dry. 'Because it has nothing to do with any of *this*.'

'I'll be the judge of that.'

Ray shook his head. 'No. First of all, you tell me how you heard she'd been arrested. We weren't in Hampshire when it happened, and as she was never charged there should be no formal record of what happened.'

Trent kept her voice low and calm. 'That's why I want you to explain it to me. Come on, Ray, you know I have to turn over every stone. Don't make me bring Alex in to explain it herself. I already have an idea of what went on, but I'd rather hear it from you than rely on office gossip.'

'Gossip? Who else knows?'

'Nobody here, I assure you. Listen, one of my old DCs from when I worked in Manchester called me when he heard about yesterday's appeal. We got chatting and *he* brought it up in conversation. I hadn't even mentioned either of your names and he asked if I remembered the wife of one of the DSs down here who was pinched at the back end of last year. Of course, I knew nothing about it, but he remembered Alex's name. He wasn't lying, was he, Ray?'

Closing his eyes, Ray wished he was anywhere else right now. Realistically it had only ever been a matter of time until she'd found out about what had happened, and why his sister had been so keen to come and visit.

'We were on holiday,' he said, finally opening his eyes and admitting defeat. 'A week away in Lancashire, staying in a caravan on a holiday park. It was Carol-Anne's first trip away, and a break away we all needed. You have to understand it wasn't *Alex's* fault. What happened, I mean.'

'My source said it had something to do with some type of medication?'

Ray nodded. 'After the miscarriage, Alex hit rock bottom. She attended counselling, but it did very little to improve her symptoms of depression, and she was eventually prescribed a mild antidepressant. It wasn't until the third day we'd been away that she admitted she'd accidentally left the pills at home.'

'Did she volunteer that information, or did she try to hide it from you?'

He didn't like the implication in the question. 'Why?'

'Please, Ray, humour me.'

'She didn't tell me straight away. I was looking through her handbag for my phone and noticed she didn't have the pills. That's when she told me. She said it wouldn't be a problem. She said she was feeling good about things, and would simply start them again when we were home. She thought it would be too big a challenge to get a fresh prescription issued while we were away and it was too far to drive home to get them. What can I say? She seemed happy enough, and as far as I was concerned the sooner she was off those pills the better. So, we proceeded with the holiday.'

'When did you first become aware something was wrong?'

'We had booked the caravan from Saturday to Friday and on the Thursday morning she woke with a migraine. I asked if she wanted me to go out and get her some medication but she said she thought a walk and fresh air would clear her head. She left Carol-Anne with me as I was planning to take her to the paddling pool on site.

'I started to worry when I hadn't heard from Alex by lunchtime. Her phone was switched off, and I had no way of tracing her. At two, I was starting to panic that she might have been knocked over or rushed to hospital or something, and that's when there was a knock on the caravan door, and I saw two uniformed officers there. They told me Alex had been arrested and that she had been asking for me. She'd told them my rank and had kept insisting it had all been a big misunderstanding.'

'She abducted a child from a park, Ray. That's more than a misunderstanding.'

He sighed, his heart aching at the trauma of those days in Manchester. 'She didn't think she'd taken a child. She thought she'd collected Carol-Anne, and it was only when the child's mother saw her leading the girl away that all hell broke loose. When the arresting officer allowed me to see Alex I realized just how bad a state she was in. Wandering the streets outside the holiday park, she'd come across a small local park. Her counsellor later said that without the antidepressant, and with the migraine

140

tearing at her every thought, Alex must have become disoriented. Even after we'd explained to her what had happened, she looked at me like I was crazy.

'She kept insisting that she'd taken Carol-Anne to the park, and as they'd tried to leave, she'd been apprehended by a crazy woman claiming that Carol-Anne was hers. And then the police had been called, and Alex had been cuffed. She resisted when they'd given the girl back to her real mother which obviously didn't help the situation. Even when I told her Carol-Anne had been with me all day, she claimed I was wrong. It was a genuine mistake: in her mind she hadn't intended the little girl any harm. It wasn't Alex's fault.'

'She was lucky the other mother and the detectives in charge were so understanding. She could easily have been prosecuted regardless of the mitigating circumstances.'

Ray knew she was right, and that was why he'd insisted she continue her counselling and the prescribed medication. 'As I said, *that* has nothing to do with *this*.'

Trent sat forward. 'Are you sure?'

'Absolutely!'

'Is she still taking antidepressants?'

This was his chance to come clean and to tell Trent his own fears about Alex's mental health. She hadn't been acting irrationally. He hadn't noticed her acting any differently, and maybe it was possible that she no longer needed the pills, or maybe she was still taking them and it was just that they hadn't been in her handbag.

Biting his lip, he said, 'As far as I'm aware.'

'The evening after the abduction I asked Alex whether she was on any medication, or whether she'd had anything alcoholic to drink prior to her trip to the car park. She answered no to both questions.'

'She must have been confused.'

Trent was now shaking her head in sympathy. 'We spoke to

her counsellor – Dr Kirkman – and although he couldn't tell us the reason for her appointments with him, he did say that she hadn't been to see him in over two months. Be honest with me, Ray: when did you last see your wife take her medication?'

He closed his eyes again, trying to recall any memories of the two of them from the last couple of months. He'd spent so much time out of the house, he could barely remember a single conversation they'd shared in all that time.

'We know that Alex drove into that car park when she said she did,' Trent continued, 'we know she had an interview lined up, for which she was running late. And we know that there was no child in that car when we arrived at the car park. Those are the only facts that are irrefutable. There is *no* evidence that Carol-Anne was in the car with Alex when she arrived in the car park, and there is no evidence that the car was tampered with in any way.'

Ray's eyes snapped open. 'What are you saying?'

Trent leaned closer to him. 'I'm only telling you this because we're friends and I consider you a damned fine detective, *but* as of this moment Alex is our prime suspect in the disappearance of Carol-Anne.'

27

Trent's questions had lasted for half an hour, yet it had felt so much longer to Alex. How many different ways could she tell her what had happened at the car park? It felt like she'd repeated the same story more than a hundred times, and now even she was beginning to doubt the key facts. Were they all right? Had she fabricated the entire story?

The truth was she couldn't be certain of anything anymore. And she desperately needed someone she could pour out her heart to. Sophie next door was the closest thing she had to a friend. There was Noemi as well, but she was more Sophie's friend than Alex's, and although they got on well enough, they'd never met up without Sophie there to rely on. Noemi always seemed so busy, though Alex couldn't recall mention of any serious boyfriend. With her stunning looks and job at a major IT company, no doubt she'd had plenty of offers.

Alex sent Sophie a quick message, hoping she would be able to spare a few minutes for a phone call.

'You're out of milk,' Isla said, poking her head around the door. 'I'll nip to the shop to get some, unless you want to go …?'

Alex looked up from the phone's screen. 'No, I don't think I can manage even a simple conversation in a shop. Do you need any money?'

Isla remained where she was, considering Alex's fragile state. 'Are you sure you don't want to come? It might do you some good to get some fresh air.'

Alex didn't want to go anywhere. Just the thought of bumping into a neighbour terrified her. Either they'd stare at her with pitying, judgemental eyes because they'd figured out the girl in the police appeal was hers, or worse still, they'd notice she didn't have Carol-Anne with her and would ask where she was. Neither outcome filled Alex with inspiration.

Isla continued to stare at Alex for a moment as if expecting her to change her mind. As Alex's gaze returned to the phone, Isla closed the door and made her way outside.

'Where are you, my precious angel?' she asked as she caught sight of a photo hanging on the wall.

The snap had been taken by a professional photographer in a studio after Alex had won a competition for the shoot. The prize had included one free image and a ten per cent discount on any other images they purchased afterwards. It had been so tough to narrow it down to just one image, and this had been the best of the lot. Carol-Anne had been sitting playing with a stuffed zebra that she had found in the photographer's box of toys and games. He'd told Alex to call to Carol-Anne and he'd managed to capture the image just as her innocent eyes had met with Alex's, the first glint of a smile spreading across her cheeks. If ever an image screamed how precious, vulnerable and innocent she was, this was it. Trent had asked if they could use the image for the appeal, but Alex had been unable to bring herself to agree. If she had, the image would have been forever tarnished. This way she got to keep her child's sweetness to herself.

The ringing doorbell caught her attention, and as she looked at her watch, she realized Isla had been gone for ten minutes already. Rehanging the frame, Alex left the living room and was about to open the door when the caller thumped an angry fist against the door, causing Alex to gasp.

'I know you're in there,' a gruff voice boomed from outside. 'Open the fucking door!'

Alex froze, her hand at her mouth. She wasn't expecting a visitor, least of all an angry man whose voice she didn't recognize.

The banging continued. 'Oi, let me in! It's fucking freezing out here.'

Alex remained rooted to the spot, terrified that any movement would confirm her presence inside. Maybe whoever it was would go away if he thought she wasn't home. Then another thought stuck in her mind: what if this was *Simon*?

'I'm getting fucking angry! You'll let me in if you know what's good for you.'

Why had he come here? He'd only sent the email last night. Did he now know the police were hunting for him? Had he come to kill her?

The door shook as the banging grew louder and more violent. 'You'd better fucking let me in!'

Alex dived into the kitchen, dropping to her knees so she would be out of sight of the outside world. Sliding across the cold linoleum, she stopped when she reached the sink, and remained there while her mind debated whether she could risk a look at the man still banging on the front door. If he continued much longer, he was sure to burst through.

Gripping the edge of the counter with her fingers, she took a deep breath, gradually straightening her legs, just enough so she could see over the lower edge of the window frame. Heart thundering in her chest, her eyes fell on a scrawny young man in a torn and weathered leather jacket, his T-shirt flapping in the wind, and long greasy hair like the mane of a lion.

Who the hell was he, and why was he so desperate to get in? His face was gaunt and covered in acne scars, and she would swear she'd never seen him before in her life. She was just about to drop down again when their eyes met for the briefest of moments, and he was banging on the window before her hands made it back to the floor.

'I fucking saw you. Let me in now!'

Alex cursed herself for allowing him to see her. 'I'm calling the police,' she yelled back, still crouched against the under-sink cupboard.

'Let me in so we can sort this out. I know she's in there with you.'

'Just go away!' Alex yelled back.

The banging stopped almost as quickly as it had started. With a sigh of relief, Alex gradually straightened once again, relieved to see Isla had returned and was now berating the young man. To her surprise, Isla then unlocked the door and brought him inside, dragging him into the kitchen and closing the door without a word to Alex.

'What the bloody hell do you think you're doing coming here?' Isla growled from the other side of the door.

Isla knew him.

That much was clear from the muffled conversation that was now underway. And although Alex knew it was rude to eavesdrop, she couldn't stop herself leaning closer to the wooden frame and pressing her ear as close as she dared.

'What the fuck are *you* doing here?' the young man fired back. 'You weren't at home.'

'I'm on a case,' Isla ground out. 'Not that that's any of your business. How did you even find me?'

'I went to your house and you wasn't there, so I used the app to find your phone and that said you'd been here overnight, so I figured you must have shacked up with some other bloke. Didn't realize you was a fucking lesbian.'

'Is that really what you think? Just tell me what you're doing here, Luke. Is it money again?'

'I'm in trouble, Mum.'

Alex's eyes widened, as she took two steps back. He was Isla's son? He didn't look anything like her, and Alex couldn't recall Isla mentioning having children, but she was certainly old enough to have an adult son. Alex felt even worse for listening in, and she was creeping back to the living room when the kitchen door flew open and Isla stormed out, yanking the front door open and pointing out.

'I told you before, I cannot keep bailing you out of these messes.'

'Mum, please, you don't understand—'

'The hell I don't! Did you think you could just rock up here and I would give you what's left of my pay cheque? You're an adult now, Luke, and it's time you stood on your own two feet.'

'Mum, I'm desperate. I need you—'

Isla glared at him. 'After what you did before … there's no way back from something like that. Get out before I have you arrested for scaring the living shit out of this poor woman.'

Luke took another look at Alex, before dropping his head and skulking out through the door. He turned as if to try one final plea, with Isla slamming the door before he had the chance.

Isla remained by the door for several minutes, not speaking, either uncertain what to say, or too embarrassed to try and make excuses for her son's errant behaviour. Alex half-expected her to throw the door open and chase off down the road after him, but she remained resolute.

It was Alex who made the first move to ease the tension. 'I'll fix us some tea.'

Isla's lips parted with no words emerging. As she nodded her head in gratitude a single tear rolled down her cheek.

Alex headed into the kitchen, filling the kettle from the tap and setting it back on its stand.

'I'm so sorry you had to see and hear any of that,' Isla said as she eventually entered the room, her head dipped.

It wasn't Alex's place to judge, so she waved away Isla's concern with a flick of the wrist.

'What must you think of me?' Isla continued, still avoiding eye contact. 'First of all I disappear for hours last night, and now my addict son turns up on your doorstep, making a real scene. It is totally unprofessional, and I think it only right that I speak to DI Trent and have a new FLO assigned to support you.'

Alex watched her. 'Can I be honest with you? I'm actually quite glad to learn that you're not as perfect as I pictured in my over-active imagination. I'm not exactly mother of the year, am I? Since you arrived yesterday morning I've been walking on eggshells around here, desperate not to say or do something that could be misconstrued or reflect even worse on me. I kept wondering what you must think of me. The mother who leaves her toddler unattended in a car, allowing some sick bastard to snatch her. So, it's a relief to come across another mother who has issues, albeit with an older son.'

'He's twenty-six, unemployed, and addicted to pain medica-tion. I used to joke with my ex-husband that at least he wasn't on heroin. We – my husband and I – decided we would start a family early. This was before I joined the force. The pregnancy wasn't easy and resulted in a hysterectomy. We nearly lost Luke, so I suppose I always considered him a bit of a miracle baby, and … I don't know … maybe it meant I was too soft on him.

'Anyway, fast-forward nineteen years, and he decided he wanted to be an artist. We paid for him to go to university, and he dropped out after eight months. At that point I should have been firmer and forced him to knuckle down and get a regular job. He said he wanted to do a gap year, go abroad and discover himself, assist charitable organizations in developing countries. Against my better judgement I thought it might make a man of him, and paid for his ticket.

'What I now know is he spent the year travelling from one hippy commune to another, smoking or inhaling God knows what. Every now and again we'd receive a postcard, or phone call where he'd make up stories of what he'd been up to. We later learned it was all a pack of lies.

'Then one day I received a call at work from the British embassy in Bangkok. Luke had been beaten and left for dead in the city and was in intensive care in hospital with a fractured skull and double leg break. I was horrified and caught the next flight over there, and I stayed there for three weeks with him, until he was fit enough to fly home. Of course we had to sort him a new passport and plane ticket as he claimed his had been stolen when he'd been attacked, but I was never certain. It was something the embassy worker said to me about the street value of a British passport, and it wouldn't surprise me if he'd sold it to fund his habit.

'Anyway, I brought him home and tried to get him into a rehabilitation programme. His leg and head were still in pretty bad shape and the doctor over here prescribed some pretty strong painkillers to help his pain. I kept him at home with me, so I could keep an eye on him. He was soon mobile again and, with me working shifts, it was impossible to know what he was up to while I was at work. He soon fell back into bad habits.'

Alex handed Isla a mug of tea. 'I had no idea you had all that going on in your life.'

Isla sipped the tea. 'Yes, well, we've always been a family of good liars. My husband managed to cover up the fact he was sleeping with my best friend for nearly two years.'

Alex's eyes widened.

'It was many years ago, and we've all moved on since then. He has *literally* moved on: remarried and has two young daughters with his new wife – and I hate him for it – but he's happy. He has very little to do with our son, which is why I'm always the first port of call when Luke runs out of money.'

'Is that why you were running late last night? Because of Luke?'

Isla nodded. 'I bet you're reconsidering my offer to have DI Trent trade me in for a new FLO now, aren't you?'

Alex shook her head sincerely. 'I'm really not.'

'I hope you and Ray are able to support each other through all this. I've seen first-hand how these situations can tear a marriage apart. I've also seen how they can strengthen the bond.'

It was strange having someone she felt so able to share with. Maybe it was the fact that Isla had revealed her own family issues, or maybe it was just because she hadn't managed to confide in anyone else, but it felt almost natural to admit the truth.

'I suspect Ray is having an affair. I don't know for certain. In my gut I think he is.'

'My husband changed his aftershave,' Isla said. 'That was the first clue for me. Suddenly he started focusing on his diet. I'd tried for years to make him more health-conscious and had given up when he suddenly started making smoothies for breakfast, going for runs and taking better care of himself. At first I hoped it was just a midlife crisis. He started working later and taking more business trips, and eventually I found a message from her to him when he left his phone unattended. At least he did the decent thing then and came clean. I mean, I had him banged to rights, but men will still often lie in those situations. He moved out the next day and didn't contest when I instigated divorce proceedings against him.'

'Ray's been playing squash without taking his kit with him. And he's never home. I can't remember the last time we made love.'

Isla stepped closer. 'I don't really know Ray, but for my money he doesn't seem the type. In this job I've seen plenty of colleagues' marriages end in divorce, and ninety-nine times out a hundred it has nothing to do with infidelity. On the whole police officers just don't have the time to have an affair. It's a pretty intense job and if he says he's working late, he more than likely is. Most marriages that end – where one of the partners is in the job – do so because of neglect; the demanding hours and mental focus required to fight crime do not go hand in hand with a loving relationship. Marriage is a union that requires work and effort, and sometimes it's impossible to find that balance. I don't blame my ex for seeking solace elsewhere, I just wish he'd been honest with me sooner.'

A knock at the door caught both their attention. Glancing at Isla for confirmation that Luke hadn't returned, Alex moved to the kitchen, gasping when she recognized the tall man on the doorstep.

28

The knot in Ray's stomach tightened, not because Trent's words had come as a shock, more because they had echoed the niggling voice in his head he'd been trying to ignore.

'I'm stepping over the line by even telling you,' Trent warned, placing her hands on the steering wheel as if she needed additional support, 'but I thought it only fair you hear it from me.'

He grunted, refusing to make eye contact with her, staring at his hands as his fingers entwined involuntarily. 'You must suspect I'm involved too then. I mean, that's a reasonable deduction if you're serious about Alex being a suspect.'

Trent didn't respond initially, though he saw her head bobbing in his periphery. There had to be more she wasn't telling him. To come clean about her suspicions so early into the search wouldn't have been a decision she'd have taken lightly. She was putting both the investigation and her own career in jeopardy; there had to be more.

'You get one "get out of jail free" card with me, Ray. Lie to me, or I sense you're not flying straight, I'll personally snap the cuffs around your wrists. So, this is it, the million-pound question: has Alex done something to hurt Carol-Anne?'

His eyes shone as his head snapped up. 'No ... I mean, I-I ... don't want to believe she has.'

His heart ached at the possibility that Alex could have made up the story about the abduction in order to cover up something she'd done herself. She loved their daughter, of that he had no doubt. So to even contemplate that something had happened – something Alex was desperately trying to cover up – chilled him to the core.

Trent was watching him carefully. 'Do you have reason to suspect Alex isn't telling the truth?'

He thought about the Manchester incident, how Alex had been so convinced she'd collected Carol-Anne from the park, rather than that other woman's daughter; how even when he'd told her he'd had Carol-Anne all morning, she'd thought he was lying to her. She was just as adamant that their daughter had been in the car on Tuesday, and he didn't doubt she believed she was telling the truth, but that wasn't the same thing as *actually* telling the truth. If she'd been off her medication for as long as he suspected, was it possible her mental health had been worsening for weeks without him noticing? What with work and the affair, he hadn't been around for long enough to really notice her decline.

'Ray? What is it?' Trent pressed as she saw his eyes darting as his mind worked.

How could he tell her and hammer the final nail into Alex's coffin himself? He had promised to be at her side for better, for worse, in sickness and in health. She deserved the benefit of the doubt, didn't she?

What if there was more going on than he was prepared to acknowledge? What if Carol-Anne hadn't been in the car when Alex had arrived at the Woodside car park? What if something bad had happened before then? Didn't he owe it to his little girl to find out the truth and bring her home regardless?

He swallowed hard, feeling the tears splash against his cheeks. 'Her pills: I don't think she's been taking them.'

It was all Trent had been looking for. Without another word, she started the engine and pulled off.

'I want you to come in and speak with the team,' Trent said, as they made their way up the stairs to the third floor. 'That means I will allow you into MIR-1 temporarily, only so you can speak as a witness, and not so you can be involved in the investigation.' She paused and reached for his arm to stop him too. 'God knows, I hope we're wrong about Alex. I know this can't be easy for you. We have to look at every angle if we're to discover what really happened to Carol-Anne. You understand that, don't you? This isn't about apportioning blame, it's about getting your daughter back. So I don't want you taking any of what is said in there to heart. The team realize what a shit situation this is, but they have to look at the case objectively. Do you understand? Try to think about Alex as a potential suspect, rather than your wife, if you can manage that.'

He nodded his understanding, wondering whether she realized how much more difficult she was making matters.

She punched in the door code to MIR-1 as they arrived, covering the keypad with her hand, and led him in.

'Right, ladies and gents,' she declared to the room. 'Pens down, calls ended and all eyes on me.'

The general chatter died almost instantly, swiftly followed by an echo of telephones and stationery being dropped on desks.

'I have advised Ray of our latest thinking, and he has agreed to fully cooperate, and answer our questions with the utmost honesty.'

Ray could feel the eyes of the half dozen men and women in the room on him, and he'd never felt so self-conscious. His gaze met Owen's and there was a shared moment of empathy before both looked away, Ray's stare falling to the floor.

'Ray?' Trent said, to capture his attention. 'Start by telling us what Alex's state of mind has been like in the past couple of weeks: has she seemed different in any way; has she seemed stressed, or worried by anything; has she been more argumentative with you or distant from Carol-Anne?'

How could he even begin to try and answer such a leading question? The first rule of investigation was to *assume nothing*, yet Trent had clearly decided Alex was to blame and was determined to tighten the net around their prime suspect, despite her previous statement to the contrary.

He allowed his eyes to circle the group gathered around the main dry-wipe board. 'I can't say I've noticed any particular change in Alex's temperament in the last week. Having been away on the course, I really haven't spent all that much time with either Alex or Carol-Anne.'

'I know this isn't easy for you,' Trent said calmly. 'You need to be objective in your recollection. Alex said her reason for being in town on Tuesday was for an interview. Is that correct?'

He nodded. 'Yes, she's looking to return to work on a part-time basis to begin with, taking on more hours when Carol-Anne starts at pre-school.'

'Was she feeling stressed about the interview? Or maybe at the prospect of returning to work after … how long has she been a stay-at-home mum?'

'It's nearly three years since she last worked; firstly maternity leave and then leaving altogether.'

'So it's fair to say that re-entering the workforce would be a significant change to her routine? Has she discussed her feelings about it with you?'

He took a deep breath, trying to relax his shoulders. 'She hasn't said she's feeling stressed by the prospect of returning to work. If anything, I'd say she was excited by it.'

Trent's eyes darted as her mind processed the information. 'Excited? So the thought of being free of the constraints of motherhood is her primary motive for returning to work?'

Why was she twisting his words like that? Alex had been looking forward to interacting with other people on a more frequent basis. That didn't mean she wouldn't miss Carol-Anne like crazy when she did secure new employment. She hadn't found being a full-time mum as easy as she'd thought. That didn't mean she would ever even think about harming Carol-Anne.

'Yes … well, no … not exactly. What I mean is: I wouldn't phrase it like that. It can be isolating being stuck in doors all day – and I think the possibility of holding adult conversations and not staring at the same four walls is what she's finding exciting.'

'And the interview itself? Had she done much preparation for it? Had she asked you for any guidance or interview technique, for example?'

He thought carefully about the question. 'No, I think it was quite a last-minute appointment, and since I was away, I didn't learn about it until Monday afternoon.'

'Did she have any support when you were away last week?' Owen asked.

'She was on her own. Her parents died years ago, and she doesn't get on well with my sister, who isn't local anyway.'

'Rattling about at home – just the two of them – can't have been easy,' Trent concluded.

Ray didn't like where this was headed. It was one thing to suspect Alex, but the team were acting like judge, jury, and executioner. All of it based on supposition rather than clear evidence.

'You're trying to paint my wife as a woman on the verge of a nervous breakdown,' he barked. 'Just because she's had *issues* historically, doesn't mean they've returned. And what exactly do you think she's done? You're trying to put words into my mouth to meet some predetermined view of her as prime suspect in your case. I don't know what it is you're constructing. Honesty is a two-way street, so why don't you tell me exactly what you think she's done and what evidence you have to support such a theory?'

He hadn't meant to raise his voice. He owed Alex a defence

against allegations she knew nothing about. And more importantly, if she *was* somehow responsible for his daughter's absence, he needed to know.

'And what about other suspects?' he asked, lowering his voice. 'What about finding someone who might have taken Carol-Anne to get back at me for locking them up? Huh? I've sent plenty of weirdoes down in my time, where's the list of them?'

Trent narrowed her eyes. 'Of course we are chasing down every possible angle, but ...' she paused and nodded.

One of the team flipped on the dry-wipe board's backlight, revealing the writing he'd been unable to decipher from where he was standing.

'Using traffic camera footage, we've managed to retrace some of Alex's vehicle's movements prior to her arrival at the car park,' Trent said, using a pen to point at key locations on a printed road map hanging from the board. 'We believe this is the route she took based on what we have found, and that it is the most direct route from your house to the Woodside car park. Unfortunately none of the shots give us a clear view of who is inside the vehicle. What it doesn't show is whether Carol-Anne was in the car at the start of the journey, or whether Alex stopped anywhere along the way to drop her off.'

Trent fixed him with a questioning stare. 'Did Alex have plans to go anywhere else earlier in the day that you know of?'

Ray shook his head as no memory fired. 'Not that I'm aware of.'

Trent kept her eyes on him. 'We also picked up her car earlier in the day – mid-morning – heading north on the M3 motorway. She is seen leaving the motorway at Fleet. Camera footage in the town is intermittent. We know she was in the area for at least half an hour, before she's seen returning to the motorway and heading back to Southampton. To your knowledge, was there any reason for her to be in Fleet on Tuesday morning?'

Alex hadn't mentioned any plans to go to Fleet, nor had she

told him that she had been there later on. Given everything that had happened since he'd seen her on Tuesday morning, it was hardly surprising if it had slipped her mind.

'Does she have any friends in Fleet?' Trent pressed. 'Are you aware of any reason she would drive forty-five minutes down the motorway to get there, spend only half an hour and then drive all the way home?'

Ray's brow furrowed as he tried to recall any acquaintances who lived in the area, returning a nil response.

'There's a nature reserve called Fleet Pond near where we believe Alex stopped,' Trent continued grimly. 'Unless you can offer me a reason not to, I'm about to authorize a search team to head there immediately with sniffer dogs. Please convince me that I'm barking up the wrong tree here, Ray.'

As he raised his head and their eyes made contact, he could offer nothing more than a quivering lip.

29

Alex's heart was racing as she opened the door and looked into the eyes of Dr Kirkman.

'I'm sorry to call around like this unannounced,' he said, his amber skin contrasting with the sky of cloud overhead, his jet-black hair parted to the side as it always was. He offered a hopeful smile. 'May I come in?'

Alex's frown deepened. 'What are you doing here?'

He looked down at his hands as he searched for the right explanation. It was strange seeing him outside of the safety of his office, even stranger that he had appeared here in this world, the one she kept compartmentalized from the counselling sessions. He didn't seem his usual, confident self, and it was unclear if it was because he was out of his comfort zone, or if he was breaching some kind of code of practice.

'The police called round at my office last night,' he began, still staring at his hands. 'They wouldn't tell me what it was regarding. They asked questions about you and wanted to know why you'd been coming to me for counselling.' He looked up, panic in his eyes. 'I didn't tell them anything, of course, that would have been a breach of the confidentiality agreement we both signed. They kept asking and asking, and by the time they left I couldn't stop thinking about you either. I was going to phone, but I thought it would be better to come in person. I got your address from our files, and I hope you don't mind me just turning up like this. I sense you might need me now, more than ever, though, so I wanted to offer my services.'

Suddenly Isla appeared, pushing herself into the gap between Alex and the doorframe, fixing Dr Kirkman with a forceful stare. 'And who might you be, sir?'

'Dr Saeed Kirkman,' he said, a confused look on his face. 'Who are ...?' His words trailed off as Isla raised her identification. 'Oh, I see.'

Isla's eyes remained on him as she spoke. 'Do you know this man, Mrs Granger?'

Alex's cheeks flushed slightly. 'Dr Kirkman is ... my counsellor.'

'I wasn't aware you had a counselling appointment today,' Isla continued, still giving him an untrusting evil eye.

'I don't ... I mean, I didn't ... I mean—'

'Would you like me to ask Dr Kirkman to leave, Mrs Granger?'

Alex remained still. On the one hand, allowing Kirkman in would only reinforce the police view that she was somehow cracking up, yet it would also be good to talk with a familiar face, free from the usual judgement.

Pulling the door wider, Alex ignored Isla's question. 'Do come in, Dr Kirkman.'

He stepped into the house, and Alex steered him towards the living room. She was about to follow him in, when Isla reached for her arm, pulling her close.

'Just be careful what you tell him. Your name is already in the public arena after yesterday. The last thing you need is more rumours leaking—'

Alex pulled her arm free, speaking in a hard whisper. 'What leaked yesterday didn't come from *my* side. Just remember that. I trust Dr Kirkman, and what I discuss with him will remain private.'

She didn't wait for a challenge, instead heading into the living room and closing the door behind her. Kirkman was standing by the patio doors, staring out into the garden.

'You have a lovely home,' he commented.

'You must be joking!' Alex gasped back. 'I'm embarrassed by the state of the place.'

'You're being hard on yourself, Alex. Believe me, next to the state of my flat, this place is a palace.'

They shared a smile, before an uncomfortable silence descended rapidly, with neither sure how to move past small talk to what was on both of their minds.

'Shall we sit?' he eventually suggested, and Alex nodded, delicately perching in her usual spot, while he made himself comfortable on the larger sofa. 'I do just want to reassure you again that I didn't share the nature of any of our conversations with the detectives who visited. I can't stress enough the importance of patient-doctor confidentiality. All I confirmed was that I had seen you in the past, and that I hadn't seen you recently. They already seemed to know those details anyway.'

Ray had probably told them all about her alleged breakdown following the miscarriage. She was certain that Trent already thought she'd made up Carol-Anne's disappearance, and she had probably hoped Kirkman would confirm just how batty she was.

Kirkman rested his elbows on his knees, interlocking his fingers into a bridge for his chin to rest on. 'Would you like to tell me what's been going on, Alex?'

'I'm not sure where to start.'

'Okay, then perhaps I may ask you a question?'

She nodded.

'Why did you stop coming to see me?'

Alex studied his face, looking for any trace of hurt or any sign that he had taken her absence personally. 'I …' She took a deep breath. 'To be honest, I didn't think the sessions were helping anymore.'

His face remained emotionless. 'And the medication I recommended, are you still taking that?'

She began to nod before realizing it was pointless lying. He'd probably already checked with her GP and would know she hadn't requested a repeat prescription in several weeks. 'They were making me feel nauseous all the time. I was a shadow of myself when I was taking them. And I need all my faculties about me if I'm to return to work, so I gradually stopped taking them. I've been so much better since,' she added to alleviate any growing concern he might have been feeling.

'That's good,' he said with a smile. 'I'm pleased you seem to be approaching the light at the end of your tunnel. I wish you'd let me know this was your plan, so I could have been on hand to provide support. It's positive news that you're feeling better.' He lowered his hands to his lap. 'There's a stigma attached to the broad range of mental health conditions that are talked about these days. People always assume that once you start seeking counselling and are prescribed antidepressants it's a life sentence. That isn't the case. There are plenty of success stories: men and women like you who make changes in their lives, and manage to drag themselves into better mental health. I'm really pleased for you, Alex. Genuinely.'

She didn't doubt that he was. In the months she'd been a regular visitor to his office, he'd never once given her the impression that his motives towards her were anything but supportive. She'd been referred by her GP, so the cost was covered by the NHS, and he always seemed pleased to see her, never pressed her to talk about anything she didn't want to, and never passed judgement on the terrible thoughts she'd shared with him.

'Thank you. I'm sorry I didn't call you to explain all this. I guess … I wasn't convinced that I would manage to break the cycle, and I didn't want to do anything to tempt fate.'

'I understand, and it makes me glad that I made the effort to come here today to check on you.' He paused, looking around the room, before plucking up the courage to look back at her again. 'Can I ask you a second question?'

She already knew what he was going to ask before the words tumbled from his mouth.

'Why is there a police officer in your kitchen, and why did those detectives come and speak to me yesterday?'

There was no point in dressing up the truth. No version of the event made it look any better than it was. 'Someone abducted my daughter from a car park on Tuesday afternoon. The police are searching for her and the man who took her.'

Kirkman remained silent. Alex sensed he was studying her body language, tinted by all she had shared with him previously.

'The little girl in the televised appeal: that was *your* daughter?'

Alex nodded despite the sting of tears in her eyes. 'You must be the only person who didn't know.'

'Now that I think about it … yes, I can see the family resemblance. At the risk of asking an obvious question: how are you *feeling*?'

The words were said with such sincerity that she couldn't help the tears running down her cheeks. 'Like I failed her.'

'You blame yourself for what happened?'

Her voice cracked with the strain. 'It was my fault.'

'It's natural for a mother to blame herself when something bad happens to their child. Unless you were the one who directly harmed your daughter, then it's not your fault.'

'I left her in the car unattended. Had I taken her with me to the ticket machine, none of this would have happened. It *is* my fault.' As she spoke the words, finally admitting what she'd been so afraid to accept, the burden of guilt lifted just a fraction, for just a moment.

30

Leaning back in his chair, Ray didn't want his imagination to run amok but he had little way of preventing it. Having been escorted back out of the Major Incident Room where the operation was in full force, he no longer had access to Trent and the team, which meant he was no longer entrusted in the inner circle.

He wanted to phone Alex and demand an answer to why she had driven to Fleet. To contact her would be to warn her of what was coming, and he was duty-bound not to let anything slip. Wasn't he also duty-bound to stop Trent making a fool of herself by ordering a search of the Fleet Pond Nature Reserve? She had to be wrong, right? Alex couldn't have …

He couldn't bring himself to finish the thought. Alex was many things, but a killer? No way.

Absolutely not!

This was the woman he had fallen in love with at first sight. The woman he had vowed to marry and cherish. The woman who had carried Carol-Anne for nine months, and was besotted with their daughter.

Trent had to be way off base.

He froze as his mind continued to process everything he knew. This was also the woman he had grown apart from. He still loved her – he thought – even though they weren't as close as they once were. That was his fault. He was the one who had changed, hadn't he? He was the one who had strayed; Alex was still Alex.

Wasn't she?

He leapt to his feet, pacing the room. This was getting him nowhere. He needed to know what was going on in the Incident Room. He needed to know whether Trent had withheld anything from him. They said they knew Alex had stopped for half an hour in Fleet, but they hadn't said *how* they knew. Which meant they had to have held something back. What could it be? What could they possibly have that made them so certain Alex had driven Carol-Anne to the nature reserve and left her there?

Half an hour wasn't long enough to dig a grave; at least, not a very deep one. And Alex wouldn't be stupid enough to think she could cover up such a crime by fabricating an abduction story. Would she?

'Jeez, you're going to wear a hole in that carpet,' DS Jodie Crichton said, as she arrived in MIR-2, a stack of papers precariously held in her arms. 'What's wrong?'

'They think Alex killed our daughter,' he said without missing a beat.

Jodie's eyes widened, but she didn't respond, presumably not wanting to be dragged into a conversation that could one day be reviewed by the Professional Standards governing board.

He met her gaze. 'I need to know what's going on in that room. Can you go in there and relay to me?'

'Only if I want to be suspended for interfering with an active investigation. You know I can't do that, Ray.'

He hadn't expected her to agree. 'Please? I hate to ask. If …' His voice cracked under the strain. '*If* Carol-Anne is dead, then I deserve to know.'

Jodie looked like she wished she was anywhere else but in the room with him. 'I'm sorry, Ray, you know I can't. The best thing you can do is go home and wait for Trent to update you. I'm surprised to even find you in here now.'

'I don't want to go home,' he growled. 'How can I look at Alex, knowing what they think she's done?'

Jodie bit her lip. 'I would help you if I could – you know I would – but I'm not on that investigation and have even less business being in there than you.'

'You could just make up an excuse to go in there.' He snapped his fingers together. 'You could go and give Trent an update on our progress and while you're in there, casually ask how things are progressing.'

'Are you kidding? She would see it coming a mile off. She was the one who paired you with me, so I could keep you away from the case. Remember? If I go in there, she'll know I'm doing it for you, and she'll have me on paid suspension before the sun sets. I'm sorry, Ray, you have to let it go.'

'Would you *let it go* if you were in my shoes?'

He was being unreasonable, but what choice did he have? Just asking Jodie to spy on the team for him was grounds for a disciplinary hearing. If allowing his career to go up in smoke brought him closer to the truth about his daughter, wasn't it worth it?

Jodie lowered the papers to the desk and let out a long sigh. 'I would hate it, but yes I would, because I know the rules.'

It was no use keeping on at her. It had been a risk to even ask Jodie to get involved, and he now regretted broaching the topic with her. He knew, too, that Owen wouldn't dare risk his neck anymore than he already had. Ray was running out of options.

If he couldn't get into MIR-1 and there was nobody who would keep him in the loop, he could only think of one possible solution, but it would mean risking everything he had worked so hard for.

His mind made up, he reached for the squad car keys, dropping them into his pocket without Jodie noticing. Reaching for his jacket, he glanced at his watch, surprised to see it was already early afternoon – he had no idea where the day had gone.

'I'm going to grab something to eat. I'll call you later.'

Her face was already buried in the files – she was clearly relieved he'd dropped his request.

Jogging along the corridor to the staircase, he was down the stairs and out of the building in under a minute, and was soon behind the wheel of the car. Starting the engine, he pulled out his phone and searched for the address of his destination. If he was lucky, he'd be at Fleet Pond Nature Reserve within the hour.

31

Alex fired up the laptop and tilted the screen so Kirkman would be able to see it. 'You'll see what I mean in a moment.'

'I have to admit,' Kirkman said, taking up the seat next to Alex, 'I saw the televised appeal, but never in a million years did I think it could relate to one of my patients.'

'The woman in charge – DI Trent – said they would keep our names away from the appeal, for fear of a possible backlash. They might as well have plastered our names all over it for the good it did. Some of the messages and comments have been just … vicious.'

'Crimes against children are incredibly emotive,' Kirkman answered solemnly. 'Even those without children of their own feel protective towards younger members of society. It's evolution: it's in our programming to take care of those more vulnerable than ourselves.'

Alex snorted. 'You wouldn't have thought from reading the messages.' She opened them for him to read. 'Just look.'

Kirkman leaned closer as he processed each spiteful word. 'This is the one of the reasons why I don't get involved in social media. It's tough in my line of business *not* to have more of an online presence. This kind of abuse – where the bully gets to hide behind a fake name and picture – it's inhumane if you ask me.'

'Isla suggested I should delete the accounts, and I was going to after last night's abuse, but I've now decided to leave it.'

He raised a sceptical eyebrow. 'I can't for the life of me see why.'

'Two reasons, I think,' she mused. 'Firstly, if people are still talking about it then it means Carol-Anne's abduction will remain in the public eye for longer. And the longer people are talking about it, the better the chance that someone will find her or come forward with information.'

'And the second reason? I hope it's not so you can continually beat yourself up over what happened?'

Her brow furrowed as she shook her head. 'I'm not a masochist!'

'Then why keep them?'

'I have to keep believing Carol-Anne is still alive and that she will be returned to me one day soon. And when that day comes, I will message each of these people back, and … I don't know … vindicate myself in some way. Silly, right?'

'The desire for revenge is a base human instinct; however it's true what they say: it doesn't help. Can I be blunt with you, Alex? I'm asking as a friend as much as a therapist.'

She nodded.

'You've already been through so much in the past year without welcoming more pain into your life. I don't believe that replying to any of these bullies will make you feel better. In fact, I think you'll feel worse for it. It's good that your focus is on getting your daughter back, and I would strongly encourage that optimism; just don't let the temptation of getting back at your accusers taint your focus. Clearly, these messages are truly hurtful; I'm not sure you're strong enough for another battle.'

She looked down, suddenly noticing his hand on hers.

He withdrew it as soon as she noticed, standing suddenly and moving back to the patio door. 'Forgive me, I overstepped my position.'

Alex was about to respond when a gentle knock at the living room door caused them both to look around.

'You have a visitor,' Isla said quietly, poking her head through from the kitchen.

The door opened wider and Sophie scuttled in. 'I got your message … oh, I'm sorry,' she said when she saw Dr Kirkman, 'I didn't realize you had a guest. I can come back—'

'No, it's okay,' Alex interrupted, pleased to see her friend. 'Please stay. Sophie, this is Dr Saeed Kirkman, my counsellor.'

Kirkman smiled broadly at Sophie, extending his hand for her to shake, which she did.

'Sophie's my next-door neighbour,' Alex explained.

Kirkman turned to face Alex. 'I should get going. Will you show me to the door?'

Alex nodded and stood, telling Sophie she would return in a moment. She closed the door as they left the room and then proceeded to the front door.

'Listen, Alex,' Kirkman said as Alex reached for the lock, 'I really think it would be a benefit to you to make another appointment to see me, and *soon*. The last thing you want is additional stress to drag you back down.' He eyed her wrists where the scars from her past selfmutilation remained.

Alex folded her arms. 'I told you, Dr Kirkman, I'm doing a lot better. If I feel things starting to get on top of me, I promise I will call you.'

'We don't even have to meet in my office,' he said, rubbing her arm gently. 'We could go for a coffee, or some food, and just talk. As a friend, I mean. Just because I was your counsellor doesn't mean …' He stopped himself before he said anymore. 'And I'm sure whoever has taken your daughter will let her go soon enough. I've always believed that good things happen to good people, and I think you're a good person, Alex.'

170

She didn't agree with him, but appreciated the sentiment.

'You have my number,' he added, and then he stepped out, glaring at the rain clouds overhead and jogging back to his car parked at the bottom of the driveway.

Alex closed the door and made her way back to the living room, where Sophie was waiting patiently.

'I didn't expect you to come over,' Alex said apologetically, feeling her conversation with Dr Kirkman had done more to ease the burden than anything Sophie could offer.

'Nonsense. I told you I'm here for whatever you need. You helped me in my hour of need, and I'm here for you.'

Alex rubbed her arm to show her gratitude. 'I hope you didn't change any plans to come over?'

'I was relieved to get your message to be honest. I was supposed to be meeting up with Noemi, but she cancelled at the last minute. A work thing apparently.'

The laptop beeped, and Alex remembered she hadn't logged back out of Twitter. Lifting the laptop, she was surprised to see no new notifications on the internet page, and then saw the email icon flashing in the corner of the screen. She clicked on it without thinking, and her heart skipped a beat as she saw who the new message was from.

Simon Says …
    Carol-Anne is such a cutie, do your maternal duty.
    He deserves to die, and he knows why.
    If you don't fulfil my wish, I will gut her like a fish.
    2 days.

32

Ray lowered his window a fraction. The car felt stuffy, despite the heavy rain now splashing against the windscreen. Ahead of him a sea of red tail lights stretched as far as the eye could see. Ironically, although he'd joined the motorway half an hour ago, he was actually closer to home than when he'd started, having not moved in some time.

The M3 could be bad at the best of times, but there had to have been an accident causing this kind of tailback. He was still at least forty miles from his destination, and according to his phone he wouldn't make it there in over an hour, with the ETA rising by the minute.

He looked up at his reflection in the mirror. The anxiety had passed, and he now felt frustration and anger. 'Maybe you should take it as a sign,' he told his bloodshot eyes, knowing it would take more than heavy traffic to deter him from his end goal. Trent felt justified in sending a team to examine the Fleet Pond Nature Reserve, and if she had reason, then he had to see what was there.

He tried to push the worst fears from his mind, reminding himself who Alex was and the love she'd shown their daughter every day since she'd conceived.

He lifted his bottom slightly to try to get a better view of what could be holding up the cars in front. It didn't look like there would be any movement anytime soon. And it wasn't like he could find an alternative route to his destination, nor could he make any attempt to leave the motorway and give up on his quest, as he was stuck in the outside lane, and the next exit was still half a mile away. It was hard to imagine how regular users could put up with this kind of jam on a daily basis.

Reaching into his jacket he pulled out the packet of cigarettes and removed the last one, screwing up the packet and dropping it back on the seat.

'What?' he shouted at his judgemental reflection. 'It's my last one.'

He lit it, savouring the burn against the back of his throat and the familiar smell of the smoke that only smokers could truly appreciate. He exhaled through the tiny gap in the window. Smoking in a squad car was a strict no-no, but at this point in time he didn't care; there was every chance he would be unemployed soon enough in any case for violating Trent's order to stay away.

He nearly dropped the cigarette when his mobile phone erupted to life, and he answered it without checking the display.

'Ray?' Jodie said urgently. 'Silly question: did you borrow the squad car? I swear I left the keys on the desk, and now I can't find them and nobody has checked them back in.'

He closed his eyes, tempted to lie and cover his deceit, knowing it would only come back to haunt him at some point in the future. 'Um, yeah, I have it. Sorry.'

'Oh thank God,' she said, the relief obvious from her tone, 'I was starting to think I was losing my marbles. Are you happy for me to put your name in the log book?'

'Yeah, of course. Sorry, I should have said before I took off.'

'Where are you going anyway? I thought you were heading home?'

'I was, but then I remembered there was something I needed to follow up.'

'*For the robbery case?*'

'Yeah,' he said quickly. 'I wanted to … um … speak to the team looking at the other robberies in Berkshire. I thought I could share the image from the traffic camera with them and see if they recognized the face.'

'*I was going to email them a copy tonight. There was no need to drive there.*'

'Yeah, I know, but … I needed some space and thought the drive would do me some good.'

'*Oh, fair enough I suppose. If you'd said I'd have tagged along with you.*'

'No offence, Jodie, I wanted to be on my own to clear my head. With everything that's going on at home—'

'*Say no more,*' she interrupted, '*I do understand, Ray. Are you nearly there?*'

'I wish! Been jammed in traffic for twenty minutes. The M3 is at a standstill.'

'*Overturned lorry just before Junction 9,*' Jodie explained. '*Diesel all over the bypass, so they've had to shut the road while a clean-up crew sorts it. You're going to be stuck there for a while.*'

He cursed under his breath. 'Screw it then. You send them the email and let me know what they say. I'll do my best to get off the road and head back to the station.'

'*Will do. Good luck!*' She hung up.

Finishing the cigarette, he flicked the butt out of the window, watching as a tiny trail of sparks temporarily lit the road before it fizzled out in a puddle. Staring down at the screwedup packet, he wished he'd bought some more before joining the motorway. He was sure Alex must have noticed the smell by now, yet she still hadn't mentioned it. He wondered what else she might not be discussing with him.

The car in front moved forward ten yards as someone further up left the lane. Ray edged forward as the phone came to life in his hand again. Applying the handbrake, he answered it.

'Alex? I can't really talk, I'm—'

'*He sent another one, Ray,*' she interjected, her voice quivering as she spoke.

'*Who* sent another *what?*'

'*Simon … he emailed me again. This time there's a picture of our baby …*' Her voice broke under the strain, making her words almost inaudible. '*Carol-Anne and a copy of today's newspaper.*'

Ray narrowed his eyes, no longer looking at the road ahead. 'Hold on, wait, you mean the guy who emailed yesterday? He sent another message?'

'*Yes! I told you it was real! He has our baby.*'

'Calm down, Alex, you're not making any sense. I can hear you're upset, but I need you to calmly tell me what the email says.'

Alex took a deep breath, trying to regain her composure. '"*Simon Says: Carol-Anne is such a cutie, do your maternal duty. He deserves to die, and he knows why. If you don't fulfil my wish, I will gut her like a fish. 2 days.*"'

Bile bubbled at the back of his throat and he choked it back, his mind racing with a cocktail of terror and confusion.

A second message.

But from who?

And why?

And who *deserves to die*?

'When did you receive it?' he asked, his vision blurring.

'*Just now. Don't you see what this means? She's still alive, Ray. Wherever she is, she's safe and well.*'

Until Trent had mentioned her suspicions about Alex's reasons for visiting Fleet, he'd refused to even consider the possibility that Carol-Anne could be dead. What did this mean for Trent's supposition about Alex? She couldn't have harmed Carol-Anne if there was proof that she was alive and well today.

He didn't know whether to be relieved or shocked, the butter-flies in his gut fluttering wildly.

'Does it say anything else? Is there any clue who sent it?'

'No. There are two images this time. The one with Carol-Anne and then a picture of a man.'

Ray's pulse quickened. 'A man? Who?'

'I don't know! I've never seen him before.'

'What does he look like?'

'The picture is black and white, but I'd say he's in his sixties – his hair looks white as snow – his face is wrinkled and he's snarling.'

'Snarling?'

'Yeah, like a cowboy. I need you to come home. Now.'

Ray stared at the line of red lights ahead of him and to his left. 'Okay, I'm stuck in traffic, but I'll do whatever I can to get home. What does Isla say about the message?'

'She's been trying to get hold of DI Trent. Apparently she isn't in the office and isn't answering her phone.'

Ray put on the car's indicator, looking over his shoulder for a chance to cut into the middle lane. 'I'm going to have to go, Alex. Listen to me, tell Isla to keep trying Trent.'

'Please hurry, Ray.'

'I'll be there as quickly as I can. I swear,' he said, meaning every word, and desperately wanting to take Alex into his arms and apologize for ever doubting her story.

Dropping the phone on the seat, he switched on the blue lights built in to the vehicle's grill. Then, spotting a gap, he quickly pulled into the middle lane to a cacophony of horns. He didn't care. Right now, he needed to be home, and he wasn't going to let anything get in his way. If he could make it to the hard shoulder, he could cut through the traffic and reach the next exit in no time.

'I'm coming, baby,' he muttered under his breath. 'Daddy's coming.'

33

Alex was still perched on the edge of the sofa, gently rocking, when Isla returned to the room, the anxious look on her face reflecting how Alex was feeling. Sophie had offered to stay, but had made herself scarce while Alex had been on the phone to Ray.

'Well?' Alex asked, unable to contain herself any longer.

Isla shook her head. 'Still nothing. I've reported it to the team and forwarded the message for forensic examination. I still can't get hold of DI Trent. Did you manage to get through to Ray?'

Alex nodded, feeling jittery. She hadn't even realized that she'd allowed herself to question whether Carol-Anne was still alive. Now the relief was palpable. She didn't even look upset in the picture, which meant whoever had her was treating her well.

That was a good sign, wasn't it? Carol-Anne had always been a happy, smiley child – to see her smiling now brought an element of comfort in what had been a harrowing couple of days.

'I'll keep trying DI Trent,' Isla said. 'She needs to know we've received proof of life.'

Isla's hand shot up to her mouth, as she realized what it was she'd said and how it could be misconstrued. 'I'm sorry, I meant it's good that she looks well and healthy. That's really positive. The last thing you should do right now is panic—'

'I *shouldn't panic?* I can't believe you just told me that!'

Isla was clearly used to handling out-of-control parents. Right now Alex needed more. Being told to relax and stay calm wasn't going to help Carol-Anne. She needed someone to take charge, to find the cruel bastard who was sending the emails and to get her daughter back. Right now, Isla looked like she couldn't even organize a three-course dinner.

She needed Ray to take charge of the situation.

Who the hell was the man in the other image? She certainly didn't recognize him. Why weren't the police more interested in that side of the message? Both rhymes had stated this *Jack* – whoever he was – had to die in order for Carol-Anne to be returned.

Were they even looking into who Jack could be? Or why someone wanted him dead? If they could identify Jack, then maybe they could trace the threat back to whoever had sent the message in the first place.

'Do you know who this man is yet?' Alex asked, lifting the laptop and carrying it to where Isla was standing. 'Hmm? Who is he, and what does he have to do with my daughter?'

Isla didn't look at the screen, keeping her eyes trained on Alex. 'I don't know who that person is or what he has to do with any of this. I assure you the team is investigating that side of things.'

Alex studied Isla's face, certain there was more behind those dark eyes than she was saying. 'They can do facial recognition, right? Like on the television? They can scan his face and see if it matches any known criminals; they can do that, can't they?'

Isla's lips tightened. 'I will keep trying to get hold of DI Trent,' she said soothingly. 'Until that time there really isn't anything else we can—'

'How would you feel if someone kidnapped Luke?' Alex interrupted.

Isla's confusion was all too apparent.

'Your son, Isla, what if someone emailed you with his picture and said they were going to kill him if you didn't do as they said?

How would you react? Would you stay calm? Huh?' Alex leapt to her feet and moved to the back door, staring out as the rain continued to fall, the puddles now resting on the top of the grass.

'I understand your anxiety, Alex, and if lashing out at me helps then so be it. I am here to help you, and to help bring Carol-Anne back to you.' She tapped the phone against her cheek, adding, 'I'll keep trying,' before heading out of the room and closing the door behind her.

Alex's legs felt like they were going to cave at any moment as the room began to spin. How could this be happening? How could she have allowed it to happen? A year ago, they had been so happy. Since discovering she was pregnant again, everything had begun to fall apart. And now, just as she was starting to get back to something resembling normality, the rug had been pulled out again.

Where the hell was Ray? It had been almost half an hour since she'd called him, and he had yet to make an appearance. She needed his paternal instinct to take control and do whatever it took to get their little girl back.

As if she had willed it, the living room door burst open as Ray rushed through. 'Where's the laptop? Show me what he sent,' he demanded.

Alex handed it to him.

'Is this even today's paper?' he asked, opening a new search window and typing in the journal's name. The headline on the page was a perfect match.

'What did Trent say?' he continued. 'Do we know if the picture is genuine, or has been Photoshopped? Did it definitely come from the same account as yesterday?'

'Isla's still trying to get hold of her.'

'At least Carol-Anne is smiling,' he said evenly, his eyes glued to the screen.

The statement was bittersweet. 'Do you reckon the picture is real?'

Ray zoomed in, examining the outline of Carol-Anne's body, looking for any jagged edges suggesting it had been cut from a corresponding image and pasted onto the image of the newspaper. 'Why wouldn't it be real?'

'You said last night you thought the person who emailed was a crank. I told you there was more to it than that!'

His head snapped up, but there was no anger. 'I'm sorry I doubted you,' he said.

The apology brought a lump to her throat, and going over to him she wrapped her arms around his shoulders, relieved when he returned the gesture.

'I knew I hadn't imagined it,' she said, her head buried in his shoulder. 'I always said I was telling the truth – that someone had taken Carol-Anne from the car – and now this *proves* I wasn't lying.'

She enjoyed the feeling of him holding her close: the warmth of his embrace, the way she could feel his heart beating through his chest, and the intoxicating aroma of his cologne. She couldn't remember the last time they'd shared this level of intimacy. And she didn't want to let go.

The moment ended as quickly as it had begun, with Ray's attention once again diverted by the grizzled nose and snarl of the old man on the screen.

'Do you know him?' she asked.

'Maybe … I don't know. It could be someone I arrested once? It's impossible to remember every face in my line of work.'

'What if he *is* someone you arrested? Maybe he's the one behind all this. Maybe he did it to get at you. We need to find him to get Carol-Anne back.'

Their eyes met for a fraction of a second, and she could tell he was thinking the same thing. He broke free of her grip, closing the laptop lid and moving across to the window. 'It's all my fault, isn't it? Someone's done this to get back at me, and now Carol-Anne's life is in danger.'

She immediately crossed the room, but rather than welcoming her embrace, he shrugged it off, eyes shining as he stormed away, slamming the door behind him.

34

Dropping the cigarette to the floor, Ray pulled the collar of his overcoat around his neck, doing his best to ignore the rain passing through the leaves of the tree he was sheltered beneath. He stared out at the approaching headlights, relieved to recognize the anxious face behind the wheel. Darting from the tree, he reached for the door handle as the car pulled to a stop at the kerbside.

'Thanks for coming,' he said, as he brushed excess water from his shoulders and swung himself into the passenger seat.

'You're lucky I did,' Owen replied, staring out into the darkness as the windscreen began to mist up. 'I kept telling myself to turn around at every set of lights on the journey over.'

'Well, I appreciate you coming,' Ray said, meaning every word.

Owen's patience was already waning. 'Why am I here, Ray?'

'I tried calling Trent; she wasn't in the office.'

'No, she's still in—' Owen froze, narrowing his eyes in Ray's direction. 'Wait, if you called me over here just to ask for more details about the case, then you can get out now. For fuck's sake, Ray! You said it was an emergency. You ever heard of the boy who cried wolf?'

'No, listen to me, Owen, that's not why I called you.' Ray fished into his coat and pulled out his phone, opening the email message he'd forwarded from the laptop.

Owen read the message: "'Simon Says … Carol-Anne is such a cutie, do your maternal duty. He deserves to die, and he knows why. If you don't fulfil my wish, I will gut her like a fish. 2 days.'"

'Where did this come from?' he asked, his eyes widening.

'Someone sent it to Alex about an hour ago. As far as I can tell it's from the same person who sent the message yesterday.'

'Shit! Does Trent know?'

'That's why I was phoning the office. She's off at the nature reserve in Fleet; I presume that's where she is?'

'You know I can't answer that.'

'I was in the Incident Room when she ordered SSD to go and search for shallow graves. Remember? It was her who involved me in this investigation, not the other way around.'

'She also said none of us were to talk to you without her prior consent or presence in the room. I'm risking my job just being here.'

'You didn't have a choice. I'm your superior and you only acted under orders; that's what I'll tell her if it comes to anything – which it won't – okay?'

'She needs to know that a second message came through.'

'The FLO is still trying to reach her. Listen, there's more.' Ray took the phone and opened the first of the images. 'It's from today's newspaper. Do you realize what this means? Carol-Anne is still alive; she isn't buried in some nature reserve in the middle of nowhere. I was wrong about Alex; we all were.'

Owen didn't answer, unable to meet Ray's gaze.

'This was also attached to the message,' Ray continued. 'You recognize him?'

The look of wide-eyed surprise on Owen's face spoke volumes.

'You recognize him, don't you? Who is he?'

Owen was glaring angrily at Ray. 'If this is some kind of joke, it's fucking sick!'

'I swear to you, this is no joke. Who is he?'

Owen shook his head, unwilling to believe Ray's story. 'Get the fuck out of my car, Ray.'

Ray wasn't moving without an answer. 'Who's the old man, Owen? If he's the one who's got Carol-Anne, then—'

'Jack Whitchurch,' Owen interrupted. 'Okay? His name's Jack Whitchurch.'

Ray's mind raced to find out why the name was ringing an enormous bell in his head. 'Whitchurch, wait isn't that …?'

'He's the recently released sex offender we had to rehome this week. I mentioned it in the brief on Tuesday morning. Remember now?'

'He's a paedophile?'

Again, Owen's face told Ray all he needed to know.

Ray's brain was already two steps ahead. 'If you rehomed him, you must know where he lives now.'

Owen quickly shook his head. 'Oh no, no way am I taking you to his house.'

'Please, Owen, you've got to. If he's got Carol-Anne, then we can save her tonight. *Now!*'

'I can't and I won't take you anywhere, Ray. I promise you, I will find Trent and update her. You need to go back inside.'

'Bullshit! You owe me, Owen. And I have seniority. You *will* drive me, or I will raise a complaint of insubordination against you.'

'Go ahead! I'm pretty sure we both know whose side Trent will take. We're even now. I don't owe you anything. Besides, there's no evidence to suggest he has any involvement in what happened on Tuesday afternoon. In fact, I can say beyond a reasonable doubt that he couldn't have been the one who snatched Carol-Anne, as he had a police guard outside his new home on Tuesday afternoon. Officers were with him from one until six while he settled in.'

'That doesn't mean he isn't involved. His alibi is a little too convenient, don't you think? It couldn't have been him because he had a police alibi? Sounds fabricated. Come on, Owen, I'm

183

not saying we have to arrest him on the spot. We could just drive to his house and have a look around.'

'There's no evidence, Ray.'

'You know as well as I do that lots of these sex pests know one another. They meet in online chat rooms and talk about their desires. He may not have physically taken her, but that doesn't mean he didn't orchestrate it, or know who's behind it.'

Owen paused. 'Wait a second, what did the first message say? Have you got a copy?'

Ray flicked through his emails. '"Simon Says … If you ever want to see Carol-Anne, all you need to do is kill a man. If you kill Jack, I will give her back. Refuse to comply and Carol-Anne will die. 3 days."'

'"Kill Jack",' Owen repeated. 'Read the messages together, and you'll see the picture of Jack isn't confirmation that he took her, it's telling you – or rather Alex – to kill Whitchurch. I need to phone this in immediately.'

In all the confusion of the day, Ray had forgotten about the content of the original email, and now, all of a sudden, Owen's words slotted the pieces into place.

'Threat to life,' Ray suddenly blurted. 'That's all you need to visit him at home. For all we know, the person who took Carol-Anne is watching Whitchurch's home now, and means to do him harm. Come on, Owen, you are duty-bound to check he's okay. We both are.'

Owen made no attempt to restart the engine, fixing Ray with a pained expression. 'No, Ray, I am duty-bound to check on him. You're not. You're not on this case. Can't you see that you're too close to help Carol-Anne? Earlier you were convinced that your wife had killed her, and when you got in the car you assumed Whitchurch was involved, and now you think he's a victim instead. Your mind is all over the place, mate, and I'm not about to let you screw things up anymore. I will check on Whitchurch and speak to Trent. I'm not taking you with me, and I don't care if that pisses you off; you'll thank me for it one day.'

35

Like wasps that had scented jam, the uniformed officers swarmed around Alex's house. No matter which room she entered, she would find at least one of them – offering that empathetic look they wore permanently – if not two, whispering in a corner. The conversations always ceased the second she stepped into the room. She just wanted to run, to leave the home and memories behind her.

Owen had been the first to arrive at the house, to advise her that a team would be coming over. He and Ray must have had some kind of argument outside, as Ray had been moping ever since, getting under everyone's feet. He had only agreed to go upstairs when DI Trent had finally arrived and barked orders to everyone who had descended on what had once been a happy home.

How Alex missed those days now.

There'd been no sign of Isla since Owen's arrival. Maybe she'd been deemed surplus to requirements.

What they'd all wanted to see was the laptop where the email message had been received. If only they'd taken last night's message as seriously, maybe Carol-Anne would already be home. Trent had yet to come and speak to her, though the furtive glances she kept firing in Alex's direction suggested she had something she wanted to say.

And then she came over. 'I wondered whether we could have a word in private, Mrs Granger.'

'Um, of course,' Alex said, sliding from the kitchen stool.

Trent stepped into the kitchen, closing the door behind her. 'I will need to conduct a formal interview with you at the station, Alex. For now I'm hoping you can answer a few pressing questions for me.'

Trent's tone made Alex feel uneasy. 'Do I need to call a solicitor of some kind? Or maybe Ray? He's just upstairs—'

'That won't be necessary,' Trent said, cutting her off. 'Tell me, Alex, do you recognize the man in the picture that was attached to the email?'

Alex shook her head. 'As I told Owen and the other officer who asked, no I do not.'

Trent's eyes narrowed. 'And when you showed the picture to Ray, did he say he recognized the man?'

'No. He said he looked familiar but couldn't place why. Who is he?'

'You're certain you've never seen his face before?'

'No! I mean, yes, I'm certain.'

'You haven't seen him hanging around outside in the days since the abduction?'

'No.'

'You didn't see him at the car park on Tuesday?'

'No. Why? How is he involved in this? Did he take my daughter?'

Trent shook her head, her expression unchanged. 'There's nothing to suggest he's involved in the abduction, save for the fact that his picture has been sent to you.'

'So why all the questions about him, and why won't you tell me who he is?'

'Does the name Jack Whitchurch mean anything to you, Mrs Granger?'

Alex considered the name. 'No, I'm afraid not.'

'And Ray hasn't mentioned the name Jack Whitchurch? Particularly in the last couple of days?'

Alex snorted. 'We've barely spoken all week, so no, he hasn't mentioned the name.'

'And this is the only email you've received since the one yesterday evening?'

Alex sighed at the constant questions without answers. 'Yes this is the only email since yesterday. Don't you think I would have told you?'

'So to clarify, you don't recognize the man in the picture, nor the name Jack Whitchurch?'

'How many times! *No, I do not.*'

'Where did you grow up, Alex?'

The change of tack threw her for a moment. 'Salisbury, why?'

'And when did you move to Southampton?'

'Seven years ago, when I came to university.'

'You would have been what …?'

'Nineteen.'

'Did you ever come to the city before you attended university?'

'Probably. I'm sure my mum would have brought me to the shops at some point. What does all this have to do with Carol-Anne?'

Trent checked the door was closed properly before taking a step closer to Alex, lowering her voice. 'Ordinarily I wouldn't share this information with you, but given Ray is in the force and probably already knows, it's better you hear it from me. The man in the photograph – Jack Whitchurch – is a convicted sex offender.'

Alex gripped the edge of the stool as she felt her legs wobbling.

'He has been behind bars for the last nine years,' Trent continued plainly. 'Before that he was under investigation for allegations of child abuse. He was groundskeeper at a school, you see. The investigating team couldn't secure the evidence they needed to press charges. That was until …' her words trailed off, as if she was unsure whether Alex had the strength to hear the conclusion.

Alex's knuckles were white as they clung to the stool, her breathing shallow. 'Tell me.'

The skin around Trent's eyes tightened. 'Until he was caught in his office with a fiveyearold girl.'

Alex gasped, and the stool went crashing to the floor, with her tumbling after.

Trent's grasp was too late to catch her, but she promptly pulled Alex back to her feet, securing the stool and sitting Alex on it. 'Whitchurch was released on parole on Tuesday morning and relocated to a safe location in the county.'

'And you think …' Alex took a deep breath to enable her to utter the words, 'he's responsible for my daughter's abduction? That's why you were asking whether I'd seen him hanging around, right?'

'I can't say for certain how he's involved in your case. Somebody obviously thinks he's connected, which is why they sent you his picture. At the moment I can't determine whether he's involved and toying with us by sending the picture, or whether whoever took Carol-Anne wants revenge on him for some reason.'

'"Revenge"?'

'The two emails have told you he must die for you to get Carol-Anne back, so what I need to determine is whether one of his former victims is using you and your daughter to seek the justice they felt they never got.'

36

Ray could hear people moving about on the landing, though what exactly they were searching for was beyond him. Did they still doubt Alex's or his credibility? Despite the messages, did they still think either – or both – of them were involved in their daughter's abduction?

Alex would undoubtedly be up here soon enough, but what could he say to her? She seemed to think that he somehow had the ability to solve their crisis and get Carol-Anne back. And as much as he wished that was the case, the truth was he was just as powerless as she was. There was no way for him to locate Whitchurch, and deep down he knew the best people were trying to identify the message sender.

Still, none of that explained what Alex had been doing in Fleet for half an hour on the morning of the abduction. There had to be a perfectly reasonable explanation for it. Having checked the calendar downstairs, he'd found no trace of an appointment or reason for her to be there.

He had noticed she'd started wearing long-sleeve tops again, despite the humid weather they'd faced recently. When Trent had asked him about the counselling he had neglected to mention Alex's history of self-harming. It was something she'd only told him about after he'd proposed. She'd said it was during a difficult time at university, and that the act of drawing blood from her own limbs somehow helped alleviate the pressure building inside. He'd never quite understood how inflicting pain on oneself could relieve stress. She'd assured him it had. When he'd come upstairs earlier today he'd found the remains of a bloody tissue floating in the toilet bowl – he was afraid she might be harming again to deal with the pressure.

Swinging his legs over the edge of the bed, he lurched towards Alex's dressing table, opening the small drawer at the front and pulling out the address book she kept in there. If she'd been visiting a friend in Fleet then their address would undoubtedly be in this book. As he flicked through the pages, skimming the addresses, he realized it was a waste of time: she didn't know anybody in Fleet, at least, nobody she deemed worthy enough to keep a note of their address.

Returning the book to its space in the drawer, he slumped back onto the bed. Why would she not tell him she was going to Fleet on Tuesday?

He closed his eyes as the answer presented itself to him.

He had strayed from their marriage vows, so wasn't it feasible that Alex had too? She hadn't initiated sex for months, and save for the drunken fumble a few weeks ago neither had shown the other any real affection. How many other times could she have taken trips to Fleet without him knowing? What did she do with Carol-Anne while she was off screwing this guy?

He was surprised by the feelings of jealousy coursing through his veins. Was it really possible that Alex had also been cheating? He'd been working late, and playing away himself, so what was to stop her seeking comfort in another man's arms?

The first time he'd slept with *her*, the guilt the following day had been overwhelming. That was what had led to the heavy drinking and desire to show Alex that he still loved her. The fumble had been ill-advised and had only shown him how out of sync they'd become. He'd told himself he wouldn't allow himself to cheat again. But after a week of flirtatious and suggestive messages they'd hooked up again. And again. And again.

He still loved Alex, and he didn't want to hurt her. He knew just how devastating a blow his infidelity would be when she did eventually find out, but he was starting to develop strong feelings for his lover; and deep down he knew that she was falling for him too.

Why did life have to be so complicated? He wanted to come clean, to admit the truth; it was the least Alex deserved and the shame of lying was killing him. How could he, with Carol-Anne still out there? It would be enough to push Alex over the edge.

His phone vibrated on the duvet next to him.

Are you alone?

He listened for any sound of Alex nearby before punching in his response.

Yeah, but now isn't a good time. I meant what I said the other night. We should cool things until I've had chance to speak to Alex.

He was taking a huge risk messaging her from the house. Alex could walk in any minute and demand to see his phone. And although he'd logged *her* in his phone as "Nigel", the content of some of their exchanges left little to the imagination. The phone vibrated again.

I know. I just thought you might need a friend. Is there any news?

The bedroom door opened before he could reply. Quickly locking the phone, he feigned interest in the football match playing quietly on the television as his teary-eyed wife appeared in the doorway.

'Can I come in?' she asked softly.

He waved her over, muting the television.

She climbed onto the bed and snuggled into his armpit as he rested his arm around her. 'Who's winning?'

He quickly glanced at the score in the top corner. 'Drab draw so far. Are they still buzzing around downstairs?'

He felt her nodding. 'Trent said the man in the photograph is someone called Jack Whitchurch. Do you know him?'

Ray swallowed hard, keen to protect her from the truth. 'Only by reputation.'

'So you know he's a … paedophile then?'

'Yes,' he replied, the word getting stuck in his throat. 'That doesn't mean he has Carol-Anne.'

'That's what Trent said too,' she said as she wiped her eyes with the back of her hand. 'She thinks whoever sent the messages wants to see harm done to him.'

'Did she say if they're going to bring him in for questioning?'

Alex was shaking her head now.

He let out a sigh of exasperation. 'They should be bringing him in to see what he knows. I bet they haven't even visited his home yet. I sometimes wonder …' He knew the thought wasn't what Alex needed to hear. 'I'm going to have a word with her,' he said, straightening and raising his arm.

'Don't rush off,' Alex said, pulling his arm back around her. 'Will you stay with me? We don't have to talk; I just don't want to be on my own right now.'

And in that moment, he knew the right thing to do was to be the support she needed. Carol-Anne needed both her parents to be ready to fight for her, and Alex would be no good to her in this fragile state.

They stayed in silence and as halftime drew near in the football match, he said, 'Do you want me to change the channel?'

Alex didn't answer, and as he looked down, the gentle rise and fall of her chest and closed eyes indicated she had fallen asleep. Pulling her closer, he kissed the top of her head.

37

Her nose rubbing against the damp spot on the pillow was enough to wake Alex from her slumber. For the briefest of moments she was convinced she could hear Carol-Anne giggling in her bedroom again, and then the harsh reality hit her like a locomotive. Seeing the creased sweatshirt and jogging bottoms she'd sported yesterday, she vaguely remembered coming up to see Ray, but had no recollection of falling asleep. Evidently she had, though, fully clothed.

Looking around the room, there was no sign of Ray. The light beneath the curtains suggested it was morning. She couldn't understand how he managed to take himself to work each day. Her every waking thought was splintered by worries for Carol-Anne, in the hands of either Jack Whitchurch or someone out to do him harm. Either way, the truth was, Carol-Anne was in grave danger.

Alex's tongue stuck to the roof of her mouth as the dryness took hold. She crawled to the bathroom, locking the door behind her and stripping off for a shower. Pulling her hair back, she squashed her face beneath the basin tap and switched on the cold water, lapping up the refreshment, before running the shower.

Once washed and dried, she made her way back to her

bedroom, checking her phone, hoping for any kind of update from Ray. Under the showerhead's relaxing jet, she had remembered resting her head on Ray's chest and him draping an arm around her. She couldn't remember the last time he had willingly hugged her to sleep, and it filled her with renewed hope that there might just be a spark left in their marriage that – with delicate nurturing – could once again roar.

Based on what Trent had told her last night in the kitchen, the team would be visiting Whitchurch at his home this morning to check for any sign of Carol-Anne and see whether anyone had formally threatened him.

In a week of heartache, it was all Alex could hope for; right now she had little else.

Looking down at the pile of clothes she'd carried back from the bathroom, Alex resisted the temptation to slip them back on.

No, today was a day to stay positive.

She'd once read a book by some motivational speaker who had claimed the key to a successful career was to visualize the life you wanted every day until you found it. Well, desperate times called for desperate measures so, stepping into a svelte purple dress, Alex pulled her hair back, tying it in a thin, wet ponytail. Blasting it with the hairdryer would take an age, and she didn't want to spend anymore time in the house than was utterly necessary. If she wanted Carol-Anne back, she had to act.

The kitchen door was ajar, and inside she could hear Isla in hushed conversation with someone. As Alex pushed the door open, the phone at Isla's ear explained why the conversation was one-sided. Isla spun round at the sound of the door and her cheeks flushed slightly.

'Is it news?' Alex mouthed.

Isla lowered the phone to her chest. 'Uh, no … it's personal.' She didn't wait any longer to offer further explanation, diving past Alex and continuing the call behind the safety of the closed living room door.

Alex put the kettle on and focused on the breathing exercises Dr Kirkman had shown her for when she was feeling stressed and needed to relax. They hadn't helped before, but she was willing to give anything a go at this stage.

That's when she stopped still, as a crazy idea pushed itself to the forefront of her mind. She almost laughed at the ridiculousness of it, yet the more she considered it, the more it offered a chink of hope.

Reaching for her phone, she typed the word 'Psychic' into an internet search engine. She was stunned by the number of hits of clairvoyants advertising their services in the Southampton area alone. How could she choose one who might hold answers, and how would she know if they were just a fraud?

She needed advice, and that was what drove her to knock on her neighbour's door.

Sophie's silhouette appeared behind the frosted glass a moment later, and as she pulled open the door, dressed in a kimono and looking bleary-eyed, Alex's fresh face clearly caught her off guard.

'Alex? What …?' she said, yawning, unable to finish the question.

'I need a favour,' Alex said, already regretting calling on her friend so early in the morning. 'This is going to sound crazy, and if you think I'm being an idiot, I want you to tell me …'

Sophie blinked several times, trying to clear the sleep from her eyes.

'I need answers about my little girl. My car's still with forensics, and I was wondering whether you would – and you can say no if you're too busy – drive me to see a psychic.'

Alex's cheeks burned as the words tumbled out. How must she look right now? It felt like the world was already judging her for being unstable, and now she was contemplating reaching out to an unproven spiritual world for guidance. It had been a mistake coming here.

Sophie looked away for a moment, and it was then that Alex realized the reason Sophie wasn't dressed was because she had company.

'Oh, Sophie, I'm so sorry, I hadn't realized … do you know what? Don't worry about it. Forget I asked.' She turned to leave.

'Alex, wait,' Sophie said stepping out into the cool morning air, pulling the door closed. 'Who am I to judge? I think it's a great idea. Promise not to laugh? I went to see a psychic a couple of years ago, right before all *that* mess. I just wanted someone to tell me everything would work out for the best. Silly, right? Anyway, he told me that it would end badly, and that I would come through the other side a stronger person. I didn't believe him at the time, but in hindsight …'

Alex's cheeks were still burning.

'Give me a few minutes to get dressed,' Sophie said, heading back inside, 'and then I'll come round to pick you up. Oh, and it might be an idea to bring something of Carol-Anne's with you, so that he can get a sense of her. You know, like a toy or some clothing?'

The bungalow Sophie parked outside of had seen better days. The brickwork looked weathered by time, and the thatch roof didn't look capable of withstanding a heavy downpour. Even the paint on the window frames was peeling. As they walked along the gravel path, Alex couldn't escape the feeling that she was making a huge mistake coming here.

At the front door, a large bell hung from a piece of frayed rope, and Sophie bashed the inner hammer against it. 'I should warn you,' she said leaning in to Alex, 'he was a bit of an oddball. He was sweet, but some of his ways were … well, let's just say not based in our current time period. What I'm trying to say is some of his mannerisms – and the way he dressed – were a bit out there.'

As soon as the splintered door creaked open, Alex realized

what Sophie had meant, as a white-haired man emerged, his red bow tie in stark contrast to the blue buttoned shirt with yellow polka dots on it. His tan-coloured waistcoat matched his trousers, and the lime green socks that finished the outfit bore the signs of recent darning.

Alex was too embarrassed to speak, and appreciated Sophie explaining the reason for their visit.

A narrow corridor led to a large kitchen-diner at the rear of the property; however, he led Alex and Sophie into a front-facing sitting room, shrouded in the morning's bright rays coming through the window.

'And how may one as humble as I aid you two beautiful angels?' he said, as he squashed himself into a worn brown leather armchair.

Sophie beckoned to Alex to join her on the tattered cloth two-seater opposite him.

'My daughter was abducted on Tuesday,' Alex began. 'You may have heard about it on the news?'

The man shook his head, waving his arm around the room. 'I don't watch television, my dear.'

For the second time, Alex wondered exactly what she'd expected to find from an individual who claimed to be able to foresee the future. Removing a stuffed green dragon toy from her handbag, she offered it forward. 'This is my daughter's. I want you to tell me where she is, and if she's okay.'

He looked sceptically at the toy. 'You say somebody *took* your daughter from you?'

'That's right.'

He pressed his splayed fingertips together and rested them beneath his chin. 'The world has a plan for all of us,' he began. 'We can sometimes stray from our predetermined path, but one way or another the forces will align to set our course straight once more. Sometimes, what feels like an intentional course change can be the chosen path to begin with. All of Mother

Nature is in sync, so the trees talk to the land, the land talks to the animals, the animals talk to the air and sea. It is all interconnected and a chosen few,' he paused and gestured towards himself, 'are lucky enough to be able to hear all this traffic. As much as I would like to be able to stare into a crystal ball and see the future playing like some kind of theatrical show, it doesn't work like that. I can only tell you what the trees are saying. Do you follow?'

Alex offered the dragon forward again. 'Are you able to tell me where she is or not?'

The man shuffled forward without standing and grasped the toy, examining it carefully, before placing it to his nose and inhaling deeply. 'A little girl, you say?'

'Yes.'

He closed his eyes, and raised the dragon into the air over his head, mumbling as he did. And just when it seemed like he would never stop, he suddenly pulled the dragon to his chest, ceased the chant, and slowly opened his eyes. 'The owner of this toy is no longer of this plane,' he declared matter-of-factly.

It was the last thing Alex had expected to hear. 'What does that mean?' She glanced at Sophie for reassurance.

'I am sorry, but nature is telling me she is no more.'

The hurt burned inside Alex, as she chided herself for even daring to consider such an absurd idea. Even so, she was terrified by the possibility that his mumbo jumbo might bear the fruit of truth. Snatching the dragon from him, she made for the front door, and heard him call out, 'Was it something I said?'

38

Waking with a start, Ray peeled his face from the pillow. Caught in limbo between sleep and realization, it took a moment for him to remember where he was. As he turned over, he was surprised to find he was alone, though the impression of her head, and the scent of her Italian perfume remained on the pillow.

At first he didn't know what had woken him, until he heard the incessant buzzing again. Reaching down to where his trousers and socks lay, he grabbed for the mobile phone, checking the display, before putting it to his ear.

'DS Granger,' he mumbled, rubbing his eyes with his palm.

'*Ray? I'm sorry to call, but I need you,*' Jodie Crichton pleaded into the phone.

Checking the display again he saw he'd missed a dozen calls while he'd slept. That could only mean bad news. 'What's going on? Is it Carol-Anne?'

Her tone was cautious. '*No, I'm sorry, it isn't about your daughter. The gang – our gang – hit another post office while they were taking a foreign exchange delivery at dawn. They were foiled and one of them is trapped inside with the delivery driver, and he's threatening to kill her if he isn't allowed to go free. I've emailed you the address. Get over here pronto and grab a coffee. Trent said you'd been on hostage negotiation training? I really wouldn't ask if there was anyone closer.'*

He stretched the last weary remnants of sleep from his body. 'Okay, I'm on my way.'

Scooping his crumpled shirt from the carpet, he would have to make his excuses before leaving. Coming over this morning had been a bad idea, but she'd offered him a shoulder to cry on. The image of Carol-Anne filling his mind now was almost unbearable, though, and he made a silent promise to end the affair once and for all.

Looking at the clock, he realized that Alex would be awake soon, if she wasn't already, which meant he didn't have time to sneak home and get back in to bed before she noticed he was gone. He hadn't meant to fall asleep in this bed.

He gave his shirt a sniff. It would have been better to go home and change, but if Jodie was right, the delivery driver didn't have a second to spare.

The road into Hedge End village had been closed to the public, with diversions set up to loop rush-hour commuters around the cordon which stretched across the normally busy main road. Having taken the squad car home last night, Ray was relieved that he didn't have to call a taxi to get to the scene. Presenting his identification at the start of the outer cordon, he sped to the inner cordon before parking up, leaving a notice in the windscreen, confirming he was responsible for the vehicle. He found Jodie gathered by the mobile van being used as the central command post. Trent was on the phone, presumably to Gold Command back at the station, while a uniformed officer was recording her instructions.

'I told the DI you were at the dentist,' Jodie said, pulling him to one side. 'If she asks, it was a medical emergency, and you've had a filling replaced.'

'Can you get me up to speed with what's gone on?' he asked as he lit up his first cigarette of the day.

'The post office doesn't officially open until nine a.m., but was due to receive a delivery of foreign exchange shortly after five. The manager usually opens the rear door, to allow the security guard to make the deposit. For some reason he wasn't able to do so this morning, and told her to go around the front. We now believe the rear door was tampered with by the group, forcing the exchange to take place at the front, where security is more vulnerable.

'The manager let her in, and as he was relocking the front door, a large white van – which may or may not have been a Transit – appeared from nowhere and two armed men dressed head-to-toe in black emerged and forced their way in. A third man subdued the second security guard, and we believe a fourth man remained in the van in the driver's seat. The gang forced the security guard to unlock the crates with the cash, which was then bundled into bags and shoved into the rear of the van. While this was occurring, a patrol car on its return from a domestic abuse call was passing and saw what was unfolding. They immediately called it in and did what they could to detain the gang.

'The gang leader called an abort, and fired shots in the direction of the two uniformed officers, with one of the gang still inside. The shop manager and second security guard were able to run to safety, but the robber inside forced the shutters down and has been holed up ever since.

'Trent was put in temporary charge as the nearest SIO in the area, but having been up most of the night working on Carol-Anne's disappearance, she's just holding the fort until an alternative SIO arrives.'

Ray looked over at Trent, still jabbering into her phone, now sitting on the step into the command post van. She looked exhausted, and he could only hope the unfolding scene wouldn't detract attention from getting his little girl back. The best thing

201

he could do now was help resolve the situation so Trent wasn't unnecessarily detained.

'Has she managed to communicate with the thief yet?' Ray asked, looking back at the shop front, the shutters down.

'There's a landline into the building, which has been called every twenty minutes since the cordon was set up. So far he's refused to answer the calls.'

'And is he definitely armed?'

'The manager thinks so. Either way, we can't take the chance that he isn't.'

'What happened to the Transit?'

'The other two bundled in and it tore off. It was found abandoned at a petrol station five minutes down the road. The attendant inside couldn't give a description of the vehicle they escaped in. They're gone. For now.'

Next door to the post office was a takeaway pizza restaurant and a barber's shop, and across the street a grocers was also still closed for business. The hum of traffic nearby could be heard on the wind. Otherwise the village resembled a ghost town.

'Ray?' Trent called out, as she finished her call with the super-intendent. 'Thanks for coming. I know – given everything else you've got going on – this is probably the last place you want to be, but I appreciate you coming. I've put a call in to a trained negotiator, but he's coming from Aldershot and his ETA is currently unknown. I want you here so you can help us better understand this man's thought processes. You've had the most recent training, so what can you tell us?'

Ray finished his cigarette and squashed it under foot. 'He'll be feeling isolated, and that isn't a good thing for us or the woman he's taken hostage. The rest of the gang have abandoned him, and as far as they're concerned he's dead to them. These are the thoughts that will be going around in his head. We also don't know if the security guard will be making matters worse. If she has any sense she'll keep quiet. We need to get through to him.'

'We've tried calling, but he refuses to answer,' Trent said, echoing Jodie's earlier statement.

'Where are armed response?'

'They're waiting for the green light, but they're a last resource. There's no reason for this not to end peacefully.'

'You need to keep them out of sight for as long as possible,' Ray urged. 'If he is armed, seeing other men with guns is just going to make matters worse.'

39

Legs burning from exhaustion, Alex marched onwards, with no clue where she was headed.

'Hey, hey,' Sophie panted from behind, racing to catch up. 'Alex, stop!'

She obliged, though more because her legs ached than because she actually wanted to talk. 'Did you hear what he said? Fucking fraud!'

Sophie rested her hands on her hips, and stooped as she tried to catch her breath. 'I know … and I'm sorry. I didn't think he would say … that. I'm so sorry.'

'There's no way Carol-Anne is dead.' Alex brought a hand to her chest. 'I feel it in *here*. She's scared and she's confused about why I'm not around, but she is definitely still alive.'

Sophie nodded, though the look on her face suggested she wasn't convinced by Alex's assertion. 'Where were you headed anyway? The car is back up by his bungalow.'

'I just needed to get out of there,' Alex replied, as the lactic acid in her muscles began to slowly dissipate.

She didn't know this area of the city well, and looking at the properties lining the hill, she had to assume the residents within must have been fairly comfortable financially. The gardens here were well-tended, the vehicles in the driveways only a few years old at most. It felt like the sort of place she wouldn't mind moving to one day when Carol-Anne was older. They'd passed a park on the drive up to the bungalow with a large green grass area and a small playground with swings and slides that Carol-Anne would love.

She wondered how many of the street's residents knew there was a fraud living at the top of the hill.

The two friends set off back towards the bungalow and Sophie's waiting car. Alex couldn't escape the feeling of remorse settling in. She'd come here – against her better judgement – hoping to somehow learn where Carol-Anne was being held. She hadn't stopped to think what she would have done with that information had it been forthcoming. She doubted Trent or Ray would have paid it much heed, in the same way she was now refusing to believe what the socalled psychic had told her.

'I'm half-tempted to report him,' Alex said, as she climbed into the passenger seat. 'It isn't right that people like him are free to play on others' emotions. I mean, what was all that claptrap about talking to Mother Nature?' She pulled a face. 'We live in an age where meteorologists still can't accurately predict whether or not it will rain, and this guy expects people to believe that he is on speaking terms with her?'

Sophie simply shrugged. 'We've all got to have something to believe in, right? I gave up religion as a teenager, and I know he sounded a bit nuts, but there was – at least for me – something in what he said. I like the idea that we're all heading in the same direction, even if we don't know where that is. For example, when my mum died a few years ago, I was adamant I didn't want to live in her house and was all set to sell up and buy a swanky apartment in the centre of town, and for some unknown reason I changed my mind. Had I not done that I might never have met you and Ray.'

'If his spouting is to be believed, we were always destined to meet at some point. Maybe if you'd bought that swanky flat, Ray and I would have moved somewhere else too. Maybe we would have ended up working together or would have met through a friend of a friend or something.'

'Exactly!' Sophie said, fixing her with a stare. 'That's my point – or rather his philosophy – that it's all predetermined. You and I would always have met somehow.'

Alex shuddered at the idea that Carol-Anne was always destined to be snatched, and that all of their actions were essentially controlled by some invisible force she couldn't see.

Sophie started the engine, and as she did, the clairvoyant suddenly appeared at Alex's side of the car, tapping frantically on the window.

'You don't have to speak to him again,' Sophie said. 'I'll tell him to go away.'

'No, wait,' Alex said, before lowering the window. 'Yes?'

He was swaying, nervously bouncing from one foot to another. 'I am frightfully sorry if I upset you,' he said, though it wasn't an acceptance of blame, more like he was apologizing for the message he had received.

Alex considered her response, before choosing not to let her emotions get the better of her again. 'Don't worry about it. It was my mistake.'

'That's kind of you to say, but my apology stands. I hope you find your child soon, and if you do ever decide to return to see me, I would be willing to offer you another reading free of charge. Not now, of course. Maybe when things settle down with you and your son?'

'It's my daughter who's missing. I don't have a son.'

His eyes twinkled for a moment. 'Not yet, but it won't be long now.'

Alex stared into his eyes, searching for any flicker of dishonesty, but he simply smiled through the window before turning and heading back to the bungalow.

'Everything okay?' Sophie asked, as Alex felt the blood draining from her face.

Alex didn't answer, gazing out of the window and wondering how he could have possibly known.

Sophie tentatively carried the tray of drinks over to the picnic bench, lowering a cardboard cup in front of Alex. 'Here you go, I put a load of sugar in it for you, supposed to be good for shock.'

Alex accepted the cup and strained a smile. 'Thank you.'

It had been Sophie's idea to stop at the park for refreshment. The small hut offered hot drinks, cakes and snacks, and was perched on the periphery of the large field of grass, the playground about halfway along and to the right-hand side of where they were seated. Of the six picnic tables near the hut, this one had had the least amount of bird poo on it.

Sipping the drink, Alex grimaced; Sophie hadn't been exaggerating when she said she'd put a lot of sugar in it.

'Too sweet?' Sophie asked. 'Sorry, you can swap with me if you prefer?'

Alex lowered the cup, keeping her cold fingers wrapped tightly around it. 'I'm pregnant,' she said, before she could stop herself.

Sophie nearly spat out her drink as she took a long sip. 'Crikey.'

Alex allowed her eyes to drift as she took in the wide-open space, wishing she could stand and race towards the horizon. 'You can't say a word to anybody. Okay? And I mean *anybody*. Ray doesn't know and that's how I want it to stay for now.'

'My lips are sealed. How far gone are you?'

'I don't know for certain – maybe ten weeks – but that's an estimate based on my regular dates.'

'You don't look too happy about it.'

'I don't know how to feel about it. On the one hand, the prospect of a brother or sister for Carol-Anne is something I should be thrilled about. I think because I miscarried last time, and with me trying to return to work, the issues between me and

Ray, and of course Carol-Anne still missing, my head's a bit all over the place.'

'Have you done a test?'

Alex nodded. 'Three of them last week when Ray was away on his course. All of them came back with two stripes.'

'Have you been to see your GP for a blood test?'

Alex shook her head. 'I don't want to go until I've decided what I'm going to do. You won't understand – nobody would – but the miscarriage was so painful emotionally that I don't think I could cope if it happened again.'

'Are you thinking of … terminating it?'

'No … I don't know what I'm going to do.' Alex looked away as the tears bit at her eyelids, and a shock of bright red in the playground caught her attention.

'You poor thing,' Sophie continued. 'I'm pleased you felt able to confide in me.'

Alex wasn't listening, still staring at the red anorak rising and falling in one of the swings. Straining to focus, Alex stood and moved closer.

Yes, it had to be.

She'd know that bright red anorak anywhere.

It was the one Carol-Anne had been wearing when she disappeared.

Without a second's thought, she burst into a sprint, racing towards the playground.

40

It was impossible to see any movement inside the shop from where the command van was parked. To move any closer risked painting a target on his back. Ray tried to get a better viewing angle. With the shutters down and lights off inside, they could only guess where the security guard and her captor were located.

Ray picked up the phone and tried the number to the shop again. The line was engaged. Their suspect must have grown fed up of them trying to call and left if off the receiver.

He turned to face Trent. Her face bore the strain of leading the uncertain operation.

'Are we able to take a look at the back door, to see what the group did to disable it? Maybe if we could get it open from the outside we could get a better idea of what we're dealing with.'

Trent considered the question, before calling over the tactical command leader and relaying the instruction.

'Be careful,' Ray added. 'You can't let him know what you're doing. Any sound could make him nervous.' He turned back to Trent. 'We need to get him to communicate with us. We don't know if he's definitely armed, and what state either of them are in. Communication is the key to resolving these situations peacefully.'

Trent fought a yawn. 'I'm open to any and all ideas. They've been in there for four hours already.'

And that meant four hours had passed where recovering Carol-Anne wasn't at the forefront of her mind. He had to get things moving, no matter the cost.

Stepping out from behind the van, he removed his jacket so his shirt and tie were in full view. He then proceeded very slowly out into the road in front of the shop.

'Ray, what are you doing?' Trent called out from the van.

He didn't respond, his eyes scanning the shuttered windows for any sign of movement.

The sun was still relatively low in the sky for the time of day, and even though a cool breeze was blowing, his forehead was dripping with sweat. Keeping his hands raised in a nonthreatening position he continued along the road, stopping only when he was directly in front of the shop.

'My name is Detective Sergeant Ray Granger,' he called out. 'I am unarmed and want to speak to you. It is in everyone's best interests for this situation to be resolved peacefully.' Ray lowered one of his hands, reaching slowly into his pocket and carefully withdrawing his mobile phone. 'I am going to phone you now. Please answer so we can talk and I can help you.' He typed in the number and placed the phone to his ear.

He was greeted with the engaged signal again.

'Please return the phone to the receiver so we can talk. I assure you, we are going to stay out here for as long as necessary.'

He waited a moment before pressing redial. The engaged signal again.

'I only want to talk,' he called out again, louder this time. 'I understand you are not alone in there, and I want to check on the condition of the security guard with you. Her name is Vicky. Is she okay?'

No response, and no sign of movement beyond the shutters.

With Trent and Jodie watching from the cover of the van, he'd never felt under such intense pressure. It was one thing attending the training, enacting role-plays, listening to the constructive feedback of the trained tutor, applying that knowledge to a real-life situation was nothing like he'd expected.

He tried the number again. It still didn't connect.

'Your friends aren't coming back for you. They're long gone. They took off and left you here, didn't they? Left you to take the fall for their crimes. They dumped the van and are long gone. They can't help you now, but I can.' He paused, staring at the phone in his hand, trying to recall what they'd practised on the course last week.

'Listen, I know you're scared. We – you and me – can work out a plan for you to come out safely. I'm going to call again so we can speak without me having to shout. Please return the phone to the receiver so we can talk man to man.'

He waited fifteen seconds and pressed redial.

From within the shop he could hear the faint tone of a phone ringing inside.

He breathed a sigh of relief. The phone rang three times before finally connecting.

'*Yeah?*' the voice said, the tone gruff, and with a definite Scouse twang.

'Hi, who am I speaking to?'

'*No names.*'

'Okay, I understand you might not want to give me your real name. Is there any name I can address you by? I don't mind if you want to give me a false name for now. My name is Ray.'

'*John.*'

'Thank you, John. How are you in there? How is Vicky?'

'*She's fine.*'

'That's good to hear. Are either of you in need of any medical assistance?'

'*No.*'

'Again, I'm really pleased to hear that, John. Now, given that

I've asked you a couple of questions, which you've willingly answered, is there anything you'd like to ask me?'

'*I want you to let me go.*'

The sweat continued to cling to Ray's neck. 'There's nothing more I'd like, John, but I'm not the one keeping you in there. I'd prefer to speak with you face-to-face than over a phone. To do that, you need to open the shutters and the door.'

'*You're going to shoot me.*'

'Nobody is going to shoot you, John. You have my word.'

'*I don't believe you. There's armed police out there.*'

'I'm not going to lie to you, John. Whatever happens from this point, you have my word I will only tell you the truth. You're right that there is a weapons-trained team out here. That's a natural response given you and your friends entered the post office with semi-automatic weapons. Are you armed now, John?'

'*Yeah I am,*' he said, his tone rising, '*and I'll fucking kill her if you try and come in.*'

'Nobody wants Vicky or you to be hurt, John, so we won't try and come in without your permission.'

'*I'm sorry.*'

The sudden change in tone caught Ray by surprise. On the one hand, it was positive that 'John' hadn't put up any barrier to their talk, or made any ridiculous demands; on the other hand, sudden remorse could be a symptom of darker thoughts.

'You don't need to apologize to me, John,' Ray said evenly. 'You sound like a really switched-on guy; would that be fair to say?'

'*Yeah, I suppose.*'

'I thought so. Sometimes I just get a feeling when I'm talking to a good person, even in difficult circumstances. I'm right about you, John, aren't I? You don't want to hurt Vicky, do you?'

'*No, I don't want to hurt anybody. I just want to go home.*'

'And I want to get you home, John. Is there a way I can get you to come outside with Vicky so we can all go home?'

'*You're lying to me. You won't let me go home. You'll arrest me, or shoot me.*'

'I promised you I wouldn't lie, John, and I don't intend to. We will need to ask you some questions about what has gone on today, that's true. I know you're a smart guy and you understand that you've broken the law today. You'll have the right to tell us what happened, to explain how you made this poor choice. It'll go in your favour if you surrender to us willingly.'

And it was then that Ray realized 'John' was crying.

'*I don't want to go to prison. I just want to go home. I want to see my kids.*'

Ray felt a lump in his throat. 'You're a father?'

'*Yeah, twin boys.*'

He thought about Carol-Anne. The course instructor had told them not to give away too much personal information as it could impact on objectivity. 'I have a daughter. She's two. How old are your boys?'

'*Four. They're a right couple of scallywags.*'

'I bet you love them to bits, right?'

'*I'd do anything for them lads.*'

Ray wasn't even thinking about his training anymore. Establishing rapport, finding a common ground, humanizing the hostage: these were the tasks he'd been working towards. None of the training seemed to matter in that moment.

'I'm just the same, John. I'd do anything for my little girl. *Anything.*'

'*They're the only reason I agreed to do this stupid job. I'd swap all the money in the world just to hold them in my arms again.*'

Ray would give every penny he'd ever earned just to see Carol-Anne again. 'Then let me help you do that, John. You're the key to making that happen. Open those shutters and the door and come outside.'

'*You promise I won't get shot?*'

'You have my word. In fact, you've seen I'm unarmed, would

you be happy if I escorted you from the door? Nobody will shoot with me at your side. How does that sound?'

The line disconnected, and a moment later the electric shutters whirred to life, slowly rising. Ray spotted movement in his periphery, holding his hand out to warn the armed unit to hold their position.

As the shutter disappeared up into its fixing, the door to the shop slowly opened and a large black woman in a navy uniform with a mop of bleached hair slowly emerged with both hands raised in the air. Behind her a smaller, frailer-looking figure dressed in black kept his head bent forward.

Ray took several steps towards them as calmly as he could manage, swallowing up the distance between them. 'Are you okay, Vicky?' he asked softly; to which she nodded frantically.

Her captor raised his head just above her shoulder and the two men made eye contact. For the briefest of moments they weren't detective and criminal, just two dads struggling to provide a good life for their children. As Ray saw both of his hands – no weapon in either – he swiftly grabbed 'John' by the wrists, yanked them behind his back and read him his rights.

41

Alex had never run so hard and fast in all her life. The grass was slippery with the recent downpours, but she didn't care, nearly losing her footing on several occasions, and just about managing to stay level.

Carol-Anne.

What were the chances that they'd stop at this random park, miles from home, and find her? It had to be a million-to-one, and she wasn't ready to look a gift horse in the mouth.

As her lungs felt ready to burst out of her chest, closely followed by her racing heart, she reached the railings to the playground. Rather than wasting time circling the perimeter looking for the gated entrance, she vaulted over them, landing awkwardly on her ankle, choking down the sudden twinge and ploughing towards the little roundabout: Carol-Anne's favourite.

At first she could only see the back of the red coat – definitely Carol-Anne's coat – and as the roundabout continued to spin, the little girl's face came into view. The short blonde curls, that infectious giggle; it was *her*.

Alex no longer cared that Carol-Anne's abductor – her tormentor – was probably nearby. She just knew she had to scoop her daughter up, and never *ever* let her go again.

Her vision was misting as her eyes welled up. Lurching forward, she reached out and grabbed one of the roundabout's handlebars, bringing it to an abrupt halt, almost causing Carol-Anne to stumble.

Alex dropped to her knees, wrapping her arms around Carol-Anne's waist. 'Oh my darling, I thought I'd lost you. Mummy will never let you go again. I promise.'

She continued to squeeze, ready to remain in that position for the rest of her life if necessary, desperate to take in every detail: Carol-Anne's smell, her giggle, the gentle rise and fall of her chest.

Her prayers had been answered. Maybe there was more to what that clairvoyant had said about destiny and predetermined plans than she'd thought. After all, if she hadn't gone to see him, she never would have found Carol-Anne. None of that mattered now.

'Get away from her!' a woman's voice screeched from somewhere behind them. Alex ignored it, her eyes closed, her chin resting on Carol-Anne's shoulder.

'Oi!' the woman yelled. 'Get your flaming hands off her, you skank!'

Alex felt a sharp pull on her shoulder and reluctantly released her grip on Carol-Anne for fear of sending her daughter tumbling. Reaching for Carol-Anne's hand, Alex straightened, going nose to nose with the woman, ready to fight tooth and nail to keep her daughter safe.

The woman who had grabbed her had spotty cheeks which had been poorly covered by foundation. Her bleached hair was pulled back into a greasy ponytail, the dark roots showing, and she was dressed in a vest top, despite the cool wind, with a large gold medallion hanging from her neck.

'What the fuck do you think you're doing with my daughter?' the woman growled.

Alex stood her ground, adrenaline flooding her system. 'I could ask you the same question.'

The woman's brow furrowed, showing more streaks of foundation. 'Are you out of your fucking mind?'

The woman reached down for Carol-Anne's free hand, but Alex stepped across, shielding her daughter with a leg.

'If you want her back, you're going to have to go through me. I should warn you that the police are on their way here now, and they will not hesitate to arrest you for what you've done. Make it easier on yourself, and walk away. I'm sure you don't want to add assault to your growing list of charges.'

The woman's lips curled into a snarl, revealing yellow teeth, and a gap where one of her front teeth should be. 'If you don't let go of my daughter's hand, I'm gonna bitch-slap you. You feel me?'

Sophie appeared at the railings, panting, and struggled to get her leg over the top. She eventually settled for using the gate several yards down.

'Oh good,' Alex said, smiling with satisfaction. 'Now my friend is here, so if you want to assault me, go ahead; I have a witness.'

'Alex,' Sophie said breathlessly, 'what are you doing, hun?'

'I found Carol-Anne, and this woman is trying to take her from me.'

The woman sized up Sophie. 'Is your mate for real?'

'Alex, you need to come with me, sweetie. Okay?'

Alex frowned at her friend. 'What are you saying? Call the police. We need to have this woman arrested, and let them know Carol-Anne is safe. Oh, and phone Ray too. He needs to see this.'

Sophie rested her hand on Alex's forearm. 'Alex, that isn't Carol-Anne. You need to let go of that little girl's hand. You're scaring her.'

Alex's frown deepened. 'What do you mean this isn't …?' She couldn't finish the sentence. She turned and her eyes fell on the little girl's face, and, letting go of the hand, Alex's legs gave way and she crashed to the playground floor.

The little girl did have blonde hair, but on closer inspection, it was straight, and not as bright as Carol-Anne's. The coat was definitely familiar, but no longer an exact match to the one that Carol-Anne owned. And the girl wasn't giggling, she was now in a fit of tears, her face red from the fear Alex had instilled.

The woman with the medallion snatched the girl's hand and dragged her away from the roundabout.

Alex couldn't breathe, it was like someone had kicked the wind out of her, and her tears of joy were suddenly replaced by anguish. How could she have made such a mistake? That poor child. The woman in the vest top must have thought she was crazy.

Sophie crouched down, her face a mix of shock and pity. 'Oh, Alex, I don't know what to say.'

'I-I-I thought it was …' Alex stammered

'I know, hun. I'm so sorry.'

'I saw her; it was her, Sophie. I swear to you, it was her!'

'At the risk of sounding totally insensitive and a bitch, isn't it possible you saw what you *wanted* to see? I could tell even from where we were sitting that it wasn't Carol-Anne. Given the news you just shared, and the shock of what that psychic said, and the stress you've been under, it's understandable you would see something that wasn't there.'

Alex buried her face in Sophie's shoulder and let the tears go, sobbing for the terrible mistake she'd made, for the life of the innocent child growing inside her, and for the loss of her little girl. Behind them, the woman with the medallion had finished her phone call and was now filming the two of them on her phone.

A Police Community Support Officer was the first to arrive at the playground, and having taken a statement from the woman with the medallion, he moved across to where Sophie and Alex were seated on a bench. After taking Alex's name and address he asked her to explain what had happened. Alex couldn't bring herself to say the words.

'You need to understand my friend's situation,' Sophie tried to explain. 'Her daughter has been missing since Tuesday, and the little girl over there does resemble her daughter. It's an easy mistake to make. No harm has been done. I'm sure Alex will apologize, won't you, Alex? Alex?'

Alex nodded quickly, daring to glance over at the woman with the medallion who was now regaling two other mums with her story of peril, undoubtedly exaggerating the tale.

'I'll need to call it in,' the young PCSO said, looking empathetically at Alex, before stepping away and putting the radio to his mouth.

'You must think I'm crazy,' Alex finally whispered to Sophie, staring at the horizon.

'Not crazy. I can't begin to imagine what you're going through.'

'Everyone thinks I'm crazy, even Ray. Maybe they're all right. I would have sworn to you that Carol-Anne was spinning on that roundabout. Now I see I imagined the whole thing. I would swear she was in the car when I parked at the car park, but what if she wasn't? What if I imagined that too?' She dabbed her eyes with a tissue.

'Because I know you're not crazy, and I believe you when you say she was in that car park with you. I don't think you're crazy, Alex. Under a helluva lot of pressure, but not crazy.'

'If I'm not crazy, then where is she?'

'I don't know. When did you last speak to that policewoman at your house?'

'I haven't spoken to Isla since last night.'

'It might be an idea to give her a call. At the very least to tell her where we are, and maybe mention what just happened. If that mum does want to press charges, I'm sure Ray can have a word and get it sorted.'

Alex looked back at the woman with the medallion who was now deep in conversation with the PCSO again. At least she wasn't still filming them.

'It isn't the first time something like this has happened,' Alex admitted quietly.

'Hold on,' Sophie hushed her, 'they're coming over.'

Alex looked up as the woman and the PCSO appeared in front of them.

'He says you want to apologize,' the woman with the medallion grizzled.

Alex forced herself to make eye contact, remaining seated. 'I am so sorry for frightening your daughter. Is she okay now?'

'She'll live. He tells me you're the mum of the little girl who went missing in town on Tuesday.'

Alex nodded.

'Listen, no hard feelings, yeah? I heard about your story, and I-I hope you find your little girl. Yeah? I'm happy to let this go.'

Alex was tempted to reach out and hug the woman, but didn't want the action to be misconstrued, and instead offered a simple, 'Thank you.'

The woman with the medallion returned to where her daughter was now tucking in to a chocolate bar, with one of the other mums sitting beside her.

'I think you should take your friend home,' the PCSO said to Sophie, who promptly nodded, helping Alex to her feet, and leading her towards the gate.

42

'Are you ready to do this?' Jodie asked, fixing Ray with a look of concern.

They were now back at the station with 'John' in custody, waiting to be interviewed. Trent had gone home for a few hours' sleep after leaving her team with instructions. Ray had once again offered his support, but she'd told him to go home and wait for news, or help Jodie process the prisoner. Carol-Anne wouldn't want him to wallow, and work might help serve as a distraction, so he'd stuck around.

'Why wouldn't I be?' he replied.

She sighed and stood to leave, before thinking better of it and turning back to face him. 'I get what you're doing: burying yourself in work. Given the circumstances, I probably would too. Look, you said yesterday you were going to take a few days off. I know I probably shouldn't have called you this morning, but you've played your part now. I don't think anyone else could have ended the siege so swiftly and with no harm caused.'

'I'm sure the guy from Aldershot probably would have done it quicker had he not been stuck in traffic.'

'Even so, Ray, you deserve a lot of credit for what you did. I don't need you to babysit me in the interview, though. It was my case to begin with – and while your support has been beneficial – I can close it alone.'

'Sounds like you want to get rid of me.'

'Not the case, I'm just conscious it's now been three days since your daughter went missing and it must be eating you up inside. And you know as well as I do that this guy is probably going to give us the usual "No Comment" interview at this point. God knows he's been in with his brief for long enough.'

He appreciated her show of support. But being at the station was better than being at home. Any breaking news would filter along the corridors quicker than it would through the Family Liaison Officer. If there was a chance they discovered where Carol-Anne was being held, he wanted to be the first on site.

Grabbing his notepad and the images from the CCTV cameras, he followed Jodie out of the room, along the corridor and down the stairs to the row of interview rooms, each soundproofed and fitted with the latest in video recording equipment.

'John' – or Michael 'Mikey' Tannenbaum as he'd subsequently been identified – was sitting low in his seat, his dark eyes sunken, his grade-2 crew cut shorter than the patchy stubble covering his cheeks and chin. His solicitor – tall and thin, dressed in a navy pinstripe suit –looked barely old enough to be out of school. Neither gave off a confident air.

Ray let Jodie choose her seat, before squatting down next to her. 'Anybody want a cup of tea, coffee or water?'

The solicitor tapped his pen against the bottle of sparkling mineral water on the table in front of him without making eye contact, his head buried in papers.

'Drink, Mikey?' Ray asked, keen to break the ice.

Tannenbaum simply shook his head.

'Very well,' Jodie said, before starting the recorder and introducing everyone in the room. 'Mikey, do you understand why you were arrested this morning?'

He nodded.

'For the benefit of the recording, please?' Jodie prompted.

'Yes,' he said.

'And you're happy that you've had enough time to discuss matters with the duty solicitor?'

Mikey glanced at the solicitor, before nodding. 'Yeah.'

'How about you start with what you were doing at the post office in Hedge End this morning.'

Ray began writing the phrase "No Comment," but stopped as Mikey sat up and cleared his throat.

'We went there to rob it, didn't we?'

Ray and Jodie exchanged glances.

'Who's *we*?' Jodie asked.

'There were four of us in the crew. I've already given the brief their names and addresses and he'll pass that to you when we're done. First I want to explain how I got caught up with them. I also want assurances that you'll protect my family if I come clean and tell you everything you want to know.' His Liverpudlian roots were strong as he spoke.

'Are your family in danger then?'

'Once I give you the names and addresses, I would think so, yeah.'

'Who will they be in danger from?' Jodie pressed, keen to establish some detail before making any promises.

'Casey – he's the one in charge – has all sorts of contacts. If he learns I've turned on him, he can have people at my place in no time. I need a guarantee that you will go to my house and take my wife and kids somewhere safe before I give you their names. Once I know they're okay, I'll tell you everything you want to know. That's the deal.'

'You're in no position to be making deals,' Jodie said sternly. 'We have witnesses who place you at the scene of the armed robbery this morning, who'll testify that you arrived with the other gang members and then held poor Vicky against her will. You're looking at a pretty long stretch based just on that.'

Ray forced eye contact with her, indicating for her to ease up.

'You want their names and details of where they're planning to hit next? That's what I'm offering if you protect my family.' He looked directly at Ray. 'You promised you would help get me back to my kids.'

Ray lowered his pen and rested his palms flat on the desk. 'And I meant what I said, Mikey. Has Casey threatened to hurt your family?'

'Not in so many words, but from day one he made it clear what would happen if we didn't toe the line. He's a pretty serious fucking guy.'

'And you think he would go after your family?'

'He's probably already got people on their way to my home. He'll have heard that my stand-off has ended and that I'm now in custody. Please, mate, you've got to send someone to get them. I swear I'll tell you everything you wanna know, about all the jobs we've pulled, but you need to protect them first.'

'If we agree to have a patrol car wait outside your home as a deterrent, then you'll give us those names? The sooner you tell us who your friends are, the sooner we can arrest them.'

'They're *not* my friends! That's what I'm trying to say; I didn't sign up for any of this, not at first. I answered an ad in the paper: they were looking for someone who was good with his hands, looking for cash work. I turned up thinking it would be some kind of manual labour, and that's when they told me what they had planned. I wanted to bail but I needed the money – and he was promising a decent bonus when the job was done … so I went along with it. And the first one went like clockwork: in and out with nobody hurt. I knew it wasn't for me, so I told him I didn't want to do it again, and that's when he indicated what he would do if I walked.'

'What did he say?'

'He didn't say anything, just ran a finger across his neck. One of the other lads told me about Casey's reputation, and I knew not to fuck with him. That's the only reason I was there this morning; I was too scared not to be.'

'If you were that worried, why didn't you phone the police?' Jodie interjected.

'Didn't you hear what I just said? Casey would have killed me and my family.'

'You could have called the anonymous tips line, and reported the job. We'd have been waiting and could have apprehended the lot of you in one go. Poor Vicky wouldn't now be suffering with PTSD.'

'I had no flamin' chance of making an anonymous call. He watched us at all times of the day.'

'How?'

'We was holed up together since we started all this. My wife thinks I'm working on an oil rig in the middle of the North Sea. Casey would allow me to phone her once a week, but he listened on the other line so I couldn't let anything slip. He's seriously fucking paranoid!'

Michael's forehead was shining under the overhead light, and large dark patches had appeared beneath his armpits.

'Help me to help you,' Ray suggested. 'Give us the details of one other job you've pulled so we know we can trust you, and then we will send someone to find your wife and boys.'

'There isn't time! You need to go now!'

'We will, Mikey, just calm down. We will put in the call as soon as you tell us what we need to know. The sooner you speak, the safer they will be. Tell us about the bookies in Shirley. Why were there only three of you that day?'

His voice raised an octave. 'Bookies? What fucking bookies? We robbed post offices, that's all! Casey had an inside man who gave us details of delivery times, likely cash values, and police response times.'

Ray's pulse quickened. 'We know you lot were there, we have

you on CCTV pulling the job.' He pulled out the picture of Scarface from the traffic camera. 'Is this Casey?'

Mikey's face contorted in confusion. 'Who the hell is that? That's not Casey. That's not *us*! I swear we only did post offices. Whoever that is, he's nothing to do with us.'

A memory fired in the back of Ray's mind. Suspending the interview, he ushered Jodie from the room.

'What is up with you?' she asked, when the door was closed.

'It's Gianni Demetrios,' he said confidently. 'Has to be. That's why he sent his goon round to Delilah's flat; she must be his insider and he wanted to make sure she kept her mouth shut. When we first looked into the job at the bookies some things didn't add up, and you heard what Mikey said: they only did post office jobs. Demetrios must have told his boys to make it look like it was the same gang, to cover his tracks.'

'It's a good theory, Ray. Where's your evidence?'

He snapped his fingers. 'We need to get to Delilah. She's the key.'

'She wasn't willing to talk the other day.'

'That was before we knew what had happened. We can offer her protection if she comes clean.'

'What about Mikey?'

Ray stared back at the door. 'He's not going anywhere, and he won't give us anymore until we get his family to safety. I'll go and speak with the inspector and see if he can get a couple of units to their house. Meanwhile, put Mikey back in cells and let him know what we're doing.'

'And then what?'

He fixed her with a look of determination. 'Then we prove that Gianni Demetrios planned the robbery at the bookies.' And for the briefest of moments he felt the respite of satisfaction.

43

Alex didn't notice the young man leaving her house until she'd nearly bumped into him.

'Sorry,' she said absently, before studying the figure closer.

He was wearing the same torn and weathered leather jacket he'd had on when he'd come banging at her door yesterday. It didn't look like he'd washed his long, greasy hair either. Keeping his head down, he didn't turn to acknowledge her apology, reaching the end of the driveway and darting to the right, soon disappearing from view behind the neighbour's overgrown hedgerows.

'Ah there you are,' Isla said as Alex pushed the front door open. 'I was starting to worry. You weren't here when I finished my call.'

'Is there any news? Are they any closer to finding her?'

Isla shook her head. 'I'm sorry, no. I would have phoned if there'd been a breakthrough.'

Alex saw her push a cheque book into her handbag.

'Was that Luke I just saw?'

Isla's cheeks flushed a little, and she nodded. 'I'm sorry, I've told him he can't keep coming here when I'm on duty.' She took a breath to compose herself. 'Where've you been?'

Alex was too embarrassed to tell her about her encounter with the so-called psychic and then the mistaken identity at the park. 'I just needed to get some air; staring at these same walls was driving me crazy.'

'Cabin fever. Did you go anywhere nice? Even a visit to the supermarket can be a good way of getting a break from all the waiting around.'

'Actually, I've got a bit of a headache,' Alex said, squinting against the light escaping from the kitchen. 'I might go and have a lie-down. I want you to come and get me if you hear from DI Trent.'

Isla nodded. 'Understood. Do you want me to make you a drink?'

'Thanks, but I'll be okay. Just need a couple of painkillers and I'll be right as rain in no time.'

With that, she slowly climbed the stairs, closing the bedroom door behind her. She didn't even bother stripping off before climbing under the duvet and pulling it up to her chin. She knew sleep wouldn't come, but it was safer to be here where she couldn't terrify any other children.

Her hand instinctively formed a protective shield around her abdomen. A single tear rolled down her cheek, and she made no effort to wipe it away allowing the duvet to soak it up. Why was it time only flew when you were having fun? Why did it drag so much when things were bad?

Turning onto her side, she stared at Ray's pillow, wishing once again that he was here with her. She could only assume he had returned to work. He could never just sit idly by and wait for things to happen. He'd probably already pulled up the criminal history of Jack Whitchurch, searching for clues as to how he could be involved in Carol-Anne's disappearance.

Her thinking came to an abrupt halt.

If he could do investigating of his own, why couldn't she? In this day and age, it was rare for anyone to go through life without leaving a digital footprint; just look at how easy it had been for *Simon* to find her email address. What was stopping her trying to find Jack Whitchurch?

Reaching into her handbag she pulled out her mobile phone and opened an internet search engine, typing in his name. The usual hits came up first: Facebook, Instagram and LinkedIn, and after clicking on each link, she couldn't find a single profile picture that resembled the man in the image she'd been sent.

Then there was a link to a pub in Whitchurch in Shropshire, as well as links to other businesses in the same town. Changing the search parameters to include the word 'news', she searched again. This time the first hits were for a couple of local newspapers reporting Jack Whitchurch's sentencing almost a decade ago. She read the stories one after another, feeling physically sickened by the accusations made against him, yet compelled to continue reading.

He'd held one five-year-old girl in his basement for more than three months. Her parents had given up hope of ever seeing her again, but she'd managed to escape when he'd inadvertently left the door unlocked one night. Apparently, she'd crept out of the basement, made it to the front door and ran out into the street, screaming for anyone to help her. And luckily, a passing milkman had come to her rescue before Whitchurch had realized she'd gone. The police had found evidence that she wasn't the only girl he had held captive in that cellar, but they had failed to trace several sources of DNA back to their original owners.

How could someone be so cruel to another person, especially a child? What was wrong with people like that?

How could he have been allowed to go free again? Surely, he was still a danger to other children? Why hadn't they locked him up and thrown away the key? Or couldn't they have chemically castrated him, so he wasn't a danger?

People like that didn't deserve to be free, let alone breathe the same air as innocent children like her daughter.

Alex lowered her phone, gulping at what she'd just thought. Maybe there was more to what the police had said: maybe whoever was behind the emails had sent them because they shared her thoughts on the wicked nature of Jack Whitchurch.

If they wanted him dead, why go to the elaborate method of snatching Carol-Anne? Why not just go and kill him? Why target Alex? She wasn't a killer, nor was she capable of ending another person's life; she didn't have it in her.

She subconsciously rubbed her abdomen, thinking of the tiny life growing within.

If *Simon*'s motive was revenge, why didn't he just go and kill Whitchurch himself? Was it because he didn't know the address? Maybe he thought Alex would be able to get hold of the address from Ray, or one of Ray's colleagues. Maybe *that* was why he'd targeted her. Maybe his messages weren't demanding she kill Jack; maybe he meant he wanted her to find him the address.

But she wasn't convinced that was the answer.

If someone was holding a loaded gun, and she had to choose between her daughter and this convicted sex offender, the answer was obvious: she'd choose Carol-Anne every time. If she had to hold the gun, she couldn't be sure she'd be able to squeeze the trigger. The consequences of killing Jack – a life in prison, the shame, not being around to see her daughter grow up – were just too much to even consider what was being demanded.

What would happen if she failed to meet *Simon*'s deadline tomorrow? Ever since the first message had come through, she'd worked on the assumption that Trent's team would resolve matters before they escalated. Suddenly the ticking clock was sounding loudly in her head.

'I brought you a cuppa,' Isla said, pushing through the door without knocking. 'How's your head now? Did you manage to get some sleep?'

Alex had lost track of time, but the ache in her head was at least gone.

Alex kept the phone's screen pointed away from Isla. 'Have they arrested that Jack Whitchurch yet?'

Isla returned her stare cautiously. 'They've spoken to him, but I don't believe there are any plans to arrest him.'

'Why not?'

'Because they don't believe he's involved.'

'Then why did someone send me his picture?'

'I don't know, Alex. I don't think you should worry about him. We're doing everything we can to find out who sent you those messages. It's only a matter of time.' She paused, a forced smile taking hold of the lower half of her face. 'Is there anything you want me to ask the investigative team when they call through later? Hopefully they should be able to give me more of an update than you've had so far.'

'I want to know what they plan to do when tomorrow's deadline arrives. *Simon* said he would kill Carol-Anne if I didn't meet his demands.'

Isla's cheeks flushed. 'Hopefully it won't come to that. I know some of the team have been strategizing, and they will have a plan.'

Alex watched her leave, knowing she was right about one thing: it *was* only a matter of time. As Isla closed the door, Alex opened the email app on her phone and began to type a reply to *Simon*.

44

The lift to the seventh floor was still out of order as Ray and Jodie made their way into the communal entrance of Delilah's Millbrook tower block. Even in the bright afternoon sunshine, the grey soulless tower had gained little additional charm. In the adjacent building, lines of clothes hung from the balconies as the residents desperately tried to dry their laundry before the next downpour.

Ray led the way up the stairs this time, and although he heaved as he reached the seventh floor, he was undeterred in his objective. Thumping his fist against the door, he wasn't surprised when his banging went unanswered.

Crouching, he lifted the lid of the letter box and bellowed, 'Delilah! Police. Open up.' He listened for any sound of movement from within; only silence greeted him. 'Delilah? You have one minute to open this door or we're going to bust through it.'

Jodie pulled on his shoulder. 'Uh, we have no grounds to bust any doors in.'

He lowered the letter box and stood. 'Just a threat.'

'She may have gone to work,' Jodie offered sincerely.

Ray wasn't so easily persuaded. 'Or Demetrios has started tying up his loose ends.'

Jodie rolled her eyes. 'What is it with you and him? There's no evidence to suggest he had anything to do with the robbery at the bookies.'

'That's the difference between being taught how to be a detective and learning from experience.' He hadn't intended to be so curt in his response, but it was too late to cover his tracks.

Jodie glared angrily at him. 'And what the hell is that supposed to mean?'

'Forget about it. Forget I said anything.' He thumped the door again, still no sound within.

Jodie wasn't prepared to let the dig lie. 'If you have something to say, spit it out. What? You think I'm not as a good a detective as you because I was fast-tracked through the system? You really think that my serving two years walking the beat in uniform would make me any better at my job now?'

He turned to face her. 'Truthfully? Yes, I do. It takes years to hone the necessary skills to do this job properly, to understand the risks and the way the criminal mind operates. You're barely old enough to be out of school, yet you're entrusted to protect public safety and prosecute those who deserve it. Quite frankly, it's a joke. The criminal justice system is on its arse, and the powers that be think the best way to tackle the issue is to throw more shit at the wall and hope some of it sticks.'

Jodie's cheeks were burning, and he wasn't sure she wouldn't slap him there and then, but her self-control was stronger than he'd given her credit for. She didn't respond, shaking her head in disappointment and stomping back along the corridor to the staircase.

Ray clamped his eyes shut in frustration. He hadn't meant to have a go at her, and he wasn't even sure he believed half of what he'd just said. It had felt good to vent, though. He would have to apologize, and he suspected Jodie would struggle to forgive him, but that was just a chance he would have to take. Punching the doorframe, the sting in his knuckles felt good as he turned his back on the door and made his own way to the stairs.

It was time for Plan B.

Their journey to the bookies was made in complete silence, with Jodie refusing to even look at him. As he'd made it out of the block of flats, he'd half-expected to find she'd driven off and left him there. He wouldn't have blamed her if she had. He didn't deserve her respect after his outburst, and apologizing wasn't a skill he had ever mastered. Every time he tried to spit out the words, she would sigh or the car would jerk suddenly and he'd be put off.

Despite the front door to the bookies being boarded up where one of the robbers had fired his shotgun, the shop otherwise bore no hint of the heinous crime that had occurred there a couple of days before.

A customer dressed in denim jeans and matching denim jacket was just entering the venue as they pulled up outside. It seemed business was open as usual as Papadopoulos did his best to recoup what the robbery had taken from him.

Ray was out of the car before Jodie had killed the engine. Jogging down the pavement, he stopped at the small newsagents on the corner, purchasing crisps, cigarettes and a chocolate bar. Lighting one of the cigarettes he walked slowly back to where Jodie was leaning against the bonnet of the car. He threw the chocolate bar in her direction, and she caught it with one hand.

'Thought you might be peckish,' he said sheepishly, before taking up position next to her.

She looked scornfully at him, before opening the packet and taking a bite. 'You know I'm just as good a detective as you are.'

'I know,' he said, bowing his head. 'I was out of order.'

'And because I *have* been trained properly, I know that doing my job effectively takes more than instinct and street smarts. I don't doubt that those things can be beneficial, but they're worth shit when the scumbags are on trial.'

He nodded, squinting against the sunshine peeking over the edge of the roof of the bookies. 'Alex has been cutting herself,' he suddenly blurted, unsure why it was so easy to talk to her. 'You know, like self-harming? I can't help thinking that maybe … I don't know. It's all such a mess. I can't seem to figure out who to trust and what has happened to my little girl. Every time I come up with one theory, I find plenty of holes in it, and I can't seem to see the wood for the trees.'

'That's probably because you're too close to it, Ray.'

'I don't have a choice though, do I? She's my daughter, and Alex is my wife. I don't want to believe that Alex could have hurt her, but there are just too many holes in her story for me to unequivocally believe her. Why was she at that nature reserve in Fleet? She's never mentioned having been there.'

'Have you asked her?'

He shook his head. 'Trent swore me to secrecy. They don't want her to know what they're looking for in case it tips her off.'

'Have they found anything of concern there?'

He shrugged. His calls to Owen were now going unanswered, and he couldn't blame his younger colleague for wanting to keep his nose clean.

'I'm …' he began, a lump forming in the back of his throat, 'I'm terrified I'll never see my little girl again. And it's killing me. I've not slept properly since she went missing and I no longer know whether I'm coming or going.'

Jodie looked away, clearly struggling to cope with the weight of what he was unburdening. It wasn't fair of him to be dropping his deepest fears on her.

Sniffing, he wiped his nose with the back of his hand, finished the cigarette, and choked down the urge to break down anymore. He had to stay strong; that's what he'd say to any other father in his position. There wasn't time for negativity.

'Shall we go in and see if Delilah is inside?' he said, ushering Jodie to take the lead, as she threw the chocolate wrapper in the nearby bin.

Inside the bookies, it was suffocatingly warm, with half a dozen men leaning up against the betting stations, half with one eye on the horse racing on the large television screen above the counter, and the remainder studying the form guide in their newspaper. There was no sign of Delilah or Papadopoulos, but Ray immediately recognized the student worker behind the counter, who gave a nervous nod in their direction.

Ray was about to ask if Papadopoulos was around, when Jodie raised the counter like a drawbridge and ducked through, holding the counter for Ray to slip beneath it too. The student didn't give them a second consideration, instead reaching for the next punter's slip and processing the payment.

Ray heard Papadopoulos's voice inside the small office. Putting his finger to his lips, Ray beckoned Jodie over, and they both leaned closer.

'It'll just be for a few days,' Papadopoulos said to whomever he was speaking. 'I'll get everything sorted out there, and then you can join me. Okay? It'll look less suspicious if we go separately.'

'What if *he* comes asking after you again?' Delilah replied quietly.

'He won't. They arrested someone from the gang this morning, so as far as Gianni is aware it's done with.'

'And when the truth comes out and this group tell the police they didn't touch this place?'

'Don't worry about that. We'll be long gone by then. Okay?'

'And what if the police come asking questions again? The two who came to my flat aren't stupid. They'll figure out I was involved soon enough. I told you I shouldn't have been off sick the day of the job.'

'I couldn't risk any harm coming to you and our baby, could I? What if something had gone wrong? I never would have been able to forgive myself. It was better this way. Gianni can go screw himself, and you and I get to spend the rest of our lives in some tropical paradise.'

Jodie was about to burst through the door when Ray pulled her away. Dragging her from the shop, he didn't speak until they were outside.

'What the hell are you doing?' she demanded.

'We can't arrest them. Not like this. You said yourself we need evidence of wrongdoing first.'

'He just confessed to organizing the robbery!'

'Hearsay. We need to catch him with the money, making his escape. We now know who's responsible. If we stick to him like glue, he'll lead us to the evidence.'

Jodie scowled at him, before sighing in frustration. 'What do you suggest?'

'We're going to need backup.'

45

Alex continued to pace the small space between the bed and the window, looking back over her shoulder. The laptop remained on the bed, the screen was open on the email app, but nothing new had been received in the last twenty minutes.

What if he *didn't* reply?

She'd written her message to *Simon* three times before sending it. The first version was too tentative, and the second too aggressive. Had the third option really been the best? As the inbox remained empty she was beginning to doubt whether she should have replied at all.

Isla could probably hear the pacing and would soon be wondering exactly what was going on. The right thing to do would be to call Isla up, show her the email and explain that she'd made a terrible mistake. Isla could then contact DI Trent and explain that it had been a stressful day – what with the incident at the park, and the meeting with the alleged clairvoyant – and it was a natural response to force things to move along. What if they arrested her for engaging with the abductor?

She paused, and looked at the door. It would be easy to call for Isla. She was supposed to be the mediator between the family and the police, after all, yet Alex couldn't help but feel she'd done a pretty lousy job so far.

She gently rubbed her abdomen. None of the stress would be doing the innocent life inside her any good. If she didn't do everything in her power to get Carol-Anne back, how would she ever be able to look her new baby in the eye and explain why his or her sister was no longer around?

She felt sick just thinking about the email she'd sent, and hated the fact that she was all alone. What other choice did she have? She didn't want to entangle Sophie in a conspiracy, and telling Ray or Isla would only wind her in more trouble. For now, she'd just have to wait and see what happened, and involve them if it got to the point where she couldn't cope.

Why hadn't *Simon* replied to her question?

Snatching up the laptop she opened the 'Sent' folder and reread her message again.

Dear Simon,

Prove to me that Carol-Anne is alive and well, and I'll do what you ask. I need more details. Where is Jack? And how will you return Carol-Anne when the deed is done?

Regards, Alex Granger

It seemed so ridiculously formal now, like she'd just written to a casual acquaintance to arrange a get-together. How else was she supposed to engage with someone who had abducted her daughter and had clearly been planning this horror for a long time?

Alex wondered whether she should send a second message, apologizing for the first one and trying to stress that she just wanted to know when she would see Carol-Anne again. It would be so much easier over the phone. The tone of an email could be misinterpreted, and it was never possible to invoke any real empathy like you could in a phone call.

Simon wouldn't be stupid enough to give her his number. The police could trace phone numbers via cell towers. She'd also thought they would have been able to trace where the email originated. Thus far Isla hadn't relayed any such information. In fact, she'd provided no updates so far today at all.

Slamming the lid of the laptop, Alex yanked her door open, taking the stairs down two at a time, hearing Isla in a hushed whisper on the phone in the kitchen.

'I understand that, but if she doesn't … no, of course I trust you. Okay, I'll see what I can find out from this end.'

Pushing the door open with her foot, Alex burst into the room. Isla quickly ended the call.

'Was that Trent? What did she say?' Alex asked urgently, the hairs on the back of her neck on end.

Isla's eyes looked away for the briefest moment. 'Uh, no. I'm due to speak to her soon. Are you okay? You look exhausted.'

Why was Isla lying to her? Did Trent still secretly suspect she was involved in the disappearance? Or worse, had they put a tracer on her email activity, and knew what message she had sent?

'Can I talk to Trent when you speak to her later? I want to know what they intend to do if they haven't found this *Simon* by tomorrow.'

Isla leaned back against the counter, the blood slowly disappearing from her cheeks. 'They're doing all they can to find Carol-Anne, Alex. You have to understand these things aren't easy. It requires a lot of painstaking work. I know in television shows things seem to move at a lightning-fast speed. In reality it doesn't work like that.'

'Surely you can trace where an email was sent from, right? I mean, I'm not very technology-aware, but even I know you have to provide a name and address to register for an email address.'

'The assigned email identification was false,' Isla said, as she placed the kettle on its stand. 'Ordinarily, we can trace the IP address of the computer used to send the message. On this occasion the recipient used software to hide his IP address. That tells us something about our suspect, though: he has a bit of IT knowledge.'

'How does that help?'

'It helps us narrow down the suspect-pool. I believe the team are now reviewing paroled convicts with similar MOs to see if they can shake a name. We *are* closing the net, Alex, I promise you.'

'And what about Jack Whitchurch? What's his involvement in all this?'

'The team have had him in for questioning and, as I told you, he has been ruled out as a suspect.'

'He is involved somehow, right? I mean, that's why *Simon* has demanded he die.'

'We don't know what his involvement is at this point. We have offered him protection, and are keeping a close eye on his activity.'

Alex thought back to the stories she'd read earlier. 'What's he like?'

'I don't think it's healthy for you to be thinking about any of that.'

'I read about him; I know what he was sent to prison for.'

There was a curious look on Isla's face, like she was searching for the right words; she'd seen the same look on Ray's face every time he'd said he was going to play squash.

'I don't want you spending too much time worrying about Whitchurch. Let us handle him.'

'Have you ever met him?'

Isla's stare met Alex's suddenly. 'Why does that matter?'

Alex could read it all over her face. 'Oh my, you *do* know him.'

Isla looked away. 'I've had the displeasure of coming into contact with all number of horrible people.'

Alex wasn't willing to let it go so easily. 'Is he as bad as the reports said? Some of the things I read made me want to be sick.'

Isla sighed. 'I'm not at liberty to discuss things like that. Take it from me, you really don't want to know. And besides, he isn't considered a suspect in what's going on with your daughter.'

Alex's back was beginning to ache, and she shuffled awkwardly until the pain subsided. 'I'm just trying to understand why *Simon* wants him dead. Maybe he was one of Whitchurch's victims.'

The kettle began to whistle before disconnecting. 'I'll be speaking to Trent again soon. I'll let her know you'd like a word.'

She was trying to pacify her again, treating her with kid gloves, when all she wanted was the truth. Why did everything Isla say seem shrouded in mystery?

'Why don't you just use him?' Alex asked. '*Simon* said Jack needs to die, so why not fake his death and draw *Simon* out? I could pretend to kill him; you could pretend to arrest me; we leak it to the press; *Simon* sees it, and releases Carol-Anne.'

'Things are never that easy. For all we know, a report that Whitchurch is dead could give *Simon* the satisfaction he craves and then he could kill Carol-Anne. If she's seen his face and can identify him then there are no guarantees he'll live up to his end of the bargain. We have to tread very carefully.'

Alex glared at her, as the implication of the words bit deep. 'You don't think she's coming back, do you?'

'I didn't say that—'

'That's what you think.'

'I'm not an expert, Alex. My role is to answer your questions as best as I can. I can't predict what goes through criminals' minds. I'm sorry.'

Alex spun on her heels, racing up the stairs, away from Isla's doubts, away from the cruel world that continued to keep her daughter from her. Slamming the door behind her, she slumped on the bed. The laptop screen was still bare, as *Simon* continued to ignore her.

46

He felt eyes on him the moment he pulled up on the road. As Ray turned and saw her leap from her car and hurry across the street, he knew things were not going to end well.

'What are you doing here?' he demanded, as he pushed his door open, grabbing her arm and pulling her out of sight of the house. 'Are you crazy?'

The fire in her eyes burned bright, and despite the reapplied make-up, it was clear she'd been crying. 'What's the meaning of this?' She raised her hand for him to see.

He cocked his head, trying to determine exactly what it was she was holding – pages of some kind – and why she would risk exposing their relationship so close to home?

'These were emailed to my boss this afternoon,' she growled. 'Have you been videoing us? Is that how you get your kicks?'

Her bitter tone confirmed she wasn't playing some elaborate prank. Reaching for the pages, he slowly turned them over. Even under the dim glow of the street light, it wasn't too difficult to realize what they depicted.

Edging her further down the street, he looked at each printed image carefully. It was impossible to tell where they'd been taken. The two of them could clearly be seen kissing and caressing one another through the view of an open window. It was all he could do to stop himself retching.

'Well?' she demanded, her eyes shining as she struggled to contain her emotions.

'I didn't send these, if that's what you're suggesting,' he began, glancing back over his shoulder to the house. 'Do you think I want to expose … what we've been doing?'

She wiped her nose with a well-used, scraggy piece of tissue. 'My boss called me into his office this afternoon and dropped these on the desk. He told me they had been emailed to all the senior managers in the business, telling them they have a …' She steadied herself. 'A *whore* working for the company. He wanted to know who'd sent them and why.'

Her dark maroon hair looked almost black in the faint orange glow overhead, and her Italian ancestry was clearly visible in those chocolate-like eyes, and the slight hue of her skin.

'I was shocked … no, *stunned* to see images of the two of us … like that. My boss made it clear that cavorting in any way that could besmirch the company's reputation was unacceptable. I've been suspended, Ray, with immediate effect.'

He ground his teeth as the anger slowly began to boil within him. Not only had someone been following and recording them, they'd now detonated the bomb. This was the last place he needed to be comforting her, in full view of his curtain-twitching neighbours, and at the same time the compassion flowing through him couldn't be ignored.

He reached out and pulled her into him, feeling the warmth of her tears as they blotted against his shirt. 'I'm so sorry. I don't know what else to say.'

She pulled back slightly so she could look him in the eye, her forehead only inches from his chin. 'Somebody knows about us.'

It was the same thought that had been running through his head since he'd turned over the first image. The question was: who, and who else had they told? He glanced back at the house again, fearing what he might find when he trundled through the door.

'I know I shouldn't have come here,' she continued, maybe sensing his anger. 'I didn't know where else to go. I wrote down the email address of the person who sent it. You can track them, right? Find out who they are and stop them?'

He thought about how the tech guys had tried and failed to locate *Simon*, but he couldn't go to them with something like this. For one thing it was a personal matter, unconnected to any ongoing investigation. And for another, it would mean exposing his own sordid secret to colleagues, and he knew how quickly gossip could spread through a station, even one as big as HQ.

He checked his watch. He'd told Jodie he would nip home to collect clothes and have a bite to eat and would then relieve her. She was probably still stuck outside Papadopoulos's two-bed mid-terraced property in the suburbs of Woolston, wondering how much longer he would be.

'Let me handle this. Okay? Leave these with me, and I'll do what I can to get to the bottom of it. Does anybody else know?'

The look of hurt that now gripped her face told him he'd asked the question in the wrong way.

'That's all you care about, isn't it?' she scowled. 'Whether or not your wife finds out about it. My career is up in smoke, and all you're worried about is covering your back.' She pulled away from him and turned to stomp off.

'Noemi, wait,' he called after her, but she was already halfway across the street and heading back to her car.

She turned suddenly, pointing at him. 'You know the saddest part of this whole thing? I was really starting to care for you, Ray.' She poked her tongue into her cheek and shook her head sorrowfully. 'More fool me for thinking you were different to the usual sleaze I allow into my bedroom. I was stupid to think I was ever anything more than a quick shag for you.'

He felt the weight of the world on his shoulders as he reached this critical fork in the road. On the one hand he feared what she might do, the tears streaming down her cheeks once more, but at the same time it would be in both of their best interests for her not to be outside his home for another minute.

'And another thing,' she spat bitterly, as she reached her car door, 'when my boss showed me the images, my first thought wasn't for my career, it was for *you*. I thought this mess was the last thing you needed with everything else you've got going on.'

He moved across and pulled her into him again. 'I'm sorry, Noemi, my head's all over the place. I don't mean to sound cold, but I need to—'

He froze when he heard his name being called from behind them. He felt Noemi's spine tense in the exact same moment.

'Ray? Is that you?'

He didn't need to turn around to know who was now standing outside their front door watching them.

'Oh shit, oh God, oh no,' he mumbled painfully under his breath.

This couldn't be happening. In all the scenarios he'd imagined Alex stumbling across the affair, this had never been one of them. It was too late to leap into the car and hurry away, as her footsteps were already clip-clopping down the driveway.

'Ray?' Alex called out again, much closer this time. 'What are you doing out here, and …' Her words broke off as she saw who he was standing with. 'Noemi? What on earth are you doing here? Ray, what's going …?'

Again she didn't finish the sentence.

Ray felt the photos being ripped from his hands, and as he turned to try and snatch them back before it was too late, he saw the anguish in Alex's eyes, and knew there was no way to brazen it out.

47

It was like looking at somebody else's life unfolding before her eyes, as if she wasn't in control of her own movements. As image after image of her husband and friend emerged from the pile, she desperately wanted to stop herself from looking. It was like a motorway car wreck that she couldn't help but gawp at.

Ray had made no movement towards her, instead remaining where he was with Noemi, guilty looks plastered over their faces. Sophie had described Noemi as 'a flake', someone who frequently pulled out of get-togethers with feeble excuses. Only now it seemed obvious why she had cancelled so many times. In fact, Alex would bet the house that, on most of those occasions, Ray had also not been home.

She felt sick to her stomach. Despite her suspicions that Ray had been seeing someone behind her back, a small part of her had hoped – beyond reason – that she was mistaken. And in the days since Carol-Anne had gone missing, she'd desperately clawed to that faint trail of optimism.

'Let me explain,' Ray began to say, until Alex cut him off with a raised hand. For once he didn't argue.

'How long?' Alex asked, unable to look at him, fighting to keep the building tears from bursting through the dam. She wouldn't give them the satisfaction of seeing how hurt she was.

'Please, Alex, let's go inside so we can talk about this calmly.'

Alex suddenly became aware that they were still standing in the middle of the road, and although she hadn't seen any of the neighbours checking to see what was going on, it wouldn't be long.

'How long?' she repeated, firmer this time.

Neither replied, and neither did either of them deny it. Was that a kindness? Or were they simply not imaginative to come up with a better ruse for why she'd caught them talking secretively outside with a handful of – frankly pornographic – photographs?

It felt like someone had punctured the boat that was her life, and she'd been desperately trying to plug the hole, but now her hands were being torn away from it. Her boat was going down and the only remaining question was whether she would go down with it.

The first spits of rain, offering a cooling sensation on her forehead, was her cue for going inside. Turning, she marched back towards the driveway, past Isla's small red car and into the open doorway, not daring to turn back and see if Ray would make any effort to salvage what remained of their relationship.

'Alex, wait,' Ray shouted, as he chased her in through the door. 'Please, let me explain.'

Alex wasn't listening. She needed space to process the revelation, but given her most recent episode at the playground this morning, she wasn't sure she trusted herself to be alone. Where else could she turn, though? Who could she trust enough to share the burden?

Isla immediately appeared in the kitchen doorway, a look of confusion on her face. 'What's going …?' she began.

The appointed Family Liaison Officer was the last person she wanted marital advice from, and, swerving away from the kitchen, Alex took the stairs two at a time, closing the bedroom door, frustrated that they'd never fitted a lock. Scraping a chair across the carpet, she barricaded the door instead. He could get in if he was desperate to, but he would think twice about it.

She heard him tapping against the doorframe a few moments later, his voice barely more than a whisper. 'Alex? I'm so sorry. You have to believe I never meant for it to happen. I know you hate me, and you've got every right to. I don't think you ought to be on your own. Please let me in so we can talk.'

Sorry. Five letters, and one of the most overused adjectives in the English language, and rarely truly meant. As a word it was often used to paper over mistakes and misdemeanours; it would take more than that now. She wanted to tell him to just go away and leave her alone, but she didn't have the energy.

He was tapping again, his words reverberating off the door's wooden panels. 'Alex, please? I'm sorry you had to find out that way; I should have told you. I should have come clean. I didn't know how. The last thing I wanted was to hurt you. God knows I didn't want it to happen like this. Despite everything, I still love you, Alex, and it's my responsibility to make sure you're okay.'

She silently scoffed. If he still loved her, he never would have allowed his head to be turned. Plenty of marriages hit bumpy roads, but not all of them ended in one spouse jumping into bed with another person. Hadn't their marriage been made of stronger stuff? Both of them had come from happy homes, with marriages that had lasted until death. Both sets of parents had set good examples of what marriage should be, so how had she and Ray allowed theirs to turn to shit?

'What's going on? Has something happened?' Alex heard Isla say from the top of the stairs. 'Alex?' she called out, louder this time. 'Can you tell me what's going on? Is everything okay?'

My twat of a husband has been banging a woman I thought was a friend, she wanted to fire back, but resisted, as a new thought entered her mind. A thought so terrifying it took forced effort to breathe in again.

Tearing the chair out of the way, Alex ripped the door open.

Pushing through Ray and Isla, she hurried down the stairs and out into the heavier rain, searching left and right for any sign of Noemi. The car was still parked across the street; however, she didn't appear to be in it. She turned to Sophie's house and saw the back-stabber, sheltering beneath the porch.

Noemi's eyes widened as they met Alex's frosty stare. 'Wait, Alex, wait.'

Alex had waited too long already. Racing across the driveway, not caring that her top and cardigan were getting soaked, she went nose to nose with Noemi. 'Where's my daughter? It was you, wasn't it? You took her. Where is she?'

Noemi was cowering, her lips moving, no sound escaping.

'Where is she?' Alex screamed, leaning closer as Noemi continued to shrink within herself.

'I-I-I don't know what you're talking about,' Noemi pleaded.

'Not happy with stealing my husband, now you've stolen my daughter too.'

Ray ran over from their own house and restrained Alex, pulling her back out into the rain. 'Alex, stop this, please.'

Something Isla had said before rattled through her mind: *in those successful cases, we identified the perpetrator as a relative or family friend.*

She looked up at him. 'Are you part of this too? Did you conspire with her to take our daughter away?'

The rain splashed off his shaved head, forming tiny rivers down the side of his face. 'How could you …?' He didn't finish the sentence, dragging her back towards their house, beckoning for Noemi to stay where she was.

Isla's curiosity had her standing at the door, a questioning look on her face as she tried to make sense of what was unfolding. She stepped aside as Ray manhandled Alex through the door and towards the living room.

'Please sit down and let's talk about this,' he said, moving across to the drinks cabinet, then thinking better of it. 'I know this has come as a shock, and I understand how confused you must be, but you can't go around shouting accusations like that. You must know I could never do anything to put our daughter's life in danger.'

Alex studied his face, looking for any hint of further deceit, any twinge that would confirm he was a part of what had happened, yet she saw only pained empathy.

She sighed in defeat. 'Don't you see? It all fits. She works for an IT company, doesn't she? She probably knows how to hide the origins of an email. And she knows Carol-Anne, and what's more, she would be a face that Carol-Anne wouldn't be afraid to go with. Isla said more often than not it's a relative or family friend responsible for the abduction of a child. Have you even stopped to consider whether she could have taken Carol-Anne?'

He took a deep breath. 'Of course I have! I had to give Trent a list of friends and acquaintances just as you did. I didn't go so far as to admit why I named her, but they did their routine background checks. She was at work at the time Carol-Anne was taken. It isn't Noemi.'

'Have the police checked her house? What if she's been stashing our daughter there this whole time?'

'Carol-Anne isn't in Noemi's flat.'

'Did they search it?'

'No …' he closed his eyes and lowered his head. 'I know because I was at her flat this morning. It isn't big enough to hide a two-year-old. I would have heard her or seen some evidence of her.'

Alex wasn't sure what hurt the most: the fact that he was defending his lover, or that he'd still been sleeping with Noemi even though Carol-Anne's life was in the balance.

For the second time that week, her heart felt like it was splintering into a thousand tiny pieces, impossible to reconstruct. She wasn't sure she wanted the answer to her next question. 'Do you love her?'

His eyes remained closed, his breathing steady, without offering a response.

'Well?' Alex repeated, as he remained silent. 'Do you love her?'

He either didn't know the answer, or couldn't find the words to reply.

'Does she love you?' Alex tried again, the words almost catching in her throat.

'I don't know,' he whispered. 'I'm sorry. I don't know what else to say.'

'How long have you been screwing her? Months? Years?'

'What does it matter?' he replied, dejected.

In truth, it didn't matter. The damage had been done the first time he'd even considered sleeping with her. 'I need to know how long you've been lying to me, Ray. I deserve that much. Before Christmas, or just this year?'

Ray ground his teeth. 'Before Christmas. Bonfire night.'

Alex's eyes widened further as the memory of that night fired behind her eyes. 'I took Carol-Anne to the display at the local comprehensive. You said you had to work late.'

'I did ... I mean I was ... I got called to an incident in town; a woman had been attacked in the street and uniform needed support. I tagged along, and was shocked to find Noemi was the victim. I offered to drive her home, and ... I don't even know who made the first move.

'I felt so guilty afterwards, and even though we both knew it was wrong ... I'm not going to make excuses. What we did was horrible, and you will never know how truly sorry I am – we both are – and you should know that none of this is your fault—'

It was like waving a red rag at a bull.

'My *fault*?' she shouted, lunging towards him, just resisting the urge to slap him. 'You're damned right this isn't *my* fault! I'm not the one who deliberately sought out someone else to shag. I'm not the one who betrayed our wedding vows.'

The panic in his eyes told her he regretted his choice of words. 'I know that. That's what I meant. This is all on me. And I'm sorry.'

'Are you a hundred per cent sure she doesn't have our daughter?'

Ray stood aghast. 'No. I told you, Noemi has nothing to do with what happened on Tuesday.'

She hadn't blinked in ages and her eyes were starting to water as a result. 'It would make sense; the two of you plotting behind my back to make me look stupid. I go crazy with worry and the three of you stride off into the sunset, leaving me in some loony asylum.'

'Alex, no! The two things have absolutely nothing to do with one another. How can you even think such a thing?'

'What do you expect me to think? You've been lying to me for months about your affair, so what else could you have been lying about?'

'Nothing, I swear.'

'And last week, were you really on a training course, or were the two of you away somewhere together?'

He fixed her with a stare, as if trying to burrow the words into her head telepathically. 'I was on a training course. You can check with Trent if you don't believe me. Besides, you met up with Noemi and Sophie last week, didn't you? I thought you had a girly night in watching *Dirty Dancing* and eating popcorn.'

A moment of doubt flashed through Alex's mind, swiftly followed by a feeling of nausea. Noemi had been here last Wednesday, acting as if everything was normal; lying to Alex's face. What she would give now for someone like Patrick Swayze's character to stand up for her and sweep her off her feet.

'On the subject of lies,' Ray interjected, 'you haven't been so honest with me either, have you?'

The question caught her off guard. 'What is that supposed to mean?'

He reached down and rested his hands on her arms, looking into her eyes again. 'What were you doing in Fleet on Tuesday morning, Alex?'

48

It wasn't the best time to flip the tables on her, but for the first time in months it felt like they were actually talking, being honest with one another. And as she now knew his darkest secret, Ray felt it only fair to try and understand what it was that she'd been keeping from him. Despite the threatening emails from *Simon*, Trent hadn't called off the search at the Fleet Nature Reserve. And although in the deepest recesses of his heart he refused to believe that Alex could have hurt Carol-Anne, she'd given him sufficient reason to consider the possibility.

A look of shock and surprise gripped her face. 'What? How do you …?'

Twisting her arms so he could see the scars on her wrists, he pressed on. 'We know you were in Fleet on Tuesday morning. Trent has sent a team to the nature reserve to examine the grounds. What were you doing there, Alex?'

She blinked several times, looking at him like he had said the most ridiculous thing. 'I wasn't there.'

'We have you on a traffic camera driving to Fleet. I've seen the footage myself. We don't know anyone who lives in Fleet, and you didn't write an appointment on the calendar, so what were you doing there?'

She pulled away from him. 'That's none of your business. That has nothing to do with what we're discussing here.'

'No? Are you sure? Or am I not the only one who's been seeing someone else on the side?'

She spun back and this time did slap him across the face, before he had time to flinch. 'How dare you! I haven't and would never betray you like that.'

He rubbed his cheek gingerly. 'No? Then what were you doing there, Alex? Why is Trent so focused on the nature reserve?'

A fog of confusion once again descended on her face. 'I have no idea.'

'Was Carol-Anne with you?'

'Yes.'

'And did she return with you?'

Her jaw dropped. 'What's that supposed to mean? Of course she did.'

He pointed at her wrists. 'How long have you been off your medication, Alex? When was the last time you saw your psychiatrist?'

She looked like she'd been kicked to the ground, and each challenge and question he fired was like another kick while she failed to crawl back to her feet. Now that he was on a roll, he knew he couldn't stop. After what had happened, she was sure to kick him out of the house, and he might not get another opportunity to find out the truth.

'I-I-I,' she stuttered.

He took a step closer to her, softening his tone. 'I want to help, Alex. I really do. And I don't want to think that you may have done something to put Carol-Anne's life in danger, but there are too many question marks about your recent behaviour. After what happened in Manchester when you last came off your medication …' He paused. 'Please just tell me why you were in Fleet. Put my mind at ease.'

'I didn't do … Carol-Anne was with me, and we came home

together. You know she was in the car park when she was taken.'

It wasn't the convincing explanation he'd been hoping for. 'Do I? We have your car arriving at the car park on Tuesday afternoon, and there's no sign of Carol-Anne being taken. Trent has reservations about your version of events.'

Alex's hand shot up to her mouth. 'No! I wouldn't …'

Ray had seen the flicker of doubt in her eyes.

'How do you know, Alex? How long has it been since you last took one of your antidepressants? I had to call in so many favours to stop you incurring a criminal record in Manchester. Now I'm terrified it was a warning sign that I failed to act upon.'

The doubt flickered again. 'What about the email messages? What about *Simon*?'

It was a fair challenge, and given the lack of apparent progress Trent's team had made with tracing the source of the emails, he could only guess at the cause.

'For all I know, you could be the one sending them … or you've paid someone to do it for you.'

This time fury fired in her eyes. 'You think …?' She turned away from him, scanning the floor for something and then strode to her handbag, lifted it, and pulled something out. She thrust it towards him.

His brow furrowed as he read it. 'What the hell is this?'

'That's where I was on Tuesday morning. That's why I was in Fleet.'

He studied the business card. 'A private investigator?'

She sighed. 'I've suspected your cheating for a couple of months, and I was hoping an investigator could follow you around and put my suspicions to rest one way or another. I knew if I confronted you about it without proof you'd say it was all in my head. I figured you might know all of the private investigators in Southampton, given your job, and I found this woman on the internet.'

He stepped backwards. 'You hired a private investigator?'

'I was going to, but then she told me how much it would cost and I knew I couldn't afford to do it without you finding out.'

'Why now, Alex? If you've suspected for so long, what made you decide to see her this week?'

Alex pulled a pregnancy testing stick out of her bag next. 'Two lines. I was going to tell you tonight ... I'm pregnant, Ray.'

He took two steps backwards. 'How ...? With whom?'

'You and me a few weeks ago: our drunken fumble. Remember? And it *is* yours before you ask. Unlike you, I've never been unfaithful. I found out last week, and I panicked. I didn't think I'd be able to raise a baby on my own, and I needed to know whether you were loyal. When she quoted the price, I told her I'd think about it and let her know, and then hightailed it out of her office. And then ... Carol-Anne was abducted, and the world spun on its head again. I have no idea what the police have discovered in Fleet, but I can tell you, without a doubt, it isn't our daughter, and it has nothing to do with me.'

The ice cubes rattled in the tumbler as Ray raised the glass to his lips, grimacing as the bourbon burned the back of his tongue and numbed his throat. Alex had asked him for space and time, and he had agreed to leave her alone upstairs, having first removed anything he thought she could use to do herself further damage.

Sitting alone in the darkness of the lounge wasn't what he'd intended, but the outside light had drifted so quickly and he hadn't been bothered to close the curtains and switch on the lights. He could hear movement through the ceiling, so at least he knew she hadn't done anything stupid. Probably packing his stuff into a bag if she had any sense, although he hoped she wouldn't insist he move out.

The ice rattled again as he lowered the glass to the coaster and checked his phone. Jodie had phoned three times before leaving him a message asking him to call her. He hadn't known how to explain what had happened and had simply sent her a message saying he had some personal shit to sort out and would be back in touch in the morning. It was a lousy way to treat her. His philandering ways had been exposed in the worst possible way, and he was now hoping his wife wouldn't throw him out.

He heard Isla approaching and quickly drained his drink. He'd relayed what Alex had told him about the appointment in Fleet to her, and although it was outside of the investigator's published hours, it wouldn't be too difficult for the team to check that Alex had indeed been there at the time she had indicated.

'Ah you're still here? Good,' Isla said as she entered the room and caught sight of him. 'Is Alex upstairs?'

He nodded, avoiding eye contact.

'Well, you'll be relieved to hear that the bones discovered in the nature reserve are that of an elderly male, rather than a child. After what you told me that probably isn't a surprise.'

'Do they know who he is yet?'

'The grave was shallow and from all accounts limbs have been separated from the body and most likely dragged away by foraging animals. It would seem he has been in the ground for a considerable amount of time, so your wife is in the clear as far as that goes.'

'Hopefully that means Trent will focus on the likelihood that my daughter is being held by someone then?'

Isla shrugged. 'I don't know what it all means to be honest. I've never known a case quite like this one.' She nodded at his glass. 'Do you mind if I join you?'

He passed her his glass, shaking his head, and watched as she carried it to the drinks cabinet, poured an equal measure for them both and handed his back to him.

'My ex-husband was a bourbon man too,' she said, sniffing the glass. 'The smell still brings back pleasant memories.'

'Why did the two of you split, if you don't mind me asking?'

She took a sip. 'We were never meant to last; or at least that's my outlook now, as I near my twilight years. We were young and

258

in love: a terrible combination. I thought he would learn to be better and he thought I would learn to adjust to his mannerisms.' She shrugged again. 'Turned out we were both wrong. After my son was born, I decided I wanted to do something worthwhile with my life and applied for the police force. I was young enough to be in decent shape, and old enough that I had some life experience. Bundle that up with the fact that I'm a woman and my application was accepted. I think I used my newfound responsibility as a springboard to avoid my shaky marriage. I applied for overtime whenever it was going, leaving my ex-husband and his overbearing mother to raise our son. Not that I shirked my parental responsibility, but it was easier not having to worry about school runs, the PTA and packed lunches. It's no wonder Luke despises me so much.'

'So being in the police didn't cause your relationship to go tits up?'

'No, it was virtually over before I started. Even so, I have no regrets. My ex-husband is remarried with stepchildren he adores, and we're still on good terms; he still sends me flowers every year on my birthday.'

'Something tells me Alex won't be quite so forgiving of my failings.'

Isla considered him for a moment. 'Do you want her to? Forgive me for speaking out of turn – and this is based solely on my interactions with you since Wednesday – neither of you strike me as being particularly happy with how things are. I appreciate I've probably met you at the worst time of your lives, yet I sense the two of you haven't been happy for some time.'

He couldn't argue, and he didn't have an answer for her question. What was making him feel most guilty wasn't that he'd been caught, but the feeling of relief that it was now out in the open.

The ringing doorbell stopped him responding to the question, and as he opened the door and saw a tearful Noemi on the doorstep, he wasn't sure what to do. Closing the door behind him, he joined her outside. The rain had now passed and a gentle breeze blew around them.

'She hasn't killed you yet then?' Noemi said, forcing a pained smile.

He reciprocated the gesture. 'Not yet. How are you?'

'I feel awful. Sophie came out when she heard us arguing. I told her what happened, and we've been sat in my car talking. How is Alex?'

'Wearing a hole in the bedroom carpet with her pacing I think. She wants time.'

'What has she said? Has she asked how it happened? What did you tell her? You'd better not paint me as the villain of the piece.'

He raised his arms in a calming gesture. 'Hey, why would I?'

'It's what most men would do: blame it on the woman. You know I never intended for what happened, and you need to tell her that.'

Ray put his arm around her, resting his chin on her head, as she snuggled into his shoulder. He'd screwed up both of their lives and would be paying penance for the rest of his.

'Has she kicked you out?' Noemi mumbled. 'I'd offer to let you stay at mine, but … it might not look right.'

'She hasn't thrown me out yet. I'll probably sleep in Carol-Anne's room for tonight at least. I'll have to try and find a hotel for tomorrow night and then work out a plan thereafter.'

She looked up at him, wiping her eyes with the back of her hand. 'Tell me one thing: do you regret it?'

He could see the look of longing in her eyes, striving for validation that what they'd shared had been more than just lust. Before he could answer, a scream from inside had him rushing through the door, finding Isla and Alex hovered over the laptop.

'What is it? What's happened?' he shouted.

Neither woman could respond, as Alex turned the laptop around so he could see the screen.

49

Alex threw her arms around Ray's neck, his infidelity temporarily forgotten as she craved to be held and assured that everything would be okay. Behind them the video of Carol-Anne singing to herself played on a loop on the laptop screen.

'Who's doing this to us?' Alex wailed.

Ray didn't answer, angling her so he could read the message that had been sent with the video.

Simon Says …
  One day to go and still you delay,
  Someone will die come what may.
  If you love your daughter,
  Do what you ought to.
  I'm sharpening my knife,
  Kill him to save her life.

He was rubbing his hand in circles on her back, but that wasn't what she wanted. Pulling away from him, she turned her back and pulled the laptop close to her chest.

As soon as Ray had returned to the room, Isla had left, dialling the office and demanding Trent come and see the latest message for herself. That had been twenty minutes ago, and voices in the corridor confirmed that Trent and team had arrived.

On the surface, the video message wasn't sinister at all. Carol-Anne had been able to sing a selection of nursery rhymes to herself for some time, but 'Ring a ring a roses' wasn't one Alex had ever taught her. So while the video provided hope that Carol-Anne was not only alive, and well, it also meant that whoever had her was in control, and Alex didn't doubt the threat to Carol-Anne's life was real.

Yet, as sinister as the recording was intended to be, Alex didn't want to stop listening to her beautiful child's sweet angelic tones.

As soon as Trent entered the room, though, the first thing she did was to seize the laptop and stop the video.

Alex wanted to speak out and demand she put the song back on, knowing she would be ignored. The fact that Trent had managed to get into Ray's head and have even him doubting her mental health and motivations told Alex all she needed to know about the detective inspector.

Alex continued to watch Trent speaking quietly to Isla, glancing over to her and Ray every few seconds, like she was still trying to assess their level of involvement in the whole sordid affair.

'Okay, okay,' Trent said, before peeling away and approaching the two of them. 'This message is in response to something *you* sent?' she asked, staring straight at Alex.

Alex looked away. 'I-I-I was just trying to get his attention.'

'Who told you to engage with the kidnapper?' Trent pressed.

'Nobody, it was my idea.'

'What did you hope to achieve?'

'I don't know. I just …'

Trent looked at her notebook. 'You wrote: "Prove to me that Carol-Anne is alive and well, and I'll do what you ask. I need more details. Where is Jack? And how will you return Carol-Anne when the deed is done?" Why did you ask these questions?'

'I wanted proof that she was still alive—'

Trent wasn't buying the act. 'Do you intend to carry out what *Simon* has asked? Because if you're conspiring to kill Jack Whitchurch I'll arrest you here and now.'

Ray put a protective arm in front of Alex. 'Now just wait right there. She's told you why she sent it.'

Trent ignored him and focused on Alex. 'Why did you say you'd go through with the act?'

'I was stringing him along, I didn't mean it.' Alex wasn't sure she believed the words herself as they tumbled from her lips, yet she hoped she was putting on a convincing act.

'Why did you ask him where Jack was? If you only wanted to string him along, why ask that?'

'I thought it would make me seem more serious. I promise you: I'm not a killer. I just wanted proof that she was still alive.'

'I don't believe you, Alex.'

'I saw a clairvoyant earlier,' Alex said, lowering her eyes. 'He said Carol-Anne was dead, and I-I wanted proof that he was wrong.'

'The one thing I told you at the outset of all this was *not* to engage with this person. By emailing him you have given him the power and attention he craves. I have no doubt now that the messages are from the same person who has your daughter. Still, we have no way of knowing whether this video was made today or on the first day he took her. Forgive my bluntness: you haven't helped matters at all.'

'Hey, ease off,' Ray warned. 'She made a mistake, let's not keep going on about it. Tell me you're closer to tracing where these messages originate, or who's sending them.'

'The perpetrator is using a Virtual Private Network to protect their location. When we traced the IP credentials, it flagged up in Belgium the first time, and then Azerbaijan, and God knows where this one is from.'

'So, what, you're giving up?'

'Of course not! We're continuing to trawl through the local

video coverage we've got, looking for out-of-place vehicles leaving the vicinity, and you know how painstaking that can be.'

'If nothing is done before tomorrow's deadline, this man is going to kill my daughter,' Alex wailed, pulling herself clear of Ray and storming from the room, hurrying up the stairs and slamming the door behind her. If only they'd listened to her when the first message came, maybe Carol-Anne would already be home. How much time had Trent wasted assuming she was guilty of harming Carol-Anne?

The bedroom door burst open and Ray rushed in, closing it behind him. 'Are you okay?'

'No I'm bloody not! What if *Simon* carries out his threat? What if he kills Carol-Anne and we never get to see her again?'

'I know how you feel, and I too wish there was something we could do to—'

'There is. You could man up and take care of this Whitchurch.'

'What are you saying, Alex?'

She glared at him, grinding her teeth to cover what she really thought of him. 'If you really loved this family you'd have found Jack's location on day one and killed him.'

He grunted disbelievingly. 'Are you out of your mind?'

Her eyes remained fixed on his. 'Do you really think it's a coincidence that he targeted *us*? The wife of a policeman who can get close to Jack and kill him? I can't believe it's me having to suggest this.'

Ray narrowed his eyes. 'I can't believe you *are* even suggesting this. What the hell has happened to you?'

'You've abandoned our daughter, Ray! You abandoned me when you unzipped your trousers and screwed Noemi, and now you've turned your back on Carol-Anne.'

'I haven't turned my back on our daughter.'

'Then why aren't you out there killing that monster to get her back?'

Ray glanced nervously at the door. 'You need to lower your

voice. If Trent hears what we're discussing she'll have us both cuffed.'

'Do you know what? I don't even care anymore. I said from the outset that I'd do whatever it took to get my little girl back, and if you haven't got the balls to do it, then I'll bloody well do it myself.'

'Don't be ridiculous, Alex! What about the baby?'

She hadn't realized her hand had been gently rubbing her abdomen since she'd made it to the top of the stairs. She didn't answer his challenge, feeling helplessness flowing over her.

'We have no clue who's behind any of this,' Ray continued evenly, 'and whether he'd even return her if Whitchurch died. For all you know, you could kill him and then *Simon* could still kill Carol-Anne. We've talked about this before, Alex, and I know you're desperate, but this line of thought is ludicrous. You'd probably be arrested and charged before you even got fifty feet from him, and then what? Even if you did do what *Simon* asked, and he *did* live up to his side, what good would it do? You'd be in prison and you still wouldn't get to see Carol-Anne.'

At least she'd know her daughter was safe, even if she only got to see her under watchful supervision.

'And how exactly would you do it, Alex? Have you even thought about that? You won't even kill spiders when they leap at you in the shower. How the hell are you going to be able to kill another human being?'

She opened her mouth to answer, but she hadn't thought that far ahead. 'I'd find a way.'

His voice was rising again. 'Oh yeah? It's not like the US where you can walk into your nearest supermarket and just buy a gun. You could always stab him, I suppose, but it can be hard work pressing a blade through human tissue, especially if he's wriggling around and fighting for survival. Or then there are a number of poisons out there. With less than a day to go, how are you going to get your hands on one of those? And of course making him ingest the poison would be challenging too. But then maybe—'

'Enough, Ray!' she said, deflated. 'You've made your point.'

Placing his hands on her shoulders, he shook his head. 'I'm not sure I have, Alex. I appreciate that the idea of killing Jack Whitchurch seems the easy answer – particularly given his criminal history –the practicality of it is a lot tougher. I need you to promise me that you'll stop thinking like this.'

She was struggling to focus on his face through the fog of tears. 'It wouldn't have to be *us* who killed him though, Ray. You must have come into contact with killers before: people who can be paid to kill?'

The lines around his eyes deepened in shock. 'A contract killer? I can't believe my ears. Alex, no. Enough of this, please? Paying a killer makes us just as guilty of the crime. Can't you see that? Can you even hear what you're saying?'

She could see the doubt in his face, and while he seemed to be questioning the person he'd married, it was she who felt let down by the man who'd once claimed he would do anything to protect their daughter.

50

Isla had seemed only too pleased to escape the house for the safety of her own flat, but had claimed it was to give them the space they needed to talk through the revelations of the night. Ray had roughed it on the couch. Not that he'd managed to get much sleep. Not even a half bottle of whiskey had been enough to switch off his over-engaged mind. The look Alex had given him last night left him in no doubt that she would do everything in her power to find and kill Jack Whitchurch, and the only thing stopping him from turning her in to Trent was the belief that her efforts would inevitably fail.

While her attitude to the ultimatum had shocked him, he knew she wasn't capable of going through with murder, and a lot of what had been said was in the heat of the moment. She wasn't a killer, and that was a fact. There was too much kindness and positivity running through her veins.

He hadn't heard back from Jodie since he'd messaged her last night, and wasn't surprised to find she wasn't in the office when he arrived. Her coat wasn't hanging from her usual chair, and her large handbag wasn't beneath the desk. He hadn't originally planned to come in himself, as there was so much to sort out with Alex, but when Owen had messaged to say they were bringing in Jack Whitchurch for a second time, and that Trent had agreed Ray could observe the interview from the viewing suite, he'd been unable to refuse the offer. It wouldn't hurt to give Alex some space to decide what the future held. He was determined not to become an absent father, and if that meant jumping through hoops for Alex, then it was a step he was prepared to take.

Owen's message had told him to watch from Trent's personal office, and Owen was sitting in Trent's chair as Ray entered the room, the two exchanging silent nods, with neither willing to engage in small talk prior to something with such grave potential repercussions.

'I got you a coffee,' Owen eventually said, sliding the paper cup across the desk.

'Oh, cheers,' Ray said, reaching for it and taking a sip. Owen had forgotten to put sugar in it, but Ray choked back the bitterness. 'Thanks.'

On the screen before them, the door to the interview suite opened and Whitchurch shuffled in, dragging his feet on the carpet, and immediately reached for the table to steady himself. He looked every one of his seventy-odd years, older even. He wasn't the first former convict who had aged badly while behind bars, though Ray couldn't be certain that the vulnerability wasn't being exaggerated for their benefit.

'Jack?' Trent began, when they were all seated and she had completed the formalities for the recording. *'I understand from my colleague here that you've been having some issues with your hearing since you were released from prison?'*

Whitchurch leaned forward and mumbled something inaudible.

Trent began emphasizing each vowel sound, *'I said you've been having some problems with your hearing. Is that right?'*

'Oh yes,' he grumbled gruffly, sounding as if he hadn't put in his dentures.

'Okay, well if you don't hear something I say, or you don't understand, I want you to tell me so I can repeat it. Okay?'

'Oh yes.'

'And to confirm,' Trent continued, 'you are not under arrest, and have attended the police station voluntarily.'

'That's right.'

'Jack, can you tell me if any threats were made against you in the months prior to your release from prison? Or if you were contacted by anyone who made you feel uncomfortable in any way?'

'No.'

'And since you were released from prison earlier this week, has anyone tried to contact you or made any threats towards you?'

'How would they do that then? It's only you lot who know where I am.'

'As we told you last time, your name has come up in a current investigation, and as there is a threat to your life, we're trying to identify who the aggressor is.'

'Yes, the other lady explained all this the other day.'

'That's right, Jack. Another threat was received last night, and we have reason to believe you are being targeted by someone.'

'Who?'

'That's what we're trying to work out, Jack.'

'Eh? Come again?'

'I said that's what we're trying to work out. Can you think of anyone specifically who would want to see harm come to you?'

He grunted. 'I can think of a pretty long list as it goes.'

Trent picked up her pen. 'Can you tell me who?'

'Names? You want names? I don't know who they are. I'm talking about the families of the ... of those I harmed because of my sickness, like.'

'Have any of the victims' families tried to make contact with you?'

'No, you asked who has it in for me.'

The coffee swayed as Ray squeezed the paper cup. 'This is a

269

waste of time,' he said openly to Owen. 'Give me ten minutes alone with him, and I'd have a better chance of working out who's behind all this.'

'I know what you mean,' Owen agreed. 'I said to the boss we should use him as some kind of bait, try and lure the suspect out, but she says we can't gamble with his safety.'

Back on the screen, Trent looked like she was equally frustrated. *'Has anyone contacted you since your release, Jack? Old friends? Anyone?'*

'No, not that I can think of.'

'You're in sheltered accommodation now, aren't you? Have you met any of your fellow residents yet?'

'Eh?'

'Have you met any of your neighbours, Jack?' she repeated, louder this time.

'Oh, no, I keep myself to myself. Better that way.'

'We have reason to believe that whoever intends to do you harm is looking for it to be carried out in the next day or so. I'd like to leave one of my team with you for a few days for your own protection. Would that be okay?'

'One of your lot in my home?'

'That's right, or positioned closely nearby. If this person comes for you, we would be on hand to stop them.'

He snorted. *'You must think I was born yesterday!'*

'I don't follow.'

'Eh?'

'Why don't you want us to protect you?'

'You just want to get inside my place so you can stitch me up again. I told that prison governor there was no way I was going to die behind bars, and you lot seem determined to put me back in there.'

Bewilderment cloaked Trent's face. *'That's not what this is about.'*

'No, of course it isn't,' he mocked. *'I suppose you offer to protect all people like me, don't you?'*

'If I had reason to fear for their safety I would. Let me make it clear, Jack, I believe the threat to your life is genuine, and I don't want to see any danger come to you.'

This time Whitchurch actually roared with laughter. *'Pull the other one. I can see how much you despise me. You lot are all the same. You're not concerned about my welfare.'*

'You've served time for your offences, Jack, so I am duty-bound to protect you as much as anyone else.'

'How many people know my address?'

'Five police officers – including me – are aware of your new identity and home location, and I can vouch for all of them.'

'Well, then, how can I be in any danger? If the only people who know won't say anything, I'm safer at home than in here.'

'I agree, Jack, but I prefer to be cautious and would still like to—'

He stood suddenly, again supporting his weight against the table. *'Have you anything else to say, or can I go now?'*

Trent stopped the recording as he shuffled out of the room. She turned and stared straight into the camera. *'Well, Ray? Got any other ideas?'*

51

Alex was convinced she hadn't slept well, yet when the alarm sounded, it was a struggle to open her eyes and reach out to switch it off. The space in the bed next to her remained flat and unslept in. She hadn't specifically told Ray he wasn't welcome in their bed, but she'd been relieved to see him take a blanket from the airing cupboard when he'd headed downstairs. Of course, for all she knew he could have spent the night at Noemi's. She hadn't heard him leave this morning.

Alex's chest tightened as the memory of yesterday's revelation hit her. Although she'd suspected for some time that Ray had been playing away, a tiny part of her had desperately clung to the hope that she was being paranoid. To have it confirmed in such a hurtful way was something she knew she would never forget.

Alex had never felt so alone. The affair and the betrayal felt so meaningless with what had transpired afterwards. Seeing Carol-Anne happy and smiling on the video had given her a jolt of adrenaline, but Trent had now confiscated her laptop to prevent her replying to *Simon* again.

Swinging her legs over the side of the bed, Alex stumbled as she tried to stand, having to suddenly grip the bed to prevent herself falling forward. The wave of nausea passed within seconds – a gentle reminder of the new life growing inside her. Yet as she gently rubbed her belly, she caught herself smiling. Carol-Anne would make a great big sister to a little boy or girl. And although raising a child on her own without Ray would be hard, the excitement slowly built, and she could almost picture the baby being born. In the vision, Carol-Anne was being led into the maternity ward, in a pretty pink and purple dress, carrying a small wrapped parcel for her new brother or sister: a teddy of some sort.

Alex's eyes snapped open. Staggering to the bathroom, she heaved into the toilet, before showering and dressing. Then she headed to the kitchen, where she poured herself a glass of cold water. The thought of eating made her stomach turn, so she grabbed a slice of bread from the packet and nibbled on it. There was no sign of Isla yet, and Alex wondered whether Luke was the reason she was late once again.

She spotted Isla's handbag on the kitchen counter where it had been yesterday. Surprised, and now wondering whether Isla was already here and she just hadn't seen her yet, Alex lifted the bag to carry it through to the living room. But it slipped and fell to the floor, some of the contents spilling onto the linoleum.

Alex crouched and quickly gathered up a lipstick, a purse and a packet of chewing gum, before stretching for the chequebook, lying open and just out of reach. She shuffled forward and gripped the edge, amazed that anyone still wrote cheques in this day and age when payments could be made with a tap of a card and by text message. As she moved to close the front cover, her eyes fell on a name that chilled her to her core.

Dropping to her bottom, and pressing her back into the cupboard door for support, Alex felt the walls of the kitchen closing in around her. On the balances page, Isla had scrawled the names and amounts paid, and the last three were all to the same name:

Luke Simon Murphy.

The last entry was dated yesterday when Alex had nearly bumped into Isla's son leaving the property. Isla had been too ashamed to admit she'd yet again bowed to her son's demands for financial support. Was it possible there was another reason Isla had been so willing to give him money? Why she'd been only too happy to act as Family Liaison on their case?

Panic swamped her every thought as flashes of the conversations they'd shared filled her mind.

It was impossible, surely; there was no way Isla and her son could be involved in the abduction of Carol-Anne.

And yet, somehow *Simon* had managed to stay one step ahead of the police for all this time. And yesterday Isla had practically admitted to knowing Whitchurch.

Clambering unsteadily to her feet, Alex looked for her phone. She needed to call Ray or Trent or somebody and pass on what she suspected, but she must have left it charging upstairs. She was about to head up and collect it when the doorbell rang.

She opened the door, surprised to see a man with large tattooed arms standing there, smiling at her.

'Alex Granger?' he said, his voice gruff.

She nodded. 'Yes, who are …?'

He thumbed at the van on the street. 'Delivery, luv. I've got a parcel for you. Sorry, wasn't sure if you were home as there was no car in the driveway. If you can print and sign your name, I'll go and fetch it.'

'There must be some mistake. I haven't ordered anything.'

He passed her the paddle for signing. 'You are Alex Granger?'

'Yes, but—'

'Well, the parcel is for that name at this address. You can refuse it if you want, and I can return it to the depot. If you then find out that it's something from your husband, partner, or whatever, you'll have to come down and collect it or call up and arrange a second delivery. Up to you.' His broad smile was warm, even if his teeth were stained from nicotine.

'Um … no … it's okay,' Alex said, the feeling of unease slowly passing. 'Print and sign, right?'

'That's right,' he said cheerily, whistling through his teeth as he returned to the rear of his van, opening the doors and pulling out a small rectangular package the size of a shoebox. He took the paddle from her and handed over the item. 'You have a nice day now.'

And with that, he turned and headed back down the driveway, not looking back.

Alex returned to the kitchen, all thoughts of Isla's chequebook temporarily forgotten as she tore at the lid of the box. As she saw what glinted back at her from inside, she screamed at the top of her lungs.

The kettle whistled, and Sophie filled two mugs, swishing the teabags around. 'I'm glad you called me,' she said, offering another sympathetic look.

Alex's eyes hadn't left the contents of the shoebox on the counter in front of her, where she'd been standing since Sophie had arrived.

'And you're sure the stuffed toy is Carol-Anne's?' Sophie asked as she slid a mug of tea over to Alex.

'It's Ballet Bunny, her favourite,' Alex replied, her voice distant as she stared at the streaks of red now covering the bunny's torso. 'She had it with her in the car when she was …'

'Have you phoned the police yet?'

Alex shook her head. 'I don't know what to do for the best. I called you because I didn't know where else to turn.'

Sophie offered her an empathetic frown. 'I'm the last person who would know what to do in this situation. Based on what you told me about that Isla woman and her son, and considering the other item in the box, I don't think you have a choice: phone the police.'

The gun sitting on the base of the box was still partly obscured

275

by the bloody bunny, and Alex had yet to check whether it was loaded.

'Where's Ray? Do you want me to call him?' Sophie cautioned.

Alex shook her head. 'No, don't call Ray. Don't call anyone. Not yet.'

Sophie pointed at the box in exasperation. 'Alex, somebody has just sent you your daughter's favourite toy, smeared with blood, along with a gun of some sort. What if it's from *Simon*?'

'Who else would it be from?' Alex whispered, lifting the bunny out of the box and putting it to her nose, instantly recognizing Carol-Anne's delicate scent.

'I don't think you should touch any of it,' Sophie warned. 'Maybe the bastard left his prints or DNA. That's what happens in those cop shows, isn't it?'

Alex inhaled the bunny's smell again, before gently putting it to one side, for the first time spotting a typed note stuck to the inside of the box. Pulling it out, she unfolded it. 'It's an address.'

'Alex, I don't like this. You *need* to phone the police.' Sophie marched out of the room, returning a moment later with the phone in her hand. 'What's the number for the woman in charge?' Sophie froze as she saw Alex handling the gun, checking its weight. 'What the hell are you doing?'

Alex hadn't felt this calm and in control for as long as she could remember. 'I'm doing what I should have done from day one: whatever it takes to get my daughter back.' She fixed Sophie with an assured stare. '*Simon* wants Jack Whitchurch dead, and that's what I'm going to do. I'd rather spend the rest of my life behind bars than bury my daughter. If you want to be a friend, you'll drive me to this address and wait for me.'

52

Flooring the accelerator, Ray dragged the squad car off the round-about to a blare of horns. Raising an apologetic hand in acknowledgement, he gripped the wheel with both hands, swerving in and out of traffic. With the grill lights flashing and the siren loud and clear, he made light work of Thomas Lewis Way, and as the signs for the airport came into view he sneaked a glance at the dashboard clock.

Not bad; the station to the airport in under ten minutes had to be some kind of record. He thought back to Jodie's anxious call. *Papadopoulos is fleeing this morning. You need to get to the boarding gate and stop him.*

She hadn't wanted to admit where she was or why she'd abandoned her post outside Papadopoulos's door, and there hadn't been time to press her. If the Greek bookie made it past passport control and out to a non-extradition country, they'd never catch him.

He couldn't escape the guilt regarding his own part in Papadopoulos's escape. Had he done as he'd said he would and relieved Jodie last night, he would have been there to stop Papadopoulos. Instead of doing his duty, he'd drowned his sorrows.

And neither the bourbon nor his current course of action was bringing him any closer to finding his daughter. He'd been pestering Trent all morning about the last email Alex had received, and what action she was going to take to find Carol-Anne before it was too late. She'd been evasive, asking him to trust her. It was nigh on impossible to concentrate on anything but his daughter, though.

Earlier today Alex had sent him a garbled message that he hadn't understood. Something about Isla's son. The message hadn't been clear, and as he'd been about to phone Alex to ask her what it was about, Jodie's call had interrupted proceedings. He'd left Owen to follow up with Alex directly.

Forcing it from his mind, he narrowly avoided another collision at the next roundabout, not slowing for the speed bumps on the approach to the airport at Eastleigh. Skidding to a halt at the departures drop-off point, he waved his badge at the security guard in the high-visibility jacket and dived through the automatic doors, searching high and low for any sign of the short, balding Greek. There were too many people to see clearly and backup had yet to arrive.

Racing to the departures screen, he looked for the flight Papadopoulos was due to board. The screen was flashing a 'Final Call' warning, and Ray took off again, heading for security control and running to the head of the queue.

'My colleague should have called ahead,' he shouted at the stern-faced woman in the navy uniform. 'My suspect has gone through and is boarding now. Please, you have to let me through.'

She looked at his badge, nodding at one of the other border force officers to escort him.

'It's Gate 12,' Ray panted as the two of them darted through the security barrier and into the departures lounge.

Three people were queuing at the door, where the boarding agent was reviewing passes, and that's when Ray spotted him: not in the queue, instead sitting in the seats closest to Gate 4.

'Wait, wait,' Ray said breathlessly. 'That's him.'

Papadopoulos seemed oblivious to the commotion. With large headphones around his head and his face buried in a magazine, it had been lucky that Ray had noticed him. As he approached and his eyes made contact with Papadopoulos, the bookie's mouth dropped.

'That's funny,' Ray said with a frown. 'You're due to board the flight to Skiathos, yet here you are waiting for the flight to Geneva. Last-minute change of mind, was it?'

Papadopoulos looked left and right, searching for an exit, before reaching for his carry-on bag. 'There's no crime against going on holiday. What are you doing here anyway?'

'We know you masterminded the raid on your own shop. We've been waiting for you to make your move, and I'd bet there's a Swiss bank account in your name where the laundered cash is sitting for collection? Where's your passport?'

'Listen, unless you plan to arrest me, I have a flight to catch.'

'Draco Papadopoulos, I am arresting you on suspicion of—'

'Stop,' Papadopoulos barked, before softening his tone. 'Listen, there must be some kind of arrangement we can come to. Hmm?'

Ray raised his eyebrows at the border guard, whose expression remained fixed on the two of them.

The bookie's eyes were twinkling. 'What if you were to let me go, and then I was to send a gift your way? To both of you I mean. All you have to do is look the other way and you can earn yourselves a small nest egg for the future, or even a holiday of your own.' He leaned closer to Ray. 'What do you say?'

Ray didn't respond, instead snapping a cuff on the shorter man's wrist. As they made their way back through a discreet security-controlled side door and out to the waiting transport van, Ray couldn't help noticing the man in the shiny black Mercedes observing their every move.

'How long have you been in the bookmaking business?' Ray asked, as the elevator doors opened, and he found himself face-to-face with Gianni Demetrios for the second time in a week. 'I mean, that is why you've had your man sniffing around the heist, right? You're Papadopoulos's silent partner? At first I thought you might be involved, somehow, but it seemed too small-time for you.'

Demetrios grinned from ear-to-ear, leaning against the door. 'Can I fix you a drink?'

Ray exited the elevator and followed him through to the secluded office. 'It's a bit early.'

Demetrios moved across to the drinks trolley and poured himself a Scotch. 'I haven't been to bed yet, so this is late to me.'

'You said you wanted to see me about something?' Ray said, keen to get back to the station as quickly as possible. 'I don't take kindly to being summoned.'

'Please, take a seat.'

'I'll remain on my feet if it's all the same to you. Last time I was in here, a picture of us together wound up on my boss's desk.'

'And you think I sent it?'

'Honestly, I don't know.'

'Yet you still returned.'

'Full disclosure: my boss knows that I'm here, so if your plan is to fabricate something, in order to blackmail me, then—'

Demetrios snorted. 'Blackmail? You think that's my game?'

Ray bit his tongue. 'Nothing would surprise me with you. What do you want?'

'Papadopoulos stole from me; I'd like to know if he was acting alone.'

'I can't tell you anything about an open investigation.'

'It was *my* money he stole.'

'And when the investigation is concluded, we will update you. In the meantime—'

'She phoned me, you know? That woman who works in the office. Delilah, is it? She knew he was planning something and she tipped me off after he'd done it.'

'That's why you had your man intimidating her at her flat?'

'"Intimidation"? Reassurance more like. I wanted her to know that we would take care of her. I reward loyalty in my organization. She was terrified Papadopoulos would find out and come after her, so I told her to go along with his plan, and that we would take care of him. She's pregnant with his kid, but there's no love there. We'll look after her now.'

Ray couldn't determine if Delilah would be better off or not. 'He's in custody now, and all things being equal will be charged before the end of the day.'

Demetrios sipped his drink. 'Lucky for him that you got there first then. He'd be in the ground now otherwise.'

'Is there anything else?' Ray asked, looking at his watch.

'I wanted to thank you for bringing a guilty man to justice. I take it my funds will be returned after the case is concluded?'

'It might take a little longer, as we believe the funds may have already been laundered. Our Fraud Team will be in touch about that.'

Demetrios narrowed his eyes. 'I'm very impressed with the speed at which you have handled all this. I've had my eye on you for some time, and despite our differences the other night, I think you have a bright future.' He paused. 'I would like to offer you a permanent membership here, at my casino, free of charge by way of showing you my gratitude.'

Ray waved his hand. 'No thanks.'

'No strings attached, DS Granger. I told you I like to reward loyalty in my organization.'

'Well, I'm not part of your organization.'

'It doesn't have to be that way. The cost of information is always on the rise. You wouldn't be the first to take a retainer – untraceable, you understand.'

'Why do I have to keep telling people that I'm not bent?' He sighed. 'I appreciate your offer, but I don't want to muddy my view.'

'I understand. Perhaps there is something else I can assist you with.'

Ray turned on his heel. 'I'd best be off.'

'Your daughter, for example,' Demetrios called out.

Ray froze.

'A source tells me that you need Jack Whitchurch taken care of. Say the word and it will be done.'

Ray slowly turned back to face him. 'What do you know about that?'

'Only what I was told.'

It didn't surprise Ray that there could be leaks in the department. 'Who spoke to you?'

'One of my paid friends. See, I told you information had a value. You want me to have Whitchurch dealt with?'

'You'd do that? Just like that?'

'One less paedophile on this planet would be good for everyone, no?'

Ray thought back to what Alex had said last night: *it wouldn't have to be us who killed him.*

'Say yes and my debt to you will be repaid,' Demetrios continued swishing the drink around his glass.

Ray knew he could never accept such an offer, but he'd be lying if he said he didn't consider it for a split second. 'I don't want you to kill anyone for me. Let's be clear about that.'

Demetrios lowered his glass and moved across, his voice little more than a whisper. 'From what I understand, if he's still breathing by the end of today, your little girl won't be. What means more to you: your principles, or her life?'

53

Looking out the window at the three-storey block of flats, Alex reread the note she'd found in the delivered package. 'Are you sure this is the right place?' she asked the minicab driver, who had already demonstrated English was not his first language.

The accommodation certainly wasn't what she'd pictured, and just as she was doubting whether Carol-Anne's abductor had made a huge mistake, a police car pulled up outside the flats. Alex instantly lay back on the seat, panicked that one of the uniformed officers might recognize her or demand to know what she was doing at the address. And if they looked in her handbag and found the gun …

The taxi driver had turned in his seat and was giving her a confused look. She forced a smile, hoping to offer some kind of reassurance, praying he didn't turf her out or draw unwanted attention to their arrival.

'You pay now?' he asked, unable to keep the concern from his voice.

'Yes, yes,' Alex whispered, doing her best to reach into her bag and find her purse without looking, worried about inadvertently firing the gun. Clasping the purse, she pulled it out, removing a £20 note. 'Can I stay here for a bit, please?'

The driver eyed the money and the metre before nodding. 'Okay.'

Alex took a deep breath and counted to five before slowly sitting back up, keeping her head as low as possible, and peeking out over the bottom edge of the window. The two officers were now out of the car. One was holding the rear passenger door open, while the other helped the old man emerge from the vehicle. From this distance it was impossible to tell whether it was definitely Jack Whitchurch, but the ivory-coloured hair was a giveaway.

She hadn't expected him to look so frail, and she had to fight the urge to feel any kind of sympathy for him, forcing herself to remember all the news stories she'd read detailing his crimes against children. She continued to watch as the two officers escorted him in to the building.

This wasn't any good. How could she get close to him if he had a police escort with him for the rest of the day? She still wasn't convinced she'd be able to squeeze the trigger when the time was right, but she knew she would definitely never be able to kill two innocents as well. Fishing into her purse, she found another £20 note and passed it to the driver.

The confusion remained strained on his face, as he accepted the money.

The three men were now inside, and from where Alex was hunched it was impossible to see inside. The address card hadn't mentioned that it was a small block of flats. She had no way of knowing which floor he lived on, let alone which flat number was his. The thought of going door-to-door, growing a list of witnesses who would be able to describe her and confirm her presence there, just wasn't practicable.

There was no other choice: she would have to get a closer look.

With another deep breath, she carefully prised the door open and slipped her legs out.

'Wait for me, please' she pleaded at the taxi driver, hoping he wouldn't take off the moment she'd closed the door.

The breeze felt cool against her face. Now she was out in the open, any casual observer in the houses lining both sides of the road could also see her. It had been a terrible idea to come out in broad daylight. But waiting for darkness brought a greater threat to Carol-Anne's life. Darting across the road so she was now on the same side as the flats, she tried to act as casually as she could, welcoming the slight cover of a line of trees that led from the large patch of grass to the side of the first of the small blocks.

The flats were protected by a weathered picket fence, too high to climb over, but a hinged gate allowed access to the inner perimeter. There were four blocks in total, at perpendicular angles to one another, obviously some architect's idea of giving the formerly council-owned buildings some kind of artistic feel. The brickwork looked cold and uninviting, and as she approached Alex wondered how many of the residents realized exactly who their new neighbour was. And in fact, how many of the neighbours bore similar criminal histories. For all she knew, she was in the presence of some of the country's most vicious former convicts.

She didn't have time to worry about that now.

The gate creaked as she opened it. As she stared at the four entranceways, it wasn't obvious which of the front doors the three men had entered. Glancing back over her shoulder, she was relieved to see the taxi still parked, and as she calculated the angles, she headed for the only door visible from the cab.

Three small glass panels in the uPVC door gave an obscured view of the inner corridor, where there was no sign of the three men. A staircase to the right led upstairs. Without gaining entrance into the building, she would have no way of determining where they were. Taking a step backwards, she stared up to the top row of windows, looking for any movement or change in shadow that would indicate where they were, but there was nothing.

The panel next to the door showed twelve flat numbers and buzzers, but none of the flats showed the resident's name. Twelve meant there would be four flats per floor, and if he was in one of the flats towards the rear of the building, she wouldn't see any movement this side. A pathway off to the right led around the back of the building, and as she followed it, she was surprised to see a freshly dug flowerbed and neatly mowed lawn space. Clearly one of the residents was green-fingered.

Alex's efforts to see into any of the flats were spoiled by the angle of the sun behind the heavy cloud pattern. Every passing second felt like a step further from Carol-Anne, and the tension in her hands was causing her to ball her fists and dig her nails into her palms for any kind of relief.

'Are you all right, luv?' a male voice called out over her shoulder.

Turning, Alex's eyes widened as she came face-to-face with one of the police officers now standing outside the block.

'You look lost,' the officer commented, giving her a curious look.

A single bead of sweat ran down the length of Alex's spine; her heart was thumping so loud in her chest it was all she could hear.

The officer took a step closer. 'Are you all right, luv?' he asked again.

Alex willed herself to say something – *anything* – to explain why she was skulking in the vicinity of a man whose life was being threatened.

The officer took a second step closer, the confusion on his face descending into concern.

Alex reached into her handbag, feeling the cool frame of the gun pressing against her fingers.

She could run, but he could give chase and would undoubtedly catch up with her.

She could pull out the gun and threaten him, but that wouldn't get Carol-Anne back.

Willing the ground to open up and swallow her whole, Alex's mind suddenly fired to life. 'I've lost my dog,' she blurted. 'Have you seen him?'

The officer's attention was suddenly diverted, as he looked left and right. 'What sort of dog is he?'

'A Yorkshire Terrier,' she said: the first breed that had come to mind.

'Where was he when you last saw him?'

'He was running near those trees,' she said, indicating towards the treeline which had provided her with cover moments earlier. 'One minute he was there, and the next, gone.'

'What's his name?'

Alex's mind blanked again as she strived to think of any dog's name. 'Jock.'

'Are you local to the area? Is it possible he might have run home?'

'Um … no, well not that local.'

'Okay, well, while searching for dogs isn't really part of our role, I can help you look for a few minutes until my colleague returns.' As he said the words, the second officer reappeared at the door. 'This lady's lost her dog,' the first explained.

'And?' the second officer commented, with an uninterested grunt.

The first officer turned back to Alex. 'I'm sure he'll find you when he realizes you're not there. The best thing I can suggest is you keep looking for now, and if you still don't have any luck, ring around the local vets and find out if anyone has reported him. Is he chipped?'

Alex frowned at the question.

'Does he have a microchip in his neck?' the officer clarified.

'Um, yes,' Alex said quickly, uncertain how long she could sustain the lie.

'We have to go,' the second officer said, heading back towards their car.

The first officer offered an apologetic nod at Alex. 'I'm sure he'll surface. I'm sorry.' And with that he joined his colleague in the car.

Alex waited until they'd pulled away before making her way back to the waiting taxi. Her heart was still racing, though there was a sense of relief starting to settle her nerves.

'You want to go somewhere else?' the taxi driver asked, as she leaned against the car.

She was about to answer when she spotted Whitchurch exit the flats, walk to the end of the path and look both ways, before opening the gate and making his way along the pavement in the opposite direction to her. And for a man who had struggled to get out of the police car, he was moving briskly.

Alex didn't answer the taxi driver, pulling up her shirt collar and setting off in pursuit.

54

'Where the hell have you been?' Trent shouted from the Incident Room, as Ray made his way along the corridor.

Ray ducked in, not wanting to shout his business to the whole room. 'You know where I was,' he whispered.

'Demetrios confirmed he's the silent partner?'

Ray nodded.

'Did he say anything else?'

'Nothing that will aid our investigation,' Ray replied curtly.

'And did Jodie Crichton go with you?'

Ray frowned. 'No, ma'am, I figured she'd be here interviewing Papadopoulos.'

Trent's face remained emotionless, which was a sign she was keeping something from him. 'How is Alex holding up?'

'She's terrified we're never going to see Carol-Anne again. Tell me you've found something.'

She stared at him for a long moment, as if trying to determine whether or not to say anymore. 'Maybe.' She headed to the back of the room, ushering with her head for him to follow. 'I've had Owen trawling the case notes of the original investigation into Whitchurch, on the theory that the person behind all this is one of his former victims.'

289

'And?'

Trent raised her eyebrows at Owen. 'Tell him.'

Owen sat up in his chair, the desk in front of him covered in pages, while three boxes of files stood at the side of his desk. 'We know that Whitchurch was convicted on three counts of indecent activity with minors, but those three weren't the only ones to make statements to the police. Bear in mind, we're going back fourteen years in investigative terms, and techniques and procedures have improved since then. In total, statements were taken from eight victims. Because their allegations weren't taken forward by the CPS, references to those statements have been largely redacted, which isn't a great deal of help to us. However, what I also found were the notes of the SIO from the time, which did name – first name only – the witnesses, and included the reasons why the CPS didn't deem those cases strong enough to pursue.'

Ray perched on a nearby desk, wishing Owen would hurry up and get to the point, not willing to interrupt his flow.

'When Whitchurch was arrested and his computer seized, the technicians managed to find images of the three victims they successfully prosecuted for. That was what helped push those charges over the line, according to the SIO's notes. We've made contact with those three victims – each of whom is living under a new name outside of the county – and there is nothing to suggest they have anything to do with this. They all have cast-iron alibis for the time of the abduction, and lack the motive to exact revenge in this way.'

'How can you be certain they lack the motive?' Ray questioned. 'They were his victims: it's human nature to want to seek revenge against a bully and abuser like that.'

'I appreciate that, sarge, but they saw justice. I've spoken to each of them, and I just don't see it. However, one of the victims from the unsuccessful prosecutions? I find that much easier to believe.'

'We don't know who they are.'

'We have first names,' Owen corrected. 'And one jumped off the page at me.'

'Who?' Ray encouraged, narrowing his eyes.

'One of the first victims to come forward was a ten-year-old who was already known to the authorities. She'd been served an ASBO, and was described as a bit of a tearaway. Her mother had died about a year before, and her dad drank heavily. Anyway, she was caught shoplifting, and when she was brought in for questioning, that's when she made the allegation against Whitchurch. She couldn't name him, but gave an adequate description and was able to confirm his address. Obviously the interviewing officers had to take the allegation seriously and brought Whitchurch in for questioning. He denied the allegation, and was released on police bail while further enquiries were made.

'While he was out, the girl's father died in a hit-and-run. There was no reason to believe the two incidents were connected, and she was taken in by social care, disappearing off the radar as far as this case was concerned. Her father's death took a toll on her, and as the case grew against Whitchurch she withdrew her complaint.'

'Who is she? What's her name?'

Owen rifled through the papers on his desk before locating what he was searching for and handing it to Ray.

'A DNA report? I don't understand.'

'The girl's father's death was unsolved. It was assumed that the hit-and-run was as a result of joyriders, and nobody was ever brought to trial for his death. Turns out his DNA was still on file, and when we ran it, there was a hit. A sample of familial DNA – his child's – was just pulled from the back of your wife's car.'

'You're saying this girl – this *woman* – has been in Alex's car?'

'Only one sample was found: a single hair in one of the hinges in the child seat; it is a positive match to the profile we have,'

Owen concluded. 'It doesn't necessarily mean that this woman took your daughter; however, unless you know who she is and can think of a reason a single strand of her hair would be anywhere near your daughter's car seat, I think it requires further investigation.'

'Who is she? What's her name? How do we find her? Can we speak to the original SIO and see if he remembers her surname?'

'He's dead,' Owen said with regret. 'We reached out to other members of the team, and while two of them could vaguely remember what she looked like, nobody could recall a surname.'

'What about social services? They must be able to tell you what happened to her; where she went, where she might be now.'

'We've asked the questions, and we're waiting for a response,' Trent confirmed.

'And this DNA match: any other hits in the system? Has she broken the law since she made the allegation?'

Both shook their heads grimly.

'Why does it feel like we're putting all our eggs in one basket?' Ray asked.

'Because we're running out of time, and we have nothing else we can use. CCTV was a bust; all the IT guys can tell us is that whoever is behind this is using a VPN to mask their IP address, and our enquiries on the street have turned up zilch. Whitchurch is refusing to comply with our offer of protection, so unless the abductor comes out into the light, we have no way of tracking him or her.'

Ray fixed Owen with a look. 'What made this kid jump off the page to you? You said something caught your eye, which you initially dismissed.'

Owen passed him another sheet of paper. 'These are the SIO's notes I mentioned. The second name on the list. It's Simone. I just thought it was a bit of a coincidence, what with the *Simon Says* messages.'

'What would this Simone have against me or Alex?'

Owen could only shrug.

'That's why we're sharing this with you, Ray,' Trent replied. 'Do you know anyone called Simone?'

'No.'

'Well, the girl was ten when she made the allegation, which would make her twenty-four now … she might have changed her name and appearance. Is there anyone around that age that you know who might have an axe to grind?'

'No, I can't. I …' His words trailed off as his mind began to whir into action: a woman aged twenty-four, whose father had died when she was younger, and someone who would understand the complexities of an investigation like this.

'What is it, Ray?' Trent asked as she watched Ray's eyes glaze over.

There was only one person's face that appeared in his mind, but surely she wouldn't risk everything over something so manipulative and horrific. Would she?

Ray reached for the phone and punched in a number. It went straight to answerphone. 'Owen, I need you to trace a mobile number for me. I need to know where it was last broadcasting from.' Ray scribbled the number and handed it over, reaching for the phone again.

'Talk to me, Ray,' Trent demanded. 'Who are you calling?'

'Alex. I think she's in serious danger.'

55

At the end of the road, Whitchurch turned sharply, disappearing into yet another line of trees. Sensing he may suspect he was being tailed, Alex upped her own pace, relieved to find a public footpath cut between the trees. Whitchurch was fifty or so yards along it, and he was turning to look back. Alex quickly dove out of the line of sight, her heart galloping.

For a man who had given the impression he was near death when exiting the police car, he was disproving the theory with every step he took. It had already been tough for Alex's fast walking pace to keep up; she had practically jogged to get to the footpath.

Where was he going? It was too coincidental that he had happened to come out of his building immediately after the police car had pulled away, which had to mean he'd been watching and waiting for them to go. Had he seen the officers' exchange with Alex? Had he seen and recognized her? Was that why he was checking back to see if she was following?

It had been thirty seconds since she'd jumped out of the way. Would that be long enough for him to gain confidence that he was alone? Alex was unfamiliar with this town, and she feared losing sight of him would mean losing him altogether.

Taking a deep breath, she peeled back onto the footpath just in time to see Whitchurch turn left at the end of it. Clutching her bag at her side, Alex burst into a sprint, quickly eating up the distance between them, and stopped herself at the end before casually strolling out and looking to the left. He was ten yards ahead, at the start of a small run of shops: a barber's, a newsagents and a bank. There was only one other person on the street – a vicar by the look of him – across the road, and busy chatting on his phone as he walked. If Alex continued her pursuit, she would be exposed. Two glances back and he would spot she was following him.

Quickly crossing the road, she hurried up to the vicar, waving him down. He had to be a good foot taller than her, with a barrel-like chest: clearly a man who enjoyed his food and drink. His receding hair was copper-coloured, and a cut on his chin suggested he'd not long since shaved. He couldn't keep the look of frustration from his brow as he lowered the phone and pressed it to his purple shirt.

Ducking behind his substantial frame, Alex kept one eye on Whitchurch over the vicar's shoulder.

'Can I help you with something?' the vicar asked.

Alex's mind raced for an excuse for interrupting him. 'Church,' she blurted. 'I'm looking for a church. Is there one nearby?'

'What denomination are you? Anglican? Catholic? Lutheran?'

'C of E,' she said without thinking.

'Ah, I'm the reverend at St Edmund's. I'm on my way there now if you wish to accompany me. Are you looking for confession?'

Her head snapped up and she looked at him. Could he somehow read her mind? Did he know what she was planning? 'Confession?'

'We open for Reconciliations at 10 a.m., I assume that's why you were looking to attend church?'

Alex looked away, grinding her teeth. Whitchurch had now

crossed onto the same side of the road as them, still heading away. He'd looked back at the footpath once and there was no way he could have seen her talking to the vicar.

'You're not from around here, are you?' the vicar asked.

Patting his arm, Alex offered a smile. 'You've no idea. Thanks for your time,' and then she moved off in the direction of Whitchurch, leaving the vicar flabbergasted by the whole encounter.

Alex didn't look back or make any attempt to explain her actions. Whitchurch was now thirty yards ahead, but the road was windy, so she would be able to take cover as they went. A brown sign on a lamppost indicated they were heading into the town centre, and a further sign indicated a car park with a hundred spaces was a few minutes away.

He had to be meeting someone: that was why he was acting so surreptitiously, and why he'd dropped the decrepit old man act as soon as the police had departed. But who, why and where? Was it something to do with Carol-Anne's abduction? Had he been behind the whole thing after all?

Alex's mind raced with conspiracy theory after conspiracy theory, none of which rang true in her head. Wherever he was headed though, at least he was currently alone.

At the next bend, Alex's heart skipped, as she realized Whitchurch was no longer ahead of her. Had he ducked into one of the houses along the road? If he had, she'd have no chance of finding out which one, without going door-to-door. He was her only link to Carol-Anne and now she had lost him.

She stopped, trying to calm the growing ache in her heart, looking around for any sign as to where he might have gone. There was a side road across the street, but no sign of him on either pavement there. Left with two choices – carry on, or retrace her steps back to his flat – she opted for the former and ploughed onwards. As she did, she spotted a second footpath, which had been invisible to the naked eye earlier. That had to be where he'd gone.

Turning onto it, she raced along the path. At the end, it opened onto a much more open space, with pavement at forty-five degree angles to the left and right, and directly in front of her there was a building site of some sort. Tall wooden fences enclosed the large space, with a wire gate off to one side, and it was here she spotted Whitchurch, slipping through the gap between the gates. He was alone, with no business being on a building site. There was nobody else in sight, and there was no sound of machinery being operated inside either.

Darting across the road, Alex looked through the wire gate and into the site, seeing a small two-level multistorey car park inside. Despite the secured perimeter this had to be the car park that had been signposted earlier. It was out of use and destined for demolition, according to the site plan on the fence nearest to her. The developer had acquired the land and planned to build a luxury apartment building.

Alex didn't like the nervous anxiety flooding her body. If Whitchurch was an innocent party in this whole mess, he was acting very suspiciously. The logical step would be to phone Trent and explain what was going on; however, to do so would be to admit that she'd been sent his address and had followed him from there. Even if Alex professed she had no intention of doing harm to Whitchurch, it would be a hard sell to Trent.

Against her better judgement, and chiding her own curiosity, Alex pulled on the gates and ducked beneath the chain and padlock as Whitchurch had done moments earlier, heading inside. She'd seen him enter the car park via the car ramp, and as she did the same, she desperately tried to listen for any sound to indicate where he was and why he'd come here.

The ground level was clear, with only a smattering of litter where the wind had blown it in. Quickening her pace, she headed along the up ramp to the second level, and that's when she spotted him, at the far side, looking out at the church in the distance. He must have sensed her movement behind him, as he turned and stared at her. There was no alarm or concern in his eyes. It was as if he'd been expecting her.

With no other choice, Alex moved forward, reaching into her bag for the secure feeling of the gun between her fingers. 'Jack Whitchurch?'

'Aye, that's me, luv,' he said passively. 'I know why you're here.'

Alex frowned with surprise. Had the abductor told him she was coming? That didn't make sense. 'You do?'

'You want me dead. I understand that ... after everything I've done, I suppose it's what I deserve.'

Simon had to have told him. Either that or he was acting on the police warning that his life was in danger, and he'd connected the dots. Either way: he'd anticipated her, and that's why he'd come to somewhere so deserted. Did he want to die?

'You know who I am?' Alex asked, her voice straining.

'Aye, I know who you are. And you should know that I'm sorry for what I did.'

He turned suddenly, and Alex's instinct kicked in: dropping the handbag, she held the weapon in her hand and brought it up to arm's length.

Whitchurch took an unsteady step back, his hands apart. 'Whoa, whoa, whoa, I didn't mean to startle you. Please, I want you to hear me out first.'

'Just shut up,' Alex said, as her vision blurred with tears. 'I don't want to hear anything you have to say.'

'I know my apology will mean nothing to you—'

'Shut up!' Alex yelled, gripping the gun tighter, her finger hovering near the trigger guard.

'Not until you let me explain,' he growled back. 'I never meant to hurt you. The things I did, the things I said, it wasn't right, but I was ill – *am* ill. This ... *thing* inside me, it's a sickness, a curse. I couldn't stop myself. It was almost as if someone was pulling my strings.'

The thought of him interfering with Carol-Anne made her stomach turn. 'Just shut up!'

'If I could go back to that time and stop myself, I would. In prison I had so long to contemplate what I've done in my life, and I am ashamed of the person I became. I'm sorry if I hurt you, Simone. You've got the right to kill me, and I'll—'

'Wait,' Alex interrupted. 'What did you call me?'

'That's your name, isn't it? Simone?'

Alex's arm lowered a fraction. 'I don't know anyone by that name. Who exactly do you think I am?'

'You're the woman who called and told me to meet you here.' For the first time there was concern in his eyes. 'You said you wanted to talk about what I'd done to you all those years ago … are you *not* Simone?'

Alex couldn't get the thoughts straight in her head. He thought she was one of his victims, someone who had contacted him and told him to meet her here. It couldn't be coincidence, could it?

A whirring noise snapped her back to reality. From the floor, her mobile phone was vibrating and glowing inside the handbag. Keeping the gun trained on Whitchurch, Alex bent low and scooped it up. Unlocking the screen with her thumb, she gasped as Carol-Anne's face filled the screen. It was a live video call, and there was her daughter, strapped into a child seat, smiling as she recognized her mother's face on the alternate phone screen.

A voice boomed through the phone's speaker, '*Simon Says: kill him now, or say ciao.*'

'Who's that? Who's on the phone?' Whitchurch demanded, rushing towards Alex.

Before she could stop herself, the shot rang out, the sound echoing off the low ceiling.

56

The adrenaline coursed through every sinew in Ray's body as he hammered the accelerator, rarely releasing it for bends and traffic lights.

'Jesus Christ, Ray!' Owen bellowed as he gripped the safety handle above his head.

'Where's the mobile signal now?' Ray barked, without taking his eyes off the road ahead.

'It's come to a stop, not far from the centre of Salisbury. Should I try and phone it?'

'God, no! We don't want to tip her off. Try Alex's phone again.'

Owen punched in the number and held it to his ear. 'It's gone straight to answerphone. Either she's on a call, or she's switched it off.'

Ray had never known Alex turn off her phone. It was permanently on, even at night because – in her words – you never knew when bad news would come.

'And her phone is in the same area?' Ray questioned.

'According to the cell phone tower. The two phones are practically on top of one another.'

Ray crossed lanes to overtake a camper van, only just managing to get back over before an oncoming car collided with them.

'I know you're worried about Alex,' Owen warned, 'but we need to get there in one piece.'

Ray's mind was no longer on his own safety. Something hadn't felt right since Tuesday. At first he'd put it down to his personal conflicting emotions about Alex's part in Carol-Anne's abduction. Now things were starting to make more sense. She'd pretended to show little interest in the return of his daughter. She'd asked how Alex and he were coping, but never anything specific about Carol-Anne. He'd put it down to her immaturity – not under-standing the extent of the parental bond – and now he could see it had just been a smokescreen to keep him from connecting the dots sooner. He didn't want to believe that Jodie and Simone could be one and the same person, but there were too many clues to ignore. And if she was indeed one of Whitchurch's victims, and had been biding her time to get revenge, then there was no knowing what lengths she would go to in order to get her revenge.

Someone who understood the inner workings of an investiga-tion, someone smart enough to know how to mask her IP address and send messages. Someone who would manipulate it so Ray would join her on a separate investigation, giving her insight into how he and Alex were coping.

Would Jodie really be able to kill Carol-Anne if Alex didn't go through with the demands? That was the only part of the puzzle that didn't fit in his mind. Even if Jodie's personality had become warped by what Whitchurch had done to her as a child, he couldn't see her capable of taking another person's life, let alone that of an innocent child. Then, an hour ago, he never would have pegged her as capable of abducting Carol-Anne and threatening him and Alex.

That brought him to the question he'd been avoiding asking since they'd tumbled out of the station and into the car: what was Alex doing in Salisbury? She wasn't familiar with the city as far as he knew, and without a car and with everything else going on, it wasn't like she would go there for retail therapy. There was only one reason he could think of, and as he overtook a second vehicle, he dared himself to ask Owen.

'Whitchurch was moved to Salisbury, wasn't he?'

Owen's wide-eyed stare answered the question for him. 'I can't tell—'

'Cut the crap, Owen! There's no other reason why Alex *and* Jodie would both be there right now. He's there, isn't he?'

Owen sighed in frustration. 'Yes, he is. There's only a handful of people who know that. Okay? Even when it was mentioned in the team brief the other day, we insinuated he was still in Hampshire, when in fact we'd moved him to Wiltshire. His location and new identity have been top secret.'

'And you haven't discussed it with Jodie Crichton at any point?'

'No, I swear to you. I know, and DI Trent knows, and then just a couple of uniforms.'

'Well if her phone is there, it's a reasonable assumption that she found out somehow.'

He thought back to the conversation he'd had with her earlier that morning. She'd called in a blind panic to say Papadopoulos was on his way to the airport, and hadn't wanted to admit why she wasn't at his flat, or why she couldn't tail him to the airport. She'd never made it back to the station, so he hadn't been able to question her about it after the arrest. It wasn't her scheduled day off, and she hadn't called in sick, so what the hell was she now doing in Salisbury, almost next to his wife?

'Two minutes out,' Owen jabbered into his radio, as Trent demanded an update.

'Earlier this morning, Alex sent me that message about the FLO and her son,' Ray questioned. 'Did you follow up on it?'

'I was, but then Trent told me to drop everything and focus on Whitchurch's victims. Trent said she would handle it directly.'

Ray pulled across the road to overtake a caravan. He hated what he had become, and there was no forgiveness he could seek for any of his extramarital wanderings. Alex deserved better. Carol-Anne deserved better. And in that moment he made a vow to the God he didn't believe in: if they both came back safe and alive, he would do whatever was expected of him. He would be a better father, and if Alex would still have him he would spend the rest of his life making it up to her.

'Right, slow down,' Owen ordered. 'It should be just around this bend ...'

Ray dragged the car around the corner, releasing his foot from the accelerator, not touching the brake. Up ahead a two-storey car park – surrounded by tall wooden fences – the roof of which could still just be seen.

'This can't be it,' Ray said with a confused tone.

'These are the coordinates,' Owen confirmed. 'Maybe they're around the rear of the site. Looks like some kind of development is planned.'

Ray continued around the next corner where there was still no sign of Jodie or Alex. Then as they turned to the third side of the square site, he spotted two cars parked at the side of the road, and beside one of them was a familiar face. Flooring the accelerator, he skidded the car as close to the front of the vehicle as he could manage without hitting it, and was out of his seat a second later. As he approached the stationary vehicle, and saw a shocked-looking Jodie beside it, he froze as his eyes fell on the precious child giggling to herself inside.

Ray dropped to his knees as his legs gave way. Pinching himself in case it was the cruellest of dreams, it took him a moment to regain his composure.

Owen helped him to his feet.

'Thank God you two are here,' Jodie began, 'I was just about to call it in.'

Ray looked from his daughter to the woman he'd once considered a friend. 'What are you doing here, Jodie? What are you doing with that phone?'

'I was tailing someone when I came across this little girl in the car. I was just about to call when you appeared.'

Ray pushed past her, opening the door, terrified that the mirage of his daughter would disappear when he reached for her, but her eyes lit up as they met his and she uttered the words he'd been longing to hear.

'Da-da, da-da.'

His fingers trembled as they fiddled with the belt around her middle, and he silently cursed as his sweaty fingertips failed to unfasten the clasp. Finally it came apart, and he pulled her out, breathing in her scent, unable to believe he was holding her again. He held her close, and in that split second the world around them dissolved and it was just the two of them lost in the magic of unbreakable love.

'Listen guys,' Jodie interrupted, 'I heard a gunshot a few seconds ago. And I think it came from inside. We need to get in there.'

Ray kept his eyes closed, determined to save the memory of the moment for the long-term.

'Did you hear what I said?' Jodie repeated. 'There was a gunshot from inside the site. We need to go and investigate.'

Owen looked from her to Ray. 'Sarge?'

Ray finally opened his eyes, checking that Carol-Anne was still in his arms, taking the opportunity to kiss the top of her head as his eyes watered. Then, taking a deep breath, he turned his attention back to Jodie, unsure what to say to her, angry that she was continuing to keep the pretence up, even though they'd caught her red-handed.

'Call it in to Trent,' he said to Owen, his eyes never leaving Jodie's. 'Tell her my daughter is safe, and we've apprehended Simone.'

57

'Carol-Anne! Carol-Anne!' Alex yelled at the screen as it shook in her hands. 'Give me back my daughter!'

The call had been ended. The picture of Carol-Anne was gone, and with it the connection to *Simon*. Five yards away, Jack Whitchurch wailed in agony, a puddle of crimson spreading from where he lay. Alex looked down at the gun, lying on the floor where she'd discarded it, her mind racing to understand what had just happened.

She hadn't meant to squeeze the trigger. In fact, she couldn't even be sure her finger had been within the trigger guard, yet she had felt the recoil as it had fired, and the explosive sound which had reverberated off the low ceiling. She had dropped the weapon instinctively, desperate to make sure it didn't fire a second time. What was supposed to happen now? She'd shot Whitchurch – even if she hadn't intended to – and with the line dead, *Simon* was gone. Shouldn't he be calling back to confirm where she could find Carol-Anne? That had been the deal, but had it been his plan all along to deceive her?

Whitchurch cried out again.

Alex had shot him, and if he died it would be at her hands. She couldn't allow that to happen. Even if Carol-Anne was close by, she couldn't turn her back on the wounded man right in front of her. It wasn't in her nature to be so cruel.

Pressing her hands into the cold concrete floor, Alex forced herself upwards, willing her legs to move closer to him, her eyes darting in all directions as her mind still refused to process the situation.

He was on his back, facing towards her, and the puddle of blood was emanating from the side closest to her. The bottom half of his sky-blue shirt was stained with blood, and the stain was spreading further up his shirt as the material acted like blotting paper. His hands dripped with blood too where he had attempted to somehow stem the blood. Without proper treatment he wouldn't last long. Alex knew little about first aid. She could put someone in the recovery position but that wouldn't help him now.

Stumbling closer, she dropped to her knees, away from the blood, and scoured her memory for anything that would prove useful. If she'd struck him in the arm or leg, she would use her scarf to make a ligature and stem the blood. A shot to the abdomen wouldn't be as straightforward.

'Ambulance,' Whitchurch muttered, his lips dry, his cheeks paling by the second.

'Yes, of course,' Alex replied, scrambling to unlock her phone and call the emergency services. The phone fell from her hands as she struggled to control her trembling fingers. Sliding the scarf from her neck, she dared to press it where she assumed the wound was below his shirt, and he winced as she pressed harder.

'We need to stop you bleeding,' she tried to pacify him.

'I can't believe you shot me,' he mumbled in disbelief.

'I know, I know, and I'm sorry. I'm so sorry, I didn't mean to do it. Don't worry, it's all going to be okay. I'll call an ambulance and they'll save you. Okay?'

Alex wasn't convinced by her tone and doubted Whitchurch was either. Moving his hand so it held the scarf in position, she unlocked the phone and dialled 999.

'Hang up the phone,' a familiar voice called from over her shoulder.

Alex instantly tensed, but she held onto the phone.

'I said: hang up the phone,' the voice repeated, as footsteps approached.

Alex dared herself to turn and look, confusion taking hold as her eyes met Sophie's. 'What are you …? Never mind. You changed your mind and decided to help me. He's been shot. We need to get him to hospital …' Alex's words trailed off as her eyes fell upon the gun, no longer on the floor where she'd left it, now in Sophie's hands and pointing straight at them.

'Hang up the phone, Alex. You've done what was asked of you. Move away from him.'

The fog of confusion remained where it was, and it was only Whitchurch's groaning as he moved for a better look that snapped her back to reality.

'You!' he spluttered, his lips cracking.

Sophie turned her attention to him. 'You recognize me then? I wasn't sure you would after so long. I'm older now; my hair is a different colour and length. A small part of me suspected you would remember my eyes. That was always your thing, wasn't it, Jack? You liked to stare into the eyes of your victims while you satisfied yourself.'

Alex's mouth opened and closed, but no words would emerge.

'I didn't think you'd go through with it,' Sophie continued, her stare falling on Alex. 'That's why I had to come here myself. I underestimated you. Were you aiming for an artery?'

A warm tear ran down Alex's cheek as the truth became apparent.

'A slow and painful death,' Sophie added. 'It's no less than he deserves.'

'H-h-h-how? Why? I don't … You were the one behind all this? Where's Carol-Anne?'

307

'She's close by. If you're lucky you might get to see her once more before they arrest you.'

Alex's blood ran cold. 'You said you'd give her back to me.'

A sickening smile broke out across Sophie's face. 'It's out of my hands now. It seems unlikely that the police will give Carol-Anne back to someone who just shot and killed a man.'

Alex's gaze darted back to Whitchurch. He was still alive for now, but his breathing had become more laboured, and she had no idea how much longer he would survive untreated.

58

'Wait, this is *your* daughter?' Jodie asked, glancing back to the car Ray and Owen had arrived in.

Ray continued to hold Carol-Anne close to him. 'Save it. Okay? Spare us the rest of your bullshit, Jodie. We know about your plan for Whitchurch. The game is up. How do you think we managed to track you here?'

'Track me? I was following up on a lead.'

Ray shook his head dismissively at her. 'Don't lie to me! We tracked you here. You've been in Salisbury for at least half an hour, and I want to know why. I also want to know why you abandoned your post outside Papadopoulos's place this morning.'

'Can we talk alone?' she said, eyeing Owen guiltily.

'No, whatever you have to say can be said in front of Owen. He knows why you're here as well as I do.'

'Please, Ray,' she begged. 'It's for *your* sake.'

'It's fine,' Owen offered. 'I'll go and see what's going on up there.' And with that he jogged back around the corner, ducking under the loose security chain and into the building site.

Ray carried Carol-Anne back to the squad car. 'I'm listening,' he said impatiently, as Jodie joined him at the front of the vehicle.

'This isn't easy,' she began, 'and I know I should have said something to you sooner, but I wanted to be sure before I led everyone on a wild goose chase.'

'Spit it out, Jodie. I don't have time for your games. How is it you came to be standing next to a car where my missing daughter was strapped in?'

Jodie looked up at the sky. 'I was really pissed off with you for not coming to relieve me last night,' she began, avoiding eye contact. 'I stayed up all bloody night and you didn't even have the decency to phone me back. I was so angry, and then I saw Papadopoulos emerge from his house and jump in the back of a taxi. It was one of those firms that specializes in airport trips, so I was pretty sure I knew where he was going. That's why I phoned you and told you to get your arse there. The tyre on my car had burst and I didn't have a spare, so I had to wait for the breakdown truck to tow me to a garage in the middle of nowhere. They replaced the tyre, and I was about to head to your place to give you a bloody piece of my mind when I spotted someone I thought I recognized. I hadn't seen her for years, and as I approached her to say hello, she acted strangely. She looked terri-fied to see me, and when I offered to buy her a coffee so we could catch up she said she had to get to work. It was all very odd. Considering what she'd been through, I wasn't totally surprised.'

'What does any of this have to do with you being in Salisbury?'

'We were friends ... must be seven, eight years ago. It was right after my dad died. I met her at a support group for grieving teenagers. We were about the same age, and had both lost our fathers tragically. I guess we just hit it off. Then after a year, she just disappeared, moved out of her flat and left without a word. I hadn't heard from her since.

'Anyway, she said she was late for work, so I gave her my card and asked her to give me a call if she wanted to catch up. And then the funniest thing happened: I heard a child crying from inside the house. It was strange as she'd once told me she couldn't have children, so I wondered whether she'd adopted.

310

'I asked her if I could meet the child, and she said she didn't have the time, and would call me later. I returned to my car, and continued to watch as I saw her put the hooded child in the back seat and speed away. Her reaction to me was just so strange, and it spiked my interest. I decided to follow her, and this is where she ended up. I saw her get out of the car and take a phone call. She was chatting to the child in the back and then the next minute she took off, leaving the child there. Given everything that's happened with you over the last week, I panicked and rushed over to the car to check the girl was okay. I was waiting for her to return, and warn her of the dangers of leaving a child unattended. And then you two showed up.' She stared directly at him. 'I swear it's the truth, Ray!'

Ray blinked several times. 'This friend of yours, what's her name?'

Jodie fixed him with a defiant stare. 'Simone Moreau. Do you know her?'

Ray didn't answer, trying to determine whether her appearance here was an alarming coincidence or whether she was just stalling for time.

'I'm telling you what I saw, Ray. I have no reason to lie to you. Check my movements. Where was I prior to coming here? Check her phone signal. I'm not lying to you.'

59

Alex's head snapped back to Sophie, who was still training the gun on her. 'I thought we were supposed to be friends.'

Sophie scoffed. 'I tried to be, Alex, God knows I tried. You're not an easy person to get along with.'

Each word felt like a dagger to the heart, freezing Alex to the spot.

'A *real* friend wouldn't be so up her own arse. A real friend would take more interest in those around her, but not you. I remember when you moved to the street. I came around and welcomed you to the neighbourhood, brought you that bottle of wine. Do you remember what you did?'

Alex's mind was blank.

'You turned your nose up at it,' Sophie continued. 'I saw the way you looked at the brand and rolled your eyes, like it wasn't good enough that I'd bought it from the local supermarket. I didn't say anything. I let it go, put it down to you just having a bad day. Then when I'd see you in the street, I'd make an effort to come over and say hello. You'd start moaning about how much your body ached with the pregnancy, and how someone like me would never understand what you were going through. You should have heard yourself at times, Alex. At no point did you ever check whether I'd ever been pregnant. I was, you know.'

She waved the gun towards Whitchurch. 'With *his* offspring. I was only ten when he first assaulted me, and with my dad gone, I was on my own and forced to do anything to keep off the streets. And that's when he found me again. It was right before his trial, and I'd run away from the foster home they'd stuck me in. He promised me food and shelter, and then he attacked me. I was only eleven when I felt the most excruciating pain and knew that my baby had been taken from me. At the time I thought it was a blessing. What I didn't realize until years later is that the damage *he'd* caused was enough to stop me ever conceiving a child of my own again.'

Whitchurch had stopped groaning, a sure sign that he was slipping away. Alex couldn't handle the guilt of knowing what she'd caused, what she'd been manipulated into causing.

'So having to listen to your constant moaning about being blessed with such a precious gift was hard to stomach. Even as I tried to tell you how harsh you sounded, you never stopped to question why. And then Carol-Anne was born and I grew jealous of what you had: a good home, a loving husband and a beautiful baby girl. Did you ever appreciate any of that? I remember the day you first showed her to me and you made a passing comment about looking for a nanny for her so you could return to work. I remember thinking: what a bitch! Blessed with something so amazing yet so quick to want to give her away.'

'I wasn't like that,' Alex fired back, anger taking over from the fear and shock.

'Children grow up so quickly,' Sophie continued unabated. 'You'd be shocked if you could see how much Carol-Anne has changed in just the few days she's been with me. And despite your negative influence on her, she's untainted.'

'Where is my daughter?' Alex growled.

'I told you: nearby. I wasn't surprised when Ray went after

Noemi. That's what you did to him. So self-centred that you drove the man who loved you into the arms of another woman. I caught them at Christmas. He never saw me, but she did and came clean. She told me she'd fallen for him badly. I tried to tell you, as any good friend would, but you never seemed interested when I was dealing with my own issues.'

'What about your ex? We bailed you out financially when things went wrong.'

'Oh yeah,' Sophie snorted. 'And didn't you enjoy lording that over me? How you'd graciously dipped your hand in your pocket to give me a couple of grand.'

'No, I was happy to help. You're twisting everything. I never knew about your troubles, and you never told me.'

'And that's who you are,' Sophie snapped back. 'Even when you're blessed with a child as incredible as Carol-Anne you spend more of the day mourning the child you miscarried rather than celebrating the child who lived. I watched you offload her time and again as you turned your back on her and hunted for jobs. You know, for some women, being the best mother they can be is enough. But not you. You would rather pay someone to do your maternal duties and go to some dead-end job than take care of her. You don't deserve to be her mother.'

'You won't get away with this,' Alex said, as fresh salty tears fell.

'Oh darling,' Sophie cackled, 'I already have. You'll be arrested and charged with Jack's murder; Ray will realize how much he loves Noemi and leave you; and I will raise Carol-Anne far away from here and far from the ungrateful woman who bore her.'

'You're crazy,' Alex whispered.

Sophie just laughed louder. 'Jack isn't long for this world. Look at him: his eyes aren't even open anymore. He's lost too much blood, and given his age, it won't be long until he passes the point of no return. Your prints are on this gun, and at least half a dozen cameras will have picked up your arrival here. As for your phone signal, it puts you here at the time Whitchurch was shot. It's like a game of Cluedo: Alex Granger with the gun in the car park. You have motive, opportunity and method.'

'I'll tell the police all about your plan.'

'*My plan?*' Sophie scoffed. 'You don't have a clue how much planning went into this. Watching you day after day, leaving Carol-Anne unattended in the car on the driveway while you went backwards and forwards, bringing in shopping. I could have taken her on any number of occasions, but I had to wait for the police to release Jack.' Her gaze shifted back to the lifeless Whitchurch on the floor. 'Social services phoned all the victims to warm them of your imminent release. I heard about it from a friend, and then all I had to do was sit back and wait for them to collect you from the prison. They had no idea I was tailing them. I knew as soon as I saw you step out of the car that you'd strike again. Not me this time, but some other victim. And that's when I knew you had to die.'

Alex fought against the urge to vomit. 'How did you know where I'd be, or that I'd leave Carol-Anne in the car?'

Sophie's eyes returned to Alex. 'Because I know you better than you know yourself. I followed you all that day, waiting for the moment when you'd turn your back, and then you did it. And do you know the worst part of it? I actually felt sorry for you, running around that car park like a headless chicken. I knew then that you'd realized what a terrible mother you are. And you should have seen the look on your face when I played those sounds of Carol-Anne laughing in the bedroom. Just enough to push you over the edge. And now here we are.'

'The police searched your house on that first night. Where was she?'

'You think I'd be stupid enough to keep her next door? That money you gave me was part of a deposit on a second house. Close enough for me to come and go unnoticed, and you had no idea.'

The sound of a siren nearby distracted them both. It was all the time Alex needed. Diving forward she wrapped her outstretched hands around the gun's barrel and pulled it towards her. Sophie wasn't willing to release her grip so easily and pulled Alex into her, landing an elbow between Alex's shoulders. Alex yelped in pain, and drove her shoulder into Sophie's middle. The two women stumbled backwards, towards the wall.

'You're wasting your time, Alex,' Sophie grunted as they continued to pull on the gun, twirling and swatting at one another.

Alex wasn't prepared to give up on the one person who knew where her daughter was. And as they continued to spin, moving ever closer to the wall Whitchurch had been standing at earlier, Sophie drove her knee into Alex's gut and crashed the gun's butt into her face. Alex went crashing to the ground, but as Sophie stepped back in satisfaction, she lost her footing. No amount of arm flailing could stop her bottom from passing over the low wall, and she tumbled out into the open space, falling into the thin air beneath her.

60

They heard the woman's shrill scream before they caught the glimpse of her body plummeting through the sky. The sound of her landing on a parked vehicle around the corner was something that would stay with Ray for the rest of his life.

Instinct kicking in, Ray and Jodie both tore off – Ray carefully cradling Carol-Anne close to his chest – seeing the imploded roof of the utilities van as they turned the corner.

'Oh, God,' Jodie muttered as a stream of blood appeared in the cracks of the shattered windscreen.

'Call backup *and* an ambulance,' Ray said, taking control of the situation and making sure Carol-Anne couldn't see anything of what was going on.

Jodie nodded, putting the phone to her ear and calling the switchboard to report their whereabouts and what had happened.

Ray craned his neck up to where the body had to have fallen from – the first floor of the car park, just the other side of the tall fence – but there was no sign of anybody who might be able to confirm what had happened.

Carol-Anne was pulling at his nose as he cautiously moved closer. The natural first step would be to check for a pulse;

preservation of life was always the first priority. From where he was standing it was clear that nobody could survive a fall like that. And even though the van's roof had caved in, the frame had withstood the collision, so it was impossible for them to actually see more than the victim's arm – poking out at an unnatural angle – without climbing onto the van for a better viewing spot.

Still shielding Carol-Anne's face, Ray reached up and felt along the thin wrist, but no pulse was evident. 'Hello? Can you hear me? My name is Detective Sergeant Ray Granger. Help is on its way. If you can hear me, stay with us.'

There was no sound or motion to indicate whether the victim had miraculously survived the fall.

'Paramedics are on their way,' Jodie said, joining him at the front of the van.

'I think it's already too late,' Ray said, his head spinning with everything that was unfolding, none of which he seemed able to control.

'Pass her to me,' Jodie said, nodding at Carol-Anne. 'So you can climb up and check on the victim.'

He eyed her suspiciously. 'I'm not just going to hand her over. She stays with me. You check.'

It felt harsh, given the explanation she'd offered, but until he had confirmation of everything, he wasn't prepared to let Carol-Anne out of his sight.

'Fine,' Jodie sighed, stepping onto one of the rapidly deflating front tyres and hoisting herself up onto the bonnet, being careful where she placed her hands to avoid touching the blood pooling just beneath the windscreen wipers.

Ray watched as she adjusted her position, and shuddered as Jodie gasped and covered her mouth. 'What is it?'

Jodie didn't respond, promptly climbing back down, the blood drained from her face. 'It's Simone, I mean Sophie. I mean … oh God.'

Ray rested a hand on her shoulder and gently squeezed. He'd been first on the scene at several sudden deaths, and it never got easier coming face-to-face with the recently deceased.

'You two better get up here,' Owen called from somewhere above them.

Looking upwards, they couldn't see his face.

'Ray? Jodie?' Owen called again. 'You need to get up here straight away. I need your help. Yell back if you can hear me.'

'Yeah, we're on our way,' Ray shouted, looking down at his daughter's face, and then back at Jodie.

'You can trust me, Ray,' she said, but he didn't need to make that decision, as an ambulance and two marked cars approached.

Keeping Carol-Anne nuzzled into his chest, Ray, Jodie and one of the paramedics headed in through the secured perimeter, racing towards the up ramp. There they found Owen and Alex slumped over a prone male, his shirt covered in blood.

The paramedic radioed for a second ambulance, and immediately cut through the shirt, to begin treatment. Ray recognized the old man's face. A shaking Alex looked different somehow. Her hands were covered in blood, and there was a distant look in her eyes, as if she was in a trance or a state of bewilderment.

It was only Carol-Anne calling out that seemed to break the spell. Alex's head slowly turned and looked up to the giggling child in his arms, and for a moment she remained frozen to the spot, like she didn't quite believe what she was seeing. Then her anguished face broke into a smile of pure joy and the tears that had been cloaking her eyes fell freely down her face.

Rubbing her hands against the dusty floor, Alex stood, using the back of her own top to wipe off any remaining traces of blood, moving quickly over to them.

'You found her,' she said to him, barely able to maintain her standing position.

Ray quickly wrapped his free arm around his wife's back,

supporting her and Carol-Anne at the same time. Pulling Alex closer, and planting a tender kiss on her forehead, he whispered: 'We did it, Alex. We have our little girl back.'

'It was Sophie,' she whispered back. 'She was the one who—'

'I know,' he said as calmly as he could manage. 'I never should have doubted you.'

Epilogue

Three Days Later

'Whitchurch corroborated your story,' Ray said, handing Alex a fresh mug of coffee before discarding the tray on a vacant table. 'As of now, you are no longer a person of interest in the enquiry.'

Alex was tempted to lean forward and thrust her arms around his neck in gratitude, but something stopped her.

The café was about a third full, with three other pairs deep in conversation, and what looked like two undergraduates with their heads buried in their laptops.

'Sophie's – sorry, I mean Simone's – house has been covered from top to bottom, and will be carefully processed over the coming days,' he added. 'It will take time, but at least that's something we have plenty of. The usual pressures of securing evidence to charge don't apply when the chief suspect is already dead.'

Alex looked away. Learning that Sophie had been the one manipulating events had come as a huge shock, and discovering that she'd died as a result of her fall from the car park had hurt more than she'd expected it would. She knew she had every right to hate Sophie, but she missed her friend.

'And he won't change his story? Whitchurch, I mean.'

'He has nothing to gain by pointing the finger at you. He still doesn't know who you are or what led you to the car park that afternoon, but he does know what you did to stop him bleeding to death.' He paused, the hint of a smile forming on his lips. 'It's funny, even though you ultimately shot him, in his eyes you saved his life. As far as the rest of the world knows, Simone shot him before falling over the ledge. You're lucky the security cameras weren't on. I'm not one for fudging the facts; however, this really is the best outcome for all concerned.'

'Has Whitchurch admitted to what he did to Simone, all those years ago?'

Ray shook his head. 'He's sticking to his story that she must have had him confused with someone else. He says she phoned him and was threatening to publish his address online if he didn't meet her at the car park. He's claiming to have no memory of anyone called Simone.'

'He recognized her; I heard him admit it.'

'I don't think it's worth pushing it. If we try to expose him for his lie, he'll quickly drop you in it too.'

She looked away, straining to keep her frustration in check. Despite everything that had happened in the last week, didn't Simone deserve justice as well? She was as much a victim as the rest of them, and she'd been let down. Alex couldn't help thinking that had Simone's allegations against Whitchurch been dealt with more appropriately at the time, things would have unfolded very differently.

'It's for the best,' Ray said, sipping his coffee.

'You were the one who told me to say that *she* shot him,' Alex whispered back, conscious of anyone who might overhear their conversation in the small café, not far from the police station. 'I was going to tell the truth.'

Ray leaned closer. 'Then you would be facing conspiracy to murder charges and spending decades locked up. Carol-Anne needs you. And you said yourself you didn't mean to shoot him.'

'What if I did, Ray? What if on some subconscious level I deliberately squeezed the trigger?'

His eyes narrowed. 'Did you?'

'That's just it: I don't think I'll ever know for sure.'

It was a question she'd posed to Dr Kirkman in the hours following what happened in Salisbury. He'd been unable to give her an unequivocal answer either. She was glad she'd resurrected their regular appointments. Even if she was over the worst of her depression, talking through her emotions with a trained specialist didn't seem a burden. And if it meant she could be a better and stronger mother to Carol-Anne then she was willing to try.

Sophie's words on that cold concrete floor had stung. It pained Alex to admit it, but in many aspects Sophie's assessment of her behaviour over the last year had been spot on. She *had* spent too much time grieving her unborn child, rather than embracing the brilliant and breathing daughter who had nothing but love for her.

'Well, what I know for a fact is that you're a good mother and Carol-Anne is lucky to have you,' Ray said, sitting back in his chair. 'I also know that the lab boys found software on Sophie's computer which enabled her to mask her IP address. They also found the photo files that were attached to the email messages sent to you. I don't think there's any doubt she was the sole person responsible for what happened.'

Alex disagreed silently. There were plenty of people who should be sharing the blame for Sophie's downfall, including her and Ray. She knew that living with the guilt of how her own actions had been interpreted by Sophie would be a struggle for the rest of her life.

'You need to let this go, Alex, and focus on what's right in front of you. Not many people get a second chance in this life.'

Behind the counter, one of the baristas dropped a tray of plates, the erupting cacophony causing everyone to turn and stare.

Everyone except Alex. She was too busy watching Carol-Anne gnawing on the gingerbread biscuit.

'Do you think she'll remember any of this?' Alex asked after a moment.

Ray considered his daughter and pulled a face, which she instantly giggled at. 'Kids are resilient. You heard what the doctor and nurses who examined her said: they could find no evidence of injury. And you say she hasn't cried out in the night since her return – that's a good sign that she isn't suffering any kind of trauma. At most I reckon she'll remember a period of days when she didn't see either of us. I doubt she'll remember Simone at all.'

'Someone should arrange a funeral for Simone,' Alex said, unable to look at him. 'I don't think she had any relatives who would do that.'

He stared at her for a long moment. 'You know, you amaze me. After everything she did to us, you can be empathetic.'

Alex straightened and met his stare. 'She was a troubled woman, more so than either of us will probably ever know. I'm not relieving her of any blame or responsibility for her actions, but on some level she must have thought that she wasn't doing anything wrong.'

'She had one of her rooms soundproofed. That's pretty twisted if you ask me.'

'Even so, she still deserves to have her remains laid to rest. When will her body be released?'

'I haven't checked to be honest.'

'Can you find out for me? Is there someone you can speak to?'

Ray shook his head, incredulous. 'I'll see what I can find out.'

Alex sipped her coffee, quickly lowering the cup as the beverage was still too hot.

'Isla and her son have been ruled out as persons of interest in the enquiry too,' he continued. 'She doesn't bear a grudge and was pretty devastated she wasn't at the house when the gun and bunny were delivered. She's taking an extended leave of absence so she can help her son get properly rehabilitated. There will, of course, be an investigation into her behaviour through the course of what happened, but I'd be surprised if it amounted to anything more than a slapped wrist.'

A new FLO had been assigned the evening Sophie had died. She'd offered even less information than Isla had in the days she'd spent in their lives.

Ray leaned forward and spread his palms flat on the table top, separating his fingers. 'There's something I've been meaning to ask you.'

She sensed what was coming, but she wasn't about to let him off easily. 'Go on.'

'Well … I'm not sure how to say … what I mean is …'

'Spit it out, Ray.'

'What about *us*?'

'Us?'

'You and me; our marriage. I know I screwed up in the biggest way imaginable, but I don't want this to be the end.'

She took no pleasure from seeing him squirm, and she didn't doubt his sincerity, but she would never be able to trust him again. 'It was the end the moment you slipped your tongue into Noemi's mouth and allowed yourself to forget about the sacred vows we exchanged in front of our friends and family.'

'I get that – I really do – is there nothing I can say or do to change your mind? I know I was stupid, and I have no right to ask for your forgiveness—'

'So don't.'

'For the sake of our daughter I think we need to try and find a way through this. If I've learned anything from this horrific experience, it's that I love my daughter more than life itself, and I want to be in her life.'

Alex gently rubbed a hand over her abdomen. 'I won't stop you seeing her; either of them. You have as much right to play an active role in their lives as I do, but I can't have you living under the same roof as me. There are too many memories in that house, and not many of them are good. I'm going to search for somewhere a bit smaller. We can sell up and put the proceeds towards that. Whatever's left you can use to fund a place of your own. I don't mind you being nearby, and I won't ever stop you visiting. I just can't have you in my bed anymore.'

Ray closed his eyes, nodding. 'I understand. I don't agree, but I understand.' He took a long gulp of his cappuccino. 'Are you still planning to return to work?'

The truth was, Alex hadn't decided what her future held. She knew she didn't ever want to let Carol-Anne out of her sight again. In fact, since mother and daughter had been reunited, the only time Alex hadn't seen Carol-Anne was when she had been asleep, and even then she'd kept the two-year-old in the same room, the door secured by a carefully angled ironing board.

'Because if you are,' Ray continued, 'perhaps we could work something out where I have them both while you're working. I'm sure I could sort some flexible hours with work.'

'We'll see,' Alex said, as her attention turned back to the little angel she'd feared she would never see again.

There was no way of knowing what the future held for any of them, but she was just grateful that they still had a future to look forward to.

A Message from Stephen

Thank you for taking the time to read *Little Girl Gone*. If you did enjoy it, I'd love it if you would post a review on Amazon or Goodreads and share the story with your friends. If a book is written to entertain, then the reader is the target audience, and I feel honoured that you chose one of my books to read.

If you'd like to keep up-to-date with all my latest releases, you can join my mailing list (stephenedger.com). Your email address will never be shared and you can unsubscribe at any time. Alternatively you can contact me through Facebook and Twitter. And I really do respond to *every* message.

Thank you again for reading my book. I hope to hear from you soon.

Stephen Edger

www.stephenedger.com
/AuthorStephenEdger
@StephenEdger

Acknowledgements

I'd like to say special thanks to the following people, without whom *Little Girl Gone* wouldn't be in existence today:

First mention has to go to my wife, who has been my biggest supporter since day one. She is the one who gets me through when the roller-coaster of writing hits a dip. She's also the one I run crazy plot twists past, and the one who lies in bed at night, terrified by the darker side of my imagination.

As always, I'd like to thank Parashar Ramanuj, my best friend for more than twenty years and my first port of call whenever I have questions on medical procedures or body parts.

I'd also like to express my gratitude to Joanne Taylor who has been proof-reading my work since the beginning, and to Elaine Emmerick, who is also one of the first to review my work, and shout about it from the rooftops.

Finally, I'd like to thank my brilliant editor Kathryn Cheshire for giving me the chance to work with HarperCollins, and the incredible team of editors, cover designers and marketers who've helped bring this book to life.

Final thanks must go to every reader of my books for encouraging me to follow my dream and never to give up.

KILLER READS

DISCOVER THE BEST
IN CRIME AND THRILLER

Follow us on social media to get to know the team behind the books, enter exclusive giveaways, learn about the latest competitions, hear from our authors, and lots more:

/KillerReads 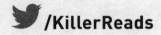 /KillerReads